SILVER SPRING

A Novel

Ivy Kaminsky

2013

This is a work of fiction. All characters and events portrayed herein are figments of the imagination of the author, and any resemblance to real people or incidents are quite probably intentional.

Silver Spring
© 2013

ISBN: 0-9815986-9-2
ISBN: 978-0-9815986-9-7

Published by:
www.lulu.com

Cover Photo Copyright © 2013 by Ivy Kaminsky
Printed in the United States of America

This book is dedicated to the real Estefan

Acknowledgements

I want to thank Marshall Sprague, author of *Money Mountain*, the real story of Cripple Creek, M. Manes for technical advice, Cherri and Rick for taking me to Cripple Creek, and all the people who have listened to me claim that I am writing a novel for the past year and believed me.

Foreword

This is a work of fiction. As such, the places and characters in it do not and never did exist. There is no town called Silver Spring except as it exists in the mind of the author. Likewise, Estefan, Dai-yu, Margarita, Estrellita, Paul and Elaine, are only figments of the author's imagination.

However, this book is a historical fiction which means that places such as Cripple Creek, Pike's Peak, Mt. Pisgah cemetery, the Old Homestead, Victor, and people such as John Calderwood, Bill Haywood, and Pearl deVere did exist, and events such as the Colorado Labor Wars and the mining strike of 1894 did occur.

The author apologizes in advance for any historical inaccuracies that may appear on the following pages. When writing a historical fiction, the author always risks making mistakes of this kind, especially when sources conflict with one another. Details such as whether or not cowboys or gentlemen took their hats off when they entered saloons or brothels could not be verified one way or the other. For example, all old historical photos from this period that the author came across showed men wearing their hats indoors; on the other hand, one could suppose that every man in the photo chose to put his hat on just for the photo. Common sense would dictate that men took their hats off indoors, but the camera doesn't lie.

All the facts about the ghosts, of course, are entirely accurate.

The author hopes the reader enjoys reading this tale as much as the author enjoyed crafting it.

The Murder

As the lovers slept, curled in spoon position, there was a soft rattle of the doorknob. Someone was testing to see if the door was locked. It was not. It was well after midnight and most of the hard partiers had gone home or were rooming with their favorite girls for the night. The Silver Spring was asleep with the exception of the person in the hallway.

Estefan's much larger body protectively enveloped Dai-yu's smaller one and the two of them didn't hear a thing. They dozed peacefully and soundly, bodies and minds exhausted.

The door opened a crack. The person in the hallway slipped inside the room. He closed the door behind him. He watched the lovers in silence. Minutes passed. He waited until his eyes were accustomed to the darkness and he could clearly see the people in the bed. They were lying on their sides; that would never do. He made a noise by scuffing the toe of one boot on the floor. They stirred in their sleep. He made another sound with his foot.

Suddenly, Estefan found himself awake. His eyes popped open, he sat bolt upright, and as quickly as he could he turned to reach the gun that was still in its holster hanging from the bed frame. As he returned to a sitting position with his gun in his hand he heard something else then. An unwelcome and ominous sound. His head jerked towards the noise.

From the foot of the bed he heard the distinctive sound of a trigger as someone cocked it. Dai-yu stirred in her sleep. He stared into the darkness, but he couldn't see anything. He did have time for two thoughts; they were: who is there, and why is he there? But there was no time left for any more thoughts because what followed next was a flash of blinding light and a very loud noise as if thunder had slapped the bed they were lying in.

Estefan felt a great pressure in the center of his chest as the air in his lungs emptied out into the room in one great rush. He could still feel the back of his head and his shoulders touching the headboard behind him. He felt the smooth wood of the bedframe hard and cool against his bare skin. He felt a sharp burning where he imagined his fractured heart might be and then he had the impression that the pain was alive and moving. It surged from the center of his chest down into his right arm.

Then he was warm all over. Finally, he felt nothing. But his brain was still awake. Aware of what was happening. He was still sitting upright. His body hadn't even moved from the impact of the bullet. He smelled the unique odor of gunpowder, something burning, bitter like sulfur. That odor mixed into the metallic odor of blood. It must be his blood!

As he watched in confusion, the sound of the first gunshot awakened Dai-yu. She too sat up. He could see her head slightly turned towards his as she stared blindly in his direction. She reached for his hand. Everything seemed to be happening in slow motion. Then there was another bright flash of light. Another gunshot exploded the silence.

Only seconds had elapsed since the first explosion tore the night into pieces.

He watched in horror as Dai-yu's small body ripped open. Her head came to rest on his shoulder. But he couldn't feel the weight of it. He couldn't feel his body at all.

He was hyper-awake. He could see perfectly now. There was a great deal of light in the room, even though the lamps were not lit, and the door to the hallway was still tightly shut. He wondered at this new perception; it was definitely not the kind of light he was used to. It was like being inside a cloud or a snowstorm. He looked over towards the door to see who had shot them but the person was no longer there.

They had been shot by a ghost! That didn't make sense, but his mind was not working correctly either. That was obvious. In fact, he wasn't even in the bed anymore, as far as he could tell, he was hovering over it. Amazing! He could fly!

His focus returned to Dai-yu's small body. She looked even smaller from up here. He tried to touch her but he couldn't use his hands anymore. She was still alive but her breath was getting slower and slower. She gasped like a fish on the banks of a dark river, a wet scaly thing trying to return to the murky water. Like a man carved of marble, he watched her helplessly from above as she tried to catch her breath. All he could do was let her lie there and die.

He concluded with some sadness, he must now be dead. He wanted to cry for his own death, for Dai-yu's short life, for all the things that could have been. But he had no body, no head, no tear ducts, no tears. The feeling of sorrow quickly passed. It was replaced with anger. How dare somebody hurt the great and powerful Estefan! How dare they!

There was noise in the hallway. The sound of people shouting. A woman screaming the same words over and over again. But all the sounds came as if from very far away. They were muffled as if they had tried and failed to pass through the cloud that encased him.

Dai-yu took a few more long shallow breaths. They were getting farther and farther apart. Then at last her body became still. Her eyes were still open but he knew they couldn't see anymore, at least not in the conventional sense. But then he felt her presence there beside him.

He felt her before he could see her. With joy he realized she was here in this place with him. He was no longer alone. They could see one another!

She looked fine. In fact, she looked even better than before. She was all light. So he guessed he must be all light too.

"Hello," he said, "How do you feel?"

"I feel wonderful," she said.

And they embraced. Without bodies, without arms, with only the love they had for one another.

Six Weeks Earlier

Estefan

Estefan was in love. Not with his wife, Margarita. Not with his three sons, not even with his current girlfriend, the bewitching Estrellita. Estefan was in love with Estefan.

Estefan regarded himself in the great mirror behind the bar. He smiled slyly at his reflection. One side of his mouth involuntarily rose a bit higher than the other as if trying to meet the dimple that appeared in the cheek below his left eye. His long straight hair was tied back in a ponytail, and was still dark. His mustache was just beginning to turn grey. Even pushing the ripe old age of 45, he was without doubt the handsomest man in the little mining town called Silver Spring. One might even venture to say further, he was the most attractive man in the territory.

Or so Estefan told himself. Not only did Estefan tell himself this, but everyone else told him this was the truth. So it had to be so. Maybe it was because he was rich. Maybe it was because he was such a generous tipper. Maybe it was because he was so clever and had an inborn ability to make money from whatever he touched. Maybe it was because he was so charming. But Estefan didn't very much care why everyone sucked up to him, as long as they did.

Estefan continued to watch himself in the long ornately framed mirror that ran the entire length of the bar. The mirror was tipped forward in such a way that the entire room could be seen in its glazed glass surface. He adjusted his flat-brimmed beaver hat a bit and smiled at the man in the distance who looked so much like he did. Their eyes never parted as he shuffled the playing cards in his hands, and set the cards down on the table to be cut by another player.

Then he smoothed his mustache hairs with the index finger and thumb of his right hand. First he rubbed his right index finger along the right side of his lip to make sure each hair lay down smoothly alongside its brethren. Then he did the same thing on the other side, running his finger from his left nostril along his lip and down his chin until it fell off into space. Lastly, he took thumb and forefinger, placed them on each side of his nose and stroked both sides of his mustache at the same time, drawing his fingers down all the way to his chin, ensuring all the wayward hairs were in proper array.

He smiled at himself again in the mirror. Seeing his reflection gazing back at him with such genuine affection was very reassuring. It was like reaching towards and touching the soul of a best friend, a good-looking, wise, and confident best friend, the best kind.

Estefan was a wealthy landowner, a gentleman rancher with fine horses, and a great hacienda, with a spacious Spanish-style mansion house and outbuildings. The great estate was located about a mile outside of the town proper. He had amassed hundreds of acres of forest and scrub, and had drilled several wells into the water table below at considerable cost. This enabled him to irrigate, at one time, cattle, and at the present time, hundreds of noble steeds that were part-Andalusian, part Thoroughbred, and part Mustang. Estefan was a bit of an entrepreneur when it came to horses. In fact, it was his love of horses and animal husbandry that led him to his wife, Margarita, in the first place.

Estefan had always dabbled in horses; from the time he was large enough to ride, he was taking care of other people's horses. By the time he was 12, and as tall as a man Estefan had wheeled-and-dealed his way into possession of several mounts of his own. He even specialized in breaking wild mustangs, some of which he was then allowed to keep. He was a natural with the animals. He loved them, respected their power, he even worshipped them a little. In return, they loved him back and did whatever he asked of them. If the truth be told, he loved these great snorting hoofed beasts more than he liked people. Horses were always reliable, trustworthy, honest, selfless, and, if not always, almost always, predictable. They did not lie, steal and cheat you if they got the opportunity. They were exactly what they seemed to be. Nothing more. Nothing less. If you treated them with kindness, they reciprocated with gentleness. If you treated them with respect, they willingly did what you asked of them. If you were cruel to them, they went crazy.

Not like humans. Even if you treated people kindly sometimes they would treat you badly or betray you. For the most part, people acted unpredictably. The only predictable thing about people was that one could not with any accuracy forecast how they would behave. With humans, one never knew with certainty what was coming next. One couldn't trust them with one's gold, one's gun, one's horses, or one's wife. At least these were the lessons that Estefan had learned in his hard scrabbling youth. And these were the rules he lived by.

By the time he was 30, Estefan was traveling all the way down to Mexico City to swap stallions and mares with rich horse traders who specialized in breeding carefully selected Spanish flowers like Andalusians, and horses of oriental original like Arabians and Barbs. The Andalusians were prized for their long swanlike necks, even gait, and stamina. It was Estefan's aesthetic opinion that they ought to be crossed with thoroughbreds and mustangs because they brought style into the mix. Style was the missing ingredient; mustangs were hardy, and thoroughbreds had speed.

It was on one such trip down to an estate just outside of Mexico City, where he spied Margarita for the first time. She was only 14, a beautiful dark-haired maiden of Spanish descent, so her skin was much lighter than Estefan's. Her father had raised her and her sisters in great luxury. She was spoiled but beautiful, but beauty always trumps manners and personality. Even though it was well into the 19th century, Margarita still chose to dress in the style of the Spanish royalty; she piled her coal black hair high atop her head and secured it there with ivory combs. She also loved to go about in mantillas and other fancy lace affectations.

They were soon very much in love, that is to say, Estefan was madly in love with her. He pursued her for more than a year, traveling back and forth to Mexico City as much as possible. He wrote love letters to the girl, and entreated her father to take him on as a horse trainer. More wheeling and dealing ensued and he had bargained away one of his prize stallions and two mares to persuade Margarita's father to give her to him, a man with little monetary wealth at the time. They were soon married and Estefan went to work for her father. It was while working for the rich Senor Martinez that he perfected his horsemanship. He learned to ride the way the royals did, became a show rider, skilled in dressage. He was no longer a vaquero, or cowboy, roping cattle and risking bodily injury on a daily basis as he shepherded the dumb beasts about.

But the call of The West kept eating at him. Eventually he convinced Margarita's father to allow her to return with him to the new territories up north. To new frontiers.

By the time Estefan was 35 he had jockeyed his horse trading money into a thriving cattle business. He had more than 500 head of cattle and employed a small army of ranch hands of his own. They lived in little camps scattered over the six hundred acres he called home.

When Estefan was 40 years old, gold was found in the region. It was this miniature gold rush that successfully propelled Estefan into a state of excessive wealth.

***

Before Silver Spring was a mining town it was a cattle town.

In those days silver was the precious metal that brought prosperity to Colorado. People mined the streams for gold but it was the discovery of silver in towns like Leadville, Central City and Idaho Springs that made many people rich. Hundreds of silver mines employed thousands of workers. The demand for silver was high because the United States government was minting gold and silver coins for use as currency. Meanwhile, the be-alls and have-alls back East decided this was not the way they wanted things to continue. As Colorado's rich got richer, those betting on gold lost out. This would never do, so the Republican Party campaigned to introduce the gold standard all over the country. This would effectively devalue silver as a viable commodity.

The politicians had strong backing in 1873, so the gold standard was adopted, and overnight silver lost most of its value. By 1893, Colorado was in the grip of a terrible depression. More than four hundred silver mines closed, and tens of thousands of miners were out of work. Many moved to the capital of Denver, but there were no jobs there either. Instead, more than 45,000 unemployed people stood in bread lines.

On the other hand, things all over the state were not so grim. In 1890, gold was discovered near Cripple Creek. As it turned out, the six square miles in the vicinity of Mt. Pisgah, an extinct volcano, was full of sylvanite, a gold-silver-tellurium ore. Unlike the gold found in many other places, the veins appeared black or dark grey.

Estefan, always the opportunist, sold the rights to various fortune-seekers to dig on his land. Estefan kept half of the mineral rights. He sold hundreds of these claims to men who came from faraway lands such as Ohio and New York. He also bankrolled a few experienced prospectors in the hopes that their claims would pan out. These tenderfeet from far-off lands were naïve souls who willingly entrusted their meager fortunes to a man like Estefan, who seemed so honest and trustworthy.

Most of the diggers soon gave up after braving one or two of Colorado's harsh winters. Once their dreams of striking it rich died, and they had exhausted their meager financial resources, they left the area, and Estefan, by default, took over their claims.

Finally, as was likely in any scenario whose foundations were built on pure dumb luck and an abundance of valuable minerals buried deep within previously unexploited mountainsides, one of Estefan "inherited" mines came in. A rich vein of telluride ore was discovered inside of a drift, and after being assayed it was discovered to contain $280 an ounce in gold. The good news was the drift from which the samples had been chiseled contained ore that went back hundreds of feet. The bad news was this put the ore squarely beneath a neighboring claim. And according to the law of apex, the gold belonged to the person or persons who had staked a claim at the place where the vein originated. But since it was not known at the time where the point of origin was precisely located, Estefan and company decided instead to squirrel the ore out at night, and have it assayed elsewhere.

In this way they kept the location of their find a secret for several months. By the time the apex was located, Estefan and company had smuggled out $125,000 worth of gold, a small fortune at the time.

Once the source was discovered a flurry of lawsuits were filed. Many people owned parts of the "mother" lode. Estefan, and the other adjoining mine owners, got together like gentlemen and decided to form a single mining company and share the profits. The lawyers hammered out the necessary agreements.

As it turned out, finding the gold was just the beginning. Getting the ore out, having it assayed and then milled was a costly proposition. It was only with Estefan's financial backing that the mine could be developed. And so it was.

Meanwhile, it became more profitable for Estefan's ranch hands to dig for gold on his land than to raise cattle, so he put them to work pulling ore from the mine.

This happy turn of events, ensured that the young baron never had to do an honest day's work again. Eventually Estefan sold all his cattle off, but he kept the horses, because they were now a beloved hobby, not a livelihood.

***

In his personal life, Estefan was also quite happy. Margarita had borne him three strong, handsome dark-haired sons. There had been two daughters who had died in childbirth. They were buried high on a hill in the cemetery that stood watch over the town of Silver Spring. Estefan, the devoted father, visited their little graves every week, sometimes even more often.

Estefan gave his wife every material possession she desired and she had dozens of embroidered dresses of silk, satin, and velvet, in her multiple armoires. She also had so many pieces of jewelry, that most of them lay silently, and unused, in one of her many jewelry boxes and never beheld the light of day, or evening, for that matter. She had ruby bracelets, diamonds rings, and pendants emblazoned with emeralds and sapphires. She had many pairs of silk or leather shoes, fine lace and silk undergarments imported from Paris and other European cities, and every other creature comfort in abundance. Everything she asked for she received and she asked often.

Like his wife, Estefan's sons were spoiled, too. They were tall and handsome and hadn't an ambition in the world. They expected Estefan would take care of them, and their eventual brides, and children, forever. Maybe they were correct. Estefan did put his family first, if only for the sake of his pride.

He smiled sadly as he recalled how he had given his oldest son, Estefan, Jr., his favorite black mare, Ashara, on his 15th birthday, just because he had wanted her. Estefan firmly believed that Ashara had Arabian blood in her, but he didn't have any documentation to prove it. He loved that horse. He had picked her out especially for himself. Then he frowned when he remembered how his son had abused that horse, tried to turn it into a bucking horse, like he had seen in the rodeos. Estefan, Jr. and his sidekicks put a rudely fashioned bucking strap on her and spurred her to make her perform. This was the first and only time Estefan lost his temper with his son. This he regretted almost as much as the fact that he had put this fine mare in harm's way in the first place.

It was a mystery; not a one of his sons revered horses like he did. They were pretty much indifferent to horses, the horses that meant so much to him.

Maybe it was because they had never had to work hard like he had, or never starved as he had. Never gone without. Never had to pay for anything they wanted. So, as if he were the first to stumble upon this great new truth, he concluded, a thing only has value if you earn it yourself. He wanted his sons to value things like he valued them. But it was not turning out that way.

When it came to his wife or his sons he could deny them nothing. For he loved his sons even more than he loved horses, he had to admit. He loved them even more than he loved his wife, for she was, after all, only a woman, one that could be easily replaced.

His wife, Margarita, was merely a vehicle that provided children, and to her credit, she had done so admirably. But now she was a little older, and the distance around her equator had expanded a few inches since the day of their wedding, and most of her hair had thinned and fallen out. But no one was the wiser, because most of the time she wore one of the wigs she had special ordered from a wig-maker out East, and her custom-made dresses, with built-in corsets still accentuated her narrow waist.

Margarita was just another one of Estefan's status symbols, alongside the hacienda, the servants, the ranch hands, and the horses. She was just another object that demonstrated to the world that he was a success. He was rich, he was strong, he was powerful, he was respected, and everyone who was anyone, already knew that.

***

It hadn't always been that way. Quite the opposite. Estefan had worked his way up from nothing, and over his dead body, and over the dead bodies of his beloved sons, would he return to such a life of poverty. His mother, Esperanza, had washed floors, emptied chamber pots, hauled water from a spring, and washed the clothes for the family of a rich man, much like Estefan himself now was, in order to survive. She had suffered the indignities of being the target of a spoiled young hacienda wife, who treated her like a dog. No, she was treated worse than a dog, because at least a dog does not have the self-awareness to know it is being mistreated.

Not only did she work like a dog, but Esperanza was also subjected to the unwanted and unwelcome sexual desires of the master of the hacienda. He used her sexually whenever and wherever he desired. His young wife understood and accepted this reality, but punished Esperanza for her, albeit unintentional, participation in this reality of life. Outwardly, the young wife claimed she didn't care what her husband did; she insisted it was one less odious task she had to perform, but inwardly she seethed. Her ego strongly resisted that idea that her husband needed other women to satisfy him. She loved him; at the same time she despised him.

The bastard children of the young housemaids were shipped off to distant relatives, for the young wife did not want them reared in her house or anywhere within her sight. For some reason, the hacienda owner neglected to send Estefan away. Perhaps it was because he was a male, a son, and the first one at that. It was generally believed that Estefan was the hacienda owner's son. Yet, another reason the young hacienda wife hated Esperanza.

Esperanza grew old well before her time. She was sent away from the hacienda house when Estefan was only two years old; from there she went to live in Guanajuato with some of her relatives. Estefan was sent to visit her several times but for the most part he stayed on the hacienda. Eventually Esperanza came back to live on the ranch in one of the cowboy camps. There she had a place of their own, but Esperanza had to cook and clean and sleep with several of the ranch hands who lived in shacks nearby.

By the time she was a middle aged woman, her breasts sagged, and her shoulders stooped. Her hair had turned entirely grey; most of her teeth were gone, even though she was only in her thirties. It seemed Estefan's mother had not had a life that was easy or very much filled with love.

***

When Estefan thought of love, he remembered back to the first living thing he had ever loved. Or that he remembered loving. It was a pinto gelding named Spike. Spike was black and white, a graceful gentle creature, and he smelled good. Estefan loved to stick his nose right up against the taught ligaments of Spike's neck, and inhale the scent that spoke of newly shorn hay. Estefan loved to watch Spike's huge neck muscles ripple as he shook off the ubiquitous flies that dogged him. As he stood with his neck pressed against Spike's own, Estefan could feel the blood pulsing forcefully through the bulging veins. Spike's smooth coat was mottled with black and white patches, and his black mane hair had been cropped close and stuck straight up like a bottle brush.

The young Estefan loved stroking Spike's short body hair with a curry comb, and rubbing the fur with his other hand after each pass of the wood and bristle brush. He'd hold onto Spike's bridle with one hand as he worked over every inch of this horse, his most prized, and, if truth be told, only real possession. Spike had been given to him by the owner of the hacienda himself when he was eight years old. No doubt because he was also Estefan's father, the hacienda owner, a lover of horses, spotted in young Estefan a protégé, a person like himself, another worshipper who knelt before the shrine of massive power embodied by these enchanted hoofed beasts.

After he finished grooming the animal, Estefan would carefully inspect every inch of Spike's body, and tenderly lift each hoof, checking the condition of the soft inner frog, and making sure no rocks or pebbles had become lodged between metal and bone. His inspection concluded when he assured himself that the growing hooves weren't in need of a trim.

The farrier on the hacienda had trained Estefan well. As an apprentice farrier Estefan gladly tended to the needs of his horse as well as the thirty or so others that resided on the hacienda property at any one time.

***

When Estefan thought of sex, he often thought of horses mating. For horses, the sex act was wild and sinister, full of tension and domination. The mares were often bit or kicked until they bled. The male horse's reproductive organs were colossal and menacing. Nevertheless, Estefan was fascinated by the entire ballet.

First the pair of animals would court, as the agitated stallion would chase the seemingly reluctant mare in circles. Eventually the female would relent, slow down, and allow the stallion to mount her; a frothy eruption of foam from beneath her long flowing tail revealed the truth; she was ready to accept him. The stallion would rise up on his hind legs and endeavor to insert himself into all that dripping foam. Then he would jostle around behind her, performing a bit of a balancing act using her hindquarters for support. At the same time his teeth would find themselves firmly embedded in her withers. It was like watching a couple of housecats. Sometimes those sharp implements would even draw blood. The actual coupling didn't last long but it was full of drama.

***

The first time Estefan saw people have sex was when he was only 4 years old. And then he really didn't *see* anything. He heard it. He was sleeping with his mother in her bed when a man entered the wooden shack they called home. It was dark outside, and darker inside their single roomed structure. The man gruffly crawled under the covers, and Estefan's mother, told the child Estefan to go outside.

"Please go. Quickly, Niño," she said. He left the bed, and went outside where he lay down in the dust outside the front door. He could hear noises coming from inside. Sounds like an animal growling or panting loudly and irregularly. These noises were interrupted sporadically by a rough man's voice, and his mother's voice; then it sounded like his mother was crying.

He got up then and opened the front door a crack. He peered inside the room, but his mother cried out to him, "Go away, Nino!"

He went outside again, but he could not sleep. He lay on the ground outside their shack, and listened to the feral sounds coming from inside. Not understanding, but not sleeping either.

At last it became quiet in the shack. He got up, and looked inside. This time his mother didn't say anything. She appeared to be sleeping. He curled up on the floor like a small dog next to her side of the bed and fell asleep. In the morning, the man was gone and his mother sat in front of a little dressing table, looking in the glass above it, as she brushed her long black hair. She hummed abstractedly to herself. It was a Spanish love song she was humming, and she was smiling.

So Estefan was happy too.

***

When Estefan was 12 years old he and his mother were living on the great hacienda after returning from Guanajuato. They still dwelt in a one-room shack that had been roughly fashioned from birch wood. The single room had been divided into two sleeping rooms, one for Estefan and one for his mother and his stepfather, the man she now lived with. Their home huddled alongside several others in another camp where the ranch hands lived on the great hacienda.

One night, Estefan's stepfather was out tending cattle. It was well after sunset. Estefan heard a horse approaching, someone dismounting, someone snagging the railing outside the door with leather reins. Then he heard the door open, and a man's footfalls echoing on the raised wood floor. He smelled cigar smoke and whiskey so he knew it wasn't his stepfather.

Suddenly he heard his mother's low voice, "No, don't! You have to leave!" Stop it! No you can't!" There was the sound of loud breathing, grunting noises, and sounds like someone struggling to breathe. Estefan wasn't sure what he was hearing. He crossed the room, pulled back the curtained partition, and saw a man on top of his mother. She was trying to push him off but he was bigger and stronger than she was. Her efforts were fruitless. He had her nightgown shoved up around her waist and Estefan could barely see the pale skin of her calves peeking out from beneath his much darker legs.

"What are you doing!?" Get out of here!!" he shouted as he charged towards the man and started pounding him on the back.

"What's this?" The big man turned, looked at Estefan, and grabbed him by the wrists. He wore a broad smile on his face. As he held Estefan off, he said in a mixture of Spanish and English, "Get out of here, Pequeño! Veté!" Then he laughed loudly as if he was enjoying a very big joke. Estefan was furious and frightened at the same time.

"Nino, get out of here! Salvarte a ti mismo!!" Estefan's mother almost screamed the words. She gestured towards the door. He froze. But instead of obeying his mother, he made a small fist and punched the man in the face as hard as he could. Estefan was tall and thin. He was muscular from much hard work but he was no match for the adult cowboys who worked the ranch.

The man was angry now. With a much larger fist he punched Estefan squarely in the chest knocking him to the floor. The man was still wearing his cowboy boots, so as if to ensure the kid couldn't get back up, he kicked Estefan hard in the gut with the toe of his right boot as Estefan struggled to catch his breath.

Then he turned back towards Estefan's mother to finish what he had started. When Estefan could breathe again, he attacked anew. This time the man wasn't fooling around. He grabbed Estefan and beat him until he was unconscious.

When Estefan awoke, he was in his own bed and his mother was tending his bruised face and trying to repair his bruised ego. "Please, Nino, do not try to protect me," she was pleading. "The next time he will kill you. And that would kill me."

"I will kill him if he comes back; I swear it to you, Mother. I will kill him if he ever comes back."

"No, you mustn't hurt him," was all she said.

"Why not?" demanded Estefan.

"Because, my dear child," he is your father.

***

And this is how he came to be where he was, at the apex of Silver Spring's society. This is how he rose to his current position. He was proud of his position in life and he was proud of himself for being so clever.

One great thing about being rich and powerful was that one didn't have to play by or abide by the rules made for everybody else. According to Estefan's book, the rich had their own set of special rules.

For instance, if one could afford a mistress and desired one, one had a mistress. If one could afford several mistresses and desired several mistresses, then one had several mistresses. And Estefan always had a mistress. Just as his wife tolerated his sporadic dalliances with the housekeepers so too she lived with this fact of life. Margarita knew he had a mistress, or two, she just didn't know who they were, and most importantly, she didn't want to know. Or so Estefan was content to believe.

Estefan knew she knew and he thought her a very level-headed and sane woman who knew her place and kept her tongue. She was the ideal wife. He really didn't care whether or not she was happy with the reality that he slept with and kept other women, for he gave her whatever she wanted. So who was she to complain? In fact, how dare she complain!

It did amuse him, when from time to time Margarita would feign jealousy. She would express, quite inappropriately he should add, interest in his comings and goings. She might ask him where he was heading, or who he would be seeing, as he mounted one of his favorite horses, and prepared to ride into town.

At such times, he just ignored her questions, and smiled smugly, as he often did while regarding his handsome face in one of the many mirrors adorning the walls of his home, as he combed his mustache and reassured himself, "Yes, she wants me! All the women want me! I am one handsome hombre!"

Then he'd spur his pony gently and rein its big heavy head toward town and gallop off. He loved the town full of noise, excitement, music, and gambling, where there were tall tales to be told, fine hand-rolled cigars to be smoked, old perfectly aged whiskey to be swilled, and beautiful young women to be bedded.

So many women. Young women. Ripe, but not yet sullied. And yes, there were lots of older saloon girls too. They each had their advantages. The young girls were tight and fit like perfectly stitched pairs of new kid leather gloves. The older ones didn't look as pink and fresh but they did know more tricks and were better at sex in general, and at making a man feel as if his heart might explode. They also were better at acting like they enjoyed sex, probably just because they smiled and joked about it more.

The young girls often wore no expression at all and one had to work really hard to make them smile. On the other hand, Estefan loved to make people laugh. So all in all, he would have to say, he preferred the young ones, even if they did require more effort on his part. As he saw it, what else did he have to exert effort on these days? He had people to manage his finances, and he had people to run his mine. Aside from riding horses once in a while he didn't do much physical labor on the ranch anymore. He did like to occasionally break in especially fine pieces of horseflesh that arrived on the hacienda every spring, if nothing else, to stay in practice.

But most of the work now went to his paid laborers and he was recently reminded of the unwelcome truth that he was getting too old to be riding wild horses. This revelation came as he fell off of one and seriously injured himself. Luckily nobody was watching. Nobody of any import anyway. Those that watched didn't dare laugh.

It took weeks for the pain to go away and the muscles to heal themselves. His leg still ached occasionally where he had twisted the knee. When he was a young man, a minor mishap like that wouldn't have slowed him down longer than the time it took to get back to his dusty feet.

Getting old was no picnic or place for old men. But once he entered the Grand Salon of his favorite brothel, everything became better instantly. The smell of cigar smoke, beer, and perfume, made him feel younger and stronger and more virile. This was especially so after two or three shots of whiskey administered orally had been delivered via esophagus to the neighborhood of his stomach.

Once a week or so, warm and secure in his "home away from home," he'd spend a few hours at a table with some of his good buddies, shuffling cards, swapping coins and wild stories, puffing away on cigars that purported to be imported from Havana. He highly doubted the veracity of that place of origin but he was willing to ignore this discrepancy for he was in the mood to enjoy the taste of the tobacco and the way the smoke tickled the inside of his nose and the back of his throat. So he didn't argue, just flipped a coin to the barmaid, and ordered another shot of whiskey. After three shots he had a good buzz going and it was time to attend to other needs.

Da-yu

Dai-yu was new at the Silver Spring. She stood out from the other girls for several reasons. For one thing, she was the only non-Hispanic or Anglo girl working and living at the Silver Spring. In fact she was one of the only Chinese girls to be employed in the Cripple Creek mining district. Even though there was a "No Chinese" law in the town of Cripple Creek itself, there was no such law in Silver Spring yet, and even in Cripple Creek, the law was not strictly enforced when it came to the "sporting girls." However, to be on the safe side, and to overcome local prejudices, the Madam dressed Dai-yu up as a Japanese Geisha; she knew nobody would be the wiser.

There were two other things that set Dai-yu apart. These were her extraordinary otherworldly green-blue eyes. Her eyes actually changed color, not with the light in the room, or with the sun's light, but with her moods. When she was angry, they were one color, when she was frightened, they were another. When she was happy, they were yet a third hue. They hadn't been the happy color in a very long time.

It was time to go to work. Dai-yu looked in the wardrobe that, along with the wooden framed bed, almost filled her small room. There were only three kimonos hanging inside. She slipped on the silver one, tied a silver belt around her waist and bundled it at the back as if it were a real obi, stabbed her lips and cheeks with red rouge, combed her long black hair with a faux-ivory handled brush, and pinned it atop her head in a semblance of a geisha. These Western men loved the exotic, or anything that hinted of it.

Even though Dai-yu knew she was one of the few lucky Chinese people to survive conditions in the untamed Colorado territory, something rankled at her when she was for all practical purposes ordered to dress up and pretend to be Japanese. Despite the fact that she was a whore, she often had to remind herself that she was lucky to even be alive.

Her parents had named her Lin Dai-yu after the heroine of the ancient Chinese story, "Red Chamber Dream," or as it was called in English, "Dream of the Red Chamber." As an adult she hoped it was an auspicious name but considering the outcome of the story she wasn't so sure. Her parents took one look at her sweet round baby face and pale blue eyes and the character named blue-black jade came to mind. They couldn't know at the time that these innocent eyes would turn out to be the mysterious metamorphic ones that would someday bring her both admiration and danger.

Dai-yu's parents loved her but times were tough, especially for the Chinese in the American West. There were many Chinese and few jobs open to them. Many worked and died building the Central Pacific railroad in the 1860's. Others worked hard running their own businesses and living above the shops. Some sold drugs. They paid exorbitant rent to live in horrible hovels infested by rats and cockroaches. They had barely enough food to eat. Sometimes they had none at all. Eventually, Dai-yu's parents were forced to sell her, their only daughter, to a White man when she getting close to puberty. They knew they were sentencing her to a life of prostitution but they had no choice. It was she or the family.

Dai-yu spent her early teen years in a brothel in San Francisco. She always wore a jade pendant around her neck. She never took it off. It was the only thing left that reminded her of a life she had with a family that once loved her. Her mother gave it to her for good luck. The single stone was a piece of blue-black jade.

Whenever she saw this stone reflected in a looking glass she told herself there was always hope. She still had relatives in the States. She was not completely alone.

Dai-yu worked hard and saved her money and by the time she was 18 she had enough money to buy her freedom. Even in that respect she was extremely lucky. The White man who owned her didn't have to let her go but he took pity on her and her small fortune. She was on her own for the first time in her life. She decided to make a new start in the new territory of Colorado. The gold rush was on and there would lots of opportunities to get jobs. Or so she was told.

Eventually, she hoped if she continued to work very hard, and was very careful with the money she earned, she could rejoin her parents, and brothers, in California, that is, if her parents were still alive. She had no authentic ambition about doing so, because she knew that Chinese custom dictated she could no longer return to her family once her chastity had been compromised. Not only that there was no way she could now marry a proper, respectable Chinese man, one with money and position.

But some stubborn part of her kept this fantasy of going home to her parents alive. The fantasy allowed her to get up each day, spray herself with jasmine scented perfume, put on a silver, blue, or red kimono embroidered with silver, red, blue, green, and gold threads, pin her hair up into a bun, and adorn it with a spray of cherry blossoms made of silk, and go downstairs to "entertain" the endless stream of strangers hungry for female companionship in its most primal form.

Estefan

It was late on a Saturday evening and Estefan was holding court at the Silver Spring like he did every Saturday night, and many other nights of the week as well. As he shook the dust of the road off his boots and coat, he hung his duster on a hook on the coat rack by the front door. Then he took off his Stetson, fastidiously brushed the dust off it too, and placed it back carefully over his shiny well-oiled black hair.

Then he headed for the back room. His well-worn ostrich cowboy boots clunked with conviction announcing his arrival as he traversed the wooden floor. He and his friends always sat at the same wooden table, well away from the goings on in the front parlor, and the sound of girls' high-pitched fake squealing laughter. In the parlor there were several couches and nicely upholstered chairs where the girls stood or sat posed like so many colorful pheasants on display as they waited for customers. In the parlor, the customers could purchase dances with the girls or negotiate for other services. There was a small upright piano in the front parlor awaiting nimble fingers.

Between the front parlor and the back room, a curved staircase with a finely carved bannister wound its way upwards towards the debauchery that took place on the second floor. There were four smaller rooms upstairs, two on either side of a central hallway, and two much larger rooms located closest to the back of the brothel, furthest from the noises of the street. The largest and nicest of these rooms was reserved for the use of the Madam. Her room was large enough to easily accommodate a four-poster bed with a canopy. The smaller rooms were occupied by the other girls, who came and went as semi-permanent residents of the Silver Spring.

The downstairs of the Silver Spring was taken up by one high-ceilinged multi-purpose room which served as combination bar, dance-floor, and gambling area. The dance-floor could also serve as a stage, when entertainment was available. At those times the Silver Spring might bring in a few singers, jugglers, magicians, or other performers to entertain the regulars as well as the drop-ins. At those times extra tables and chairs usually kept out of sight appeared from a storage room.

Estefan liked to be as far away from distractions as possible when he was gambling. Estefan always sat in the same chair, the one farthest from the front door. He warmed a seat that always kept itself close to the wall. Estefan didn't like people sneaking up behind him. If it was possible to do so, one might have said Estefan kept one eye on the door and one on himself in the mirror.

Nevertheless, in the Silver Spring he felt at ease. His bravery partially resided in his abundant machismo. And it partially resided in the Remington revolver he wore snuggly in his worn leather holster. Security felt a lot like the weight of the weapon pressing against his thigh.

Tonight, like every other night he spent at the Silver Spring, he joked with his friends, drank and gambled as usual. He ordered another whiskey from the waitress and downed it. For no definable reason he felt strange tonight. Expectant. Something good was going to happen. He felt it. Usually he ordered a whole bottle of whiskey, and set it on the floor by his chair leg and refilled the shot glass on his own. Tonight he felt like doing something different. Tonight he felt like trying something different.

His favorite call girl, the brassy Estrellita, came over to his table repeatedly to flirt and cadge drinks off him, and like the true gentlemen he was, he good-naturedly bought her the required bebidas. She asked him several times if he was ready to go upstairs but he politely declined. He loved her, in his own way, after all he had been making the "beast-with-two-backs" with this same woman every week for the last seven years, but tonight was a new beginning. He didn't know why that was, but he could feel it, sense it in the air.

There was a full moon out.

And then after Estrellita left the table for the third time, he knew what "it" was. He was looking across the room and he saw *Her*. She was new. She was Oriental. Where had she come from? How had she entered the room without his seeing her?

She was a little tiny thing, wearing a huge mass of black hair piled high atop her head as if it were a hat. Her hair dwarfed her face. Her skin was pale, small blushes of pink touched the highest points of her cheekbones, and lipstick so red it was almost the color of blood outlined her tiny mouth. Her eyebrows were two single arching brushstrokes that might have been drawn with an ink quill. There was no expression on her face as she stared absently at nothing.

She was wearing a Japanese kimono. The long sagging bodice was bunched up at the waist and her tiny hands and arms were well concealed within its huge voluminous sleeves. It was made of a shining silver fabric and had sparkling gold and red embroidery on it. A large four-toed dragon appeared to be climbing the back of the robe and two smaller phoenixes were winding their way up the two sides of the front of the robe. There was a large silver sash tying the entire package together, which had been knotted into a silver bundle in back and lingered just over the spot where he imagined her smooth flat behind must be concealed.

To Estefan's eyes it seemed as if she were surrounded by white light. A virgin reborn. For a moment, his perception of the world shifted. He no longer found himself at the center of the universe. He realized with a disconcerting start that he could hear his brain speaking to him. It was sending him a command, an executive order. It said, "You need to have this woman. You need to be with her." He couldn't remember the last time, or any time he had ever imagined he heard words before.

***

Estefan stared at the China Doll in disbelief. Their eyes met for an instant and she quickly looked away. But that was all the encouragement he needed. He signaled for the Madam. She hurried over to his table. He asked the woman about the new girl. When had she arrived? Where was she from?

"China? Japan? San Francisco? What's the difference?" laughed the Madam.

What was her name? How much did she cost?

"It depends," said the Madam, with playfulness in her voice. She often liked to mess around with Estefan. He was always so straight-laced in his old-fashioned ways. Sometimes she was amazed by how truly conservative, especially when it came to sex. It always seemed a little funny to her since he was the closest thing they had to a worldly character at her establishment. That's how it was in small towns like Silver Spring; things were simpler. Now in the bigger towns or the cities, like Denver or Cripple Creek, they had *real* brothels. They had women that cost $250 a night. For what, she couldn't help but wonder? She couldn't imagine sex that could be that good or that exciting, or that amazing that it could demand that sort of money. Luckily for her, neither could most of her patrons.

She teased him a little further. "What do you think she is worth? She's very special. She's very different. She's been trained in special 'techniques.'" And the way the Madam emphasized the word "techniques" made Estefan's blood pressure go up a notch. And he blushed. The Madam knew, from their own limited number of shared sexual experiences with one another that as far as sex went, Estefan was, for lack of a better word, a prude with puritanical ideas, wants, tastes, and desires, despite his outward show of bravado. The Madam knew that Estefan pretty much liked to stick to the Catholic rulebook, which did imply, if not explicitly state, that sexual intercourse was only intended for the purpose of procreation and was not necessarily designed with pleasures of the flesh in mind.

Estefan let the Madam's barbs wash over him. His thoughts were not derailed. He did possess what could only be termed as a goal-setting mentality, and his goal, at the present moment, was to obtain the favors of the new girl. When he asked how much she cost, he didn't care what the number was; he was in actuality stalling, trying to slow down the process, because, for the first time in his life, he was nervous when it came to the idea of being with a woman. He discovered, to his dismay, he was trying to prolong the eventuality of their meeting in a physical way as long as possible. He was actually afraid to meet this new woman, this exotic beauty, this lotus flower. *Where is this insane insecurity coming from?* he asked himself.

He felt an involuntary tightness in his Levis Strauss' and he broke out in a sweat. "Ask her to come over here," he managed to say to the Madam. *Ask her? Oh god. What has come over me?* The old Estefan, the self-assured Estefan, the confident Estefan would have said, "Tell her to come here!" But instead, he was asking. Not demanding.

The Madam rustled away in a flutter of green satin and muslin petticoats, and returned at once with the young woman. She was even more striking up close. Her almond-shaped eyes framed in blackest kohl, made him gasp. What color were they? Blue? Green? Aqua? All of the above? She wore a pendant around her neck; the stone was dark and had a greenish glow. He found he couldn't look her directly in the eyes without feeling about ten years old. Instead, he stared at the stone contrasting so sharply with her light skin.

"Please sit down here, my dear," he choked out the words. *Calm down,* he told himself. He flipped the Madam a couple of $20 gold pieces to seal the deal, as if to say, "Sold American!" and she rustled away. The Madam, who hardly ever showed emotions like surprise, was nevertheless, shocked to see such a lucrative amount. But she tried hard to conceal her reaction.

"Thank you," she said and disappeared quickly.

The girl sat in the chair immediately next to his, one recently vacated by one of his "good" friends. She sat down as if in slow motion. Her movements were like water; it wasn't as if she was standing at one moment, and then sitting at the next. Instead it was as if she was standing and sitting all in a single moment, a long fluidic moment. It made no sense to Estefan's befuddled brain but the universe had shifted in other ways as well. Maybe it was the alcohol, but he was certain he could see her energy pulsating in constant flux between one place and another. She was poetry. Unselfconscious. Graceful. But once she stopped moving she became a sculpture carved of antique ivory.

He distractedly played several more hands of poker while the girl sat silently and watched. He offered her a shot of whiskey but she politely turned him down. He insisted. She nodded her head slightly. He signaled to the barkeep to bring him a glass of whiskey. The barkeep never left his station behind the bar except when Estefan called.

As he was instructed, the barkeep filled the glasses served to the working girls with colored water or tea so they wouldn't get drunk. So once the drink arrived, Estefan poured some whiskey from his own glass into it. His intent was not to get her drunk. He didn't want her drunk. He just wanted her a little less stiff, cold, and rigid, a little less on guard.

His goal was to help her relax. Even as she sat beside him, so close he could feel her perfume anesthetizing his brain, she resembled a snowy white egret, waiting motionless, ready to explode into flight at the least provocation.

She sat rigidly, back straight, eyes wide, alert. He wanted her calm, relaxed, loving, open to him and all the treasures he would willingly shower upon her young translucent flesh. He kept on playing cards as she sat there quietly. He pulled out a few cigars, and offered them to his buddies. Then he pulled out his knife and cut off the tip of one. He struck a match and lit the cigar. A tendril of lazy smoke trickled up towards the high ceiling. Estefan played cards and smoked while the China Doll sat there silently like a man-made statue.

The cigar slowly burned. Estefan slowly burned. Finally the cigar was only a stub and he put it out in a small ceramic tray near the center of the table.

He lit a second cigar. He glanced at her every time he won a hand and scraped a small mound of gold and silver coins towards his ever growing pile. He laughed loudly with pleasure each time he won and hoped she would laugh along with him. But she didn't make a sound. This made her all the more desirable, because now she had become a project. A goal. A problem that required a solution. How could he make this perfect China doll come to life? How could he make her smile?

At long last he resorted to the one tried-and-true method in his bag of tricks. As the second cigar approached the end of its useful life, he stubbed it out with a flourish. Then he stuck the two just smoked cigar butts in his mouth, over his canines, and said "I am a walrus," in a badly executed British accent. He flapped his arms together touching the backs of his hands as if they were flippers and made seal sounds. He glanced to his side to see if there was any reaction from the China doll. Nothing.

She was good. So after a few minutes of that, he pulled the cigars out of his mouth and stuck them burned side down into his nostrils. Then he switched his accent to French. That was doing it, as he caught a glimpse of her face in his peripheral vision. He was getting a reaction, teasing a smile out of the young woman. He kept up the French patter, saying things like, "Comment vous s'appelez vous, mon chere?" and "Cherché la femme!" as he stroked his mustache suggestively. He repeated these two phrases over and over again because that was pretty much the length, width and depth of his familiarity with that Romance language. As he spoke he continuously leaned back in his chair trying to balance it on its rear legs as if it were a steed whittled from wood. The chair sporadically bumped the wall behind it as he rocked backwards and forwards.

All was going quite well in Estefan's estimation when the chair under him decided that it had enjoyed enough of the show. Its back legs buckled and chair and Estefan dove for the floor.

Estefan appeared to fall in slow motion, and before he or anyone else could react he hit the floor with a loud *Bang!* The noise was so sudden that everything and everyone went silent. Even the piano player's fingers froze over the ivory keys. The silence lasted for what appeared to be a long time but it was only a second or two. Then Estefan's best friends began laughing. Even Dai-yu joined in.

Her laugh was like silver forks tapping on fine crystal, pure and resonant. And Estefan knew his heart had been hijacked.

Dai-yu

Despite her desire to not reveal anything of herself or her emotional state, Dai-yu had to laugh at Estefan's graceless fall. Laughing felt like a brand new emotion to her, and she realized with a jolt she couldn't remember the last time she had laughed so freely or the last time she had felt such relief.

Then she thought of Ting-Ting II. And the first great hunt.

Ting-Ting II was a little black-and-white cat. She was named for the original Ting-Ting, who was grey.

Like the first Ting-Ting, Ting-Ting II had adopted her as cats were wont to do. Dai-yu didn't feed her. Or give her shelter. Dai-yu gave her only one thing, the thing she needed most. Love and attention.

Ting-Ting II had found a large bug and was playing with it. First she'd pick it up tenderly in her mouth. Then she'd release it. Then she'd get down on her belly until she was at bug level and carefully watch it run a few feet until it had almost made it back under the building where it had presumably originated or where its little bug relatives were hiding. Ting-Ting II's eyes never moved from their position on the insect, never blinked, but stayed rigidly fixed on the tiny brown carapace. As the bug tried, hopelessly, to ensure its survival, Ting-Ting II followed along behind it. It scrabbled as quickly as its six jointed legs could propel it. Then Ting-Ting II would delicately place her left front paw on its back and stop its forward motion. Legs kicked but to no avail. Then Ting-Ting II picked the bug up gingerly in her tiny soft mouth and moved it back to the place where it had begun its mad escape. Again and again she'd set it down in the dirt carpeting the alleyway and release it. Watch it, catch it, bring it back and set it free.

Dai-yu watched transfixed. A casual observer would not have been able to decide which of the pair was most focused, the young black-and-white feline or the small Chinese child. This game of catch-and-release would have gone on forever if not for the semi-permanent structure of the beetle's shell, which finally had to succumb to the stresses, albeit small stresses, of Ting-Ting II's paws and mouth.

It expired. Ting-Ting II kept poking it with her paw. It was no use. The bug was an ex-bug. And Ting-Ting II was so disappointed. She even looked pained. The expression on her face, one of surprise mixed with grief struck Dai-yu as terribly funny. And she laughed.

***

As Dai-yu pulled herself away from this memory and time seemed to stop, Dai-yu stared at the man on the floor. And as she stared she tried to remember how many years it had been since Ting-Ting II had killed that bug. She couldn't recall.

There was a look of surprise on Estefan's face. Then it turned red. He looked as if he might be angry. The red color deepened. Like rain bursting from a cloud in a thunderstorm he began laughing. It was loud, bold, uncensored laughter, a surprisingly wonderful sound to Dai-yu's ears. Suddenly she discovered she had revised her original assessment of the man. He was not just a conceited pheasant displaying his feathers; he was a child filled with joy, and she felt a sudden kindness towards him.

Dai-yu moved then; she was out of her chair, quickly as a cat, and she reached down to help him up. She bent forward, extended both hands towards his, and grasped the forearm nearest to her feet.

As she pulled him up by the arm, her hand moved down naturally to take his hand. It was a very strong hand. And as she experienced its strength she flashed back to a memory of a large man taking her hand – it was her father. Whenever her father took her hand she felt safe.

And as quickly as she remembered her father she returned to the Silver Spring, to the man she didn't really know at all. For a moment their eyes locked. His eyes were very dark, almost black. She couldn't help but wonder, what was in there, behind those eyes? She saw something familiar, and something foreign, something comforting and frightening at the same time.

They held hands for what seemed to be an eternity, in a dimension where time was toying with them, slowing down and speeding up in an unnatural way. But the one truth in this reality was the feel of his hand in her hand; that felt natural and comforting and good. Again Dai-yu felt surprise. And a little alarm. When had she last felt true human connection, true human warmth or true human affection? She could not say. Instantly, she let go of his hand.

Estefan grabbed her two arms for support and picked himself up from off the wood floor. Then he made a great effort to move his appearance from disheveled.

He patted and brushed at his Levis with both palms, as if they had become soiled from their momentary contact with wood christened by alcohol and cigar ash. He patted both sides of his head with his flattened palms as he groomed his unruly hair. She handed him his recently dislodged hat and he carefully placed it back where it belonged. It struck Dai-yu that this was not just a hat on his head; this piece of molded felt was a crown on the pate of a monarch. That thought made her smile silently and invisibly to herself.

Glancing up at himself in the mirror, he smiled broadly.

Brusquely Estefan took his seat again, a king returning to his throne. Everyone in the place was clapping their hands together, hooting, and laughing. Then the sounds of normal conversation resumed. The entire room was charged with excitement. Everyone seemed to be talking more loudly. For a brief moment Estefan had imposed himself onto everyone else's reality. And without missing a beat, he grabbed the deck of cards and began shuffling them, bridging them, riffling each half of the deck into the other.

And as he went back to his cards, Dai-yu was left alone with thoughts pelting the inside of her head.

Estefan's hand was firm, worn, toughened like leather, so different in texture from her own. As she leaned down to help him up her nostrils had filled with his scent. He smelled of several tangible things: whiskey, cigars, the red Colorado earth, horses, leather, *yellow* or the smell of meat, sweat from hard work, and a few nontangible ones: the sunlight, the wind, raw power and strength.

Then she thought of other things, long ago things. The recollection of Ting-Ting II and the bug sent her imagination back to another vignette from her early childhood.

***

Dai-yu was sitting in the alley behind the apartment they shared with several other Chinese families when she lived in San Francisco. In the dusk of evening she spied a little grey cat. It was not much larger than a kitten. She called out to it, and its eyes grew large with curiosity. "Here kee-kee!" She cried again. It opened its mouth, uttered an abbreviated "Me-ow!" and trotted over to her. To Dai-yu's eyes, it appeared to be smiling. Dai-yu plopped down in the dust of the street and the kitten crawled across her crossed legs. She scratched its soft dusty fur. As she reached the spot at the base of its tail it rose up on its little toes, and pushed its hindquarters upward against her tiny fingers. She was rewarded with a loud rumbling sound that came from deep within the little creature.

Dai-yu was amazed; kittens buzzed! As it relaxed it flopped over onto its side so she could reach its belly. As she petted the fur on its tummy, the tip of its tail twitched up and down. Dai-yu put her head down against the kitten's torso and was delighted to discover the entire kitten vibrated! *How wonderful!* she thought. She breathed in its fur; it smelled like the sun, fresh and clean. She picked the kitten up and squeezed it tightly against her small chest as she brought it into their apartment.

"Look mama!" She held the kitten just under its front legs and its hind legs dangled limply in the air. "Look what I found!"

"Aiee!" her mother shrieked. "Get that filthy thing out of here! Go wash your hands!" Then her mother added, as if it were a self-evident truth, "Cats are evil!"

Dai-yu fled the kitchen and set the kitten down in the alley behind the apartment. She continued to pet the little animal even though her mother seemed to believe that it single-handedly was responsible for spreading the black plague. The little cat brushed up against her knees as she sat-cross-legged in the dirt and cried. Her mama had yelled at her. She had done something very wrong.

"Poor kitty. Poor Dai-yu," she cried.

Despite her mother's dire warnings, Dai-yu started to feed the little grey cat whenever she saw it in the alley. Like many felines, the kitten had a daily routine and Dai-yu was now on its list of regular people to visit.

Dai-yu named it Ting-Ting, which in her language meant slim and graceful. She snuck out every evening at dusk and there was Ting-Ting eagerly waiting for her, greeting her with a broken "Me-ow," enthusiastic purrs and a crooked tail sticking straight up into the air.

Dai-yu had no idea what to feed a kitten, so she brought it little pieces of sticky rice ball that she smuggled out of the kitchen when her mother wasn't looking. She hid the rice under her sleeping mat. The trail of ants that led in a straight line from the outer walls to the pallet that was her makeshift bed soon attracted her mother's eagle eyes. When her mother spotted the crawling insects parading back and forth with microscopic grains of rice in their microscopic mandibles she screamed like a woman possessed by a demon, "What are you doing!? Why are you hiding rice!? Are you out of your mind!?"

Dai-yu didn't say a thing. She kept the secret of the kitten, and she continued to sneak out at night to pet Ting-Ting. Dai-yu loved that animal. It was her best friend. It was a good best friend, it was soft, and it purred when she stroked it between the ears. It smelled good when she stuck her nose deep into its fur.

After the rice incident, each time she'd apologize to the little feline, "I'm sorry, Ting-Ting, no food today." But

Ting-Ting didn't seem to mind. Ting-Ting was delighted just to see her. She waved her crooked little tail like a flag on her approach. Then she kneaded her soft paws rhythmically as she lay curled up in Dai-yu's lap, eyes closed, purring with satisfaction. Dai-yu rubbed all the right spots: the balding areas in front of each of Ting-Ting's pointed ears, the area under her chin, the lower belly and that all important spot at the base of her tail.

This went on for several weeks before they were found out. Her mother saw her slip into the alley one night and followed her. When she caught sight of Ting-Ting, she ran at her, waving her arms, hissing, and shouting loudly, "Scat! Scat!" in Chinese. She even tried to kick Ting-Ting, but the little slim one was too fast for her. Ting-Ting darted off and disappeared beneath a nearby building. Then Dai-yu's mother grabbed Dai-yu harshly by the shoulder and shook her. Once again she railed as if she was out of control. "I told you that thing is evil! What is wrong with you!?"

Then she swatted Dai-yu sharply on the behind and dragged her into their apartment. After that, Dai-yu never saw her friend again. She still went outside every evening to look for Ting-Ting but she never came. This went on for months. Dai-yu didn't dare say anything to her mama. Years later Dai-yu guessed the worst. Maybe her mother caught Ting-Ting and killed her; maybe her mother told the neighbors and they killed her. Years later, she surmised with great sadness, someone, maybe even her own family members, maybe even she herself (unwittingly) had most likely eaten Ting-Ting. Her mother had probably told them those were bits of pork in their rice. She was filled with disgust and dismay every time that thought entered her mind.

All she knew for certain was that Ting-Ting was dead. Even at that tender age, Dai-yu knew in her heart that the only reason Ting-Ting didn't return to her was that she couldn't. Ting-Ting wanted her love and her company, not her food.

When she finally came to the realization that Ting-Ting was gone for good, she cried and cried. Her mother yelled at her for crying too.

It was a mean lesson, but it taught her two things. First, don't become attached to anyone or anything. And second, if you have a secret, make sure no one else ever finds out about it.

This had been her most pertinent and dramatic lesson about love. Love was something you killed when it became too expensive, or inconvenient.

Love was something disposable.

No wonder she had not been able to let her heart trust again. She had been betrayed repeatedly by her mother and father, the two people she should have been able to trust. Dai-yu had been angry with them for years. A part of her was still angry. But she was wise beyond her years. She forgave them. She forgave them for killing her cat. She forgave them for selling her. She realized these must have been the only options open to them. She knew that a large piece of their hearts must have died on the day they sent her away. She knew her parents loved her no matter how badly they showed it. She still had the jade pendant her mother gave her before they sent her off. It was this pendant that confirmed this truth.

She knew with certainty, that someday if she ever had a daughter of her own, she would kill herself before she would send her away, or give her to a stranger.

Estefan

Estefan was tired of playing cards, and taking the money off of his foolish drunken friends. He was not tired of winning, but his mind was no longer on the game of poker. He turned towards the little China Doll sitting beside him. *My* little China Doll. Did he dare say it? He did. He was a man used to getting what he wanted, and having things his own way. Whether it was horses, or money, or women, he always set his mind on a thing and then did whatever it took to get to that goal. Horses, money, and women, these were the things he valued. These were the things he would have. In abundance, he added.

He got up, bid his partners adieu and turned to the China Doll. He held out one hand towards her and she took it in her own. As they left the room, his focus was entirely on this princess draped in silver. He was oblivious to the fact that Estrellita's eyes were burning a hole in the back of his shirt.

He led the China Doll towards the staircase that led up to the rooms where only certain types of "business transactions" took place. As they reached the staircase, he held back to let her take the lead. At this juncture in their relationship, she was the only one who knew where her room was, and where she would take him.

They entered the tiny room, and there was no place to sit but on the narrow bed with its brass frame. "This will never do," he complained. "You need a much bigger room than this one. You need chairs and a table." She stood there and said nothing. He waited for her to say something like, "Thank you, or that would be nice." But still she said nothing. And she didn't move. Finally, he said, "This won't do. Take off your things." She did obediently. He stared at her perfection. He was speechless for once.

He was too embarrassed to disrobe himself; suddenly he was shy about her seeing his big stomach. So he kicked off his boots and sat on the bed fully clothed.

He beckoned to her. "Sit here, with me," he commanded gently. She was like one of his new yearlings, cautious, wild-eyed, afraid.

She obeyed him and sat. But she sat as far away from him as she could, he on one end of the bed and she on the other. "Come closer," he commanded again. She inched closer. But she was still too far away, still no nearer to touching him. "Not like that!" he snapped. "Here, I'll sit right here at the head of the bed, and you sit here between my legs. No, not facing me, sit the same way I'm sitting." He realized this was like giving orders to a young stubborn foal. But a horse didn't understand words. Did she even understand what he was saying? Or was she being purposely obtuse?

"That's right, now lean back against me." He leaned against the pillow propped against the headboard with his pants legs spread wide, and she sat Indian style between his legs. As ordered, she leaned back until her perfect ivory skin was touching his shirt. But he could feel her tension. "This won't do at all!" he said. "Try to relax," was all he could think to say. But he knew you couldn't order a horse, or a girl, to rein in its instincts.

He realized the only weapon in his arsenal at the present moment was time. With time trust would come. He needed to gain her trust and he needed time to do that. "Close your eyes," he said.

He wrapped his large tanned hairy arms around her shoulders. His hands and forearms came to rest on her soft inner thighs. He felt her tension as her body shuddered slightly. Her straight blue-black hair was still tightly coiled atop her head, as if it were a cobra tensed for the attack. "May I?" he asked, as he began to fumble with cumbersome fingers for the pins, or whatever else was hidden in there, that held the entire mass balanced carefully in place. With no luck.

"I'll do it," were the first words she uttered. *Thank god, she could speak;* he was beginning to think he had been dealing with an actual lifeless doll. She spoke so quietly, her voice was barely a whisper.

Expertly, she removed the pin that held the shining black mass in place, and her long tresses tumbled down loosely. He could almost hear the individual blades sighing with relief as they regained their freedom. Her black hair was as long and shiny as an Arabian's tail. "That's much better," he sighed in return. Her straight thick hair was cool against his cheek. Everything about her was cool. Her demeanor, the way she walked, the way she moved, the icy distrust with which she regarded him.

She was so tiny, childlike. No wonder they called her the "China Doll." It was a cliché but one which was aptly assigned. She was like a doll, born of porcelain clay, fired in a kiln until hard as obsidian. But unlike the black translucent mineral, she was sculpted of antique ivory. A masterpiece created by a master artisan, skillfully brought to life with strategically placed dabs of black, turquoise, and cerise paint.

Her eyes, so bewitching, were safely directed away from him. As long as he didn't look into those round orbs, he could stay in control. He could be in charge and that's how he liked it.

He touched her breasts. He couldn't help himself. They were small and adolescent. He caressed her belly. He closed his eyes, inhaled her perfume. What was that scent? Jasmine? Incense? Some kind of flower? He knew he smelled flowers but they all pretty much smelled the same to him. Vanilla? Something sweet. He licked his lips as if he could taste that something.

He kissed her neck. He nuzzled it with his chin scratchy with the stubble of early evening. He couldn't tell if she liked these attentions because she did not react, either verbally or physically. Like a doll, she was motionless.

***

But he didn't care, and his eager cock didn't care either. He realized, almost in embarrassment, that his hardened member was rudely poking her tiny firm behind through his jeans. He blushed. She turned to him then and whispered, "It is okay. Let me." And she turned towards him and bent forward to unzip him and take him out.

Then she made to take it into her tiny mouth. He was aghast. No one had ever done that without being ordered. No one had ever done it so gently. So lovingly. Could this be the special "training" that that Madam had referred to?

She kissed his hard member and touched it with her small childlike hands; she examined it closely as if it were a living thing, and under her touch, it did come to life. Then she began to suck it gently. As she sucked it became a live snake, hard, scaly, full of venom. But she didn't seem to care. She was not afraid of serpents.

This went on until he felt dangerously close to losing control. Some part of him returned to propriety and he stopped her. He was filled with fear, fear that his essence might release itself in a horrific torrential outpouring and drench her perfect face, or her beautiful shining hair. Fear that he, a lowly mortal, would soil her perfection. He had never felt such reverence (or was it fear?) for a woman before. It was an odd feeling. It was not a good feeling. He found himself confused, befuddled, at a loss, for the first time in the presence of a woman. Well, maybe not the first time, he remembered his own brief deflowering. So it could more truthfully be said, he added to himself, for the first time in a very long time.

Instead of letting himself come in this way, he bade her lie on her back. He made ready to enter her, but as he tried to bury himself deep within her secret garden, he found, with some disappointment, and perhaps an inkling of relief, that the gate was frozen shut. Wasn't she a whore? Hadn't she been with more men than he or she could count?

Of course, logic said, she was a whore, but her body proclaimed otherwise...

He knew he could force his way in, but that's not what he wanted. Not with this woman, not with this girl, for she was no whore to him. She was an angel incarnate, a statue that belonged on a pedestal in a museum. A goddess to be worshipped, a living breathing idol to be prayed to, a treasure to be cherished for all eternity.

So instead of doing what he usually did, that is, relieving himself with a great beastly groan, and emptying himself into the vessel before him which symbolized all of womankind, he took her chin gently and held it lightly between his thumb and forefinger. Then he tipped her head up towards his own and kissed her respectfully on the mouth. And bid her good evening.

Estrellita

Estrellita woke up. It was five p.m. She could hear the sound of a piano playing. The music was coming from downstairs. She could hear several men talking, singing, laughing raucously. It sounded like they were having a party down there, except for the fact that she didn't hear any women, and party sounds, in her experience, were usually dominated by the high-pitched sounds coming from women. Now that she listened harder, she did hear women's voices erupting in laughter from time to time. She started to get up, until an insistent thought entered her mind. *I'm not on duty, yet. There's time to sleep a little while longer.*

Now that she became aware of her body, she noticed that she was really tired, dead tired, and her body ached everywhere. *That's okay, she reminded herself. A hit of smoke and I'll be ready to go.*

"It's showtime!" she said out loud, as she rolled out of bed. She flung open the wardrobe that held her sizeable selection of dresses, and stood staring at the many frocks hanging there before her. A red one? A blue one? Or a green one? She chose her favorite red one because she was feeling really low and the red one always made her feel a little better once she put it on and fixed her long wavy black hair. She stared at her reflection in the tiny black rimmed mirror tacked to the back of the door to her room. Besides the red one was Estefan's favorite. He had even picked it out for her and had it delivered special from Paris, France.

The blue-black circles under her eyes were getting darker, almost sinister. At least that's how they appeared to her. She dug through a drawer of her nightstand and found a pot of makeup. She slapped a coat of beige tinted powdered concealer around her eyes and hoped it would do the trick. Who was she kidding? Nobody in the room downstairs could give a rat's ass about the raccoon rings around her eyes. Nobody cared what her face looked like, or if she even had a face. All they cared about was the possibility of renting or buying for an hour or a night the two cubic feet of real estate occupying the region between her clavicle and upper thighs. She was the only person in the world who cared if she looked 12 or 24, if her eyes were clouded with fever or bright and shining with good health. She was the only one who cared if her hair was dull or clean, or greasy or curly, or if her teeth were straight and white, or missing altogether. Not a man in the world cared if her lips and cheeks were stained artificially bright red or if they glowed pink with only the assistance of nature herself.

She was, after all, a whore, and her job was to have sex with any man with silver or gold coins in his hot sweaty palm and a prick in his hot sweaty pants.

A job was a job. An occupation was an occupation. Life was what it was.

She preferred the older men, they weren't nearly as fast, or as mean, or as rough when handling her merchandise. They even said sweet things to her and made her feel attractive sometimes. But she was a whore, and she didn't get to pick. The men did the choosing. On the other hand, she did have Estefan, even if he did have a wife. He was something consistent in her life, and loyal in his own way.

She eased down the back stairs and out the back way. She found Joaquin and he got her set up with a bowlful and a pipe so she could make it through the evening. As she fidgeted impatiently, he slowly packed the green herb into the bowl and lit it for her with a match. Then he deeply sucked on the small opening and as if checking to make sure it was not poisoned, took the first draw. He always took the first toke, much to her annoyance. But beggars can't be choosers, and whores can't complain without risking a mean backhand. Once Joaquin half-emptied the bowl he handed her the pipe and she inhaled deeply, until all the green bits in the bowl turned bright orange and then turned black at the edges and drew into little curls. Then she held the sweet smoke inside her lungs as long as she could, and let it out slowly. As the smoke spun lazily upwards she waited to feel better, for the anxiety that roared into her world like a train every morning, to pass.

Then, as she did every day, she made a wish. It was always the same wish. To become the smoke. To drift up and float heavenward; to fade away a bit at a time, and then disappear once and for all. To not feel the despair she felt when the smoke was not inside her.

Without the magic of smoke she did not know how she would stand the pain, the humiliation, the hopelessness, the emptiness of her life. With the help of smoke, her life was just one long, admittedly tedious, dream. There was still no way out, no other place to go, but at least her life was bearable. Besides she always had her "girls," her sisters-in-arms, and if they could stand it, so could she.

She returned to the big house, took a long deep breath, repeated that line to herself, *It's Showtime!* As she did so, she turned the brass knob and pulled open the stained glass door and entered the Grand Salon. It wasn't very grand, and it wasn't even particularly great, in fact, it wasn't even very big, but that's what everyone called it. The paper on the ancient walls was flocked with red velvet. The lamps had red shades. The Persian rugs covering the wooden floors were many colors but mostly those colors were shades of burgundy, cherry and maroon. The bar that ran the length of the far wall was backed with a huge mirror that was surrounded by a heavy wooden frame carved in deep relief with many animals and flowered shapes. There were dragons and phoenixes wending their way along the border, carved in remarkable detail, eyes, ears, and even scales had been individually and meticulously inscribed into the wood. The frame had probably been imported, at an astronomically grand cost, from India or China, or another foreign land. Or so she imagined. Maybe that's why they called it the Grand Salon.

On the other hand, there were now so many Chinese immigrants, many of whom were skilled craftsmen, living in cities like San Francisco in the California territory, that beautifully carved frame might very well have originated right here in this country. Thousands and thousands of Chinamen had gone West to finish work on the railroad. Once it had been completed they lacked the funds or other resources to return home to their own countries and so they remained in America, and tried, often with limited success to capture a piece of the American dream for themselves and their offspring.

The Grand Salon was also the room where the men played card games and did whatever it was men did when they wanted privacy away from the company of women. She threaded her way past the card players and down the hallway and took her post in the parlor, the room closest to the front door and waited. She sat on one of the cushy sofas. This is where all the women waited for the men who came in off the street. Sometimes all a "customer" wanted was a glass of whiskey; sometimes he wanted a bath, or a shave; sometimes he wanted to dance with a pretty woman; sometimes he wanted a lot more.

She soon was picked from the crowd, if you could call five girls a crowd, and the madam tipped the doll that represented her working self, into its horizontal position to signify that her status was now "OCCUPIED." The bell above the doll sat without making a sound awaiting her imminent return.

The john was non-descript and youngish and sorely needed a shave. He smelled badly but that was only because he wore clothes that begged to be thrown out, as eager to end their misery as those unfortunate enough to smell them; mending would only give them false hope. The john was polite, made eye contact, and attempted to make small talk. He was a bit nervous around women, and, she was happy to note, one of the good ones. The good ones required little exertion on her part. She could virtually lie there and do nothing, and they were satisfied. They would grapple at her breasts for a minute or two, until their cocks became hard enough, then they would plug themselves in, swish around for five minutes and squirt, sometimes loudly, sometimes quietly, with a single loud grunt. Then they would leave, and sometimes leave her a T.I.P. to insure proper service in the future.

True to form, he ejaculated quickly, rested for a few minutes, then got out of bed and put his boots back on. He never even took his pants all the way off. He just shoved them far enough down onto his thighs to free up the necessary body parts. He seemed embarrassed and she could almost hear his mother admonishing him to stay away from those wild women of the night. But he couldn't stay away, he had to do what nature called, and he felt bad about it. The good news is, that these sweet boys were so ashamed to be there that they almost always left her a substantial "T.I.P." which went directly into her "liberation fund" and was never exactly reported to the Madam or other people who ruled her life.

After he left the room, she washed herself off as best she could with the small hand towel in her room and the water in the wash basin and went back downstairs to hopefully add to her nest egg. The room was more crowded than before even though less than 20 minutes had elapsed. Then she felt Him staring at her.

Suddenly she was transported back to another time, another place, another nightmare that took place during her waking hours.

Estrellita blinked a few times, and stopped remembering. She realized it was just a paranoid moment, just a bad memory. The man across the room wasn't staring at her anymore. It had all been a horrible flashback. And she never had to think about it again. So why did she?

Estefan

After Estefan left the China doll he almost galloped down the stairs. As if emerging from a dream, the "gentleman" Estefan turned back into the man he was before he had ever set eyes on her, a man with needs and desires that had to be satisfied immediately. When his girl, Estrellita, came around this time, he decided it was definitely time to go upstairs with her.

As soon as they entered Estrellita's big room, Estefan threw her down on the bed. He was very much a creature of habit. And the act of love was not about love at all. For him it was like channeling a wild mustang, taking what he wanted, biting a mare savagely on its neck, eyes rolled back in its head like a beast.

As he charged into his mustang fantasy he covered Estrellita with his body. Habit took over. He grabbed her arms and pinned them with one hand above her head. Then he kissed her fervently on the mouth and the breasts, alternating between those two sites. Eagerly she entered his mare/stallion fantasy and struggled, pretending she couldn't free her arms.

Just as suddenly as he was seized by this mad, habit-informed desire, he discovered an image of Dai-yu sliding itself into his consciousness. It was a most unwelcome image he realized. He cleared his mind and set himself back to the task at hand. Estrellita always leaned into his kisses, and groaned breathlessly, like he was Don Juan himself. As she sighed, he *knew* he was Don Juan reincarnated.

As he kissed Estrellita's mouth and chewed hungrily at her lips, his hand reached down to find the spot between her legs. He pushed his fingers one by one into her tightly closed box. Again he was aware that his thoughts had returned to Dai-yu. Quickly, he forced the China Doll's image from his mind. He sucked angrily at Estrellita's neck and breasts. He sucked with such passion he left bruises with his mouth.

He tried to wait until she was nice and slippery down there but it didn't much matter with Estrellita if he forced his way in. So he grabbed her roughly, turned her away from him, and entered her from behind. Again he pictured the China Doll. Again he forced her hovering angel-like presence away. Estrellita was making a lot of noises, grunting like an animal, as he began his rhythmic assault on her back entrance. He assumed she liked this kind of treatment. He really hadn't thought about it much before. It was the arrival of the China Doll that suddenly made all of this problematic. In any case, sex with Estrellita, as rough and unbounded as it was by ideas of right or wrong or other people's feelings, sure beat having sex with his silent undemonstrative wife, Margarita.

As his thoughts veered to Margarita, he had to stop. He dropped to all fours, rolled over and lay down on his back.

Fucking Margarita was like despoiling the virgin Mother, something you did but then felt guilty afterwards for doing. Margarita never made any noise, and sometimes he wasn't even sure she was awake. He wondered if she said the rosary in her head while he made love to her. He wondered where her thoughts went when they were together.

As he retreated into himself, Estrellita, who didn't like to be ignored, decided she better do something. She grabbed him then and began squeezing seductively, sliding her hands up and down the still semi-hard shaft. She squeezed gently, and a little less gently, alternating her grip until his attention was sharply refocused.

He quickly came then. Then he took a brief rest. When he woke up, everything seemed back to normal.

He started feasting on his "little star" again. He whispered, "You have the most beautiful body" and she smiled widely. And he realized he was speaking to Dai-yu as he said it. This time he gave up. He didn't even bother to try to make that idea go away.

He gazed at Estrellita's breasts and curly hair. And as he did, he felt himself rising again. Then he hungrily resumed kissing her neck and breasts, leaving a trail of blue black wherever his desperate lips touched her skin. She continued to make noises of enjoyment. Finally he climbed atop her and pumped away until he came a second time. Then he fell asleep for a long time. When he woke up again, there was little Estrellita waiting for him, curled up like a cat, but all smiles to see him again.

He beckoned to her to come closer. She snuggled her small body up against his with her head against his heart. Then he talked to her. She listened attentively, asking questions, laughing in all the right places. Hours went by. They returned to their simple life together, a life existing at the place where society bumps up against everything else. It was its own reality, outside the boundaries of other people's lives, and it had its own rules. It was a place where there were no wives, and no other women. It was a safe space, devoid of dangers and distractions like the presence of a ridiculously dressed Chinese doll. It was a world only large enough for the two of them.

It was within this shared oasis, that Estefan told Estrellita of his real life adventures. He recounted tales of horses, and cow hands, disputes he had with prospectors or neighbors over water or property. Sometimes he told her secret stories from his youth. He knew he told the same stories over and over again, and while his wife, the good and noble Margarita, never laughed at these silly anecdotes from his past, Estrellita laughed loudly at everything he said as if he were the funniest man on earth.

Do you love me, Mijo? Estrellita used the familiar term.

"Of course, I do." Estefan assured her. But now he was sure his words were full of lies.

"Did you miss me?" she went on.

"Only with every waking breath," Estefan embellished.

"Tell me the story of the thing you saw when you were eight years old," she begged.

"You know I hate that story," he smiled as he lied.

They both knew he loved telling that story. He must have told her that same story at least a dozen times already. And it always changed a little each time he told it.

"Please," she begged. It was her job to drag it out of him.

"Oh, all right," he relented as if it was causing him great pain. It was his job to pretend he didn't want to do it. It was all part of the game.

He began, "You see, after my mother was sent away from the big house on the hacienda, for a while we moved down to Guanajuato. There we lived in an old creaky house with my aunt and uncle. It was a big house, compared to the one we were used to. It even had an upstairs. I shared a room with my big brother, but we had to sleep in the same bed. Even though it was a large house, it was crowded because there were a lot of people staying there. One night when everyone else was sound asleep, I heard a noise coming from downstairs. It sounded like a scratching sound. I was the only one who heard it. I woke up my brother."

"'Did you hear that?' I demanded. He listened. We both listened. There wasn't a sound. 'Go back to sleep!' he told me. I tried to. He fell back to sleep, but I heard the scratching some more. I woke him up again. Again we listened. But there was only silence. 'Go back to sleep!' he hissed. He was mad this time. I tried to, but again I heard the sound coming from outside."

"I got out of bed, and started creeping down the stairs. The scratching sound got louder as I got closer to the bottom of the steps. It seemed to be coming from out in the yard. I walked slowly towards the back door. I kept thinking to myself, *What are you doing? Where are you going? Why do you have to know what's out there?* I was really scared but I just kept on walking. For some reason, I just had to see what it was. Closer and closer I got to the door. Suddenly I heard a sound that sounded like 'Yom! Yom! Yom!'"

"Someone or something was eating. I froze. Then I heard a terrible snarling noise as if two great beasts were trying to kill each other. I cracked the door open and peeked into the backyard. It was a chupacabra!'"

This was the place where Estrellita usually started to laugh.

And this was the place where Estefan would just ignore her and keep on spinning the tale.

He went on, "It was not just one chupacabra; there were two of them! They were fighting over something! I summoned all my courage and pushed the door open and took one step into the dirt yard. The two goat-suckers stopped in mid-bite. Their eyes were glowing green dots in the black night. They stared at me, snarling and their pointy white fangs gleamed in the moonlight. Then they screeched, dropped what they were chewing on and ran up to the fence. They leaped over it with ease, almost as if they had wings, and disappeared into the dark. When those things screamed I thought I was going to pee on myself, but I didn't. I couldn't believe everyone in the house was still sleeping. How could they sleep with that racket in the yard?"

"I stared at the spot where the chupacabras had dropped the thing they were fighting over. I knew no one would believe me when I told them what I saw so I started to walk over to the thing on the ground. This would be my proof. My legs did not want to move. As if in slow motion, I forced them to move, I had to take my hands and move my legs with them."

At this point Estefan put his hands on his thighs as if to dramatize the scene. He continued, "One step at a time. Slowly, I came closer and closer to it. At last I was close enough to see what it was."

"It looked like a human hand, gnarled fingers curled into a fist! And as I stared at the severed wrist, one of the chupacabras leaped back into the yard. I was close enough to touch it. I was close enough to smell it! I could see its face in all its gory detail. It had huge pointed ears, and a scrunched up face like a hyena or a vampire bat. Its shriveled front legs resembled raccoon paws. It smelled like spoiled milk."

"It glared defiantly at me. Then it sneered nastily with all its sharp teeth showing, snatched the hand in its misshapen jaws, and scrambled back over the fence."

"I stood there in shock. I couldn't scream even though I wanted to. The next thing I knew I felt a hand on my shoulder. It was my brother. I jumped at least a foot into the air, and the scream came out then!"

"'What did you see, brother?' He asked me."

"'I don't know. I think it was a chupacabra!'"

"He laughed. 'Oh, little brother, such an imagination!'"

"'Didn't you hear all the noise?' I asked him."

"'No, all we heard was you screaming! Come on back to bed. No more cabrito for you, little brother.' He laughed at me again."

"But I know what I saw," finished Estefan.

Estrellita laughed. "I believe you, Niño," she said. And she put her head back on his chest and listened to his heartbeat. A little faster than before, she noted.

***

It was long after midnight before they finally finished playing around beneath the sheets of Estrellita's big bed. They fell asleep in one another's arms and the image of Dai-yu was finally put to rest. For the time being, Estefan's heart was full of Estrellita.

Estefan spent the rest of the night at the Silver Spring. At the break of dawn he woke. It was still mostly dark out but the last of the red, purple, and orange clouds were still commandeering the skies over Silver Springs and the Rocky Mountains. He hurriedly tugged on his boots to catch the tail-end of the sunrise and headed back to the estate outside of town. As he rode his horse through the quiet countryside, he drank in the peace of the early morning hours.

This was a time of day when the chances of spotting wildlife was a certainty, not a probability. He caught glimpses of mule deer and elk still foraging for their breakfasts, and every so often a rabbit, coyote, or fox popped out of nowhere. He also heard the birds singing their little hearts out in the spruce trees above. It was a moment when he was sure that God was smiling down on him.

Estrellita

After Estefan left, Estrellita lay in bed for a while. She couldn't sleep. His presence, his aura, was still filling her head and her heart. She pictured him: his smile, his crooked teeth, his smooth black hair that hung down in her face loosely as he feasted intently on her body, so involved, so single in his purpose. She imagined touching his shiny waxed mustache, his brown skin. She could still hear his voice: its deep tenor vibrations, the sound of his words, the sounds of his laughter. She could still smell him: his tanned body that spoke of leather, horses and hay. She sniffed the sheets, she loved this moment right after he left, when the sweat had covered and soaked the sheets and his perfume was everywhere. In her nostrils, on her chest, even down below in her short curly hairs.

Everything about him made her smile. She was happy, content, and filled with warmth. She felt wonderfully relaxed. The world was truly a good place. She knew with certainty that the universe was good. She was loved. Estefan was a good, good man. So loving, so charming, so handsome. And he made her feel so good, so important, so desirable. She could tell he really loved her. All was well in her world and she was sure this feeling would last forever.

Then she fell asleep. And while she slept, everything changed. From white to black. From light to dark. From good to evil.

When she awoke hours later, all the good feelings were gone. She felt empty. Alone. Abandoned. She was agitated. She masturbated using the images from their recent lovemaking session to fuel this frustrating experience. Even after she came to an explosive orgasm, and fell into a relaxed sleep for a few minutes, when she woke again, she still felt bad. She was filled with fear. There was no relief.

The world was no longer a good, safe place. Nothing was right in the universe either. Estefan didn't love her. With sadness, she realized she didn't even rank a spot on the list of things he considered important. His wife, his sons, his horses, his gold, his reputation, even his mustache, everything he was or possessed came before she did!

Estefan was a bastard! A selfish, uncaring bastard! He was hurtful, false, ugly! She hated the way he looked, the way he laughed, the way he smelled. She hated everything about him. It was he that made her feel this way! Useless…valueless, a piece of flesh, a piece of rental property.

Everything was Estefan's fault! He made her feel as if she had no more value than a discarded rag used to scrub a floor! He made her feel invisible. He not only did not love her, he did not even remember she existed when they weren't in the same room. This realization struck her right in the heart.

Estrellita's thoughts spiraled down until she was at a place where the entire world seemed hopeless. To Estrellita's brain, full of negative distortions, the world had become a kind of hell. Only in hell could a man treat a woman the way Estefan treated her. Only in hell could a man get away with this bad behavior. Why did she put up with it? Why?

She broke out in feverish tears as she promised herself as she had countless times before, she would never again let him treat her this way. She cried and cried and as she cried she vaguely came to an awareness that she had to force the tears out. She had cried so many times before over this man that the crying had become a ritual, a habit. She wasn't even sure she felt any of the sorrow she used to feel after he left. Now all she felt was outrage. Her tears were tears of anger.

When her eyes were nice and puffy and red, she got out of bed, went to the mirror, splashed cold water on them, fixed her face, and went down the stairs to the Grand Salon. There she proceeded to get good and drunk.

There she went to wait for the next time Estefan showed up to start the cycle of acceptance and rejection all over again. There she went to await the next round of self-loathing.

The Lovers

The second time Estefan made love to Dai-yu was a lot easier than the first time. The terrible indecision was gone. The fear was gone. In its place was compassion and tenderness. For the first time in his life, he sensed a kindred spirit. She was another wounded creature in need of care.

He decided it would never do to rush things. He led her by the hand to the small room, sat her on the bed and regarded her for a time. She was wearing the same silver kimono as the first time he had seen her.

"So tell me," he said, what are those birds and he pointed to the phoenixes adorning the front of the robe.

"Those are called 'Feng huang,'" she said simply.

"What does that mean," asked Estefan.

"Feng huang is bird that rises from the ashes.

"Oh, a phoenix," said Estefan, "That is what we call it."

"Phoenix," said Dai-yu, emphasizing the word. "And what does phoenix do?" she asked.

"I'm not sure," laughed Estefan. "But it's a mythical beast."

"What does this Feng Huang do?" he said and as he mispronounced the word, Dai-yu corrected him; then she laughed.

"Feng huang is bird that that rules over all other birds; feng means male and huang means female. Feng huang symbolizes male and female energy; they say it is good omen if one is marrying. Feng huang is associated with fire element.

"But what does it do?" asked Estefan.

"It is ferocious bird; it kills snakes!" answered Dai-yu. They both laughed then. She went on, "Is has five tail feathers to symbolize five virtues of Confucius."

"This is pretty complicated," said Estefan.

"Everything has meaning to Chinese. Nothing is just for show. There are two phoenixes on my robe, one male and one female. Do you know which is which?"

Estefan guessed correctly.

"You are right, five tail feathers is male. Five is Yang. Yang is man. This phoenix," and she pointed to the one with five feathers, "Is you. And this one," she pointed to the other, "One feather broken into two, "Two is Yin. Yin is woman and this is me."

"Next time you can tell me about the dragon," said Estefan.

"Oh that is much longer story," she smiled.

He carefully undid the single wrap to the kimono and she stepped lightly out of the fabric that fell and bunched itself haphazardly about her small feet. She reached up and pulled the single pin that held her shiny black hair on top of her small head.

He picked her up and marveled at the amount of long black hair. It fell towards the floor, like the waves of a black waterfall. He placed her on the bed. This time he took his clothes off too. He was painfully aware of his sagging belly, but she smiled at him so he was encouraged.

This time his intent was to please her. Please her in a way he was fairly certain no one had taken the trouble to or had the desire to do so before. She was of the world but not worldly at all. Instead, the world had been chewing on her for years. The world had been chewing at her soul, chewing at her body, chewing her up without swallowing her. Leaving her wounded, but wounded in a way that could not be seen with the eyes.

As he unrobed she immediately went into her automatic mode. She grabbed for his stiff shaft, which had become erect instantly as his eyes touched her young naked body. She meant to take his member into her mouth but he stopped her. She was confused but acquiescent.

Tonight Estefan took the initiative. He was the one to bend forward and minister to her needs.

He gently moved her legs apart and with his long fingers began to brush the small, almost invisible, hairs that lived there like so many tiny trees populating a tiny forest. He moved his hand slowly, as if he were stroking a skittish cat. Little goose-bumps rose to freckle her inner thighs as if rising to greet his sweet caresses. He began to kiss the skin of her inner thighs with his soft lips, and as he did so, he inched closer and closer to the area where her two legs joined together. In response to his inward progress, her body tensed. She was tense, but not in the right way, not in the way Estefan had hoped she would be.

Suddenly, she put her hand in his hair and stopped him. Estefan guessed that she was afraid. Okay, if the filly is shy, you back off. Try again later. Meanwhile you do something else, something less threatening.

He returned to her willing mouth. He kissed her, as his tongue touched her tongue, she opened wider to allow him to penetrate her; again and again he kissed her. Their mouths merged as if they might swallow one another; they kissed until they were both out of breath. Then when he sensed her body beginning to relax again, he slowly brought his fingers down to the place hiding her most valuable treasure. Her body tensed. He backed off. Finally, he resumed his insistent stroking of the hairs there, despite her body's resistance. Slowly he stroked, and eventually she allowed her eyes to close. Her body was still tense but at least her eyes were shut. That meant she was trying to let her guard down. She was no longer staring at him in fear.

As he stroked the hairs, every so often he brushed across the place where he knew the opening lay. It was as tightly sealed as if it had been sewn shut. Eventually he felt something change; the little doorway to the cave began to open. As he continued to stroke, ever so slowly the cave yawned and with delight he found one finger damp as it crossed the threshold for the umpteenth time. Yes, this might just work, he congratulated himself. And then as if she was seized by a sensation of pain, her eyes pinched tightly, her face wrinkled into a grimace, and her buttocks tensed just slightly. The rest of her body scarcely moved but he could see from the flush that covered the upper part of her chest that he had managed to touch the trigger in just the right way and the girl's hidden weapon had discharged.

Slowly she opened her eyes. She stared at him in wonder. She reached down as if to touch herself where he had been touching her. Then she started to smile. She laughed a short laugh that resembled a snort. Then she asked him simply, "What did you do?"

It was his turn to laugh. And slowly it came to Estefan's consciousness. Like a puzzle. No one had ever done this with her or to her. She'd never had an orgasm before.

"I didn't do anything," he said, "You did, and you can do it again."

"I can do it again?" she repeated almost in disbelief.

"Sure," he said, "Anytime you want. Here, let me show you how." And he took her hand in his own and brought it back down to the relevant coordinates. This time she was eager for him to touch her. And unlike a filly, the pupil was excited about beginning its education.

***

Two days later, Estefan was sitting with his back against the pillow that was, in turn, propped against the headboard. She was sitting cross-legged between his legs, facing him, regarding him steadily with her large jade-colored eyes. *That's strange*, he thought, *her eyes were a different color before*. He decided the light from the street lamps that managed to creep past the curtains must be playing tricks on him. Her eyes used to be dark, almost pitch black.

"So tell me," he said. "What is your real name? What does it mean? Where does it come from? Where do you come from?" Everything about her was a mystery. He loved mysteries. That is, he loved solving them.

"So many questions," she stated. Then she smiled at him, and his heart was instantly warm because he knew this smile was a real one, a sincere one. There were no cigar butts in the room.

She was truly at ease, genuinely at rest, at peace. He marveled at the beauty of the smile, so childlike, yet secretive and wise at the same time. When she smiled, she resembled the all-knowing Buddha, and she seemed older, even older than he. The concept of "old-soul" crept into his consciousness from deep within his memory. It seemed that he had heard it in an old folk tale when he was a child. It had been stored alongside other foolish beliefs, beliefs where people die and come back as ravens or wolves or bears, beliefs that haunt the dark corners of rooms where old women whisper secrets to one another.

Yes, he knew with certainty, this was an old-soul before him. Here was a being that had lived before. Perhaps she had once been a wise old woman, or a man, or the Buddha himself. And now this soul inhabited the body of a young willowy maiden.

"Come here, turn around." He circled her with his arms as she leaned back against him.

Strange thoughts, indeed, thought Estefan, but this was a strange otherworldly nymph he held in his arms.

Dai-yu looked down at his arms encircling her body and took his right hand in her two smaller ones. She began to examine his palms. First she looked at his left palm;

then she spent a considerable amount of time studying the other one.

"What are you doing?" asked Estefan.

"I am reading your palm," she said simply.

"I don't believe in that! He said. That's black magic! It's evil."

"Oh no, it is not evil! It is the past, the past is not evil. The past is just the past. It cannot hurt us anymore. It is over. It is okay if you do not believe," she said. "I will believe for both of us."

He tried to pull his right hand back. But she held on defiantly. It took both of her tiny hands to secure his much larger one. She was a lot stronger than she looked. Finally, he relinquished. And her little face came very close to his curled fingers, and he could feel her warm breath on his skin. She moved her head side to side like a cat before a window studying a bird, back and forth, trying to determine if the bird is a bird or just a part of the background.

As she stared intently at his palm she traced the different lines slowly with a fingernail. He felt a tingling in his scalp at the back of his head as he felt her nails move from one part of his hand to another. After a few minutes, she spoke.

"I see that you have had much hardship in your early time. You have one love but it is over; see how it tries to escape from your palm and hide itself away? You have sickness in your heart and in your head," and as she said that she touched first the center of her chest with her first two fingers, and then the top of her head with her first three fingers and thumb spread apart. All of a sudden, Estefan was interested.

"Will I live a long life?" he asked.

"Oh no," she said, "We cannot say. "We can only say what has already happened. Your palm records past, not future. I can tell where your pain is, but not where your pain will be someday. Ah, but you will die rich man," she added.

"Well that's good to know," he said. "What about this pain in my heart? What does that mean?"

"I do not know," Dai-yu said truthfully.

"Now it's your turn, he said. "Answer my questions."

"My Chinese name is Lin Dai-yu," she said. "It means 'blue-black jade.' It is very old name from very old story. It is name of girl poet and artist. She fell in love with boy. But boy was destined to marry someone else, even though he loved her in return. So she drowned herself in sorrow."

"That is a very sad story. Does that mean it is also a very sad name?" asked Estefan.

"Yes, I believe it is very sad name," said Dai-yu.

"Does this sad name belong to a sad girl?" he continued.

"I am bird in cage," Dai-yu said somberly.

"Does the bird still sing?" asked Estefan.

"Sometimes. When bird forgets it lives in cage, yes, bird still sings."

He was sad. Sad for the bird. Sad for the life the bird lived. And he wanted to do something about it.

"We'll see about that," he said and he took her chin in his hand and kissed her small lips with his own.

The Madam

Before he left the Silver Spring that night, Estefan approached the madam with a simple request. He only asked one little thing... that Estrellita swap rooms with the China Doll. Not simple for her, simple for him.

On the one hand, the Madam was relieved to be given a chance to get rid of the mean-spirited Estrellita. On the other hand, she knew such a request would cause nothing but trouble at the Silver Spring.

She had hoped for years that Estrellita would leave on her own. But instead of leaving, as the years passed, Estrellita built up a sizable list of important clients, and the Madam was forced to put up with the prickly spines on the poisonous ivy that all but choked the cheerfulness out of her other flowers.

If she made Estrellita give up her room, she knew this was as good as kicking her out on the street. Estrellita's temper and ego would never allow such a thing. It would also signify the worst possible thing that could happen to the woman, that is, that Estefan no longer wanted her anymore. Or he didn't want her as his number one. Perhaps not even at all.

The madam was glad that she could get rid of Estrellita, but she wished it didn't have to be her doing. She did not want to be the "bad guy." She wanted Estefan to be the bad guy for once, but she knew that would never happen.

She was sure that with his charming silvery tongue he would be able to dump Estrellita and still remain friends with her. He could make Estrellita believe that the China Doll's room was better than the one she had been living in. He could spin some cock-and-bull story, tell her the room had a better view of the street, or better morning light, or was closer to the communal restroom, although she suspected Estrellita would never fall for such blatant misdirection.

The madam knew Estefan could sell anything to anyone.

Sadly, she imagined how the conversation between Estefan and Estrellita might go. He would ask her to give up her room as a favor to him. And Estrellita, who never could think clearly in her "boyfriend's" presence, would amiably agree. In fact, she would be angry with Estefan, but she would not dare let him know. Instead, true to form, she would displace her aggression onto everyone else. The Madam knew Estrellita would not attack *her* personally, and she briefly experienced a half-dose of guilt and a full-dose of sympathy for the other girls, for they were the ones who would experience Estrellita's wrath directly. She even pitied poor Dai-yu even though she didn't know her well enough to care very much about her or her well-being. Dai-yu would certainly find herself to be at the center of Hurricane Estrellita.

Then the Madam envisioned the more likely circumstance, she herself breaking the bad news to Estrellita.

Why Estefan had ever liked this nasty vetch in the first place was anyone's guess. It was a mystery to be sure. Estrellita was rude, crude, and had a mouth like a chamber pot. She had a strange looking body; her breasts were proportionally too large for her narrow hips. Her legs seemed a little too long for her torso. Her blotchy face had uneven features, and she was stupid. She didn't even dress well, despite the generous allowance Estefan bestowed upon her. She picked out garish clothes and accessorized them as if she were a gypsy. "The more colors, the better," seemed to be Estrellita's fashion creed.

Everyone assumed she had some secret sex trick she wasn't sharing with anyone else, or some strange animal magnetism only detected by men, or perhaps she cast a spell on the ones she desired. That was much more likely it was generally agreed. Black magic, dabbling in the occult, or voodoo vied as likely candidates for Estrellita's unexplainable success with persons of the opposite sex.

Whatever it was, it certainly kept her men happy and loyal; she had several clients, besides Estefan, that had been patronizing her for years.

Now that Estefan had chosen Dai-yu to be his woman, the Madam hoped that Estrellita would leave the Silver Spring peacefully. She didn't even care if Estrellita left and took her other clients with her. This would be a happy scenario all around. With what Estefan was now paying her for Dai-yu's contribution to his life Estrellita's earnings towards the upkeep of the saloon were no longer needed.

The Madam justified further in her head. She reasoned Estrellita would be better off without Estefan's patronage; she could even get married, or buy a house of her own. The Madam was certain Estrellita must have amassed a considerable nest egg by now; after all, Estefan had been giving her money for years.

Another odious thought momentarily crossed the Madam's mind; Estefan might buy Dai-yu a place of her own, a house. But she knew that was highly unlikely, it was infinitely wiser to "keep" her at the Silver Spring, where she was safe. Living alone was a dangerous proposition for any woman in the American West.

Estrellita

Estrellita had been top hen in this henhouse for years as Estefan's mistress. As Estefan's property, she had a certain prestige and status that she lauded over the other girls. Being Estefan's girl meant that she outranked all the others. He was their biggest client, and he preferred her company.

Estrellita's main function had been to service Estefan. She did flirt and mooch drinks off many of the other clients, mostly just to fill her abundant free time. She even slept with the ones she liked, as long as she was sure Estefan wasn't going to show up, especially the ones who bought her substantial gifts.

The Madam was willing to let Estrellita have her own way, and to let her live in the best quarters in the brothel, only because Estefan liked her. Otherwise, she would have put Estrellita's self-centered ill-tempered behind out on the dust-filled streets of Silver Spring long ago. The spoiled prima donna only remained at the Silver Spring thanks to Estefan's protective influence.

Estrellita hated the other girls and other women as a rule. She only had one or two friends at any time. These were the only girls she tolerated in her presence. These favorites or "pets" were allowed to brush Estrellita's long hair, cut her toenails, wash her clothes, or plait her locks into long braids, like so many servants. Estrellita would even deign to let her patsy of the present try on the many dresses that Estefan had given her. As Estefan's mistress, she was often the target of his abundant largesse. It could be said that Estefan had many faults, but generosity wasn't one of them. He loved to shower gifts upon the people he cared about. Perhaps that was why he was liked by so many people, men and women alike.

For years, Estrellita had stalked about the Silver Spring like a swan among ducks, snidely disparaging the others if they dared try to take the attention off of her, or dared to look prettier, or dared to dress more provocatively than she did. Estrellita wasn't beautiful in the normal sense of the word, and caked makeup on her face as if she were getting paid to use as much of it as possible.

It was also well known that Estrellita stole things from the other girls. If anything turned up missing, and it frequently did, it was invariably later found out to be hidden in Estrellita's room.

Behind Estrellita's back, the other girls joked, they should have named her "Estrellita Negra" or dark star.

The girls Estrellita liked all had one thing in common. Excessively low self-esteem. Wherever they came from, whatever circumstances they had endured, had symbiotically prepared them for a life as one of Estrellita's flunkies. Perhaps Estrellita felt sorry for them, but more likely she preferred them because she could bully them around and they'd still come back for more. They'd still be happy to do her hair, or nails, or grovel pitifully before her, all the while enduring Estrellita's frequent putdowns. Estrellita peppered her conversations with back-handed compliments, such as, "You are pretty, but if only you were prettier, you'd have a man like Estefan," or "You may be clever, but if only you were a little smarter, someone would notice you," or "You are a very sweet girl, but if only you had a better personality, you'd have a husband by now."

For even though it was never openly discussed, each girl hoped in her heart of hearts to leave this place, and the fastest and surest one-way ticket out was to win the love of one of the men, who crossed the threshold of places like the Silver Spring. Men who swore they'd never come back, but men who worked long hours and found themselves tired, stressed, and alone on many a night in a strange town.

Hope took the form of the fantasy that one of these worldly travelers, worldly only in comparison to the girls' limited experiences, would realize that a certain girl possessed a heart of gold, beneath a gruff exterior, and that she was not a whore in her heart, but a victim forced to sell herself by the unfair circumstances that life had heaped upon her.

Some girls even believed in the fickle hearts of the regulars, and believed those hearts could change. A regular was a man who showed up punctually every week at the same time like a train on a schedule. One could set one's pocket watch on the comings and goings of the regulars.

The Madam

Change was not necessarily a good thing, the Madam was realizing. When she broke the news to Estrellita the girl didn't say anything. She acted almost as if she hadn't heard her. Then she packed up her few personal items and moved them into the China Doll's room. She was quiet, too quiet.

Estrellita had never even spoken to Dai-yu. To Estrellita, Dai-yu was not even worth the attention of a hair on a dog. Now Dai-yu had insinuated herself into Estrellita's life in a most unwelcome and unforeseen way.

Once Estrellita gave up her room, and its accompanying status, there was hell to be paid. Punishing Dai-yu became Estrellita's new mission. She set her mind to making Dai-yu's life miserable. And that's exactly what she did. She was civil with the China doll when they were around other people, but when they were alone, she would pinch her cruelly on the arm, or pull her hair wickedly. Then she would laugh like a witch and run off. Dai-yu didn't dare fight back. Or say anything.

Behind Dai-yu's back, Estrellita would start vicious rumors. She denigrated her origin, her people, her looks, her eyes, her body, the way she spoke, the way she smelled, her accent, and anything else that came to her envious mind.

Dai-yu

Dai-yu could not believe how things had changed. Last week, she was nobody. Nothing. Invisible. She had been less than the red dirt beneath her feet. That was the way she preferred it. It was always safer to lay low than to draw attention to oneself.

Today she was the most important girl at the Silver Spring. Or so it seemed. Unfortunately now she was also the mortal enemy of the furious Estrellita.

Estrellita

Estrellita felt her world falling apart.

She already despised the Chinese girl. Now this resentment was heightened. Once everyone learned that she would be exchanging living quarters with the little Chinese slut, things got really bad. She heard the other girls sniggering behind her back. Even the men seemed to be looking at her in a new way, perhaps even with pity? And Estefan, every time she laid eyes on him now, she felt sick. Sick in her stomach, and sick in her heart.

Why was this happening? How could Estefan let this happen? It was just like him, fickle. And she had let this happen. She had let him treat her badly. When he was bad to her he could always show up later, with gift in hand, and a hangdog expression to beg forgiveness. And she would always forgive him. But not this time. It was too much.

Estefan

Estefan went on with his life as if nothing had happened. He didn't think twice about replacing Estrellita. He didn't think about anything other than what was important to him. And what was important to him was making the little China girl happy.

He was truly smitten with her. He decided to surprise her with something, something to tell her how much he cherished her, something to make her feel less sad. "I'll be back soon," he told her. Then he kissed her one last time, mounted his black horse and rode home.

The next day he visited the local jeweler. He was standing outside when the man opened his shop. The goldsmith had several fine pieces of gold and silver jewelry on display in the window. Estefan went inside and asked the man to see his finest works of art. The China doll was no ordinary woman so she deserved no ordinary piece of jewelry. She needed an extraordinary necklace to adorn her slender swanlike neck. She had to own something that celebrated the color of her eyes. It had to be something precious and unique.

He spotted a necklace in one of the glass cases. It had many small oval shaped red stones cradled in sterling silver settings that cascaded down to a point. At the point was a large blood-red inverted pear shaped stone that looked like a teardrop. It was flanked by two rows of tiny diamonds.

"That one," he gestured. "What are those stones?"

"Rubies," answered the jeweler.

"Can you make me another piece like that one, but with green stones instead?" asked Estefan.

"Certainly," said the artisan. "What sort of green stones did you have in mind? We have several kinds of green gems." He quickly listed them all, "Emerald, malachite, peridot, jade, we even have green sapphire."

"Show me what you have."

The jeweler pulled out a small selection of stones in various shades of green.

"Those ones," Estefan pointed to the emeralds.

"Good choice," said the jeweler.

"How long would it take?" asked Estefan.

"At least a week," replied the other man.

"How much would that cost?" Estefan continued the line of questioning.

The jeweler quoted the price and Estefan dug into his coin purse and pulled out ten $20 golden double-eagles. The jeweler's eyes widened perceptibly.

"Have it ready by tomorrow night," Estefan ordered.

"That is not possible," countered the jeweler.

"Make it possible," said Estefan and as he produced another gold eagle from his purse, the jeweler lapsed into his groveling mode.

"Yes Sir! Of course, Sir!" he said with enthusiasm.

"Oh, and how much for the other necklace?" continued Estefan. "The one with the rubies?"

"I can give you that one for five double eagles." Estefan reached into his pocket again and fished out some more money. "I'll take that one too. And I'll be back around 6 tomorrow night."

Estefan returned home. He was as excited as a small boy on Christmas morning. He never could stand to wait for his gifts to be opened. He always wanted to know ahead of time what he was getting. He loved to get gifts, and he loved to give them. He loved to see the surprise on other people's faces. And he loved to be able to give presents, especially fine expensive ones. He couldn't wait to see the look in Dai-yu's eyes. He very much doubted she had ever expected to one day own such a fine showpiece.

He was back at the jeweler's shop at 5 p.m. late the next afternoon. He couldn't wait until the appointed hour. He hung around and watched as the jeweler, with a magnifying loupe in his right eye, fiddled with tools at his workbench, and at last began to polish the emerald necklace with a small cloth coated with rouge. Then the jeweler thoroughly cleaned the rouge off with a brush full of soap and hot water.

The process seemed painfully slow to the impatient watcher. When Estefan thought he could wait no longer, the man finished working on the necklace. He held it up for Estefan to inspect. Estefan didn't know much of anything about jewelry but it appeared to be large and it sparkled energetically, so he was satisfied. The jeweler carefully placed the neck piece into a small wooden box lined with black velvet and handed it to Estefan.

Then the jeweler wiped the ruby necklace with a small polishing cloth before putting it into another small box. Estefan handed him the 30 gold pieces, thanked the jeweler graciously, and placed the two boxes into the left inside pocket of his overcoat.

Estefan was beside himself with excitement for it was now time to present his gift to his newly beloved.

***

After Estefan left the jewelers, he went straight home. By the time he got back to the hacienda it was after seven p.m. It was too late to give Dai-yu her necklace so he decided to wait until the next evening. Instead he had a late dinner with his wife, Margarita but his mind was elsewhere.

Margarita

Earlier that same day, Margarita was in the kitchen chewing out one of the kitchen maids. The crystal had spots on it, even though apparently she was the only person in the house observant enough to notice them.

"I'm sorry! I'm sorry!" begged the old woman. But Margarita was relentless. Finally, in a fit of pique, she fired the old lady. Then she ordered another one of the servants to rewash all the glasses, re-polish the silverware while she was at it, and scour the kitchen tiles. Then she flew up the stairs to her room to sulk. It usually made her feel better to thoroughly castigate someone of lesser social status, but this time the act was oddly unsatisfying. She flung open the doors of one of her wardrobes and tried to select something to wear. She screamed for her hand-maiden, Luisa, who was hiding somewhere. Just before her ill-tempered visit to the kitchen, she had ordered Luisa to "Go away!" and unfortunately, Luisa had. It was altogether a very bad day for the poor, spoiled Margarita.

She wanted what she wanted and she wanted it *when* she wanted it. And no one seemed to be able to anticipate her every whim in advance. It was all very unfair.

Luisa appeared quickly and helped her dress. She was sullen and silent. Margarita ordered her to smile, and to stop pouting. The maid forced a smile to her lips, but her eyes were wary. Margarita straddled her corset horse, as Luisa laced up the garment that kept all her bodily parts in their proper places. Then Margarita stood before the oval full-length clawed-footed dressing mirror and admired herself as Luisa fixed her hair.

Despite her earlier foul mood, ten minutes of beholding her own breath-taking visage, was enough to make her feel much better. As Luisa brushed her hair for her and braided it, the vestiges of bad mood departed altogether. Luisa finished wrapping the package with an ivory comb and Margarita found herself regarding a true Spanish princesa.

It would be a glorious day after all, Margarita announced to herself.

Two of the ladies who lived on the closest neighboring "haciendas" were coming for tea and to play cards. The haciendas were actually just ranches but the well-to-do nabobs or snobs preferred to call them by the Spanish word to enhance their prestige, even if only in their own eyes. There were no great haciendas in these parts.

The lion's share of the afternoon was spent in idle conversation as the three shared their respective "horror" stories of negligent, disrespectful servants, and overpriced luxuries ordered from Europe. They commiserated about the slowness of the delivery service, and the substandard quality of gourmet food items they had to settle for, items that were substantially lesser than women of their social mien deserved. They lamented the taste and texture of the locally grown beef and the scarcity of good tea. They agreed that it was only their great fortitude, ability to endure, and flexibility that enabled them to flourish under such savage and barbaric conditions.

When the girls left, Margarita puttered around in the upstairs rooms of the hacienda house, reading old love letters, and wondering what had become of the life she was supposed to have. She thought back to her life in Old Mexico and the other suitors that had come before Estefan. What had become of them? Who had they married? Were they still in love? Did they still think of her? Did their wives have it as well as she had it? She smiled at long last for she did have it very well even if at times she forgot to see it that way.

That night, Margarita's husband, Estefan, surprised her with yet another gift of fine jewelry. It was pitiable, this blind devotion he had for her. She opened the velvet lined box at once and was momentarily thrilled to discover a beautiful neckpiece inside. It was expertly crafted of sterling silver findings which protectively hugged a bevy of oval-shaped rubies. The piece culminated in a huge pear-shaped ruby surrounded by a circle of tiny twinkling diamonds. They sparkled with brilliance. She tried the necklace on immediately. Estefan stood behind her and helped her fasten the clasp at the base of her neck, and as he did so, he kissed the spot between her neck and shoulder lovingly and cooed, "To the only woman I've ever loved. Te quiero mucho, Corazón."

Dinner was a pleasant experience for a change. Margarita fingered the large ruby every couple of minutes as if to remind herself of her husband's undying love, and beamed as she did so.

**

Margarita was so thrilled by Estefan's trinket that she decided to allow him to make love to her. First, she proposed a toast, to their great fortune, to one another, to the lucky stars that had brought them together. Their glasses clinked and they sipped simultaneously. As the supper progressed, Margarita rapidly downed a couple of glasses of a fine Madeira that had been imported from France. She drank with a purpose, the purpose of accelerating the arrival of her amorous side. The sweet fortified wine went down smoothly and quickly produced the feelings she was aiming for. As she drank the cool liquid she gazed upon her husband. He was getter more handsome by the minute.

She flushed in anticipation as the temperature in the room increased. Then she rose and took Estefan's hand and led him upstairs to the bedroom. Estefan went through the motions. But his mind was elsewhere. He helped her out of her dress and underthings. They slithered underneath the bed sheets that had been warmed by the hot water in the little porcelain pig.

But Estefan just couldn't do it. For some reason, it felt wrong; he felt like he was cheating on his new Chinese mistress, cheating with his own wife. It was nuts, and it was a first. He kissed Margarita, but the kisses fell flat. There was no spark. He didn't feel anything, no lust, no heat, no hardness where he needed it.

Margarita wanted to have sex with Estefan. She wanted him like never before. She gave him her most seductive look. To her dismay he wasn't getting aroused. His member just hung there, refusing to commit itself. It became an uninvolved and unrepentant bystander.

Margarita kept trying. She initiated another kiss, but nothing happened. His return kiss felt empty, as if he was not really with her. He excused himself, then apologized. She felt the earlier anger of the day returning.

"What's the matter with you?" she demanded.

"Nothing. I'm just feeling a little scratch in my throat. Maybe I'm coming down with something," he lied.

Then he went to the other room. She could hear him getting dressed.

"You're not going out at this hour, are you?"

"Yes, I have some business to attend to," a lie was growing.

"At this hour? I thought you said you were feeling sick?" she interrogated. As her fear escalated, her temper rose in a show of support. She was close to full boil.

"Yes, I'll be back soon," as if that lame qualification might placate her.

"I don't care if you never come back, you bastard!" Estrellita screamed. Estefan mounted his horse and rode off.

And a day that started out badly ended the same way.

Estefan

It was well after nine when Estefan arrived at the Silver Spring. Eagerly he searched for the China doll. There she was, like a dazzling mountain bluebird, sporting a bright blue kimono. Apparently, that was her trademark identity in this place. The satin cloth was embroidered with pink and white flowers, and in the distance there were tree-covered mountains. The many colored threads were highlighted in places with shiny gold threads.

On his last visit, Estefan had slipped the Madam a sizable tip to ensure that Dai-yu was waiting for him, and no one else, when he arrived. Instead of playing cards or drinking, they went immediately up to her new room. He was pleased to see that Dai-yu had moved her few personal possessions into Estrellita's old room since they had last met. This room was the largest, most well-furnished room in the Silver Spring, aside from the Madam's own suite. Like the Madam's own room, it had a large four poster bed with a canopy.

"How do you like your new room?" he asked Dai-yu.

"It is very beautiful," she added, "I am grateful for your kindness."

"Don't be," he bragged. "I did it for both of us." And he laughed out loud. "My woman deserves the best of everything!" With that pronouncement as a segue he reached into the inside pocket of his overcoat, and brought out the box that protected the emerald necklace.

When she spotted the box, her eyes were a blue-green color. But once she beheld the shiny green-colored stones, her eyes turned deep blue. So that was her happy color! The first thing she did was take off the jade necklace she had been wearing for more than six years. She kissed the small stone and placed it on the nightstand.

Then as she trembled he stood behind her and secured the necklace in place. His fingers on the back of her neck made her whole body tingle. Then he continued to stand behind her and examine her in the mirror. He loved her round face, her long black hair, the tiny breasts, slender waist, delicately formed hips, and gazelle-like legs. She was so perfect, and he imagined her standing naked before him, wearing only that gleaming mass of silver and green. It seemed almost criminal that something artificial, something manmade, should try to compete for attention with her natural beauty. He made as if to take the necklace off.

"No," she said, "I will treasure this always. I will never take it off." Then she kissed him. And he thought his heart might burst open and all the blood flow out, because he could not stand so much joy.

After Dai-yu thanked him repeatedly for the necklace, she knew it was time, to give herself to this crazy, impetuous, and irresistible man. She wanted to give everything she had, everything she was, to this miracle who was the answer to the many prayers she had, until this very moment, believed had gone unheard.

She reached into the drawer of the night stand next to the bed to retrieve one of the sheepskin condoms the madam ordered specially from Paris. She began to unroll the flimsy piece of flesh when Estefan stopped her.

"There is no need for that," he said.

"What?" she asked surprised. *Condoms were a necessity for survival in this place, in this time.*

"No," Estefan said, "You belong to me now. No one else will be using this," and he gestured towards her body, "Anymore. This beautiful body belongs to me."

"But what if I don't want to belong to you?" she said playfully, teasing him.

"You don't want to be mine, my possession? You don't want this?" and he pointed to his chest, "You don't want my corazón!?" He sniffled as if he were about to break into tears.

"Oh *that*?" she said, Yes, I want *that*," and then she laughed. "And I really want *that*," and she pointed to his erect member.

"Then that is what you shall have!" His tears forgotten, he grabbed her and kissed her hard on the mouth.

"Wait," she tried one last time. "What if there is a child?"

"What if there is? That would be perfect," Estefan purred. "A beautiful bebé born of our beautiful selves." And he laughed. Then he paused as if he was actually picturing the child of their union. "Yes, that would be ideal. I will take care of you both!"

And though this fantastic future sounded too good to be true, Dai-yu believed him. She dropped the unused condom back into the drawer.

She thanked him one more time for the emerald necklace with her words, and then with her body. They made love, and her body joyously welcomed the intrusion of his. Then exhausted they fell into a deep sleep.

Margarita

The night after she received the fabulous necklace, Margarita was again in the mood to thank her husband, but instead of accommodating her, Estefan told her he had to go out. Margarita threw a minor tantrum once she got the news, and it quickly escalated into a screaming match.

Estefan left the house in a huff and Margarita went upstairs to throw things around her bed chamber and to yell at the servants, who were nowhere to be seen.

"Cowards!" she screeched. "You can't hide from me!"

Once she calmed down a bit, she decided to do something truly crazy. She decided to go into town, to see what he was up to. She wanted to find out why, all of a sudden, his visits to the Silver Spring had escalated from once a week to almost every other day. Even for Estefan, who in her estimation never tired of sexual matters, this was a bit excessive. Maybe there was something else occupying his mind. She had to know.

A small hopeful voice in her head spoke up. Maybe if she surprised Estefan, maybe he would be happy to see her. Maybe he would even want her to become a part of this other life. She knew it was insane, because going to the brothel was his thing, part of his private world. Going into town was his personal business, and they had had, up until this very moment, an unwritten understanding in this regard.

But tonight she was feeling strong, and powerful and untouchable. For after all, she reasoned, if Estefan was indeed the most powerful person in the environs of Silver Spring, and she was married to him, then by all rights, she was the second most powerful person in the region. His power, and his prestige, belonged to her.

She could do this thing! She would do this thing!

She ordered the servants to bring the horse-drawn carriage around to the front of the house, and swiftly and expertly they hitched up a pair of horses. She draped a floor-length black cape over a long dark blue velvet dress. The neckline plunged dramatically and left a wide open expanse of skin that begged to be filled with jewels. She wore the new necklace proudly; the blood red color of the stones contrasted smartly with the deep royal blue of her dress. The driver helped her into the carriage proffering one arm to her and helping her settle onto the leather seat. Then they set off.

The ride to town took almost two hours. The trip was considerably shorter for a man on horseback, but the carriage with its wood and iron wheels had to go slowly. Otherwise its passengers would be subjected to a very bumpy ride. She had much time to think about what she would say to Estefan, how she would justify her presence there, how she could explain this breech of the rules of decorum.

But there was something else at work here. It was almost as if she were possessed, and something outside her was compelling her to move forward on this path, even though she knew it was a path fraught with possible negative consequences.

Several times she almost stopped the driver and ordered him to take her back to their estate. The estate that was, in actuality, a prison for a woman like herself. A very nice, well furnished, posh prison, but a prison, nevertheless.

For the reality of Margarita's life, and all such women like herself, was that *she* was not the one who decided when or if she could leave or go into town. It was *he* who determined such things. She was not the one who decided what she could or could not have. He was. He was the jailor and she was the prisoner. At least this is where her paranoid thinking began to take her and helped her justify her somewhat senseless actions.

***

When they reached the outskirts of town, she asked the driver if he knew where her husband was. The driver didn't know or didn't want to say, so she threatened him with the same fate that befell the kitchen maid the day before. Reluctantly he offered the name of a very popular saloon.

"Take me there," ordered Margarita.

As they stopped in front of the brightly lit establishment, the driver made a weak attempt to stop her from going inside. "Are you sure you want to go in there? It's not a place for, and he hesitated while choosing the correct word, ladies."

"I'm sure," she said, although she wasn't at all sure anymore.

"Do you want me to come with you?" the driver offered.

"No, that won't be necessary." Then she thought better of that hasty decision. "Yes, come with me, she ordered the driver. You can hold my coat."

The Dancing Duck was a large, bawdy place on a side street that paralleled the main street of the town. A large tacky sign on the front of the building proclaimed, "THE DANCING DUCK," and a crudely drawn duck that appeared to be kicking up its webbed feet in merriment made sure even those who could not read could tell what sort of shenanigans took place within the walls of the building.

In addition to the dancing girls and alcohol, the Duck frequently featured entertainment: scantily clad female dancers, world class musicians, famous comedians, and magicians. Margarita had never been there herself. Nice women, wives, and schoolmarms did not go to places like this. But she had heard tales. That the girls would dance with the men for money. That some of the girls would even do more than dance.

The downstairs was taken up by a large dance floor, and a raised stage served as a venue for the traveling shows. The dance floor was flanked by a large bar and many patrons, male and female, were taking refreshment there.

As she walked into the room, she tried to take it all in. There was a lot of noise and a lot of bright light, too much smoke, too much color, too much raucous laughter. The music was playing much too loudly. The youngish girls dancing on the little raised stage kicked their long stocking-covered legs, spun their bodies, and flashed their frilly underthings, as she stared in shock. She was speechless.

As if responding to her stunned silence, the room started to quiet as her presence was detected. And as if she were foreign bacteria invading a body, a domino effect took place as the antibodies went on the alert.

Those patrons closest to the door were the first to react. Their silence spread quickly to the others occupying the interior of the brightly lit room. All the laughing and talking paused for an instant as all eyes turned towards the door.

Then, as if a stage cue had been given by an invisible director, the voices began to rise again, and the laughter started anew. Every person simultaneously decided, like the cells of one giant communal brain, to ignore her incongruous presence and unexpected arrival.

The girls at the bar went on soliciting drinks from the men, and the gamblers at the tables went on tossing coins into the pot and flipping cards.

She looked about the room, anxious to see a familiar face, the face of her husband, her beloved Estefan. Instead, she saw many familiar faces, the faces of the husbands of her female friends, the faces of people she saw every day of her life. She recognized the banker, the man who ran the general store, the owner of the livery stable. All the faces were familiar, but somehow unrecognizable. They had all been altered somewhat by the atmosphere or softened by drink. Like so many horny teenagers, they smiled lasciviously at all the women in the room, those who flirted with them and those that didn't. They even looked at her hungrily, a pack of wolves licking their lips in anticipation as they approached an injured fawn trying to regain its footing. She was taken aback. She was frightened.

She didn't see Estefan and her nerve was crumbling. She almost asked the bartender for a drink. But instead she fled to the safety of the carriage waiting for her outside.

The driver asked her, "Are you okay? Would you like me to take you home now?"

"No!" she almost screamed the word. She was adamant. The night was not over. She would see Estefan. She would find out what secrets he was keeping from her.

From the safety of her hansom she took a deep drag from the silver flask filled with bourbon whiskey she had brought along with her. She sat for a while as the driver outside on the buckboard nervously fidgeted. Finally she called to him. Where else could he be? Again the driver played dumb. And the words "Silver Spring Saloon" came to her mind. She had heard of this place. It was *the* place, the place where the high-falutin' high-steppers hung out. And where else would Estefan be? She knew the truth. He would be where *they* were, in a place where "girls of the night" were. Doing the things she had only heard about or dreamt of in her wickedest nightmares.

Take me to the "Silver Spring," she said.

"Yes, Ma'am," the driver said. He didn't even try to provide an argument this time.

He cracked the whip and started the horses up and within minutes they were down the street, in front of another building.

***

Silver Spring had only a handful of brothels, or houses of "ill-repute," compared to Cripple Creek. It even had one-women cribs that catered to the needs of the regular menfolk and poor broke miners who lived in the tents that filled the mining camps. But everybody knew the Silver Spring was the place where the "gentlemen" of the town and the "men of means" congregated.

Even in the dark she could still make out the white hand-painted sign on the front of the two-story building. Its fancy lettering proudly proclaimed, "THE SILVER SPRING." The sign hung over an ornate front door decorated with leaded-glass windows. An incandescent glow highlighting the glass panels with their fleur-de-lis promised the interior of the building would be warm and inviting.

She was a little disappointed to see there was not a trace of the sordid purpose of the building anywhere. There were no red lanterns in the downstairs windows, as she had always heard was customary in such places. There were no red curtains either. Instead the Silver Spring resembled a respectable Victorian style mansion.

She took another shot of bourbon, dismounted from the carriage, told the driver to wait outside, screwed up her courage for the second time, and went in the front door. As she entered the parlor, the three young girls that were sitting there stopped talking. They stared at her. Not rudely, but with undisguised curiosity.

She tried not to stare back. Instead she regarded them coolly. They were casually dressed and lounging about in the foyer/parlor like well-fed housecats. Their outfits had low-cut tight bodices and slit skirts, which resembled her own fancy underwear and corsets from Paris. It occurred to her then as she looked them up and down, that next to them, in her black and blue finery and a modest dress that covered every part of her body except for her décolletage, she stood out like a peacock in the middle of a flock of barn ducks.

One of the young women said, "Can I help you?"

It was obvious she had walked into the wrong room. Nevertheless, she was on a mission.

It was very warm in the parlor. She started to remove her cape, but decided against it. Instead she answered the girl. She said, "No thank you." She could hear music, laughter and conversation coming from down the hall. It seemed everything that was happening was happening in the room just past the stairway.

She took a deep breath, walked past the girls and headed in the direction of the music. Instead of the din of the previous night spot this music was pleasant, even soothing. A classical sonata greeted her ears.

Like an automaton she placed one foot in front of the other. Her body was on its own as her mind tried unsuccessfully to make it stop. She knew as she went forward, step by step, that she was making a huge mistake. But she couldn't stop herself. She could hear her steps echoing unnaturally in the hallway. They were much too loud.

At last, after what seemed an eternity, she reached the back room where the music was playing, men and women were talking, and it seemed everyone was laughing.

She couldn't go home now. She had committed herself to this course of action. And she had been seen. As her eyes roamed the room, she spotted Estefan. He was sitting at a table covered with coins, cards, ashtrays, and empty shot glasses.

Then she saw the woman. She was young, Oriental, exotic. And she was sitting very close to Estefan; if she had been any closer, they would have shared a single chair. Margarita's eyes went directly to the other woman's bosom. The Oriental woman was wearing a necklace. And it was virtually the same as the one she now possessed. Only, instead of a large pear-shaped ruby, there was a bright green emerald glittering serenely between the small perfectly shaped breasts!

***

As her focus left the necklace and traveled up to the face of the young Oriental woman, their eyes locked in a visual embrace. There was no malice in the eyes of the girl, just curiosity. She inclined her head slightly to the left as she and Margarita stared at one another. Margarita released the girl's eyes and her attention shifted slightly to Estefan. Estefan didn't even look up.

But she knew Estefan had seen her standing there at the doorway, so she hurried back to the carriage. She was crying although she couldn't feel the tears. She snapped at the driver, "Take me home!" He cracked his whip and the horse broke into a trot.

Margarita's entire body was numb; she couldn't feel the leather of the seat or the occasional bump on the rocky ride home. A jumble of thoughts jabbered away at one another in her brain. She knew she was in trouble. She knew it would only be a matter of minutes before Estefan would react to her unprecedented appearance.

Another more odious thought fought its way to the forefront ahead of the others. Her husband had another lover. Not just a girlfriend. Not just someone to fuck. This was a woman he had showered with gifts. A woman on a par with herself.

She pictured him giving this new girl the emerald necklace. She saw him standing there behind her, affixing the clasp, leaning forward to kiss her on the sacred spot between neck and shoulder, whispering as he did so, "To the only woman I have ever loved."

Wasn't *she* the only woman he had ever loved? Hadn't he used those very words when he gave her the ruby necklace? She was infuriated to think he might have said these same words to *her*. But he must have been lying to the Chinese girl, mustn't he? That possibility gave her some hope, a glimmer of satisfaction. But you couldn't tell with Estefan. On the outside, he always seemed so honest, so sincere.

Such an actor! He was evil! She had been such a fool!

As she berated herself with these horrible thoughts, she always ended up in the same place, with the same self-defeating conclusion. *She* had been a bad wife. Why else would he have strayed? *She* wasn't loveable. Why else would he have fallen in love with another? She flagellated herself without pity. She was the one who had been wronged, and yet she was feeling responsible! Why was she making excuses for him? Why was she feeling that she was somehow to blame?

More thoughts taunted her. Had he called the Chinese girl, Corazón"? Had he called her "Mija?" Had she called him "Mijo" in return? Did he tell her he loved her? Did she tell him the same thing?

She felt tension in her temples, and her head throbbed. She could not think rationally. What to do? What to do? She had to do something!

He had to be punished! The Chinese girl had to be punished as well! As she sat before the mirror at her dressing table, she wondered how she had made it up the stairs to her room. She wondered how long she had been sitting there in this same place, unmoving, staring at nothing, when she heard a door close downstairs and she heard Estefan's footfalls on the wooden staircase.

He knocked lightly at the closed door. She didn't remember shutting it. He opened it and came inside. "Were you looking for me?" was all he said.

She stared at him. She didn't know who he was. She knew it was her husband standing there before her. She knew it was he who had taken the sacred vows on the day they wed. She knew it was the same man who had shared her bed on so many cold nights. She knew he was the man she believed she loved, but he was a stranger, a betrayer, a liar, a man whose talent for acting ought to be known from the California coast to the stages of New York.

She didn't know what to say, so she said nothing. But she did feel something now. At the sight of him, she felt her heart breaking, she felt it rip, and hot tears began to drip down her nose and over her cheeks, dropping one by one onto the bodice of the dark blue dress and onto the red ruby necklace.

Dai-yu

Dai-yu was amazed and pleased she had to admit to herself finally by the necklace Estefan had given her. She knew he viewed it as a token of his esteem, but she couldn't help but view it as a ticket out, a way to escape her current living predicament. If she sold this single piece of jewelry, she could leave, she could go anywhere. She could go to San Francisco to find her family.

On the other hand, a funny thing had happened after Estefan finished making love to her. After she had experienced *it*.

Instead of being just another john or another nameless trick, Estefan was now someone she cared for. Cared for deeply. She felt her heart opening, something that hadn't happened in years. She hadn't loved something or someone in so long she thought she was no longer capable of having such feelings. The last time she had felt love, it had been in the form of a purring feline with a crooked tail. Now that she thought about it, really thought about it, she had never felt this way about a man, aside from her father, and her father didn't fit in *this* category.

Now, her world of sorrow and disappointment had been flipped on its head. There was a man, with crooked teeth, a broad grin, mischief in his eyes, sweet words on his tongue, full lips, and rough, but gentle, working hands, who loved her. There was a man who believed in her, who wanted to rescue her, someone who would be around to save her. Perhaps she would stay in Silver Spring, after all.

The Afterlife

A few weeks later Dai-yu's dreams of Prince Charming and living happily ever after came to an abrupt end. Like Romeo and Juliet, she and Estefan just weren't meant to be. As bullets tore their bodies apart and they died, Dai-yu's hopes and dreams died.

She and Estefan were murdered in their bed. And a mystery began to unfold.

After gunshots tore the silence of the Silver Spring apart, Estefan and Dai-yu found themselves beings unencumbered by bodies made of warm flesh and filled with hot blood; instead they became watchers transfixed by the events of the evening.

Many minutes passed. Or maybe it was only seconds. The ghosts Estefan and Dai-yu couldn't tell. The room was full of people now. They watched with a deepening curiosity as the people talked. The people were talking loudly and were very excited. Although people died all the time in these parts, it had been a very long time that anyone had died in the Silver Spring, especially in such a sensational and sexually compromising way. The people talked a lot and pointed a lot, and someone gently picked up Estefan's wrist to check for a pulse. Then they did the same thing with Dai-yu's slender wrist. Once it was verified that they were no longer alive someone solemnly pronounced they were dead, and as was customary, the bodies were covered up by a sheet.

The ghosts looked at each other and smiled, a little sadly, but their curiosity kept them firmly in place.

Twenty or thirty minutes must have passed. There was no way for the ghosts to tell time. But they could guess by what was happening. The doctor showed up to change their legal statuses from alive to no longer alive. The doctor signed a couple of papers and gave them to the authority, the local sheriff, who, by this time, had also made an appearance. The sheriff showed up ostensibly to begin a murder investigation, but, as was usually the case in such matters, things were pretty much cut and dry. Suspects and motives pointed to jealous spouses, jealous lovers, and crimes of passion.

Nevertheless, the sheriff made a show of gathering facts and evidence. He poked around the room, picked up a couple of spent casings, asked a lot of questions, got a lot of answers, talked to a lot of people. The Madam, as pretty much the senior authority on the site, fielded most of the questions. And most of the questions came up empty. Did anybody see anything? Did anybody hear anything, *besides* the gun going off? Did anybody know who might want Estefan dead? Lots of names came up then.

Nobody bothered to ask about the China Doll and her list of enemies. Nobody cared about the China Doll. She was just another casualty in the war against love.

The usual questions were answered with the usual answers. Nobody saw anything. Nobody heard anything, except for Estrellita. She was the one screaming. She had seen a man run down the back stairwell and disappear into the dark.

Another several hours must have passed. The town folk had searched futilely for the man Estrellita had seen. No weapon had been found.

Someone was sent out to Estefan's estate to inform Margarita of the events of the evening.

***

The next morning Margarita arrived, in tears, along with Estefan's three sons. As the ghosts watched, Estefan Jr. and Margarita entered the scene of the crime. His eldest son was supporting his mother, with arm around her waist at all times, as if she might pass out and sink to the floor at any instant. Margarita couldn't look at the body so Estefan Jr. did the honors.

Margarita's hair was a mess, and she appeared to be in shock. She didn't say a lot; mostly, she leaned on her son for support. Her eyes were glazed over, not seeing much of anything.

***

To the ghosts time lost its sense of linearity. Everything seemed to be happening in one long unending stretch of time. There were no longer divisions to break time into seconds, minutes, hours, or days.

Later, but no telling how much later, Estefan and Dai-yu found themselves alone in their own alternate reality. Their physical bodies were still there in the bed, shrouded by a bloody sheet. From what they gathered as they listened to the cacophony of voices below, the bodies would be moved in the morning when the undertaker/mortician showed up. The room still smelled sharply of blood.

The ghosts decided the only thing left to do was take a wander around the Silver Spring. First, they traveled from room to room checking out all the sleeping people. It was amazing people could sleep after such a fuss. The bodies looked strange from above. They looked even stranger as the ghosts crouched down beside each one and stared into the faces. The faces looked dead themselves, waxen and still.

The two ghosts discovered they could "touch" each slumbering body, but the sleepers only shivered a little as if they were cold.

At first, Estefan and Dai-yu didn't exactly know what they were looking for. Then it hit them. Dai-yu was the first to figure it out. They couldn't touch other people's bodies with their bodies, because they didn't have bodies anymore. But they could touch other people's minds with their minds.

Dai-yu slipped into the dream of one of her sleeping co-workers. Estefan followed her and slipped into the mind of the man sleeping next to her. Dai-yu took over the sleeping girl's dream and Estefan took over the man's dream. With delight, they discovered this is how they could be together again. Dai-yu operated the borrowed body of the girl as if she were a puppeteer deftly bringing a marionette to life. Estefan did the same with the hijacked body of the man.

They made love repeatedly during the night using the borrowed bodies. It wasn't the same as using their own bodies, but it was a still a wonderful experience. The woman's body wasn't as young and supple as Dai-yu's own had been, but it still had all the right parts in all the right places. And Estefan's body had all the right male parts in all the right places. He even beamed a little when he realized he had gained a full inch in the bargain.

In the morning though, a weird thing happened. When the girl awoke, her conscious mind was stronger than Dai-yu's consciousness. Dai-yu could not resist as her spirit was summarily pushed out of the girl's mind and she found herself bodiless once more, floating about in the Silver Spring. She looked about frantically for Estefan. She found he too had been ousted rudely from his temporary home. It was a bit of a trick, this dream-borrowing, and apparently it only worked when their hosts were asleep and their conscious minds were weak. But they soon got the hang of it. They went from host to host searching for just the right fit.

***

Back in the world of the living, the sheriff determined the murder had been committed by the Madam's 1858 Remington army revolver she had inherited from her father. He carried it with him during "the War."[1] The Remington was a sweet little gun with a polished carved wood handle and sleek styling. It had six chambers which enabled it to fire up to six .44 caliber bullets rapidly. The lawman quickly arrived at that brilliant deduction once he was informed that the Madam's gun had been stolen in close proximity to the commission of the crime. To support this conclusion, it was determined the shell casings discovered at the scene were the same kind that would have been discharged from a weapon like that. As for suspects…

It was Estrellita who rose to the forefront mainly because she disappeared right after the murder happened. To the relief of all, the case was quickly closed. It was obvious who had done it. The motive was there, the opportunity was there, and the weapon had been accounted for. No one had seen Estrellita since the night the two lovers were killed. It was assumed she left the district because she was guilty, guilty, guilty.

Estrellita had motive and more motive. It was blatantly apparent that Estefan was no longer in love with her, and as all the girls in the Silver Spring testified, she was still very much in love with him. In addition to the rejected lover motive, someone had broken into the Madam's lockbox where she kept the week's earnings and made off with several hundred dollars in the chaotic time after the murder. Estrellita was already known to be a thief and quickly rose to number one suspect in this secondary crime.

---

[1] Aka, the Civil War; at the time no one called it that. Historians today call it that.

***

When it came time to settle Estefan's affairs there were two major problems. Fortunately, for those left behind, Estefan had left a will. Unfortunately, for those left behind, the first problem soon came to light. To wit, it was discovered that Estefan's fortune, estimated in the hundreds of thousands of dollars, was missing. Estefan had never trusted banks, or anyone for that matter. Not even Margarita knew where he had hidden his gold and silver.

Then there was the second big problem. Once Estefan's death was announced in the newspapers, all sorts of people showed up to file suits against the estate. Relatives of prospectors who had worked stakes on Estefan's property showed up trying to claim proceeds earned from those original claims. Several co-owners of the mining company of which Estefan was a part made claims against the estate, accusing Estefan of high grading. There were even a handful of women Estefan had supposedly known at some time in their lives who swore Estefan was the father of their children.

All these opportunists wanted a piece of Estefan's riches. While Estefan was alive, his power and reputation had apparently been enough to keep the vultures at bay. Now that he was gone they sprung from the dark Colorado topsoil like earthworms after a good rain.

The lawyers struggled to make sense of the labyrinthine records that purported to show who owned what and which parcel of land had been leased to whom, for what purpose and for how long. They could make little sense of the spaghetti-like heap of records scrawled haphazardly in Estefan's sloppy hand.

One of the details of the will was that a small pension be set aside for Margarita to live off of for the rest of her life, which of course, presented a problem, because there was no money available to dispense. Another related problem was that Estefan had also left a little monetary bequest to Estrellita, and Estrellita, the prime suspect, was now missing. It would be difficult, if not impossible, to track her down. Even if they could track her down, she would most likely be hung for murder. And, if, in the unlikely circumstance that Estrellita was found to be innocent, there would still be no money in the estate for her to enjoy.

The three sons, who had been looking forward to spending the money Estefan had been amassing for many years and living a life of ease, were left with a bunch of horses, a good deal of land, and a much disputed part-ownership over a gold mine.

By all rights, the estate should have gone to the oldest son, but in this case, he was not the most aggressive of the boys. Estefan, Jr. was the scholarly type. He was not wild about horses, so he left Colorado and went back East to study at an institution of higher learning. He did not begrudge his brothers their desire to take over Estefan's business affairs, and once he left the two younger brothers got into it. Besides deciding who should take charge, they were left with the problem of not knowing a thing about mining. This meant they needed to become experts at mining overnight.

Digging had already come to a standstill once the ownership of the mine entered the legal process, and as it did so, the main source of income for Estefan's estate ground to a halt. Eventually Estefan's youngest son, Oscar, took control of Estefan's interests in his father's absence.

Unfortunately, Estefan's sons were no match for his shark-like business partners. They were soon forced to sell the shares that had given Estefan control of the mining company to Estefan's business partners in order to have enough working capital to run the estate. Oscar and Gilberto even toyed with the idea of selling the property and the mansion house to one of Cripple Creek's many millionaires.

Oscar turned out to be smarter than anyone had imagined. It was evident that he had inherited some of Estefan's wheeling dealing acumen.

In the end, the vultures were paid off. They skulked off to resume the lives beneath the rocks from whence they came. Most had unsubstantiated claims anyway, and the estate was settled. During the long drawn out legal battle, the two younger sons sold off most of Estefan's prized horses, since neither of them had inherited Estefan's love of the animal.

**

In the meantime, Estefan was buried in the town cemetery. The sons managed to scrape together enough money to erect a very ornate monument to their father. Everyone came to the funeral; despite the untimely circumstances surrounding his demise, Estefan was still a well-respected and well-liked townsperson.

As they laid his body to rest, Margarita wailed as if she was a paid mourner. Estefan, the ghost, of course attended the funeral. He was a little surprised to see his ex-wife so overwhelmed by grief. He had never seen her so emotionally distraught. Now that he thought back on their long marriage, he had never really seen her cry. He had seen her screaming and angry on many occasions. But up until that moment he had not realized that she could sob like that. Her grief was almost a physical entity. As he watched in wonder he could feel the vastness of it.

Other women were weeping loudly. His sons stood beside Margarita; they were silent and somber. Their eyes were filled with tears. He had no idea they cared. That anyone cared. He was a little bit in awe of the depth of the dent he must have somehow made in the universe. He must have really mattered to these people.

After the funeral a special reception was held at the great estate and all the respectable townspeople showed up. The Madam and all the girls from the Silver Spring held their own memorial service at the Silver Spring which was much more lushly attended than the one at Margarita's home.

Everyone showed up at the second reception; everyone except Margarita. Even Estefan's sons were there. They drank toasts to Estefan and told stories about his life and his legendary exploits. And everyone got very drunk as was appropriate.

The rumors and legends of the murder fueled local gossip for years.

***

Dai-yu too was buried in the local cemetery. A makeshift wooden cross, on which the undertaker had inscribed a couple of Chinese characters, marked her final resting place. The good intentioned mortician did not know what the characters meant. He copied them off the jade locket that was found in her belongings. He thought it was her name. They actually said, "Luck" and "Joy."

***

Six months later, Margarita's body was found by one of the servants. It was hanging from a banister. Blame for the double murder slowly shifted from Estrellita to Estefan's estranged wife. It was now commonly assumed she must have killed Estefan and Dai-yu while they slept.

Margarita's devoutly Catholic family in Mexico City was contacted about what to do with the body. Since Margarita's passing was a suicide, and suicide was a terrible sin to those that practiced that religion (and many others), her family refused to take her and bury her in their family cemetery.

Margarita was buried alone and in disgrace at one of the crossroads on the outskirts of the town of Silver Spring.

***

Rumor had it that Estefan had buried his treasure somewhere on the land where he pastured his horses and cattle. Other rumors spread the tale that Estefan's gold had been hidden in one of the mine shafts dug by the prospectors that had at some time searched for their own mother lodes on Estefan's estate. It was all the brothers could do to keep trespassers and treasure seekers off their estate without having to kill them.

And life, for the living, in Silver Spring went on.

***

Meanwhile, the afterlife for Estefan was considerably better than the mess that resulted from his untimely passing. He and Dai-yu spent many a night in the borrowed minds and bodies of the dreamers that still slept at the Silver Spring.

Finally, after many nights of wandering from room to room, and dreamer to dreamer, Dai-yu finally gathered up the courage to try the Madam's body on for size.

Estefan encouraged her. He urged, "Come on. Just try it. What's the worst thing that can happen? It's not like she can fire you!" he pointed out.

So as the Madam snored away, Dai-yu slipped into her slumber.

To Dai-yu's surprise, she felt right at home inside the Madam's mind. The Madam's body was much larger than the China doll's body had been, but their brains were similarly wired. Despite the differences that had existed between them in life, that is, different backgrounds, different cultures, and different experiences, on a subconscious level they were kindred spirits, so to speak.

So from that time on, night after night, Dai-yu visited the Madam in her dreams and made herself at home there.

Meanwhile, Estefan found a certain man who came often to the Silver Spring. There he drank and rarely talked to women. Once in a great while he bought one of them a drink. He was usually too shy to even ask them to dance. His name was Armando and he was a poor cattle drover. There was something special about Armando and this was evidenced because the Madam took a liking to him. There was something about him that was very familiar, but she couldn't quite put her finger on it.

The Madam almost NEVER slept with any customers anymore. One had to be a very special individual to even attract her attention.

Armando was quiet and reserved, educated, polite and handsome and at least 10 years younger than the Madam. In fact, he was almost the complete opposite of Estefan. Estefan liked Armando even though they had nothing in common. Or perhaps he liked Armando precisely because they had nothing in common. At first Armando only showed up once a week. On these occasions, Armando spent the night with the Madam. This is when Estefan became intimately acquainted with Armando.

After a very short while Armando found himself hopelessly in love with the Madam of the Silver Spring. Whether it was ghostly goings on or a true attraction between Armando and the Madam didn't matter, because they were as happy as two green lovebirds sharing the same perch in the same little cage.

In the beginning, the people of Silver Spring were surprised by this seemingly odd mismatch but the two new lovers were blissfully content. Within weeks, they were spending every night together, and Armando was hanging out at the Silver Spring whenever he had a free moment.

Because he was not already married, Armando was able to make an honest woman out of the Madam, as the expression goes. He proposed and they were soon married. The wedding took place at a small chapel on the main street of Silver Spring. A reception was held that night, so all could attend, and was of course held at the Silver Spring.

Even though the madam ran a whorehouse, she was the closest thing Silver Spring had to respectable society, since there was no such thing as respectable society in the mining town. Silver Spring wasn't like the big city of Colorado Springs, where men who made millions from Cripple Creek's gold lived well away from the rabble, in their own little enclave centered on Wood Avenue.

The Madam was Silver Spring's equivalent to its pillar of society; she gave money to the poor and all the businessmen of the town respected her. The only people who resented her with the wives whose husbands were her best customers.

At the reception the madam wore a beautiful many-tiered white dress covered with lace. It had been custom-made for her in Ireland. Armando wore a black coat and tails. His matching vest was finely embroidered. A great feast was served. The first course was turtle soup. Several different kinds of meat including duckling, veal and squab made up the main course. Only the best food was brought in from faraway places.

As the music of a harp played, the guests dined on luxury items like fried artichokes and asparagus, cherries and currants. There was a white bride's cake and a black groom's cake of figs and other sweet candied fruits. A final course of cheeses and fruit rounded off the dinner. Several kinds of wine were liberally served by an army of hired waitpersons. And there was of course, fine champagne to toast the newlyweds. It was a glorious affair and people talked about the after-party for years.

Everyone agreed it was a match that truly seemed ordained by the gods that smile upon such things.

Part II

Texas

2012

Elaine

I wonder how bad prison food is, Elaine thought as she stared out the window. Rain streaked the dusty glass from the outside and wandered slowly down to the caulking at the bottom of the sill. The sky outside was dark grey. The same color as the inside of Elaine's skull.

Prison food couldn't be any worse than food that has no flavor, Elaine thought. Food hadn't had any flavor for weeks now. Ever since she had accidently stumbled upon the texts in Paul's smartphone.

I wonder how I'll look in an orange jumpsuit, she mused. *I know orange isn't my color*, she thought. *Pink is my color. Turquoise is my color. Bright colors are my colors. I am spring, I am fall, and orange is for winter*. She had another thought. *Maybe orange is just for women who frequent the holding cells at the county jail*. Vaguely she remembered reading a book about prisons and recalled that the uniforms were supposed to be white or blue. Or maybe that was just for the men.

What did female inmates wear?

Maybe she could fall in love again if she was in prison. Maybe some husky strapping bull dyke with very short hair, and a few pre-prison tattoos stenciled onto her overdeveloped deltoids, would take pity on her and protect her.

Maybe she was supposed to be with a woman. She never liked wearing makeup or doing her hair. She never particularly enjoyed shopping for clothes or shoes. She wasn't like other women and didn't even like carrying a purse. Perfume made her sneeze. Getting flowers as a gift or romantic gesture just embarrassed her.

Love with men hadn't worked out so well over the years.

On the other hand, she never had liked the company of or appreciated other women. Maybe she could fall in love with one of the male guards. She knew a lot of them were crazy. But at least they were crazy jealous.

Not like Paul.

It turned out Paul did not have a jealous molecule in his entire body. Paul had turned out to be all kinds of disappointing.

And now, there was the specter of another woman. A she-devil named "Islandgirl." Where had they met? How did they know one another?

Men, why were they so secretive?

And why, why, why did they cheat?

Paul. Even Paul, the only man she had been one hundred and twenty percent sure wouldn't cheat. Even Paul...unimaginative, unemotional, sexually-unmotivated, Paul. Apparently, even Paul, given enough rope, wanted to wander away from the corral.

***

There were so many texts. She stopped counting when she realized there were more than 60 texts to the mysterious "Islandgirl" on the first two days alone.

Conversations that revealed the secret world of their relationship:

Islandgirl:: Nice tie.

BigP: Thank you; my wife bought it for me.

Islandgirl: She has good taste.

BigP: You like it?

Islandgirl: I love it. Your wife is a lucky woman.

BigP: You think so?

Islandgirl: I know so. (winking emoticon)

Or an interchange that seemed to bespeak worlds about Paul's still active sexual desires:

BigP: Nice blouse.

Islandgirl: You like it?

BigP: I love it!

Islandgirl: You don't think it's too much?

BigP: NO WAY (all caps!). It fits just right in all the right places!

Islandgirl: You are so bad! (wink)

BigP: You make me bad! (wink). LOL.

Islandgirl: LOL.

Elaine felt nauseous. The texts said so little, but revealed so much. The texts showed they were thinking about one another all day long.

Islandgirl: What are you doing?

BigP: Coffee here.

Islandgirl: Is it good?

BigP: Good enough to jump start the old heart! LOL.

Islandgirl: LOL.

Apparently, Paul was quite the wit on the smartphone.

BigP: Morning. Coffee here. Meeting in ten minutes. I hate meetings.

Islandgirl: Me too. Don't worry. You'll impress the heck out of all of them.

BigP: I don't think so. They sleep through meetings.

Islandgirl: LOL.

BigP: Wish I could go back to sleep.

Islandgirl: Me too. LOL.

The worst messages of all were the ones that simply stated, "Thinking of you" and "XOXO." Much worse than the little illuminated characters themselves were the evil little smiley faces and winking emoticons.

As she scrolled through screen after screen an army of LOL's scattered before her horrified eyes. Like pepper granules on the milky white part of a sunny side up egg they seemed to be laughing at her. Laughing at the fact she was surprised. Laughing at the fact she had been so naïve. What had she expected? She treated Paul as if he was a worthless, boring eunuch when they were together, even in public.

She imagined she could hear laughing, echoing within the confines of her newly anaesthetized brain. Both of them laughing.

She knew things were not the same between herself and her husband. She had known it for a long time, for most of the marriage, in fact. They were so different, but they spent a good deal of time telling one another how similar they were, and trying to convince themselves they hadn't made a mistake when they chose to marry.

The one thing they did have in common was they both wanted desperately to be in love with people they weren't in love with.

They were both good people. They were both morally upright, honest, and loyal. And they had joint custody of many good friends, nice, morally upright, honest, well-behaved friends. Paul and Elaine's cadre of friends were comprised mostly of happily married couples and most of them were on their second and third marriages. Only Paul and Elaine had survived their 30's and 40's and were still together.

Their many good friends loved both of them and believed they were the perfect couple. Everyone wanted to believe in Paul and Elaine. Even maybe more than Paul and Elaine wanted to believe.

But perfect couple they were not. Far from it. But they were perfect individuals, in their own perfect individual ways, if perfect meant unique and unlike any other human beings that found their eating, pooping, sleeping, working, breathing, animalistic selves whirling purposelessly though the universe on the same perfect planet known as Earth. But they were not perfect as the entity known to all outsiders as "Paul and Elaine."

Paul and Elaine was a two-headed one-brained creature that attended parties, drove around town in a single car, ate dinner at the same table, removed ketchup and mustard containers from the same refrigerator and placed them on the same dinner table with the same matching plates and the same matching knives and forks. Paul and Elaine was a two-headed one-purposed being that sat side-by-side on the scuffed up leather couch and argued about who should or should not take control of the remote control and which channel would or would not bathe them with its non-ionizing radiation for hours at a stretch. Paul and Elaine was a two-headed one-missioned monster that settled down to sleep every night beneath a flower-studded comforter stuffed with man-made material and smooth 400-count Indian cotton sheets that smelled a little of sweat and a lot like Downy fabric softener. Paul and Elaine was a two-headed one-bodied animal that curled up into a fetal ball, and tucked its smaller inner legs and arms into the spooning embrace of the other's larger legs and arms and fell asleep.

Paul and Elaine was an animal that looked good on the outside but was a little bit sick on the inside.

***

There were several side effects to Elaine's present psychosomatically induced "illness." Aside from not being able to sleep for more than an hour or two at a time and the fact that food no longer had any taste, she had now begun to obsess almost non-stop about the idea of murder. Paul needed to be dead. Just as people once joked that "he needed killing" was a legitimate legal defense for murder in the great state of Texas, Paul had become one of those individuals to Elaine.

Elaine had decided "Paul needed killing." So too did the unknown slut, or whore named Islandgirl.

They both had to die.

Now she just needed to figure out a way to do it. She needed to think of a way where she wouldn't get caught. Or even a way where she *would* get caught. It didn't really matter at this point. Elaine knew her sanity had long since left her.

The house was mausoleum quiet during the day. Then Paul would come home, and begin making noise. All kinds of noise. Cracking his knuckles, eating potato chips, crunching ice cubes, chewing baby carrots, talking on the telephone, watching television, playing CD's, sawing wood, running band-saws, sanding, walking around; even treading on carpet, Paul made noise. Elaine was even convinced that she could now hear him breathe, every inhalation, every exhalation grated like claws scraping a blackboard. Sounds from Paul's body were amplified to Elaine's overly sensitized ears. She was turning into the protagonist of Edgar Allen Poe's story, the one who could hear the telltale heart beating.

It was as if Paul just couldn't stand a quiet house.

Elaine preferred silence. Elaine needed silence. Silence in which to create scenarios of death. Silence in which to weave plans. Plans echoing with Paul's screams. Plans plastered with visions of Paul's deep blue eyes watering in stunned disbelief. Plans filled with images of the gurgling spluttering witch begging for her life as Elaine sliced open her jugular vein and watched the evil carmine colored blood spray all over Paul's already frigid cold body.

They had to die together. It was only fair.

They had to die horribly. That was important too.

But how? How could she pull it off? How could she make it look like an accident? What could she use as an alibi? So many questions.

She would be the first and only suspect. For everyone in the world loved Paul. Good, innocent, well-meaning Paul. Paul, who didn't have an enemy in the universe, let alone on the tiny blue planet covered with clouds circling a star affectionately referred to as Sol by its tiny insignificant humanoid inhabitants. Paul, the man who didn't have a malicious bone in his body. Paul, who was incapable of doing anything unethical, or illegal, or even a tiny bit mean.

Why on earth would anyone kill Paul? She knew it would not look good for her if he showed up dead. For, as luck would have it, she was the only person on earth who stood to benefit if Paul were to suddenly be removed from the planet.

Elaine was the beneficiary on the house. Elaine was the beneficiary on all Paul's brokerage and savings accounts. Elaine's name was the only one on Paul's big life insurance policy.

Yes, Elaine needed an alibi. And she needed it quickly. Her patience, like her sanity, was running out. She could feel the pressure building. She could tell the rattling, shaking top was getting ready to fly off the pressure cooker.

***

Elaine was standing at the front door of their house. She stared at her right hand as it tapped on the stained glass panel; it appeared to belong to someone else. There was a shuffling sound from within. Then she could feel the vibrations of soft footsteps, not particularly in a hurry, approaching her position. The door opened. Paul was standing there, an expression of neutrality covering the features of his face. There was no light of recognition in his eyes. They were blank, staring, wide open. Then a flicker started making its way from his brain to his eyes. It was a flicker of fear. Then, as if the flicker in his eyes was lonely, the corner of his right mouth began infinitesimally to rise as it to join it. Eyes and mouth joined together to create an expression that could only be described as a sneer, a sneer of distaste. As if a bad smell affronted his nostrils. The origins of a grimace.

He was definitely not pleased to see her. But that was fine with her; as long as he was unsuspecting, unprepared, and defenseless. Then she remembered why she was there. In slow motion she began to lift her right arm. It was so heavy. The gun was weighing it down. Slowly she brought the steel body concealing its cold lead bullets up until it was on the same level as the center of his chest, the place where she imagined his black heart was beating in its cold indifferent way.

The distance between Paul's cotton-swathed flesh and bare dull grey metal was only a foot, maybe even less. She hesitated for another second. His eyes flicked downward to her hand, to the gun, to his oncoming fate. Then she willed her forefinger to begin pulling the trigger. It didn't want to yield. It was as if there was no energy, no chi, left in her body. Everything was moving very slowly. She could hear no sound, even though she could see Paul's lips beginning to move. His mouth was open wide, and she smiled as she thought he resembled a big croaker with a hook through its bottom lip begging for freedom. It seemed a bit odd that that particular idealization made her smile when she usually felt so sorry for the fish. But Paul was no fish.

She pulled harder. She could feel every muscle in her forearm crying out. *What are you doing!? Leave us alone!* She pulled until the space around her was filled with an explosion. She stared ahead into Paul's eyes. They were gaping; wide open. Like the fish's mouth.

Then she saw a lot of smoke and fire and red.

She lowered her eyes to Paul's chest; now there seemed to be a yawning hole in its center. The opening appeared to be a peephole into the universe and she could see many silent, glorious, sparkling magenta, rose, and turquoise nebulas floating and motionless. Millions of white stars spun silently in the background. But they weren't moving either. And she realized that didn't make any sense. But it sure was awe-inspiring. As she stared into the chasm that was Paul's expanding chest she began to imagine she was flying through outer space. Paul was receding as she got nearer and nearer to the speed of light.

And she realized it was all a dream. She tried to wake herself up. But the dream wasn't releasing her. It insisted that she watch the story a little bit longer. She began to feel afraid, not happy.

She was happy at the idea of destroying Paul. But the message of the dream came to her then. Paul was a lot larger than she was. She could not destroy him. He was indestructible, unending, existing eternally. Paul was the beginning and the middle and the entirety of her universe. Without Paul she was nothing.

And she woke up with a start. It was all a dream. A bad dream? A nightmare? She wasn't sure yet.

She glanced over beside her in the darkness. In the blackness of their bedroom, barely illuminated by the light sneaking in past the curtains guarding the window, she could see a lump in the bed next to her. She reached over to feel Paul's rump. Yes, it was still warm. Yes, he was still alive.

Yes, it was a nightmare…

Paul

Paul stared out the window of his cubbyhole into the courtyard of the office complex. There was a duck pond out there. A couple of live oak trees hot and sweating crouched at the water's edge which was lined by a cluster of pale green waxy leafed pittosporum bushes. The well-groomed shrubs resembled small trees of their own and the ducks liked to lie on the muddy earth beneath them to keep cool in the heat of the day. The dark brown-green pond water, still and unmoving, reflected its verdant surroundings. A couple of fat white farm ducks floated lazily in the afternoon heat. But Paul didn't see any of this.

His eyes moved sluggishly from the window jamb to the accumulation of papers, folders, and open books on his desk. He didn't see any of these items either. Finally, his eyes came to rest on a photo in a gilt-bronzed frame. The photo was on the wall that faced him. It was a picture of Elaine and him, dressed to the nines, in front of a Christmas tree. Happier times. Much happier times.

Elaine was smiling broadly; all her perfect white teeth belying so well the truth known only to a few, "This is not a happy woman."

In the picture, he had on a dark blue sports jacket and a black and white silk tie with an art deco design on it. Elaine had picked out the tie and she always insisted he wear it on formal occasions. Paul was sure it was a nice tie but it was not really to his taste. He had learned long ago not to mention that fact to Elaine.

He stared into the eyes of the woman in the photograph as if she might look back at him. The brown eyes with little flecks of green were bright and shining. Her white teeth gleamed. The skin of her cheeks glowed. The photo was slightly overexposed so neither one of them appeared to have a single facial line or blemish. If, he realized, he were a vain man, and he was not, he would most definitely put this photo on his Facebook page, even if it was 10 years old. But he didn't have a Facebook page. In fact, he didn't have time for a Facebook page. He didn't text people either. To Paul both of these activities seemed a colossal waste of time.

He wondered again at the photo. What had happened since then? He answered his own question…too much had happened since then. So much that had changed the two of them. So much that had changed Elaine. She wasn't happy anymore; that much was obvious. But why did she hold *him* responsible? He hadn't changed. He had been nothing but accommodating. Emotionless. Understanding. He had displayed the patience of Job. Her frequent emotional outbursts and the overall disregard and disrespect with which he now found himself being bombarded, on an almost constant, daily basis were beginning to wearing him down.

In addition, she no longer apologized when she lost her temper. It even appeared she might not be capable anymore of behaving in a civil manner, at least not in his presence. It was a conundrum, especially to someone like Paul, who was even-tempered, and rarely, if ever, displayed anger. Yes, he got angry. He was only human, but he chose not to display this anger. Particularly not around those he cared about.

Many years of living with a woman like his mother, who was an emotional time bomb like Elaine herself, he had come to realize, had taught him an important survival mechanism. That is, to lay low, out of the storm, until it passed. At least, in defense of his mother, when it came to her volatile temper and mood swings, they passed quickly. In fact, it was almost as if they had never happened.

His mother would fume, whine, complain, kvetch, and then without warning, she would blow. Fortunately, these eruptions were so illogical and emotionally undecipherable, that Paul, and his father, had learned to tune them out. She would rant and rave with or without them. In other words, the physical presence of another human being was not necessary for her to carry out these tantrums. She could rant and rave alone, in a vacuum, so Paul and his father could simply flee from the room, or the house, as his father was wont to do, and she didn't seem to care.

But when it came to Elaine, Paul found that she wanted him there, to engage him, to castigate him, to serve as an emotional whipping boy. Elaine would say a lot of things that he tended to tune out, again, for the same reason he tuned out his mother's vindictive verbiage, because the things she said just didn't make any logical sense. But that strategy only seemed to infuriate Elaine more. She wanted him to respond. She wanted him to fight back. But he couldn't figure out what they were fighting about most of the time.

It was like being in a debate with a really rude opponent, having come into the debate with the disadvantage of not being told what subject you would be debating, which side you would be taking, pro or con, and without having done the necessary preparatory research ahead of time. At a time like that, there was no way to win. You didn't have your arguments prepared. You didn't have your facts ready. And worse, your opponent wasn't listening to your counterarguments or giving you an opportunity to respond when it was supposed to be your turn to respond.

In any case, for Paul it was a no-win proposition.

And Paul was tired of losing.

He retreated to the peace of fantasy. And the girl in the coffee shop.

***

She had young firm breasts, and a tiny waist, and straight blond hair that reached just to the top of her shoulders. She wore a name tag that said, "Cyndy."

Cyndy's hair was often several different colors. Sometimes magenta streaks danced through the gold and other times there were chunks of maroon or turquoise that often matched her flamboyant clothing. She had flawless porcelain skin that was several shades lighter than the color of natural skin. But Paul didn't mind, the whiteness of her skin contrasted dramatically with her long curly possibly fake eye lashes, and the kohl-colored flicks that emphasized her greenish eyes. Her lips too were stained in unnatural colors, sometimes rimmed in dark brown, almost

128

black, and the interiors sparkled with dark red lip gloss. She had a nose ring, and her ears were pierced repeatedly and every time he saw her she wore previously unseen ear adornments. She also bore an assortment of piercings and tattoos.

But Paul didn't mind that either because she was always smiling. And sometimes she hummed her hip-hop songs, and she and the other baristas told private little jokes to one another and laughed uproariously. He knew they were probably laughing at the customers, but he was sure they were laughing at other customers, and not him.

At times Paul wished he could work at a Starbucks or some other franchised fast food establishment. Then he could just put in 20 or 30 hours a week at the most. The rest of the time he'd become an inorganic part of the couch, watch MTV or VHS or whatever it was the young people listened to these days, or "Keeping up with the Miami Housewives at the Playboy Mansion," stuff tortilla chips into his mouth and drip salsa on the cushions without Elaine screaming at him to chew quietly and clean up after himself. He'd swig cheap beer like Lone Star, with his 20-year old homeboys.

He often pictured himself living such a life. Sometimes he even pictured himself puffing on a cigarette, the collar of his leather jacket turned up, wearing rolled up jeans, and leaning up against a coke machine on the main street of Marfa, Texas, outside the Paisano Hotel, looking as cool as James Dean.

Just as likely, as in NOT, he imagined himself hanging out on the sidewalk in front of the Starbucks and chatting with the regulars and the people who worked inside. His favorite barista always prominently starred in these little flights of fantasy.

In his dreams, Cyndy would take her break and come out and join him. And he would slyly examine her breasts as he pretended to study her tattoos and other piercings. "When did you get that one?" he'd ask her. And "What does that one stand for?"

She'd laugh with that sweet young mouth and her teeth so white and straight as she unwound the tale behind each and every bodily mutilation.

Sometimes Paul's fantasy went a little further. It was after closing time, and it was dark outside. The incandescent lights inside the store were out, for the most part, but the interior glowed eerily blue under the florescent security lights. The sodium bulb in the street lamp that lit the parking lot showered the tables and the chairs, and even the barista, with a strange orange glow. In his fantasy the furniture was still outside, unlike in real life where the baristas spent the last ten minutes before the closing bell frantically collecting these portable items and stashing them within the safety of the store itself to keep neighborhood thieves from walking off with them.

In his reverie, Cyndy sat across from him at one of the tiny metal tables as he sipped his complimentary latte and she savored a tall chai tea. Of course, in his dream she bought him coffee. In his fantasy she could not do enough for him. Love was coffee. Love was giving. Love was her bare clad foot creeping up off the cement sidewalk and finding itself snuggly lodged between his thighs. Her little tiny toes nudged him gently. He could feel himself tingling, his pants becoming slightly uncomfortable, as his constricted member hardened ever so slightly.

She smiled at him across the table, pretending she wasn't doing anything but lifting her cup of tea slowly to her lips. Her vividly decorated multi-hued fingernails gleamed in the light from the street lamp. Then she'd lick her thick red lips with anticipation, as if that nice warm liquid that was slipping down into her tiny tight belly were nurturing and fulfilling. He could see the tip of her shiny pink tongue as she flicked it out to touch the insulated cup. She sipped. The crowned green mermaid came very near her face. Silently she sipped, her eyes never parting from his. She sipped as her toes silently slipped up and down again and again. He was rock hard now. He shut his eyes and enjoyed the feeling. The feeling that he was wanted and cherished and horny.

Abruptly, flushed with disgust, he realized he had unzipped himself, and was rubbing himself at work, fortunately behind closed doors, but still at work. He had promised himself that he would not do that at work anymore. What would happen if someone came knocking at his office door?

**

Quickly Paul zipped himself back up. Mournfully, he stared at the pile of work on his desk. He endeavored to clear his head. Despite the air conditioning that was doing its best to make sure the temperature in Houston approached that of Minnesota, it was now uncomfortably warm in the office. He tried to think about what he was supposed to be doing, and not what he wanted to be doing.

Paul's eyes returned to the picture on the wall. It was taken in the good old days, when company Christmas parties were lavish affairs. When there was plenty of *free* (the *optimum* word) alcohol to go around. Those were the days when the stigma against drinking at such functions only applied to upper management. He recalled with a smile how his favorite secretary, Maryann, who technically wasn't *his* secretary, always had a great time. Maryann was the secretary to his boss.

It was Maryann and the thought of seeing her every morning and flirting harmlessly with her throughout the day with his smartphone that kept him motivated enough to get up every day and head into work. That and the lunchtime game of Spades. Work itself was painfully boring.

His actual secretary, who again wasn't technically a *secretary*, but instead performed the few secretarial tasks that still needed performing in the days of the self-sufficient engineer who knew how to do his own typing on a computer keyboard, was the secretary for the entire group of engineers/technicians. Her name was Wanda. "Wanda the witch" (the name he used only in his own head, of course), was a mean old shrew of a secretary, or administrative assistant, as she preferred to think of herself. She was a woman pushing forty who appeared much older. She was woman with no professional status. Even worse, she was a woman without personal status either, a divorcee with no husband.

The end result was Wanda was a woman who rarely smiled at anyone, and never smiled at him. She seemed to derive most of the perks she received from her work life by torturing him with mind games and pretending he didn't exist and that his requests had no importance to her. This pretense didn't take any training in the fine arts of the theatre to convey, because he was certain the truth was that she didn't like him very much at all. This seemed to be a reality with no causal component that he could comprehend. In the mysteries of the work world, which Paul never did fully manage to decipher or understand, despite his many years of living and surviving in that world, for some reason Wanda was allowed to get away with, what could only be called in Paul's book of interpersonal relationship rules, bad behavior.

As far as he could tell, the reason for this eventuality was simple; her eyes were firmly fixed on the needs of bosses, Paul's boss and Paul's boss' boss, those whose opinions mattered, those with power, those who could actually influence or decide whether or not she remained a "resource" in a company that valued "synergy" above all else, well, except for safety, of course. In other words, she kept her eyes and attention steadfastly focused on those who occupied the strata above Paul's own, those who dined on steak and seafood regularly. These upper and middle managers lived in multi-million dollar abodes in the hoity-toity mini-municipalities surrounding Galveston Bay, or the suburban neighborhoods of Clear Lake City which were infested with twisting writhing snake-like cul-de-sacs which served to keep the residents of the four and five bedroom homes, with four and five baths, and detached multi-vehicle garages, in, and undesirables out. These mini-McMansions were carefully and particularly designed with the tastes and requirements of conservative, Texas Love-it-or-Leave it types and their well-coiffed wives.

These southern Stepford wives appeared to be cracked from identical molds. They walked tall, heads back, invisible books balanced atop straight honey-blond highlighted hair usually tightly confined by scrunchies into ponytails. Their perfectly manicured nails and lips always matched; their smooth 40 and 50-something faces and necks were always tucked-and-nipped so they resembled as closely as possible their ex-cheerleader selves. Most of them were stereotypical sorority sisters from the University of Texas or other comparable institutions of higher learning in the Lone Star State.

It was hard not to like these women, for although they reeked of artificiality, on the inside they were excessively sweet. They had "manners" and called everybody "honey" and "sugar," and politeness oozed from every perfectly exfoliated pore.

Wanda and Maryann were the exact opposite of these Stepford sisters; they lived in places like Pasadena and Deer Park, and wore jeans, T-shirts and tennis shoes to work. They purchased their inexpensive clothes at Walmart.

Wanda could be very nice, nauseatingly so to those who she perceived could help her. She was Splenda® sweet to Paul's immediate supervisor, she was Sweet-n-Low® sweet to Paul's immediate supervisor's boss, and she was Equal®-ly sweet to the plant manager. Continuing on with the theme of sweetness, Wanda often brought home-cooked cookies and other desserts to work for the enjoyment of the managers. And if truth be told, and Paul always had to tell the truth, since he was an engineer and an engineer's greatest pursuit is the truth, Wanda's one redeeming asset was that she was an incredible baker. She did produce dark and delicious delights from the depths of her witchy abode. He suspected they were probably infused with slow-working poison or laced with toxins no one knew about or could taste. Even so, he found himself joining the pack of starving 10 a.m. hyenas fighting over the scraps after the lions had had their fill.

In Wanda's world, Paul was worthy of no respect, for after all, he was only an engineer. And an engineer without managerial responsibilities at that, which was an even lower life form. For this reason, the older jaded secretary who had "lost at love" and was "determined to take it out on all the men of the world" was permitted to treat him and his compatriots, peers, or equals with complete and utter disregard, disrespect, and a healthy dollop of disgust, thrown in for good measure.

On the other hand, Paul really liked Maryann, the secretary who worked for his boss. She always had a smile and a wisecrack for him. Her jokes tended towards the raunchy end of the tasteful/tasteless spectrum. These barbs were liberally sprinkled with jokes about minorities and sexual acts. He didn't like the jokes themselves as much as he liked the way she told them. Her grin was large, unaffected, and sincere, and her voice, tempered by years of cigarette smoking, was deep and husky.

Maryann smoked continuously when she was not in the office. The rest of the time she found herself scuttling out to the SMOKING ONLY PERMITTED HERE lean-to that had been grudgingly bestowed to the handful of die-hard rebels who refused to give up the nicotine habit. There the curmudgeonly remaining few who loved to say, "They will have to pry this last cold Marlboro out of my stiff dead fingers if they can," gossiped and shored up one another's opinions and attitudes. The consensus seemed to be that they were victims, martyrs of a movement of ecologically green, tree-hugging liberals, homosexuals and non-God fearing atheistic bastards who were forcing good Southern Christians like themselves to do what it wanted them to do and live the way it wanted them to live. The smokers believed these evil minions of Satan were poisoning all that was good and sacred in Texas, and by extrapolation, since Texas was the beginning, middle and end of any universe worth living in, ALL that was sacred and good.

Paul's mind returned to the Christmas party. He pictured Maryann, true to form, very drunk. It was only 9 p.m. but she could hardly stand, she could hardly dance, but that wasn't stopping her from going through the gyrations. She was even doing the bump with her new husband, Bill.

They were very much in love. And Paul envied them. Of course, they were both bona fide, certifiably, unashamedly, alcoholics. But that seemed to Paul to be a match made in heaven. They lived together on a 32-foot sailboat that was moored at one of the local yacht clubs. It was the kind of lifestyle one dreamt of in one's wildest imagination, in the same place where one can be a pirate plundering the seven seas for gold and glory. In reality, it was the kind of lifestyle a man like Paul could not even conceive of. Because it did entail getting rid of all of the stuff of life that wasn't absolutely essential. And Paul liked his "stuff." He had spent a great deal of time and money amassing his "stuff." Truthfully, Paul had to admit he probably even "loved" his "stuff."

To live on a sailboat, like young lovers, one even had to give up many conveniences. For example, the luxury of home mail delivery. On the other hand, Paul and Elaine had already given that up when they moved to the country, where the mail came by Rural Farm Delivery. They still received mail; it just was delivered to a post office box located at the next town over. It wasn't much of an inconvenience when you really thought about it, since the only snail mail one received anymore was junk mail.

But living on a boat meant other things. It meant no real privacy. If one wanted to have sex, which wasn't an issue now that Paul was permanently committed to Elaine and Elaine didn't seem to want sex anymore, one couldn't really make a lot of noise. The sound would carry to the other boats. But, for people like Maryann and her new husband, Bill, making a lot of sound whilst in the midst of passionate, albeit drunken, lovemaking was never an issue.

As he watched Maryann and Bill do the "sex-dance" on what could only be peripherally referred to as a dance floor he only envied them more. Not only did they not care that they were not great dancers, they did not care that Maryann's boss and all of Maryann's co-workers now knew they were not great dancers. It was obvious however, from their fairly well-coordinated hip movements that they were probably having a great time in their shared moments between the sheets.

Paul smiled again fondly at the memory of the Christmas Party as he thought of Maryann and Bill bumping and grinding unselfconsciously. In contrast, and sadly so, Elaine was not unself-conscious. She was completely and constantly conscious of everything. Sometimes he wished she would drink more. Or at all.

Instead, Elaine worried. She worried about how she looked. She worried that she looked fat. She worried that she looked old. She worried that he didn't look right in some way. Elaine would not even get up and dance with him even after she told him repeatedly she wanted to and even after he asked her politely. The implication of course was that he, Paul, was to blame, because she had cruelly and bluntly told him on several occasions, that he could not dance.

Nevertheless, despite the fact that Elaine sat there and watched the dancers having fun, she would not get up and dance with him, and as office decorum would have it, none of the other men in the place had the nerve, or were drunk enough to bypass the rules and their potentially jealous spouses, to ask her to. She settled for enjoying herself mildly. This meant that occasionally she said something snide to him or flirted blatantly with the other husbands. As Paul turned the events of that evening over again in his head, he had to conclude it was not altogether a pleasant memory.

***

As he pictured what Maryann and Bill might have been doing after the party, Paul was reminded of the fact that sex with Elaine had become an unpleasant task. He still got horny so he still needed some sort of outlet. In the beginning he'd reluctantly approach her. At first, she stalled him with all the standard excuses: I've got a headache, backache, neck ache, it's my period, or I'm too tired. Then she started putting physical restraints on what he could or could not do and what he could and could not touch.

"Don't touch me there! That hurts!"

After the boundaries were drawn up, there were the "lessons" and directions which effectively siphoned off whatever joy and spontaneity was left in the act. Elaine tried "show and tell" but no matter how hard Paul tried to do what she wanted him to do, he just couldn't seem to please her. It soon became obvious no matter what he did or didn't do she wasn't enjoying sex which effectively destroyed any pleasure Paul could derive from the act.

And Paul and Elaine became, for all practical purposes, roommates.

Elaine

That night Paul and Elaine had another "talk."

You need to find a hobby, Paul said for the umpteenth time.

"I know. I already have a hobby," she replied as if by rote.

"Reading is not a hobby."

"It's what I do. And I play Scrabble."

"Scrabble is not a hobby. Not the way you do it. You're too competitive. If you don't win, you're not happy, and when you do win, you gloat. You're the worst winner I've ever seen." He went on, "You did the same thing with photography. You couldn't just enjoy it. You had to compete in the club contest, and if you didn't win, I had to hear about it for hours every time we left a meeting. 'The judges weren't fair! The judges don't know art! The judges are idiots! I'm the only artist in the club! No one appreciates art. That's the reason they are photographers, they don't have any artistic training…'"

"That's just the way I am."

"I mean you need to get a real hobby. Something you do just for fun. Something like stamp collecting. Or painting. Or stained glass," Paul elaborated.

"I've done those. They don't keep my interest. As soon as I get good at them, they bore me."

"I see. What about wood-working?" he asked.

"That's your hobby. You know I'm hopeless with tools."

Elaine remembered back to the first and last time she and Paul took an educational/technical class together. They were learning how to set stones in silver and gold jewelry. Paul was the class exemplar, the teacher's pet. When the instructor wanted to illustrate how to do it correctly, he held up Paul's penny with 100 one point bead-set cubic zirconiums, all in neat little precise rows of ten, and marveled. "You are wonderful, Paul! Such technique! Such control! Such élan! Such humility!" Well that's not exactly what the instructor said, but that is what Elaine heard.

In sharp contrast to Paul's expertise with fingers and thumb, was Elaine's inability to grasp the simple techniques that men like Paul seemed destined to master. Case in point, when the instructor wanted to show the other students in the class how NOT to do something, he would sidle over to Elaine and watch over her shoulder as she attempted to carry out whatever task involving eye-hand coordination he had just finished demonstrating. Then he would laugh and ask everyone to come gather round to see what Elaine was doing.

"NO, that is *not* how you hold a graver!" he would chastise her. "Here let me show you how to do it again before you hurt yourself." He said it gently with good humor, but Elaine heard, "You f*** up!! You fumble fingered fool!" Of course, he had said nothing of the sort.

It only made sense. Paul was born with a knurled ring in one hand and a chuck key in the other. Or whatever those tools were called. Elaine was tool-disabled or gadget-disadvantaged, maybe she was even a bit retarded when it came to manual dexterity. She needed to coin a name for her particular aversion to tools.

All she knew was that one day when Paul was at work and she wanted to cut something herself, she attempted to tighten the bolts, on the table saw or hacksaw or chain saw or band saw or whatever piece of large equipment it was, after changing the blade. Unfortunately, she did something incorrectly, because the blade came loose, and while spinning at some ridiculously high velocity, somehow managed to cut into the T-shirt she was wearing at the time, directly over the spot where her heart was beating or would have been if it hadn't stopped, without nicking her skin at all. Then the blade flew across the floor and crash landed. As she looked down at her chest she found a hole burned dead center in the middle of her favorite Jimi Hendrix T-shirt.

After the incident, she again reminded herself to stay out of the garage where Paul accomplished his wood-working wonders in the first place. When Paul got home there was hell to be paid because of the damaged teeth, the saw's teeth, not Elaine's. Again, she was reminded that Paul liked things a little more than he liked people.

***

The hobby conversation ended the same way it always ended. Elaine agreed she would check out the most recent issue of "Leisure Learning" and sign up for yet another class. Paul won, as Elaine effectively surrendered, agreeing to try another hobby she would soon tire of.

Truth be told, Elaine already had a hobby. It was sex. Or once upon a time, it had been sex. When she was young she had labeled herself as "promiscuous." Then she completed a research paper on promiscuity in college and decided that that didn't really mean anything. What was promiscuity? A behavior. What kind of person engages in that behavior? A nymphomaniac. So she began to label herself as a nymphomaniac. Unfortunately, that was a just an overused term tossed about in movies or sitcoms when they wanted to describe a character whose sexual escapades usually provided comedy relief.

She knew she had a problem so she decided to go to therapy. Her therapist defined it as a "sex addiction." Or as a sex and love addiction, which sounded somewhat better. Unfortunately sex addiction too suffered from the same widespread cultural misunderstandings attached to nymphomania. That is if you told someone you had a sex addiction they: a) didn't believe it was a real thing, or b) said, "Good for you!" Particularly, if that someone was a man.

The problem with an addiction is that it interferes with one's life. With Elaine it interfered with her marriage. It interfered with her personal life. It interfered with her thought process.

Elaine didn't feel good unless she was actually engaged in some sexual episode or fantasizing about her next one. Like most sex addicts, she could spend hours or days in this pre-planning state. When she was in this state the therapist called it "acting out."

The problem with having a sex addiction was that Elaine didn't actually enjoy sex. As a sex addict, she only engaged in sex to relieve the pain she had when she didn't do it.

And to avoid feeling the feelings she had when she wasn't having sex.

Feelings like abandonment. Rejection. Fear. Anger. Anxiety. She couldn't explain the feelings to Paul and God knows she had tried. When she had sex she felt accepted and loved and powerful; it was a really, really good feeling, as in "high." But it only lasted for a few hours, like a good buzz.

On the other hand, when she didn't have sex, she felt bad, really, really bad, worthless, unattractive, hopeless, bordering on suicidal. And that feeling lasted until…she had sex again.

She guessed this must be why they called it an addiction. It was like being addicted to a drug. The therapist gave her a tape on sex addiction or sexual impulsivity. The tape said when a person has sex it releases hormones in the brain, hormones that make one feel just as good as a drug addict doing cocaine. In other words, sex acts like a drug. That is, if you are a sex addict.

***

Elaine married Paul because he wasn't interested in sex. At least that's what she thought at the time. He was safe. So even though Paul and Elaine appeared happily married to the outside world, they didn't have sex at all. In the 16 years they had been married they averaged sex once a year. Even then she only did it for Paul's sake. The therapist called this "acting in."

That's what one does when one is a sex addict and turns one's sex drive to the OFF position. Like an anorexic who cannot make him or herself eat because the sight or even the thought of food is disgusting, when Elaine's addiction flipped into its anorexic phase, sex became disgusting. The thought of having sex made Elaine physically ill. After she had sex she felt dirty. Even after a shower she still felt unclean. Every time Paul touched her she felt soiled.

Once in a great while, Elaine still agreed to sex to try and save her marriage. Whenever Paul approached her for sex, she just lay there, and let Paul do what he needed to do. She even pretended to be enjoying herself. Sometimes she would endeavor to make little happy noises from time to time, to make him think she was engaged, present, and what he was doing felt good to her too. In reality, sex didn't feel good to her at all. In reality, she couldn't wait for him to finish, and she spent her time making lists in her head of things that needed to be done, or old boyfriends she'd had sex with, or she tried to remember the name of that actress she saw the other night during the movie trailers.

She knew she had seen the actress in "Fargo" but just couldn't seem to recall her name. She could picture her, pregnant and dressed in a police uniform. What was her name? So Elaine played a game where she started with the letter "A" and tried to come up with every woman's name she could think of that began with that letter. She'd try them out, one at a time, to see if they sounded right. Then she'd start with the "B"s. She knew that once she had the first name right, the last name of the movie star would pop into her head. By the time she reached the "C"s, Paul would be done poking around down there. He would heave one last large satisfied grunt as he released; then he'd smile that same self-satisfied grin. It was the same silly grin she'd seen on the face of almost every other guy she'd had sex with.

In his defense, Paul did omit the one thing that annoyed her the most. He skipped the question that apparently plagued all of her former lovers to no end. Once they were finished gratifying themselves, they invariably asked, "So did you cum?" or worse, they'd ask, "How was it?" This was annoying because then she would almost always have to lie and exclaim, "It was great!" or "That was awesome!" or "That was really intense!" and Elaine really hated to lie. It irked her immensely that not only did she have to feign excitement, she then had to feign sexual fulfillment.

To Paul's credit, he never asked her how it was. Maybe he knew how it was. But she chose to believe instead he didn't want to know how it was.

After lovemaking, Paul was too hot to hug, so he would roll over on his side. Sometimes he fell asleep right away and slept for the rest of the night. Sometimes he only fell asleep for a few minutes; he would lay there long enough for his heart to slow down to its regular 78 beats a minute. Then he'd get up and take a shower, and go off to his part of the house and do whatever it was he liked to do till one or two o'clock in the morning.

After Paul left Elaine lay there and thought. She thought about how much the two of them had changed since they first met.

Such was life. She used to have a little tiny butt and big boobs and hated her body. Now she had a saggy butt, and saggy boobs and she still hated her body. But now she knew what real hate was. She'd look back at pictures of herself and wish a time machine could give her back that young body she used to hate.

Paul too used to be so shiny. He was so cute, and so fit. His heart used to beat at 68 beats a minute, when he was young, and athletic, and in the best shape of his life. In those days, he could run five miles a day, and he dripped with testosterone. These days his knees, or his back hurt and Elaine was amazed to see him with a hard-on.

In those days, Elaine was deep in her sex addiction. She loved sex with Paul. In fact, she loved sex with anyone.

Now that Elaine was stuck on the flip-side of her sex addition, sex had become an odious chore. Luckily she and Paul had many other interests to keep them attached to one another. They had dinners out with friends, they had semi-regular weekend get-togethers with the neighbors, and they attended the monthly meetings of the photo club and the wood turners clubs even though Elaine was more a spectator in both these days. Their most frequent bonding activity was eating out for dinner, which they did like most Houstonians at least three to four times a week to stimulate the local economy, but in reality because they couldn't agree on the same foods to eat at home.

In the old days, after sex Elaine used to watch Paul sleep. She loved to listen to him breathe and watch his lips purse as he sucked in air and blew it out gently. This was one excellent thing about the man. She needed to add that point to the list of "Good Things about Paul."

Paul did not snore. Instead, he purred like a big old tomcat. The air went in through his nostrils silently, and puffed out his lips with a little "Pooh!" sound. And sometimes, it made a little "Coo!" sound, and at other times, it even sounded more like "Kwoo!" She wondered if other women's husband's made cute little sounds when they slept. She never asked them. She didn't really have any women friends like that. All her female friends were communal or shared friends, that is, friends of "Paul-and-Elaine." These women would undoubtedly take tales of Paul's sleeping habits home to their husbands, who would then invariably repeat them back to Paul and embarrass him. Then he'd never let her watch him sleep again.

He'd sleep with one eye open for the rest of his life, she thought. She laughed at this idea. It was just like most of her other ideas – crazy. Maybe she was crazy, like Paul often teased her, after all.

***

She had another thought about how things had changed. Nowadays, immediately after sex was over, Elaine would get out of bed, and take a quick rinse to wash him off of her, to wash the sex act off of her.

In the old days, in that place and time when she was "acting out," she had loved *that* odor, the odor of male and female coming together. She even used to go to work with that smell all over her. When she used the restroom, she'd shimmy out of her underwear and inhale it. That odor, that olfactory memory, would plunge her into the place where she'd have one long sexual thought that lasted for an entire hour or an entire day.

Instead of thinking about her job and the work she had to do, she'd relive one of her favorite sexual encounters in all its graphic detail. Any encounter would do, any lover would do. They were all completely interchangeable inside the "bubble."

At work, she'd daydream through the approach. First the man in her dream would reach over and start stroking her buns, toasty under the covers. She'd smile as she thought about the way his rough fingers would try to work their way surreptitiously into her fuzzy garden. She'd always pretend to be fast asleep as he did this. She loved this little tease, this little game, as he tried to be as sneaky as he could be, and she'd never let him know she was awake and aware of what he was doing, because she was curious. She was curious to see just how sneaky he could be. She was curious to see just what kind of nasty things he would try to do.

What would he do if he thought she was asleep? How far would he go?

And the fantasy would begin…He would barely (accidentally?) brush her back door with a finger or two. He would ease a finger inside her and she would squeal with delight. Then he would slide two fingers in, then three fingers in, stretching her open in the forbidden way. Then he would ram his fingers in and out and she would be powerless as she succumbed to previously unknown pleasures beneath this sensual attack. She would screech like a female cat in heat as the male cats lined up to service her…

***

In real life, she knew Paul was thinking about it, thinking about touching her bottom, but was too scared to try anything. She knew he was afraid of what she might do or say. She knew he feared she would roll over and attack with something like, "What do you think you're doing!?"

But she wouldn't have. And one of the problems with Paul and Elaine was even though Elaine's *sex addict* liked to think about sex a lot and liked to talk about sex a lot, and made frequent inappropriate sexual jokes in public, Elaine was a prude. In reality, she was too inhibited to tell Paul, or any man for that matter, what she really wanted him to do to her.

So instead, during sex with Paul or any man for that matter, she just lay, sometimes perfectly still, as he did whatever he needed to do to reach an orgasm. And the odd thing was most men didn't seem to care if she didn't respond back. Maybe they were in their own little bubbles and the "bubble" did have a way of making one's own personal needs paramount to anything else.

As she lay there thinking about sex, next to a man who could give her sex, she wondered what had happened to her life. Where had everything gone wrong? When they got engaged? When they got married? Maybe she was one of those people meant to stay single. Where would she be now if she had never married Paul? Dead probably…

***

She realized she was thinking the bad thoughts again. As Paul liked to remind her, she was thinking too much. He was right about that. She thought too much, imagined even more, and entertained entirely too many fantasies. Especially to be married to a man like Paul, a man devoid of imagination. Or so she liked to tell herself.

But it was a good marriage, all in all, if you took sex out of the equation. On the other hand, she was sure, that over time, with the right guidance, and maybe a copy of "The Joy of Sex" or "What Women Want," strategically left on the night table, that Paul would come around.

One day, Elaine hoped, Paul might decide that other things needed to be incorporated into their lovemaking. But alas, this was not to be. He liked making love, as he called it, in exactly the same way, every single time. And as she tossed this quandary around within her overactive mind, she came to the realization that every man she had ever slept with, that is, after deducting the many one-night stands, had been the same way. When it came to sex, they all liked to do things in the same way, in the same order, only incorporating a frighteningly small selection of activities into their respective repertoires of "love-making."

***

Elaine's thoughts slipped back to the 1990's to the time before she was married to Paul and to another lover, one who epitomized this truth.

When had she dated him? Before she got married? Definitely. Before she met Paul? Possibly. But was she dating both of them at the same time? Probably. At least for a time.

His name was Skye. Skye was a semi-professional self-proclaimed punk rock musician, who composed a musical tape to be played during sexual intercourse. In real life he was an architect and when it came to sex, he liked straight intercourse. That was a little incongruous she thought; he was a strange man but his sexual proclivities were normal, run of the mill, truly mundane. At the time she thought he was a freak, in retrospect, not so much.

She clearly remembered sex with this man. She even remembered what his penis looked like. She remembered what *all* the penises looked like. That was a disturbing thought.

The prelude to sex with the musician/architect always included something a little kinky to her naïve 27-year old sensibilities. Usually a little marijuana and scented candles were employed to set the mood. And there was always a weird smell in his house in the Montrose. What was it? Something that smelled like olive oil but wasn't olive oil.

Sometimes they would take a bath in his big antique footed tub that stood aloofly on its little clawed feet well away from the rest of the bathroom fixtures. The tub was very deep and she had to stretch her legs uncomfortably high to step into it. How she missed those young beautiful legs.

They would fill the tub with bubble bath and she would soap up his back, and scribble things on it like she used to do when she took baths with her sisters. The game went like this: first, the soaper would write a letter, and the soapee would have to guess what letter it was. Then the soaper would erase that letter with water, and write another one, and finally the soapee would have to guess what message the soaper was spelling out. And the message was always the same…I-L-O-V-E-Y-O-U.

(She tried playing the game with Paul. Paul wasn't interested in taking baths together. Or showers. Paul didn't know how to play. But Elaine still tried to teach him).

Why did she always write the same message? She imagined it was because she always did "love" whoever it was she was having sex with…at the time. And "love" was, quite simply, any guy who could give her an orgasm. Was that love? Or did it just feel like it? That was a question for the therapist.

After the bath, she and Skye would dry off and jump into the water bed. And he would start the music…

The music started out slow, like a full orchestra playing the overture to an opera, then it built gradually to a crescendo, and ended up soft and anticlimactic at the end. Elaine imagined this was his way of transforming sex into something greater than it was, like an author lassoing words and changing them into his own personal thoughts, or a photographer capturing images that embodied his unique perception of the world.

Personally, Elaine didn't have a problem with the idea of sex as a symphony. Scoring the sex act was an interesting exercise in merging the sacred and the profane. The problem was that he played the same music every time he made love, with every lover he made love to. So even though he appeared to be a creative individual, he was instead mindlessly scripting the sex act, turning it into something completely unoriginal. And that, in Elaine's judgmental opinion, was not art. It was a sin to an "artist" like Elaine.

In his defense, and she always defended her ex-lovers, he was the best fuck she'd ever had. Unfortunately, and this was a truth she was not happy about having discovered, fucking was not the same thing as "making love."

151

He was versed in tantric sex and it was while making love to him that she discovered to her amazement that she was capable of multiple orgasms. She attributed it to his technique, but now that she was a lot older and considerably more experienced, she realized he had practically nothing to do with it.

At the time, in her naiveté, she thought two orgasms was a big deal; now that she was older, she found out that there was no real limit to the number of orgasms she was capable of. That is, she could experience many tiny orgasms or one large orgasm instead, which seemed a rather odd trade-off. She often wondered if she was some sort of freak, because on the television shows women achieving multiple orgasms seemed an anomaly, not the norm.

With perfect 20/20 hindsight, she had to conclude it was most likely the marijuana she and Skye smoked at the time that helped her reach the second climax.

As she lay there next to Paul, she wondered why she was reliving this sexual episode. And why did she have this bad habit of comparing Paul to every other lover she had ever had and finding him lacking?

Her thoughts quickly returned to her first tantric lover. How did she find out that he was treating all the women he had sex with in the same exact way? She thought it was a funny story, but it wasn't like she ever had the opportunity to relate it. She hadn't even told Paul about it. Paul didn't really like to hear about her previous sexual exploits. Paul was not one to kiss-and-tell, and though the sex addict in her begged to hear about his ex-lovers, Paul never obliged.

It seemed very romantic when Skye gave her a cassette tape of a song he said he wrote for her. At the beginning of the song was a dedication to her. It went, "To Elaine, you are my only one." After she played the song, she casually flipped the tape over to see what was on the other side. When she played Side B, to her horror, and subsequent amusement, she heard another woman's name in the dedication. Maybe he forgot to erase the other side. Maybe he was just stupid, forgetful, or lazy. Or crazy. Maybe he had smoked one bowlful of marijuana too many. Then again, now that she thought about it, the only reason she didn't stay with him was that he was indeed crazy. In fact, the only thing she had liked about him was the sex. And now she realized, a little sadly, he was just another sex addict.

The interesting revelation about this episode came much later. It seemed eerily familiar. Then it hit her. Another boyfriend in college had done virtually the same thing. He had given her a poem he wrote and then had given the same poem to her best friend, Layla. So neither poem meant anything. And he didn't even realize he had done something wrong!

What was the message to be gleaned here? Men are just lazy? Men will take the path of least resistance? Men will find out what works and keep on doing it? Men were just hopeless...

Maybe it wasn't she that was crazy; maybe she had just caught crazy from all the people she had been with.

She thought again about the tape, and wondered how long it had taken him to produce it. How many hours had he spent conceptualizing the task? How many hours had he combed his music library for just the right pieces, with the right rhythms, and melodies, and tones appropriate to the purpose of setting the right romantic mood? How many hours had he spent cobbling the different pieces together, cutting and splicing? In the days before YouTube and self-publishing in music, there were no software packages available to do these editing jobs for you. More importantly, why was she thinking about something and someone that she had experienced more than 20 years ago? And why were the memories of him and sex with him so vivid?

***

Elaine liked to generalize. It was just one more strategy she employed, like making lists, to keep her chaotic thoughts in order. She often wondered about males and the ways they approached the sex act. She concluded that there were three main theatres of operation if you were a man, namely: Oral, Vaginal, and Anal. That is, if a man preferred oral sex, then he only wanted oral stimulation; conversely, if he liked good old-fashioned stick-it-in the way the missionaries stick it in, then that's what he always wanted, and lastly, if he was into anal sex, then he only wanted to come and go by the rear door, so to speak.

On the other hand, she had probably only experienced sex with other sex addicts, so perhaps her generalizations about men only applied to men with sex addictions. It was strange, but it seemed to be true, in her limited experience with other sex addicts. She didn't know what it meant or if it even meant anything.

All she knew for certain was that when it came to sex, she did whatever the guy wanted. And then she felt cheated.

If asked, she would say, she loved Paul, even if she often wished he was dead, but she wanted to have sex with him that was exciting and made her feel out-of-control again.

If asked, She had to admit, she missed "acting out." She missed doing all the stuff Paul wasn't interested in doing. Paul did, once upon a time, try everything she proposed, well almost everything, once. But then she felt guilty for asking him in the first place. Paul was definitely a missionary position kind of guy. As luck, or habit, would have it, Paul never liked any of the new things they tried, so they didn't try them again, and she didn't feel guilty anymore.

At least, not when it came to sex. On the other hand, Elaine felt guilty about lots of other things.

***

Elaine realized that something had to give. Something had to change. It was a only a matter of time before she: a) killed Paul, b) or killed herself, c) began acting out, d) went completely insane, or some combination of the above. They had been married 25 very long years and the pressure cooker was about to explode.

Her solution was to say to Paul, "We need a vacation!"

A vacation was an opportunity to give her time to think, to reevaluate…or for a miracle to occur…

The good news was they always needed a vacation. They hadn't taken one in years. It was always too expensive, or one of the cars broke down, or they needed to remodel the kitchen, or the economy was bad, or her relatives came to visit or his relatives came to visit, and these "obligation vacations" left them sick and tired of other people. So they just stayed home and talked about going on holiday, and watched Rick Steves sashay throughout Europe, and Elaine made lists of all the places she wanted to visit before she died and rank ordered them with the ones she wanted most at the top. First there was Paris, then Rome, then New Zealand, then Alaska, then New York, then China, then maybe Australia.

They never left the city.

Paul never asked Elaine why all of a sudden out of the clear blue she wanted to go on vacation, even though this proposal was very suspicious coming from Elaine. Historically it had always been Paul who had suggested traveling, and it was always Elaine who put the kibosh on the idea.

And she didn't offer to tell him why. She did not mention the daydream where she shot him or the one where she had pushed him off a cliff side to his certain demise. That thought made her smile a little wickedly. She could picture it clearly.

***

They were hiking up the side of a mountain. There were a few scrubby wind-tortured mesquite and other trees lining the way. But mostly they were threading their ways between the yucca plants and cactus that lined the trail. As they walked, they carefully avoided the poky needles and spines that were everywhere.

As a matter of fact, this part of the daydream was no fantasy. Elaine was reliving a scene from Big Bend National Park. But that didn't matter, the place didn't matter, the time didn't matter, all that mattered was the end result. Dead husband. Dead husband's money. Future boyfriend. Future happiness.

The path wound back and forth in a series of switchbacks to the top of the ridge. They hiked for what seemed like hours but which turned out to be only an hour or so, a relatively short time as hikes go, once she consulted her watch. At the top of the ridge was one of the countless scenic overlooks awarded to the few, the bold, the adventurous, those willing to leave their automobiles and travel on foot into the bowels of the park. This scenic overlook, like so many others, was well marked with the CAUTION! DO NOT GO BEYOND THIS POINT sign that Paul so liked to ignore. This time, though the sign would get its revenge. Just beyond the sign was a sharp drop off.

As Elaine's murderous fantasy unwound, she envisioned every detail of Paul's appearance. He was sporting a cheap knock-off of a khaki colored photographer's vest that he bought at Target or K-Mart, its many pockets bulging with filters, spare lenses and film canisters, and he had a well-worn Tilley hat over his brown hair. It was the hat he would sleep with if he opted to sleep with any hat. He was wearing, in the place of good hiking boots, boat shoes, also known as "Topsiders." He was laden down, mule-like, with an assortment of very expensive and heavy camera equipment, including a tripod, medium format camera body with telephoto lens firmly attached, and a hand-held light meter around his neck (Why a light meter? Why not? It was a fantasy…and he had to look the part of the photographer).

Then despite the sign, Paul decided to leave the safety of the path and head down over the side of the cliff. He must have seen something; perhaps a great shot awaited his camera's lens.

Pelicula! Pelicula! Danger! Danger! Stop! Elaine screamed the words (in her head). She tried to stop him but it was no use. He took a few tentative steps, then, suddenly, he lost his balance. How that happened, Elaine had no idea. Maybe the rocks gave way, maybe the earth gave way, or maybe a malicious desert wind caught him and propelled him downward. (Maybe a disillusioned half-mad housewife gave him a small nudge...)

In the dream, she tried to hobble down to where he was, but she was afraid. And it all happened so quickly. In less than a second, Paul's topsiders were sliding (and no wonder; who wears boat shoes to go hiking?), Paul's body was sliding, Paul's cameras and camera peripherals were sliding. And then, just like smoke, they vanished over the edge.

Elaine cried out in agony. Or so the story she recounted for the authorities went. She called out for help. She hollered and hollered, until she was hoarse. She cried. There was nothing she could do. The cell phone had no signal. There was no one around to help. More importantly, there was no one around to see...and most importantly, there was no one back in the real world who cared. No one to investigate the sad series of events that led to the quick death of the short life of the great photographer...

***

After this lovely fantasy Elaine's thoughts returned to some great sex she had had once upon a time in a hotel room, in a foreign country, possibly on their honeymoon, or on one of the other trips they took together before they were actually wed. Or perhaps it was with some other man. She couldn't remember.

But it was good sex. That she remembered. It was probably back when she was deep in her addiction. But that was beside the point.

***

Paul didn't say no to the idea of the trip. In fact he was very much for it.

Road Trip

Instead of flying to Colorado, they decided to have an adventure. That is, Paul did. Elaine didn't mind, she could easily add flying to the list of things she hated to do.

Paul liked adventures. There was a subtle difference between an "adventure" and an "ordeal." An adventure was an ordeal that you could write about later with fondness. With enough time you could even laugh about the things that took place on an "adventure." Ordeals often incorporated things like severe sunburns, dehydration, headaches that lasted multiple days, insufficient restroom facilities, urinary tract infections, or too many biting insects that Elaine was invariably allergic to.

They decided to drive the two days it took to cover the 1000 miles between their home and the land of the Rocky Mountains. They started out north on I-45 and planned to be in the Dallas/Ft. Worth area by lunchtime.

They passed through a variety of small Texas towns, all with strange names that Elaine began adding to her plethora of lists.

On the road from Houston to Amarillo they passed through Corsicana, Ennis, Cleburne, Mansfield, Waxahachie, Midlothian, Forest Hill, Saginaw, Pecan Acres, Decatur, Alvord, Bowie, Henrietta, Wichita Falls, Tower Park, Electra, Vernon, Quanah, Childress, Memphis, Clarendon, and Claude. She briefly wondered about the pedigree of each peculiar name as they passed through them and she kept her eyes peeled for the local cemeteries, which were usually found just past the town proper. Some of the towns were too small for their own cemeteries so the people were buried on family plots, which were usually not visible from the interstate, or freeway.

Sometimes they would consult the Fyodor guidebook they always had on hand when they traveled. Then when they had a lull in conversation, which was most of the time, whoever was not at the wheel would read the relevant passage aloud to the driver. Then they would briefly discuss the local tourist attractions, as if they might actually stop and check some of them out, concluding with the same declaration, "Let's check it out on the way back."

They never did check anything out on the way back. They were always in a hurry to get home by that time.

This was fine with Elaine, because, for her, the whole point of traveling was being in the car with someone else at the wheel, which left her free to look out the window, and watch eagle-eyed for the hawks that perched at regular intervals on the endless telephone poles that shadowed the roads. Sometimes she would count hawks, or try to identify them in her handy Peterson's field guide to North American birds. She counted red-tailed hawks, harrier hawks, but not vultures, because those were, as she like to say, a dime a dozen. The hawks were much less likely to travel the skies and hunt for small critters that lived in the recently harvested cotton and sorghum fields by the freeways.

When Paul drove, Elaine liked to kick off her shoes, and put her bare feet up on the dashboard like she saw the young girls do on the way to and from the beach. At times like this, she felt about that age again. That is, young enough to wear a bikini and still look good in it.

As they drove, Elaine returned to thoughts of the weirdly named Texas towns. Were these Texas towns named after people that had once lived there? She had heard that Alvin, Texas, birthplace of Nolan Ryan, the Astros baseball legend, had been named after Alvin, the man who operated the local train station.

The name that often came to mind when people discussed the phenomenon of strangely named Texas towns was Cut-n-Shoot. Cut-n-Shoot didn't seem all that odd to Elaine. She found Memphis and Paris to be stranger names. Were they named after Paris, France or Memphis, Tennessee? Or did the Texas towns come first? She'd have to Google that stuff later, if she even remembered later. Maybe she should have brought her laptop. On the other hand, there were lots of stretches on this drive where they wouldn't have service anyway. Lord knows, there were hours when they didn't even have passable radio stations on this drive.

As they drove through the Texas countryside, the radio wars began. The "official" rule was whoever was at the wheel got to choose what played on the radio. However, in the interest of long-term peace they usually bent this rule to accommodate people who were not amenable to sitting civilly at the negotiating table, or to be more specific, Elaine. In real life, that is, at home, Paul liked to listen to show tunes, klezmer music, or traditional Jewish folk music, blue-grass, and classical. Elaine only listened to classic Rock-n-roll, that is, music from the Led Zeppelin/Pink Floyd era, and belly dancing music.

For this reason, they usually wound up listening to country music. This was because Paul didn't really "mind" it, and Elaine could "stand" some of the new progressive country singers and their hits as long as they clearly incorporated the "rock-n-roll" sound.

As they approached the outskirts of Bowie, Texas a great song came on the radio. Elaine, being a non-Native Texan, could so relate, and the words went something like this: "Some call it heaven, but I call it hell, living in the Bible Belt…" That song was soon followed by a Jerry Jeff Walker classic she hadn't heard since she was in college. Elaine burst out in song as the refrain came back to her…"Up against the wall red neck mothers/ mothers that have raised their sons so well/ he's 34 and drinking in a honkytonk/ just kicking hippies' asses and raising hell."

Elaine's pondering about town names continued as they spied the sign for Bowie. Was Bowie named after David Bowie or the Bowie that the knife was named after? Duh, they must have named it after the Bowie of knife fame, because as some fragment of Jeopardy trivia entered her brain, Bowie, and what on earth was his first name, had perished at the Alamo. Or had he? Time to Google again.

As they saw the first sign for Wichita Falls, she recalled some trivial fact she had once heard about that city, that it had been named after some waterfall that wasn't really a natural waterfall. It was a man-made one, and they stuck the name of the town out by the waterfall, so it could be seen from the highway. This lapse in memory again emphasized an alarming problem occurring more and more of late. Namely, that she was forgetting names, and she sighed in frustration as she remembered how good she used to be at recalling those.

Names and phone numbers. But that was another Elaine and another brain.

After they left I-45 and got on 287, the road changed from perfectly groomed interstate to a divided 4-lane highway. It was still a much better maintained thoroughfare than the 287 of her college days. The white concrete was drizzled with black snakelike trails of tar.

The speed limit dropped by increments from 75 mph to 30 mph, as they passed through each town. These signs instructing travelers to slow down popped up every half mile or so, and one had to keep alert and watch for them. If one was not careful one would find oneself passing a sign at the same time as an 18-wheeler and one's view of a sign might be obstructed altogether.

Elaine took no chances when she was driving; one speeding ticket in Palacios years ago emphatically reinforced the awful truth, that is, a single speeding ticket received in any small-town Texas resulted in a progression of more and more serious consequences. These entailed receiving points on one's record that stayed there for years, being forced to complete the odious take-home defensive driving course or alternatively to attend a local comedy club and listen to not-so-funny comedians perform not-so-funny material, in order to keep one's insurance rates from going up. This was not to mention the other two side effects of breaking the law: first, receiving the requisite dressing down from Paul the do-gooder, who was no one to talk, having received several speeding tickets himself, and second, having to pay the ridiculously steep fine for exceeding the speed limit in the first place.

Speeding was definitely not an option on this road trip because black and white Texas police cruisers were everywhere, passing out tickets as if they were "Buy one, get one free" coupons.

Instead of stopping in Ft. Worth they kept going. They ate lunch at a little town called Henrietta. Elaine would have loved to know where that name came from. She imagined it was named after Henrietta, the world famous chicken. Famous for what? Laying the most eggs in a lifetime, of course.

They took a big chance and ate at the local Dairy Queen which was not visible from the freeway. It was in fact two miles from the freeway, but at least it was a straight shot, down the main drag of the town, and getting there and back to the freeway was not a problem. Instead of looking around for a non-franchised eatery, Elaine insisted. She was a in a hurry to feed. The food was not great, and there was no ambiance to speak of, but the girl behind the counter was friendly.

No one got lost and the food was cheap.

The Dairy Queen was sparsely populated by natives, and the little girl behind the counter was not that little. She asked them if they'd like the Hunger Buster for half price and they couldn't say no. Elaine inquired as to why the hamburger was being offered at that price, and the girl told her it was a manager's special.

Unlike Paul, Elaine preferred to eat known foods at known restaurants. When it came to food, Elaine hated to try anything new. On the other hand, and she always found this an odd incongruity, she liked to try new things when it came to sex. In direct contrast to Elaine's preferences, Paul liked to try new restaurants and new foods. But when it came to sex, he wanted everything to be exactly the same, every time, and he refused to try anything new.

After Odell, they were greeted by the sight of a wind farm where more than 50 huge three-pronged wind turbines slowly rotated their appendages like strange ballerinas in the ever present breeze that rustled the Texas prairie. At Chilicothe they spotted what could only be called large bumps on the horizon, which in fact turned out to be Native American burial mounds, not the first sign of the Rocky Mountains, as Elaine had hoped.

The small town of Clarendon drew Elaine's attention because there were large white crosses in front of many of the small houses that lined the main street. They appeared to be fabricated from PVC pipe. That was odd, but outside the town there was an even larger cross that appeared to be wired with Christmas lights; maybe it was lit up all year long, but there was no way to know, since they wouldn't be passing that way again after dark. I guess, the message was clear, and harkened back to the song they heard just outside Bowie. There could be no doubt they were neck deep in the land of Christians, strangers in a strange land.

***

The plan was to stop overnight in Amarillo. Elaine wondered about that. Was Amarillo named after the color yellow? And what was yellow about Amarillo? Didn't the word "amarillo" mean yellow in Spanish? Elaine couldn't remember.

Normally it would take 12 hours to get from Houston to Amarillo but they did the tourist/photographer thing which meant they stopped whenever one of them wanted to take a picture of something or whenever they saw a promising historical marker or roadside attraction. The picture taking didn't really cut into their road time that much because, as all good photographers know, there are only two times for excellent image-making: first thing in the morning and just before sunset.

As a rule, Paul never shot at any other times of day when taking pictures of his favorite subjects, landscapes. Elaine liked to take pictures of a little of this and a little of that, but on vacation she focused on taking pictures of her favorite subject, cemeteries.

They stopped only to eat lunch and fill the tank with gas, use the restrooms, and buy snacks to munch on the road. Paul bought crunchy salty things, and plastic bottles filled with Pepsi. Elaine preferred little chocolate donuts, grape juice, and other sugar-filled edibles. At one place she bought one of her favorite childhood snacks. It was a bag of light-orange-colored larger-than-the-real-thing Circus peanuts. She hadn't tasted one in years. They weren't nearly as good as she remembered them. And after about a quarter of the bag was gone, she was sick of them and she tossed them out.

When they got to Amarillo it was getting dark. They drove from hotel to hotel as Paul was wont to do, as he tried to find the best deal on a room. If it were up to Elaine, they would stop at the first hotel or motel they came to and pay whatever the desk clerk was asking for a room with clean sheets and a working toilet. She was not into shopping for the best deal. She was not interested in saving 10 dollars one way or the other. After traveling all day on the road, the only thing she wanted to do was find a room with hot running water so she could take off her sweaty clothes and enjoy a renewing shower with that luxurious hotel shampoo that always smelled so much better than the shampoo they used at home. Then she wanted to dry herself off with one of those clean plush white towels that were always stacked three high on the racks in the bathroom.

The hotel shuffle went like this. They'd drive up to the office at the Holiday Inn, get a price, and Paul would reject it, probably just because it was the first price. Then they'd hit the nearest Day's Inn, or Drury's Inn, or Ramada Inn, ask prices, and Paul would proclaim each, in its turn, to be too expensive. Finally, they'd hit the closest Hotel 8 or the Motel 6, which happened to be available. Then Paul would ask the price in advance and ask about discounts. It used to embarrass the hell out of Elaine.

Why, with all *his* money, was Paul so unabashedly cheap? On the other hand, it was probably because he was so cheap that he had all *his* money. It was a vicious self-perpetuating circle. Eventually they would find themselves checked into the cheapest hotel Elaine could tolerate. By that time, Elaine was well past pleasant; she was tired, bitchy, and hungry and in a hurry to eat. She often had to physically drag Paul out of the room before he started unpacking his things.

After they both showered and changed into clean clothes, they went out to eat dinner at the nearest restaurant they could both agree on. This ritual took a minimum of another half hour, in its entirety, and further put Elaine in a pique, because once she was clean, she was anxious to eat.

The dinner ritual involved first asking the desk clerk which local restaurants he, or she, would recommend. This took several minutes because Paul was always very polite and never seemed in a hurry. Then they would get in the car and drive past all the recommended eateries, deciding which ones looked the best. Sometimes they would stop, go inside, and ask to see a menu which Paul would then read cover to cover before he decided if this was to be the restaurant where he deigned to dine. If Elaine was really hungry, she would canvass in favor of the first food place they saw. This didn't make any difference to Paul who was always looking for something Elaine wasn't privy to.

At last they picked a place and sat down to eat dinner. Paul ordered his usual healthy meal which involved many vegetables and fish of some kind. Elaine consumed her usual unhealthy meal of white starchy things, mashed potatoes, and chicken-fried chicken, smothered with white creamy gravy. All the things on Elaine's plate were the same bland color.

It was hard to believe the two of them ever ate dinner together. Perhaps that is why they ate out so much. Elaine didn't like what Paul liked to eat and vice versa. Even when they cooked at home, Paul liked to try out new recipes that often involved liberal use of spices such as cardamom and those nasty little seeds that infested rye bread. As usual she couldn't think of the name of that particular seed. All she remembered was that no matter what Paul cooked it always seemed to copiously exude toxic amounts of whatever spices the recipe called for. She even suspected Paul added extra amounts of the noxious substances just to annoy her, although he swore repeatedly he had followed the recipes to the letter.

In contrast to Paul's culinary habits, when Elaine cooked she stuck to the recipes she had learned as a child when she cooked at home. Tuna casserole, meatloaf and mashed potatoes, hamburgers, liver and onions. Invariably, Paul would claim the food was bland and not flavorful enough, and he began heaping salt by the teaspoon over the meat before he even tasted it. Okay, so teaspoon was an exaggeration, but the end result was the same. This act, which seemed to negate the considerable effort Elaine had expended in preparing dinner, was just one more thing that drove Elaine crazy. Maybe she really was nuts.

It was safer, for all concerned, if they ate food prepared by other people.

After dinner, they returned to the hotel room where Elaine said a little prayer to thank the gods for cool clean sheets and overstuffed pillows. Elaine slept like a baby. Paul put the television on and flipped through the many cable television stations. At last he settled on a channel and watched its shows mindlessly, at a reduced volume ostensibly out of consideration for Elaine's comfort but in reality, for his own protection. But he needn't have worried. This was one time Elaine really didn't mind Paul making noise. After driving all day by the time they got into bed, she was tired enough to fall asleep even with the sound of good guys shooting bad guys in the background.

They were up at dawn. Both of them were always anxious to get on the road again. They ate breakfast at the Kettle that was next to the hotel. The food was cheap if not great, but as they both agreed, for a change, it was hard to mess up bacon and eggs. The biscuits tasted homemade and the restaurant had little tubs of butter and several kinds of jelly on the table so Elaine was in hog heaven. Paul ordered a Spanish style omelet and the total price of the ticket was a moderate amount so he was happy.

After breakfast they packed up the room, which took another 15 minutes, because Paul was fastidious and had apparently unpacked his few things and put them in the dresser drawers and hung them on the hangars in the closet sometime after they returned from dinner. Then he had to make sure he scoured the whole room carefully so he wouldn't leave anything behind. Elaine took less than five minutes to get dressed and ready; then she sat on the single chair in the room, irritably wagging one foot, as she waited for Paul to get his stuff together.

The sun was just rising and the traffic was light even though they were hitting the tail end of the morning rush hour. From Amarillo they headed north to the town of Dumas. From Dumas Highway 87 took them due west to Hartley through a great deal of farmland. From Hartley the road again veered on its northwest path. From Hartley, they drove to Dalhart.

The town of Texline was located just before they entered New Mexico. The sign for Texline proudly boasted a population of 507. *With or without counting the cattle?* laughed Elaine to herself.

Then they saw it, the anti-climactic sign that informed road warriors they had crossed some unseen line, some invisible boundary, and had entered into a different state. Elaine couldn't help but notice from her "extensive" travels that one state always looked exactly like the one immediately adjoining it at the juncture itself.

The sign was bright yellow and said only this: WELCOME TO NEW MEXICO, LAND OF ENCHANTMENT. There were four crudely drawn red peppers on the sign. It was obvious that nobody had received a great sum of money for designing this sign.

Elaine always expected the signs that told of such demarcations to be spectacular or breathtaking or at least have some semblance of the pride that the people of that state held for their chosen residence. Or at least for their signs. And she was always disappointed. The sign always said something terse, yet accurate, direct and to the point.

Elaine also expected to feel different once they made the transition from Texas to some other place. And that never happened either. She felt the same. The car felt the same. The day felt the same.

The land did however, start to change as soon as they hit the edge of New Mexico. Small mountains or plateaus could be seen in the distance as they moved from flatland to higher ground. Strangely shaped reddish buttes incongruously popped their noses up into the blue overcast skies like mushrooms peppering an early morning lawn.

Lava flows covered with shrub were everywhere around them.

This brought to mind the mountain Elaine could see from her childhood home. They called it South Table Mountain and supposedly it was a lava flow created during a volcanic eruption. That meant that a volcano was nearby, dormant, and would erupt again someday. As if the child Elaine hadn't enough things to fret over, from the time she learned this information, she lay asleep at night worrying that she and her family would be incinerated by hot lava, or buried alive like the citizens of Pompeii, when, not if, the neighborhood volcano erupted again.

In New Mexico the weather changed. It was cool and rainy. As they entered a 20-mile Safety Corridor, where everyone had to turn on their headlights even though it was the middle of the summer, it was so foggy they actually lost sight of the road at times.

The choice of radio stations changed too. They evaporated as if the fog had gotten them. There were no rock-n-roll or country stations out here. There was one religious station devoted to spreading the good news about Jesus, a Mexican radio station energetically filling the car with throbbing Latino rhythms, and a public radio station, which, unlike Houston's NPR, was playing nothing but elevator muzak.

Just as in Texas, they passed several towns in New Mexico with names Elaine would never remember or need to remember: Clayton, Royce, Mt. Dora, Grenville, Grande, Des Moines, and Raton. Clayton was the cleanest town she'd ever seen, it looked as if someone swept the streets every hour or so, and there was a wonderful artist or craftsman cranking out yard art, that is, sculptures made of welded sheet metal. A menagerie of rust-colored bison, horses, elk and other animals filled the grounds in front of the metal works. One building on the outskirts of town even appeared to have one of these fabricated dragons winding its way in and out of it.

Elaine briefly wondered about the town of Des Moines; as they discovered the natives did not pronounce the name of the town like the other Des Moines, instead of "Day Moyn" they pronounced every letter. They called it "Dess Moyns".

As they passed by, not through, each small town, the speed limit dropped from 70 to 55, for no apparent reason. Elaine's only guess was that the locals were trying to increase revenue by asking speeders for donations to the cause.

At Raton, they stopped at a McDonalds for a cup of coffee and a bathroom break. The restaurant, whose parking lot was jammed with cars and trucks, seemed to be serving a million customers right then and there. It was located a couple of blocks from the intersection where they had to pick up I-25 to continue on into Colorado. There they had a nice conversation with two strangers who lived there. The conversation covered the usual safe subject, i.e., the weather. The New Mexicans complained about the drought. And the Texans complained about hurricanes. Everyone expressed concern for the people dealing with the rampant wildfires in Colorado.

Elaine liked to talk to strangers on trips, although she rarely did so in real life. Apparently, this was because on vacation, she was "off-script." This is what her therapist called it. On vacation, she could be whoever she wanted to be and she wasn't self-conscious and shy. Maybe, she thought, this is why people who go to Las Vegas do things they would normally never do in real life. Maybe the sign on the outskirts of Las Vegas read, WELCOME TO LAS VEGAS, LAND OF THE OFF-SCRIPTED. She smiled to herself.

She knew people who would go to Vegas two or three times a year and when they were in the City of Sin they transformed into the "beautiful people," at least in their own minds; they dressed in sexy clothes, wore too much makeup and too much glittering jewelry. They had their hair done, and they wore high heeled shoes. Oftentimes, these were dowdy people in real life. But in Las Vegas they magically turned their lackluster selves into high-rollers, slipping the ushers 20's and 50's to ensure they were close enough to see the lines around Wayne Newton's eyes as he whined out that old favorite Danke Schoen and told the same stale jokes he told from the 1960's. These Vegas regulars would instantly be transported back to the time when they were "Teenagers in Love" again.

Elaine herself was disappointed by Vegas the one time she had visited it. She just couldn't let herself become someone else. Someone who didn't worry. Someone who didn't make lists of the things that were wrong with their hotel room, or who hated the noise and smoke in the casinos. Elaine didn't know how to be someone who drank too much, and woke up the next day to do it some more. Elaine didn't enjoy plugging quarters into the slot machines, or tossing the dice on the crap tables, because she worried about how much money she was wasting. Instead, she watched other people as they had fun. Maybe that's what Elaine enjoyed about being a photographer. She could take pictures of people having fun, she could remain an outsider, witnessing life, but not really being a part of it. A silent observer. Vicarious living at its worst.

Perhaps the sign at the outskirts of Las Vegas read, WELCOME TO LAS VEGAS, LAND OF PEOPLE WHO KNOW HOW TO HAVE FUN…NOT YOU, ELAINE. Now she knew she was just being paranoid.

On that long ago trip to Las Vegas Elaine was sorely disappointed by Wayne Newton's show. Paul was the kind of guy who refused to bribe an usher because he felt he had already paid too much for the tickets. As a result, they had to sit way in the back of the auditorium so Wayne Newton was nothing but a little dot on the stage. Paul, on the other hand, was thrilled to be there, even if he couldn't really see Wayne. Elaine silently groaned at the contrived banter between the singer and the leader of the band. For some reason, it sounded rehearsed. Well, of course it was, but it also sounded strangely as if she'd heard it all before, word for word. *Déjà vu on Danke Schoen, that ought to be the name of a song*, she thought wryly. She wondered if she was imagining this too. Or if she'd seen this very same act on Public Television just months before.

After breakfast they drove from Raton, New Mexico to Trinidad Colorado through the mountains. As they passed through Raton Pass, they saw the sign that meant they were now in Colorado. It was another disappointing sign.

The pass was picturesque, but the car didn't seem to be enjoying the drive as much as they. Its engines strained a bit as they climbed upwards though the mountains. On the other hand, the car loved the downhill trip. Even on cruise control the speedometer inched past 70 mph several times.

In Raton Pass they were gently reminded they were no longer in Texas. Their ears popped as the elevation jumped. Elaine remembered back to the innocent days of her youth, the yearly sojourns through the same sort of mountainous terrain to see the aspens change color. In those days the roads were narrow and one never drove faster than 40 mph. These days, a perfectly groomed four-lane interstate highway hurried people through the mountains at 70 mph. To Elaine it seemed a travesty against nature to help people drive this quickly through places they should be savoring. God's country, if there ever was a god.

***

The sign that welcomed them to Colorado meant they were only hours from the city of Pueblo. Pueblo supposedly was named after the local Native American tribes, perhaps it was Navajo or Hopi Indians. Some factoid in the back of Elaine's mind told her that "pueblo" was the Spanish word for town and that the Spanish explorers named all the Native Americans they encountered pueblos because they lived in cliff dwellings.

These days Pueblo's claim to fame was that it was a prison town. Many criminals in Colorado called it home. Elaine wondered what the Spanish word for prison was, maybe the people of Pueblo needed to lobby to rename their city that.

They ate lunch after they passed the city of Pueblo because Elaine refused to eat in big cities when they were on road trips. She knew that leaving the safety of the interstate meant traveling on strange streets in unfamiliar places. In Houston, where life was logical, the feeders paralleled the freeway, and to get back on the interstate, all one had to do was drive along until one came to the next on ramp. In cities like Dallas, however, once one exited the freeway one had to drive through neighborhoods to get back on. Leaving the vicinity of the highway in towns other than Houston meant they were likely to get lost, and getting lost usually meant a fight. This refusal to eat in big cities was one of the few times in their marriage where Paul surrendered without a fight because the ensuing arguments that resulted just weren't worth it.

In addition to arguing about not leaving the freeway until after they passed through large cities, they often fought as they passed through these same big cities, because that was when they had to change roads, and in order to do that correctly they had to make sure they stayed in the right lanes and take the right exits. Highway signs were not like they were in Houston in other cities. Sometimes the exits just showed up unexpectedly and the signs that instructed drivers which lanes to be in were confusing.

From past experience it was proven that Elaine made a terrible navigator. Unfortunately, neither of them seemed to benefit from past experience. Paul still handed Elaine the roadmap and asked her to perform the function of navigator. So they continued to get lost on road trips, especially in the large cities and they continued to argue when they did. Paul blamed Elaine for navigating poorly, and Elaine blamed Paul for making her navigate. It was a no-win situation.

Just before they reached Colorado Springs they saw the turn off to Silver Spring. The signs also pointed out the way to Cheyenne Mountain Zoo. As Paul feared, Elaine begged to go to the zoo. One of her annoying and fairly non-negotiable demands was that whilst traveling they had to stop at all animal-related roadside attractions.

This proviso meant they once had to visit an alligator farm located on the way to the Great Sand Dunes in the southeast corner of Colorado on one of their other trips to the Centennial state. Despite Paul's reluctance on that "adventure" he had to admit he did enjoy seeing 30-foot long alligators leap into the air to grab scraps of tilapia dangled before them by the alligator wranglers who owned the ranch. Elaine was more excited about seeing the ostriches and other animals the owners of that establishment had amassed.

At the zoo atop Cheyenne Mountain, they spent half a day wandering up and down the hillside that housed the many exotic animals. Paul had to buy Elaine the requisite green kibble pellets from the feeding machines so Elaine could behave like a kid again, tossing pellets at the animals who summarily snubbed them, because they had just been fed. Then they spent an hour, at Paul's urging, talking to a zookeeper and watching a young ochre colored orangutan eat an orange. Or, more precisely, *not* eat an orange. As they watched in fascination, the great ape would chew up the orange peel; then he would spit it out, and with his lips press the orange mess up against the glass window of his enclosure. Then he would use his big flappy lips to gather up the tiny pieces of orange peel and repeat the entire process. Again and again he did this, which might have signified that he had progressed, like a human child, to Piaget's secondary circular reactions stage.

It did appear the animal was enjoying itself. On the other hand, that just might have been because it was smiling the smile permanently assigned to those big flappy lips, the same ingenuous smile that dolphins wear on their beaks.

The gloomy Elaine decided he was a sad, lonely, bored prisoner. Like herself. Smiling at people because it was easier than explaining why she was so sad all the time for no good reason.

After they finished at the zoo, they had to stop at the tomb of Will Rogers which also was atop Cheyenne Mountain for some reason. A tape of Will Rogers' voice reading snippets/witticisms from his famous writings played continuously as they wandered about looking at the various photos of the man posed with other famous now-dead people. How sad, thought Elaine, no one under 30 even knows who Will Rogers is anymore.

That was another bad thing about getting old. One found oneself frequently lamenting the loss of famous people that were dropping like flies. Elaine heard herself saying the same things her mother used to say when she was a kid. When her mother said those things Elaine would roll her eyes; now she realized her mother wasn't nearly as daft as she had believed. She clearly heard her mother's voice inside her head, *In the old days comedians could make you laugh without using filthy words or talking about sex!*

Elaine added, *Without describing bodily functions in detail!*

When had common decency become a thing of the past? Elaine consoled herself with the unarguable truth about fame. In 50 years no one would remember the heroes of reality television, people like Daniel Tosh of the inane MTV show, Tosh.O, or Honey Boo Boo Child, that were busy alienating and attempting to mortify every person of her generation with their outrageous and disgusting antics.

But she thought, with some solace, people of the future would remember the great humorists like Mark Twain, Will Rogers, Dorothy Parker and James Thurber. Or would they?

***

Once they finished sightseeing on Cheyenne Mountain it took them roughly another hour to reach the B&B in Silver Spring. As Paul drove, Elaine read the section on Silver Spring in the Fyodor book out loud. It was very short, only a paragraph covered the entire history of the town. Apparently, Silver Spring had reached its heyday in the year 1894 once they discovered gold in "them thar hills." Before that the town had been sparsely populated; only a few hundred called Silver Spring home. By 1894, four years after the first of the gold was found, its population had exploded to more than 5,000. By the 1970's the population was again only a couple of hundred. Silver Spring had become a ghost town. One could drive up and down the main street of the town and the vast majority of houses and businesses were boarded up. *Where did all the people go? What happened to the gold mines?*

***

"So what does it say about our bed and breakfast?" asked Paul.

Elaine flipped to the section on things to do and see which included small write-ups on local hotels and other places to stay.

"That's weird, said Elaine. "It isn't in here. I was sure it was in this book. Maybe it's in the other one, the one in the back seat. She grabbed that one and paged through it. It's not in here either. That's really strange. So how did we hear about this place?" she finished.

"It must have been on the internet," Paul offered. But something in the back of Elaine's mind knew that wasn't right.

"Oh well, we still have a reservation for tonight, don't we?" he asked.

Elaine dug around in her purse and pulled out the hotel information she had printed out at home. "Everything's here: king-size bed, non-smoking room, confirmation number. It looks like they are expecting us."

***

The drive through the mountains, like all mountain drives in the Rockies, was beautiful. There wasn't a direction that wasn't filled with scenery destined to be pasted onto postcards for sale in souvenir shops all over Colorful Colorado. There wasn't a spot that couldn't be deemed a "Kodak moment" demanding the service of a cheap digital camera or smartphone. The platoons of blue spruce and conifer marched up the mountainsides and the paved roads clung gingerly to the rivers that snaked and carved their ways through the mountain passes. July in Colorado was well past the aspen season but there was still much beauty to behold. Snowless ski runs, bubbling brooks, purple and white columbines planted by people in little flower boxes sat in front of Swiss-style chalets. Remote mountain vistas, once pristine, were dotted now with the multi-million dollar mansions of wealthy Coloradans or Californians or Texans who had come to paradise to live off the grid, becoming one with nature as they heated and cooled their homes with solar energy.

As late afternoon approached the sun began to play hide and seek with them, concealing itself behind the peaks and the shadows across the road became long. Luckily they made it to the town of Silver Spring before night fell.

Part III

Colorado

2012

Day One

That evening, Elaine and Paul found themselves in a little bed and breakfast in the middle of the Rocky Mountains. The B&B consisted of a large Victorian style mansion where guests could sleep and where everyone took their meals. There were also several adjacent cabins that had probably been added to accommodate more guests in the high season. The mansion was on the street and the cabins were behind it bordering a brook, which bubbled with clear Rocky Mountain spring water.

The hostel's claim to fame was that it was located on the site of a notorious local brothel. And perhaps it was haunted, something about a murder or someone dying there. The story wasn't very specific but Elaine recalled a jealous wife shot her husband to death. Now Elaine wasn't sure where she had read that information and she couldn't find the source. Maybe she had made it up.

The murderous wife wasn't what had inspired Elaine to pick this B&B. She picked it because it had a very nice website, she liked the way the main building looked, and the man on the phone sounded like he really wanted her business.

Elaine started unpacking as soon as they got up to their room. They were staying in the mansion proper. Their room was cozy and the B&B was cozy. There were framed embroidered pictures on the wall, and knickknacks on all the wooden furniture. There were even some little porcelain Lladro figurines, she was surprised to see, on the dresser and nightstand. She loved Lladros! One porcelain figure was of a tall willowy woman in a dressing gown. The other was of a pastel colored Lladro rabbit munching on a leaf with flowers. Now didn't that beat all? How on earth did they know she liked rabbits? There were several old volumes on the bookshelf, a plush hand-made quilted comforter on the bed, many overstuffed pillows, and an old-timey space heater in the corner of the room. They even had their own bathroom with a pedestal style sink and an acceptable showerhead, Paul was quick to report.

The wooden bed frame creaked and the springs squeaked as they climbed under the covers that night. Elaine snuggled up to Paul and put her arm around him. He fell asleep immediately. She listened to him breathe for a while.

Even though she was exhausted from the long drive she still pulled out her lists and checked her cell phone every so often to check the time so she would know how much more night she had to get through.

Then she went to work on her favorite list. It was not her favorite because of its content, but favorite because of the frequency with which she worked it. She worked on this list much more often and at greater depth than all the other lists. It was the list of reasons to leave her husband. It was actually a two-part list. There was one side devoted to the reasons why she should leave her husband and one side filled with reasons she should stay.

On the first side, in position number one was the fact that they didn't have sex anymore. After all those years where she didn't want to have sex with him, or anyone, for that matter, now she wanted sex again. It was like the sex addiction was back. Only it was not just back, it was back with a vengeance.

And the problem was, when she tried to initiate sex now, Paul just didn't want it. Maybe he was too old. Maybe he didn't really need sex anymore. She axed that possibility; she knew that wasn't true because he was still *pleasuring* himself and he still had his collection of porn tapes and magazines which she had accidentally stumbled upon while doing something else.

Maybe it was because he was having trouble getting a hard-on. Then again, that had always been a problem in their marriage. Under this item, she mentally penciled several questions: Is he even attracted to me? Was he ever attracted to me? Does he only like young girls? Am I too old? Is he gay?

Maybe after too long a time, intimacy just couldn't be reignited. She sighed.

She checked her phone again and it was after three a.m. Suddenly, Paul stopping his little purring and came awake. This wasn't like Paul. He never woke up in the middle of the night. And he never woke up all at once. He had a funny look in his eyes. His pupils were dilated, the eyes of a cat ready to attack. The look was funny, not funny "HaHa," but funny strange, mainly because she had never seen Paul with this look. To be sure, she was familiar with "the" look. Most of her other boyfriends had had that look at one time or another. It was what she liked to call "the predator" look.

Her first boyfriend had often had that look. They met when they were college students. She was 20 and he was 18, and they were a perfect match, since all he thought about was sex, and all she thought about was sex. He would come over, in the middle of the day, not for lunch, but to squeeze a quickie or "nooner" into a stress-filled school day, for after all, they were top students at a top university. Stress was rampant.

They would leave class, and practically run down the stairs in the building, and cross campus, to her dorm room where they would lock out her roommate and have sex for hours.

The "predator look" is the look a cat gives a small defenseless mouse as it tracks its every move. Eyes dilated, black pools dominating, colored irises retreating into afterthoughts. The predator look is the same look a shark gives a smaller fish before it snatches it by the tail and swallows it. The same look a wolf gives a crippled bison calf before its jaws bite into the wooly fur. Focused. Without conscience or remorse. Pure instinct.

In the darkness of their rented room, Paul smiled at her and he looked 30 years old again, the age he was when they met. Although, if the truth be told, Elaine always saw him as 30 years old; she never saw the wrinkles around his eyes, or the thinning hair, or the little pouch of belly fat. Of course, she knew all these things were there on an intellectual level, but on an emotional level she still saw him as he appeared at their very first meeting. She still pictured him at the Birraporetti's Italian restaurant when she asked him if he liked cats and he said yes, and she asked him if he would still be there when she got back from the restroom, and he was. And she knew she was in love with him right then and there.

Elaine still saw him just the way he looked when she was 27 and he was at the peak of his physical perfection. That is, the idea of physical perfection to her love smitten eyes.

Paul reached over to touch her but it wasn't like in the old days. He didn't grab her and start groping her breasts like a blinded beast. He didn't squeeze her nipples as if he was trying to see how structurally sound they were. He caressed them, gently, first with his fingertips, and then with his soft lips. And she realized, with a bit of fear, that this wasn't Paul touching her at all. Well, of course, it *was* Paul. But at the same time, it wasn't *Paul*. She didn't know who, or what it was, but she realized, with a sly smile, she didn't actually care. For the first time in her life, she commanded, *Brain, go to sleep*! and it did. She let her body take over. Amazingly, her brain agreed to sit back and watch.

The first orgasm was intense, even for her, and she had experienced intense orgasms before. Unfortunately, they had usually been the result of a man-made device. Or a bit of the green weed. This time it was a real orgasm. A natural one. Or was it?

Once her body stopped moving, her head was fuzzy, and she found herself listening to her own ragged breathing and pounding heart. She opened her eyes and stared around her. The room was dark except for one thing. Paul's eyes appeared to be glowing, a sultry red-orange color lighting the room like a neon sign. She gasped. She wanted to scream but stopped herself. Whoever or whatever he was, she wanted him to stay, to keep doing what he was doing, to make her feel young and wild and nasty again.

He grabbed her and this time he was not gentle at all. But she was ready for him. She was surprised by how ready she was. She was wet and slippery, anxious to feel him inside her. He jabbed his fingers into her curly pubic hairs and she felt something scratching her. Maybe it was long fingernails. An image of long curved bear claws popped into her head. Hopefully, it was only her imagination.

She didn't care and she wasn't frightened. She was excited. His long fingers were insistent, clawing into her body, pushing deep inside. Instead of pain, it felt good, and she cried with pleasure for a change. He jerked his hand (or paw) out and she felt him penetrating her, digging deeply into her garden. He pushed so hard it felt like he hit a bottom. She didn't even know she had a bottom. Then he began to thrust hard, over and over again, machine like, but she didn't wrench in pain like she had so many times before. She moaned in delight and her body joined in. For once, sexual pleasure was real, and good, and she never wanted it to end.

And when it did end finally with one explosive charge, she was so tired, happy and satisfied, that she was the one who fell asleep. She didn't mind that it was over. And she didn't feel cheated. Paul lay on top of her as she dozed, and when she woke up again to look around, the room was pitch black.

Apparently, whoever, or whatever it was, had left Paul's body.

In the morning, she asked her husband how he had slept.

"Like the dead," he said.

Day Two

The next morning Paul was shaving in front of the tiny hand mirror pinioned to the wall above the freestanding pedestal sink. The sink was crafted of white porcelain and was chipped in several places, which only added to its quaintness. Paul's face was covered in shaving cream, and the scratchy mirror was fogged up from the shower, so he was leaning forward and peering at himself in the glass to see better. That's when Elaine snuck up behind him and groped his butt.

"Nice buns," she rasped.

Paul jerked and almost cut himself.

What that was for? he thought in alarm. Then he lowered his eyes from his own in the mirror and focused his attention on her reflection. She was smiling – a wicked little smile that he hadn't seen on her face…now, that he thought about it -- ever.

It was the kind of smile worn by young girls in girlie magazines. The smile that makes you want a genie so the genie can turn you into an ink character and you can join that beautiful girl forever between the pages. The kind of smile worn by long-legged tanned girls wearing nothing but Daisy Duke cut-offs and crop tops in the beer commercials. Sweet 20-year old girls in hip-hugging jeans, with pierced belly buttons and bare tummies, tramp stamps waltzing across the soft skin of their lower backs. Girls that fix their eyes on those lucky guys, nodding at them slowly, as if to say, "Yes, that is the right kind of beer you are bringing seductively to your lips. Yes, that is the kind of beer that makes you the kind of man who will be taking me home tonight, and Yes, that is the kind of beer I want to taste on your tongue as we kiss, and then make love (substitute fuck) all night long!"

A fantasy smile. A come-hither smile. A come-take-me-now smile.

He asked her, "Are you feeling okay?"

Elaine just kept smiling and replied, "I am feeling GRRRrreat" and she dragged the word "Great" out like Tony-the-Tiger does in the breakfast cereal commercials.

Paul started to say something else but he caught himself. He knew from experience the longer they talked with one another, or, more precisely, *at* one another, the more likely they were to end up in some stupid argument about nothing at all. He didn't have to think long about his next reply because Elaine jumped in and filled the silence.

"You look delicious," she purred.

Now Paul was certain something was amiss. This woman standing before him, in nothing but an oversized Pink Floyd T-shirt and nothing else, he noted with rising alarm, appeared to be in need of SEX!

Oh no! was all his brain could muster.

What am I to do!? he thought.

It had unfortunately gotten to the point in their marriage, where Paul, if he thought about it, no longer wanted sex. That is, sex with Elaine. He wanted sex. He needed sex. He often woke up as hard as an 18-year old. It's just that sex with Elaine was such a chore.

If Paul made lists, and he didn't, he would have put sex with Elaine on the list of things he NEVER particularly wanted to do again. It was certainly not on the list of things he WANTED to do. He would have scrawled SEX with WIFE on the NEVER list way below all the other items. Even below tasks such as putting the trash out on the curb; putting the screens up on the windows; cleaning the dead oak leaves out of the gutters, which entailed getting up on ladders and he hated heights; washing the cars, putting gas in the tanks, changing the oil in the cars, and rebuilding the carburetor on his corvette which needed to be done on a fairly regular basis, tasks which involved getting his fingers greasy, which he hated; cleaning out the garage, which involved lots of sweating which he was not fond of; and mowing and edging the lawn with its never-ending grass that needed fertilizing and debugging and watering and coddling and kissing and hugging as if it were some great sod-covered living beast.

Okay, so he didn't really "hate" these tasks. He actually sort of enjoyed the fact they were mindless activities. They kept his hands busy while his mind could wander.

And his mind did wander.

It meandered from Internet porn sites, to old girlie magazines he kept squirreled away in the work bench in the garage, to the pretty young girl who worked at his favorite coffee oasis. She always greeted him with a big sincere smiling "Good Morning!" as if he were indeed her favorite customer. She always seemed to be happy to see him. It was as if she actually looked forward to his appearance at Starbucks every couple of days. Or so he imagined.

Suddenly he realized he was not back at his favorite Starbucks. He was standing in his briefs before a strange mirror, in a strange bathroom, in a strange B&B, in a strange town, with a strange woman. Not that she was strange, per se, but she was behaving in a rather peculiar way. Even for a woman her age, prone to menopausally-induced rapid-fire mood swings.

"So, what do you think?" she said, and gestured towards the bed.

"Uhm," was all he could muster.

And just as quickly as she had snuck up behind him, she was gone.

He was relieved. He felt his heart slowing down. Until that moment, he hadn't noticed that it had sped up. In fact his heart had been galloping. And he had been so ensnared in his coffee girl fantasy, he hadn't noticed.

Now he wondered if his heart was beating faster because there was a nearly naked woman out there in the other room, or was his heat thundering because...?

His thoughts were abruptly snuffed out as Elaine sidled up to him again. This time she was stark naked and frankly he was frightened.

Scared that he couldn't or wouldn't be able to perform. Too much pressure. He blushed. She must have seen his face because she whispered, "Don't worry, big boy, Mama wants to do all the dirty work."

Despite his apprehension, he suddenly felt a warm rush of hot blood shoot down into his pelvic region. He closed his eyes as Elaine kneeled down before him and slipped his shorts off. She eased him into her mouth. And despite his earlier reluctance, he felt himself growing inside her wet warm mouth. He quickly overflowed the small cavern and she grasped his hand and led him over to the creaky old bed.

This time is was Elaine who seemed to be possessed as he lay on his back and she knelt between his legs.

She morphed into a she-devil. Sucking his cock until he almost came, then backing off until the blood stopped pounding in his ears and his heart stopped battering itself birdlike against his ribs. She was playing him like a wild trout, bringing him to the surface, then releasing the line, letting him sink back down beneath the water, then teasing him closer and closer to the surface, all the time toying with him, trying to tire him out. Bringing him up and dropping him again and again. Just as he didn't think he could stand it anymore, she let him go, and sent the line reeling. With one tension-releasing groan, he fired into her eager mouth.

And it was eager.

This was a first. She never liked to suck. She never liked to swallow. And here she was before him, swallowing, and smiling as she did so.

Then to top it off, she said, "That was delicious!" Now he had nice buns *and* he tasted delicious. He liked the way she said the word, "delicious." He felt like a child who had just accomplished some great task, like tying his shoes all by himself. He smiled inwardly.

He knew it was crazy to be proud of these two things but for one moment in his crazy adult life, where everyone expected him to act grown up, and do great things, and be proper all the time and be responsible for others, he was proud to be a sexually functioning man. He grinned unselfconsciously like a little kid, and felt safe, and happy and secure in his mother's arms. And he fell asleep.

When he woke up, he felt the weight of someone's head against his chest. It wasn't his mother at all. It was Elaine, and she was different. She looked the same physically. But she was different somehow. And then he looked again and she didn't even really look the same physically. He was certain she wasn't the same woman in the car on the drive up here yesterday. Was it only yesterday? It seemed a lot longer than that. But she did appear to have changed. She was glowing, or vibrating, or…then he saw what it was that was different.

It was her eyes. As she watched him drowsily he noticed her eyes were iridescent. Glowing. Burning. They had even changed color. They used to be brown. Now they were a kind of blue-green, like the inside of an opal.

That's weird, the left side of his brain pointed out. But the right side of his brain said, *Just go with it*. And he fell back to sleep.

***

The bed and breakfast was the domain of an older couple named the Kerstetters. They had to be in their 60's or 70's. But they had the inner glow that came from living a healthy life in the cool mountain air, eating organically grown fruits and vegetables, recycling, reusing and reducing paper, plastic, and glass, conserving water, serving as good stewards of the environment, hiking or bicycling everywhere they went, and doing yoga. Mrs. K's grey hair was interspersed with auburn ones, making it evident she had once been a luscious redhead. In contrast, Mr. K had a dark swarthy complexion. The hair on Mr. K's scalp was still mostly black, even though he should have had a head full of white at his age. A few grey scout hairs were making incursions into the black, in the vicinity of his sideburns. His moustache, on the other hand, was completely grey.

They probably were much older than they seemed to be. They were tan and fit looking; their eyes sparkled, their skin was clear, their spines were supple, and like everyone else in Colorado, their colons were clean.

It was early afternoon when Paul and Elaine finally left their cozy room and headed down the stairs to the dining room for breakfast. The Kerstetters seemed overjoyed to see them. Elaine and Paul apologized repeatedly for the lateness of their appearance, but Mrs. Kerstetter would have none of that. Even though it was well past noon, she insisted on fixing them a full gourmet breakfast, with eggs and bacon (from environmentally friendly chickens and pigs), homemade jam on homemade toast with organic butter, fresh fruit from the local farmer's market, and coffee (shade-grown of course). They even brought out the proper accompaniments for coffee, according to Paul, a little blue ceramic Delft cow filled with chilled heavy whipping cream (from eco-friendly cows?) and a matching china dish laden with brown sugar cubes. It was almost as if the Kerstetters had read Paul's mind.

The Kerstetters joined them at the large wooden antique dining table even though they did not eat anything. They asked them many questions, mostly of an oddly personal nature. They wanted to know where they had met, how Paul had proposed, how long they had been married, whether or not they had any children, and whether or not they planned to have any. Paul laughed good naturedly at the thought of this because Elaine was a little too old to become pregnant – in fact, at least10 years too old. But Mrs. K pointed out that Sarah in the Bible had gotten pregnant in her winter years. They thought this biblical reference to be a bit out of place but didn't say anything. They just looked at each other and raised their eyebrows.

Mrs. K continued to press them on the issue of becoming pregnant and seemed quite pleased to find out that they had plenty of money for a child and an ideal home environment in which to raise one. Again they found this a bit disconcerting but ignored it and just chalked it up to quirkiness. Paul was a bit surprised to hear Elaine talk as if she might be considering the option of having a child at this late date. Elaine was just full of surprises all of sudden, he concluded.

The Kerstetters never asked them where they worked, or what they did, or if they liked their jobs. They didn't inquire about their retirement plans, or their hobbies. They didn't even ask about the weather where they came from, or any of the other superficial matters that people usually start out discussing when they find themselves in the company of total strangers. They talked to them as if they were already family. The usual awkwardness of getting to know one another simply disappeared.

Paul was mostly quiet unless addressed directly. But Elaine seemed to be thriving on all this attention to her personal life. She seemed quite at ease with Mrs. Kerstetter, who more than anything, seemed to embody everyone's ideal of the perfect, caring, non-judgmental, nurturing mother. She was also an exceptional hostess. Mr. K, like Paul, seemed comfortable sitting there silently listening to the women prattle on.

Each time the level of liquid in either of their coffee cups sank below the halfway mark, Mrs. K. hopped instantly to her feet and was back with the shining chrome coffee pot refilling cups as she prodded Elaine for more answers to her never-ending questions.

Paul began to feel ignored so he started studying the vast array, or flock, of carved ducks and other waterfowl decoys that filled the room. He suddenly noticed that the birds were everywhere. Some were sitting, others had wings extended. But all were amazingly lifelike and accurately portrayed the real birds. As he examined every corner of the room he saw birds roosting on the bookshelves, on the cupboards, on the china cabinets, on the fireplace mantel, even on the floor, and on the windowsills. They were very intricately carved and when Mr. Kerstetter noticed Paul's eyes landing on his birds, he launched enthusiastically into the conversation.

He carefully explained, in painstaking detail, how each duck was created, from a raw wooden form to its final embodiment of beak and feather. In fact, as Paul studied one of the birds close up he could see that each feather, and each barb on each feather, had been burned individually into the wood and then laboriously hand-painted. They were truly works of art, not craft, as duck carvings often found themselves relegated. In Paul's humble opinion, and it was true he was no expert on fine arts, these ducks belonged in an art museum. When he ventured this opinion to Mr. K, the older man beamed with satisfaction and blushed a little. Paul and Mr. K had bonded.

Elaine had already noticed the birds. Because they were so lifelike, she had assumed they were trophies so she had dismissed them as she always did such items, that is, as further barbaric evidence of cruel human behavior. She thought of hunters as mindless uneducated people who liked to slaughter defenseless animals just for pleasure. Until that moment, Mr. K had been condemned to that group. Suddenly, she felt warmth towards the older man. Just as Mrs. K. embodied some perfect mother template in her mind, Mr. K. was awarded a role as father figure.

As an avid birdwatcher, and former paying Audubon member, she noted with delight all of her favorite ducks. Blue-winged and green-winged teals, mallards, both female and male, buffleheads, shovelers, and fancy wood ducks were prominently represented. There was even a small colony of shorebirds including pipers and white ibises. There were many others she did not recognize but it was a collection worthy of a fine aviary in a zoo. Elaine decided to let Paul and Mr. K share their mutual interest in tools and creating beautiful new things from formerly living things. Playing God in a way?

The conversation naturally divided itself into two parts, men versus women, as the men went on and on about power tools versus hand tools, enamel paints versus water-based paints, chisels, files, sandpapers, flexible shaft machines, and wood burners, not to mention the various methods of fabricating realistic duck eyes and webbed feet from scratch.

Mrs. K suggested that the women do a little baking for tomorrow's breakfast and Paul's mouth almost dropped open as he watched his wife charge into the kitchen several paces ahead of the older woman. Elaine never cooked at home! What was going on here!?

The men continued to examine the ducks one by one and Paul was impressed more and more as they went through the collection. Thousands of tiny rachises and barbs made up the feathers which had been painstakingly burned into the wood and painted with shiny enamel and tiny brushes. It would have taken hundreds and hundreds of hours. Now this was a hobby! Perhaps one that could or should even replace his current hobby of fantasizing over women's bodies and other sexual things he shouldn't be thinking about in the first place. And he envisioned two big advantages to bird carving: 1) he could still joke that he liked "chicks," and 2) the guilt associated with all that lusting would go away.

In the kitchen, Mrs. K and Elaine were soon busy flipping through recipe books. In fact, Elaine did enjoy cooking, or baking, to be more exact, but Paul was not fond of baked goods like kolaches, donuts, pies, cakes, and cookies. He didn't like that sort of sweet stuff at all. His idea of dessert, much to Elaine's dismay, was a healthy fresh piece of fruit. Unlike Elaine, who couldn't seem to get enough of pastry, Paul preferred crunching away on a raw apple to devouring delectable cupcakes, muffins, or warm slices of pie garnished with whipped cream.

So Elaine never baked at home. But here, on vacation, it was different. She was excited to be puttering around in someone else's kitchen, checking out the many small jars of cloves and allspice in the spice racks Mr. K had lovingly constructed for Mrs. K, poring through recipe books she had never before seen, and trying out each list of ingredients against those tastes she remembered in her head. She spotted a recipe for peach pie. Now that sounded delicious! But she recalled poking around in the refrigerator the night before searching for a snack for Paul and finding only apples in the fruit drawer.

"Wow, this peach pie sounds delightful, especially this topping of cinnamon, brown sugar and almonds," she said.

"Well, that does sound yummy!" Mrs. K agreed. "And I believe we just happen to have some ripe peaches for such an occasion."

As Elaine watched, Mrs. K drew open the fruit drawer and the apples were no longer there. Instead the drawer was brimming with fuzzy orange-yellow peaches.

"What the...?" Elaine started to say. Then she paused. What difference did it make? Mrs. K probably went out sometime this morning and stopped at a local grocery store to pick up these gems.

Who cares? We're on vacation, and it's time to have fun, she told herself.

Meanwhile, Paul and Mr. K went outside behind the main house to check out the woodshop in the garage.

They were gone for hours.

Since they had decided on two peach pies, Mrs. K and Elaine began by peeling a mass of ripe juicy peaches. They sliced them up, and mixed in some cinnamon and brown sugar. Then they combined the ingredients for the pie dough, flour, sugar, and salt, and cut in the chilled butter with a fork; finally they added ice water to the dough until it was the right consistency. They divided the dough into four pieces, two for each pie, floured the countertop and a wooden rolling pin, and took turns rolling out crusts, and put one in the bottom of each pie tin. After they filled each crust with peaches, they covered them with the top crusts, and pinched the edges of the crusts together all around with the back of the fork. They poked some holes in the two top crusts so the pies wouldn't explode and make a mess in the oven. Lastly, they put the two tins on a cookie sheet to further protect the inside of the oven and slid the cookie sheet inside.

All the while they were creating these masterpieces of culinary delight, Elaine found herself telling the older lady everything about herself. From the time she grew up, to the time she got married, to her decision not to have children and her recent regrets regarding that decision, to the vivid details of her newly awakened love life.

Once the pies were in the oven, Elaine and Mrs. K decided to play Scrabble. They didn't actually play Scrabble. They got out the tiles, set up the board and racks, and resumed talking again, forgetting all about the game. Mrs. K made tea; she had an old copper tea kettle that whistled when the water was on the boil and Elaine was thrilled to see her put milk and sugar in it the way it's done in England, which just so happened to be the way Elaine preferred to take her tea. Then they sipped from their cups and chatted like old friends.

Mrs. K listened intently, asked the right questions, in all the right places, and kept Elaine talking, until the tape of her whole life had been unraveled and played to a total stranger.

Meanwhile the pies baked. Halfway through, Mrs. K got up to sprinkle the tops with large crystals of sugar which made the crusts sparkle. Elaine followed her to the kitchen and watched. *Nice touch*, she thought.

Then they went back to their non-game of Scrabble and waited until the top crusts of the pies were nice and brown and the whole kitchen smelled of cinnamon. Then Mrs. K slipped on a green oven mitt that looked like a fish, pulled the pies out of the oven and set them on cooling racks. Elaine smiled at the whimsical mitt.

How queer, Elaine thought. *I've told this woman, this stranger, things I've never told Paul, and he and I have been together more than 20 years. I've known this woman two days and I've been talking for,* she glanced at her wristwatch, *four hours straight.*

"I must be talking your ears off," she exclaimed.

"Oh, no dear, I very much want to hear your story. I want to hear about you and your lovely husband," said Mrs. K.

At that pronouncement, Elaine had to laugh out loud. She never thought of her husband as "lovely." Annoying maybe; perfectionistic certainly; obsessive-compulsive often; at times, self-centered; at other times giving; always loyal; picky, cheap, frugal, honest, and fastidious. But, never lovely. And yet, in light of recent events, she had to agree that Mrs. K was correct. Paul was lovely. He was sexy, he was desirable, and certain parts of his anatomy were lovelier than others.

***

That night Paul and Elaine lay in bed and tried to read. Paul had a book on wood carving, specifically dedicated to the art and craft of duck-carving, borrowed from Mr. K. Elaine was idly flipping through the pages of a book of cookie recipes. But neither of them could concentrate on the words or the glossy 4-color photographs that embellished both volumes. Instead of ducks and desserts, all the two of them could think about were their recent sexual encounters.

***

The Kerstetters too lay awake. Mr. K turned to his wife and asked, "What do you think of this couple?"

"I think they're perfect," said Mrs. K.

***

After an hour of pretending to read, Elaine yawned exaggeratedly and said, "Well, I'm all in. What about you?"

"Me too," replied Paul.

Paul flipped the switch on the lamp that sat on the little nightstand next to the bed. Then they waited. Elaine waited for Paul to reach over and begin fondling her in that exciting new way. Paul waited for Elaine to deliver some salacious sentiment intended to make his blood pressure rise. Something on the order of a Mae West line like, "Hey,

Big Boy! Is that a rocket in your pocket or are you just happy to see me?" [2]

But nothing happened. Paul didn't reach over and start rubbing. Elaine didn't say a word.

The room was silent. They could hear crickets chirping to one another in the cold Rocky Mountain summer air. They could hear the wind rustling gently through the tops of the pine trees. They could hear the floorboards of the old house creak dejectedly every few minutes. They could hear a clock ticking somewhere down the hall of the old building. When one of them rolled over or scratched, the bed squeaked with annoyance.

Each feeling frustrated and a bit rejected, at long last, they fell asleep.

Hours passed. Suddenly they were both awakened by the sound of...what else could it be...but, lovemaking?

The sounds were coming from the room down the hall, the one where the Kerstetters slept. There was a low groaning sound, followed by another and another. This was followed by loud grunting noises, and the whine of creaking box springs. Paul flipped on the light and stared at Elaine.

"You don't really think they are doing it, do you?" he whispered.

"Well, that's certainly what it sounds like," she whispered back.

They both broke out in guilty grins.

"No way," he hissed.

---

[2] Mae West actually used the word "gun" not "rocket."

"Yes, way," she hissed back, and she laughed in spite of herself.

The creaking of the bed down the hall got louder and louder and rhythmically started causing the wooden floor to creak too. Moans that sounded female got louder and louder and just as they were thinking it should be time for a man's voice to crash in with one lion-like roar, they came to the realization that this wasn't going to happen anytime soon. Minutes went by and the old couple kept at it. At first it was cute, but after a while it became a little disturbing, at least to Elaine. Paul, on the other hand, seemed to really be enjoying this voyeuristic opportunity.

They could hear what they assumed was Mrs. K's voice engaged in a conversation. This was interrupted periodically by crooning and moaning noises. Then the female voice started rising in volume and began loudly blurting out ejaculations such as "Oh!" and "Ah!" and "Stop!" and Don't Stop!" Mr. K's lower voice chimed in vociferously and gruffly with remarks of his own. "Yeah baby!" and "You like that, don't you? This is what you want, isn't it Bitch!?" He was almost shouting.

At that point, Elaine broke in with her own exclamation. "That's it, I've heard enough!"

She jumped out of bed and headed down the stairs for the kitchen. Paul, on the other hand, couldn't get enough of this unexpected audio presentation.

The kitchen was dark except for a small light that was left on over the stove so people could come and go as they liked without stubbing a toe in the dark. The oak floor was cool to her bare feet.

Elaine started for the refrigerator but she realized she wasn't hungry so she went out the back door to sit on the swing tethered to the porch overhang. It was a nice swing but it was suspended on black heavy chains that squeaked loudly as she began to rock slowly forward and back. The squeaking of the chains brought her vividly back to the squeaking bed upstairs and she pictured the old couple busily going at it like two curs in heat. She smiled despite herself. Imagine being that horny at that age.

And she thought, *Why does it bother me so? It's weird, isn't it? We like to do things that feel good, but we don't like thinking about other people doing those same things. People are so silly. Then again, Paul doesn't mind listening. What a voyeur!* Then it occurred to her, *I bet they heard us going at it the other night. I wonder if Paul realizes now they were probably listening to us. Oy!* she thought. And her head began to hurt.

She got up and started walking behind the main house along the dirt paths that connected all the cabins to one another. Then she noticed something odd, *another* something odd. There were no cars parked by the cabins, although there were parking spaces available. In fact, as she reflected on this mystery, she concluded she hadn't seen any other guests. *Wow,* she thought, *that's weird.*

She looked up at the stars. There were millions of them spray-painting the sky in Pollock-like splatters. The high altitude and thin air made this place an astronomer's wet dream. In contrast, where they used to live, in the suburbs of Houston, the neighborhoods were thick with fast growing deciduous trees, great for shading the backyards and keeping the houses cooler, but rotten if one was inclined to look up at the sky. This was not to mention the omnipresent light pollution, an orange glow on the horizon in the rare places where one could see the horizon, courtesy of the neighboring oil refineries. Even when one could see the night sky, it was usually a grey overcast one.

Even where they presently lived, on Galveston Bay and far away from the city, the lights on the neighboring piers, and from the fishing boats on the water, as well as the newly installed street lamps, effectively prevented star-, planet-, or nebula-gazing. The sad thing about the street lamps is they weren't even there until the yuppies, who fancied they were moving to the country to escape the inconveniences of the city, infested the place and brought their obnoxious big city conveniences with them.

Here, in the Rockies, the background sky was almost black and the stars glittered brightly. Elaine wondered which constellations she was looking at. When she was young, she had star charts of both Northern and Southern hemispheres. Once upon a time she knew all about the scale used to measure the difference in brightness between stars. She still recalled that the brightest stars were not actually stars, but were planets which sometimes seemed to glow red or blue, instead of yellow. Once upon a time she even knew most of the constellations by name even if she hadn't seen most of them in real life.

She had only ever seen a handful. She listed the ones she remembered and the list was disappointingly short. There was: The Big Dipper, The Little Dipper, Polaris, the Northern Star, Orion the Hunter, and the one that was shaped like a "W". What was it called? Sagittarius? No, that wasn't it. Cassiopeia? Maybe. She hated being old.

She used to have a great memory. An eidetic one, or was it photographic? Or were they the same thing? Another thing she couldn't remember. Once upon a time, if she saw something once, she remembered the image of it forever.

Now she suffered from frequent attacks of "CRS" also known as "Can't Remember Shit" as she and her old cronies joked. It wasn't really funny anymore. She sighed. *Try to focus on the positive;* she repeated one of her favorite affirmations for the umpteenth time.

As she looked upward, as if for the first time, she tried to see the Milky Way. That was a treat she recalled from the last time she went camping. How long ago had that been? 10 years? 20 years? 30 years? Was it even with Paul? Was it with her friends or family? Where had she even been camping?

Where was the time going? Now she realized why old people were always talking about past events, things that had taken place when they were children, as if they had just happened. The same thing was happening to her. Past memories were just as clear in her mind as if they were fragments of yesterday. Some past memories…that is.

She sighed again because, as she had to remind herself repeatedly, and she didn't really want to believe it, SHE was officially "old people" these days. She found herself standing in line in McDonald's and being offered a discount for the Senior Coffee without even having to ask for it. And yet, when she looked at herself in the mirror she still saw the face from 25 years ago. She suspected it was the same phenomenon that made her see Paul as if he were still the same age as on the day they first met, that is, denial.

Crazy. Crazy Crazy thoughts.

She heard the screen door creak open and it was Paul.

"May I join you?" he asked.

She was very glad to see him. Glad he still wanted
to be with her. Glad he still wanted to hold her hand as they
walked about in public. Glad he wanted to join her there on
a crystal clear Colorado night as they beheld the wonders of
the universe and rocked in unison on an old squeaky porch
swing.

"Please, do," she smiled broadly at him.

Day Three

Paul and Elaine slept late again. It was after 10 a.m.
by the time they made their way down the stairs to the
kitchen/dining room. The Kerstetters were nowhere to be
seen. Instead, there was a note on the table which read:
*Sorry we won't be able to join you for breakfast. Help
yourself to the goodies on the table. Gone to the city.*

The table was set with napkins, good china plates
and silverware that shined. There was a basket lined with a
cloth and the basket was filled with tasty breads: bagels,
croissants, whole wheat muffins, banana bread, and
something that looked suspiciously like it contained bran.
There was also a bowl of fresh fruit: bananas, apples and a
lone peach. And there was a full pot of coffee on the
countertop. Freshly brewed. That was strange; they must
have just missed them.

The cream was inside the little cobalt blue and
white porcelain cow inside the fridge and Elaine fetched it
for the both of them. They helped themselves to more of
the homemade jam, cream cheese, bagels, and the fruit. It
was a delicious breakfast, somehow made better because it
was all set out ready for them to enjoy.

Elaine wondered again about the note. There was
no city close by. The nearest large metropolis was
Colorado Springs and that was 60 miles away and it would

take twice that many minutes, driving on the winding mountain roads to get there. That was each way. Then the K's had to do whatever errands they had gone to do, so it appeared the Kerstetters would be gone most of the day. By the looks of it she and Paul were on their own, and would have to find some way to fill the time. They decided to go check out the local businesses on the main square of the town, which wasn't really a square; it was more of a straight line. There was a rotary located on the main street near the spot she surmised must be the town center. It joined together several smaller streets. Since they were in Colorado, they decided to do like the natives and actually walk on foot. It was a very long distance for city lubbers like themselves, at least half a mile, but they were game.

They ate breakfast, put on proper street attire, and grabbed a couple of jackets and a pair of ski hats. The morning was quite chilly, the sky was cerulean blue, something out of a "paint-by-number" palette, and it was at least 20 degrees cooler than it would have been back home.

The street was quiet. They walked hand in hand to the town square, or what approximated a town square, more of a motley collection of various stores, selling the everyday necessities for living. There was a main street cluttered with tourist shops, coffee shops, markets selling natural and organically grown foods, a drug store, and an apothecary where one could purchase medicinal marijuana! For the second time since they had left home Elaine knew they were strangers in a strange land. No such animal existed where they lived. Where they came from, marijuana was smoked, to be sure, but it was legal nowhere within the borders of their home state. It was however, easily attainable, because Mexico was only a stone's throw to the south.

Neither Elaine nor Paul was interested in purchasing any of the natural remedy, for recreational or any other purposes, but they were intrigued by the entire phenomenon. So they poked their heads into the store to get a glimpse of the pharmacist. They expected to see a drug-addled hippy. They were also curious to see whether or not he had a glazed look in his eyes. They were a little disappointed to see that he was a normal pharmacist, professional and average looking. His eyes were not dilated.

Then they hit the art galleries, gift shops and rock store. There was even a carousel on the street, ostensibly for the little ones, but they could tell it appealed to people of all ages. There were hundreds of human and animal figurines that had been created by a loving woodcarver, a real life Geppetto. The artist, or craftsman, depending on the way one viewed folk art, had breathed life into large lumps of wood, which had been molded, albeit crudely, into many, if not all, the animals on the ark. Many of the creatures had humanlike expressions and most of them were humorously posed. Elaine particularly liked the gorilla sitting on a park bench, with his arm slung over the empty seat that was beside him. He appeared to be waiting on a date. Paul chose the swan with its elegant simplicity as his favorite character.

Elaine found herself mentally checking off items on a list of animals in the menagerie. A for alligator, B for bear, C for caribou, D for duck, and then she had to stop herself. She skipped ahead to Z for Zebra and broke the spell. She was back with Paul, on vacation, there were no lists, because they were in "C" for "Colorado" and on "V" for "vacation."

The rock shop was filled with geodes and all the other usual suspects when it came to minerals and gems.

There was an assortment of wire-wrapped jewelry crafted from polished semi-precious cabochons. There were mineral specimens that caught her eye, particularly the malachite and azurite ones. There was also a substantial museum quality collection of prehistoric fossilized bird and plant remains. There was even a bowl of singing rocks. As they examined the shiny torpedo shaped stones, and tried to decipher the instructions to make them sing, the owner of the store came over and demonstrated how they worked. One had to toss two of the stones into the air at the same time. If you threw them just right, the two magnetized stones would stick together and break apart rapidly and repeatedly as they fell towards the ground. As they clacked against one another the noise was akin to a cricket chirping. It was a great treat for the children, or more precisely, the owner's grandchild, in the store, as well as for Paul, who easily mastered the eye-hand coordination needed to make the rocks sing.

Elaine, on the other hand, threw more like the child in the store, and just as the child's throws came precariously closer and closer to the glass display cases, and the owner of the store felt obliged to take the rocks away from the child, Paul too was forced to disarm Elaine to avert disaster.

After the rock incident, Paul and Elaine returned to examining the exciting artifacts in the store. The most exciting find, if one finds a rock shop exciting, and Paul and Elaine did, there were many hand-turned rock bowls of some type of quartz that was light green with brown and reddish striations throughout. They had been turned on some sort of lathe and the walls of the vessels were so thin they had been rendered translucent. The owner was happy to explain the origin of these bowls and the techniques used to produce them. The quartz itself came from the Middle East and many of the same type of bowls were now on display at the Smithsonian. As a result, the owner had managed to fund the rock shop with grant money. Somehow the grant money was used to import these man-made natural wonders, and all the money left over was used to pay the salary of the man who ran the shop. *Pretty sweet,* thought Elaine. Now all she needed was to come up with some sort of artistic enterprise that needed funding.

Elaine "oohed" and "aahed" over these hand-turned bowls in the hopes that maybe Paul would return and buy her one later as a surprise.

But she knew this was not to be. Paul never bought her anything she liked, or to be more precise, expressed a liking for. He spent a great deal of time and thought deciding what to give her, but invariably never showed up with anything that was to her taste. Instead, he always bought her something he thought she *ought* to like, not something she did like. It was all part of his master plan (the one she did not recall signing on for) to make her a better person.

In his defense, however, Elaine was a better person after having been with Paul. For one thing, she now appreciated the difference between freshly brewed coffee, made from freshly ground whole beans, and that swill served in fast food joints or that used to lurk inside the inner recesses of the coffee machines at work. Thanks to Paul she now was aware that the correct way to imbibe coffee was infused with heavy cream, not half-and-half, not milk, and most certainly not, heaven forbid, artificial creamer! One could go so far as to claim, before Paul, Elaine had never had a good cup of coffee and she now knew what coffee was supposed to taste like.

To be sure, she also now appreciated the difference between real butter and margarine. In fact, before Paul she had never cooked with real butter, or put it in rice, or mashed potatoes, or on bread. In fact, before Paul she had never had high cholesterol…

A third great truth Paul had instilled in Elaine was that a nicely set table made the food taste better, in other words, food should always be presented well. That meant garnishes, fancy garnishes. Or even simple ones. Silverware, napkins, and place settings. Everything had to be visually aesthetic. And one did this even when dining alone. Not just for company.

In the big scheme of things, these were not huge important matters, but in Paul's world, they meant everything. They illustrated the difference between merely existing, and living the good life. In Paul's world, they symbolized, and Paul would never admit this, the difference between being rich and being poor. The funny thing was, Paul didn't even know what being poor was. Elaine had grown up poor. But probably, even more significantly, Paul had grown up with parents who had grown up poor during the Great Depression. And their fear of being poor again must have affected Paul in some major way.

From the rock store they could see a little shop across the street that seemed to specialize in girlie things like knickknacks and purely decorative stained glass hangings and lamps. Elaine grabbed Paul's hand and practically dragged him across the empty street to check out this establishment.

The store was alive with glass vases, hand-painted pottery, and other shiny baubles. There were strings of blue Christmas lights around a mirror, and many Tiffany style stained glass shades on both floor and table lamps. There were framed original paintings of female nudes rendered rather primitively, in Elaine's overly critical artistic opinion, hanging on the walls and reclining on easels. And there was a Christmas tree, peppered with ornaments, garland, and strings of twinkle lights, boldly standing guard over the other inhabitants of the store 365 days a year. It was Elaine's kind of store. Paul obediently followed her from room to room as she pointed out more things she wouldn't mind taking home to serve as reminders of this lovely vacation.

After shopping for several hours, it was again time to feed so they stopped at one of the two coffee shops on the main street. It was not a Starbucks. Paul made a deliberate effort, especially on vacation, to patronize "onesies" as he called them. On vacation, but only on vacation, Elaine was willing to give in to Paul on this point.

Onesies were stores that used to be called "Mom-and-Pop" stores. A store qualified as a "onesie" as long as it was not part of any chain or franchise operation.

The coffee shop featured home-baked cookies, muffins, and more of the ubiquitous bran and whole wheat pastries that seemed to be everywhere in the Rocky Mountain state. The coffee was excellent, and even though the coffee shop served some generic version of Half-n-Half instead of heavy whipping cream, they had to admit it was an awesome "Cuppa Joe," as the expression goes. Paul and Elaine sat in the window and sipped coffee from porcelain mugs, and watched as the occasional passerby passed by. It was a weekday so they expected little sidewalk traffic, but this was a bit too quiet. Too quiet even for Elaine who preferred, even craved, solitude. She loved places like Big Bend National Park where one could spend an entire day without seeing another human being, if one so desired.

Things here were certainly unexpected. Here they found themselves in one of the most beautiful states in the Continental United States almost entirely alone. It was not exactly high season to be sure, but there still should have been more people around. They were the sole customers in the coffee shop, the lone patrons of the B&B, the only people in the rock shop, and now, come to think of it, the only ones in the trinket/knickknack store across the street.

It was a little bit disconcerting.

Elaine told herself it was probably like Grand Central Station around here come ski season, and she should be thankful for the peace and serenity.

When they returned to the B&B it was late afternoon. They finally acknowledged the inevitable. They had nothing to do. There wasn't a television in the room, their cell phone connection was spotty and they had just seen the town.

"Maybe we should take a drive up to the mountains tomorrow," Paul suggested.

"That sounds like an excellent idea," his wife agreed.

They put it on the agenda for the next day.

Meantime they returned to their room to shed their jackets and drop off Elaine's handbag. They came back down the stairs, hoping the Kerstetters had returned from their trip.

They were alone. So Elaine rummaged around in a desk in the living room that was adjacent to the kitchen/dining room and found a deck of playing cards. She sat down at the coffee table that crouched before the couch, and started flipping through the cards in a game of solitaire. Paul found another book on duck carving and buried his nose in that.

That night they crawled under the covers as soon as it got dark out. It was early, only eight p.m., but they had run out of things to do. This was a first. Usually Paul had planned out an extensive itinerary of activities and their vacations, chocked full of adventures or ordeals (depending on the number and severity of things that went wrong), seemed to end as soon as they had begun.

As she tried to fall asleep and Paul's breathing became regular, Elaine's mind boarded yet another train of thought.

In her fatigued state, she began to imagine Time as an entity.

It occurred to her, as if it were some great new revelation and that was why it was so seductive, that maybe she, Elaine, was having this thought for the first time in human history; maybe no other person had ever thought this thought before. And then she remembered that this was a bit akin to that something that happened whenever she got stoned. The "brilliant" ideas that flooded her mind were not so brilliant, or maybe they were brilliant but she was never able to capture them in drops of conceptual resin long enough to preserve them until she was straight again.

Or maybe, more likely, everybody had these same thoughts; they just free-floated through the universe and only the Prousts, who spent way too much time alone locked up in their own introspective prisons, and other prolific authors could write fast enough and long enough to preserve them.

Then she recalled how, in her "poetry" phase, that every time she wrote down one of these "brilliant" thoughts in the middle of the night, they didn't make much sense in the morning, and they were definitely not original or earth-shattering. She wasn't channeling some great mind like that of Plato or Aristotle. She was only experiencing that "something" that happens to a dreamer in the wee hours of the night when the succubi and incubi come out to proverbially screw with the mind.

But nevertheless, she went on following the trail that promised enlightenment.

It struck her that Time was a living immortal being, perhaps a crazed god and she could sense him speaking to her, trying to tell her something.

Why had Time chosen her? What was so special about her? Was it a warning?

The fear that always seemed to be lurking just beyond Elaine's conscious mind jumped in then. Time was an enemy, a dangerous enemy. He lay stretching out before them, before all of them, before all of mankind. He was trying to intimidate them with his enormous threatening bulk, and was doing a darn good job of it, daring humans to try to whittle him down into manageable pieces.

Time was a great self-centered malicious Greek God, like Zeus, himself. Time was taunting them, calling out to them, don't waste me, don't squander me, but don't fill me with mindless activities to make me go away. Because if you do, one day you'll be sorry, you'll wish you had me back again. One day I'll be the most important thing in your life. But I won't help you. I'll just laugh at you.

Elaine realized she was having another one of her delusional insights. She was just glad that Paul couldn't hear the drivel filling her head. And she was glad it was too cold in the room to get out of bed and try to find something with which to write it all down. She knew it wouldn't make sense once she tried to put it into words.

She looked over at Paul. He was sleeping peacefully, cat-purring as usual. So she focused on that sound to make the voice of Time go away.

As suddenly as Elaine found herself conversing with Time, she found herself dreaming…it was a dream full of sex, vivid and disturbing, but when she woke up she couldn't remember anything at all.

Day Four

When the Kerstetters got home was anybody's guess. Paul and Elaine didn't think it proper to ask and the K's didn't offer to tell them. They were at breakfast the next morning, bright and bubbly as ever.

As Elaine came into the room, she couldn't help but notice something peculiar. Mrs. K was wearing a bright fuchsia scarf. And she noticed something even stranger as breakfast went on. The scarf appeared to be covering something on the skin of her neck, something that looked remarkably similar to a hickey. Would the surprises never cease? She stared at Mrs. K's neck, and Mrs. K saw her staring, but didn't say a word.

What is going on around this place? Elaine wondered silently.

Out loud she asked, "So how was your trip to the city?"

"Wonderful!" replied Mrs. K. "Just wonderful. We accomplished a lot. And how was your day?"

"Uneventful. We did check out the town, and I saw some beautiful things to buy in the local shops."

"That's just wonderful my Dear, and did you see the lovely new maternity shop?"

"What!?" Elaine was stunned. "No, of course not! No new babies in my family!" she blurted out. Then she laughed nervously.

But Mrs. K seemed serious. "You never know about these things," she said.

***

After breakfast, Paul and Elaine hauled out the map of Colorado and decided to drive over to Victor, to see the big open pit Cripple Creek and Victor Gold Mine and then to continue on to Mueller State Park. It was only six miles to Victor, a short hop from Silver Spring. The open pit mine was huge; there was no other way to describe it. Great earth movers that looked tiny from the top of the hill dwarfed the tiny dump trucks that swarmed about them like worker ants feeding a queen.

The pit was located on the site of the famous Cresson mine which was one of the most productive mines to be discovered in the area.

The mines of the Cripple Creek district were all located within a great bowl at an elevation of 10,000 feet. As soon as the miners got down about 800 feet the mines began to fill with water. To combat this problem, pumps had to run 24 hours a day at a considerable cost, and the water in the mines prevented digging from going below a certain depth. The solution was to drill tunnels to drain the great bowl. Several tunnels were engineered over the years, at progressively deeper and deeper depths until the Carlton Tunnel was constructed; a serious engineering feat at the time. It took seven years to finish, and a great deal of money. Digging the tunnel was frightfully slow-going and expensive: eight feet a day at $20 a foot amounted to a total cost of $815,000 dollars.[3]

But the cost of the Carlton Tunnel was well worth it; at that depth, the owners of the Cresson mine made a once-in-a-lifetime discovery. Like the archeologists that stumbled into King Tut's undisturbed tomb, they stumbled into a great geode, also known as a vug. It was 20 feet long, 40 feet high and 15 feet wide. Sparkling gold crystals studded the walls. The magnificent vug brought its owners more than $1.2 million dollars[4] in four weeks!

After Elaine and Paul snapped a couple of pattern shots of the multi-colored layers of earth that had been stripped away from the mountainside, they headed to the state park.

***

In Mueller State Park Elaine and Paul did all the normal tourist things. They picked up the map at the entrance way, studied it for a while, then stopped at all the scenic overlooks, clicked away with their cameras, and smuggled "contraband" to the nuthatches, ravens, and striped ground squirrels, that were not, in fact, chipmunks, although everyone called them that. This illegal feeding of the "locals" went on even though plentiful and prominently placed signs warned tourists not to be taken in by the pitiful

---

[3] This is in 1953 dollars, based on the book, *Money Mountain*, by
   Marshall Sprague. Today this number would be much higher.
[4] See note above.

expressions on their little faces. The animals were begging, hanging around, and looking extremely hungry, mostly in Elaine's imagination, of course.

The admonition "DO NOT FEED WILD ANIMALS" was as blatantly ignored here as it was at the Denver Zoo. Paul even put little peanuts on his camera and set the self-timer to go off in order to entice the varmints to come closer and create their own self-portraits. After many failed attempts using this technique, he did manage to snag a couple of award winning mug shots of squirrel faces packed with peanuts.

The other "score" for Elaine, and she considered it a "score" whenever she saw some type of wildlife, was that they spotted several smallish herds of elk. She had seen elk before, in Rocky Mountain National Park, but it was still a thrill to see them here.

They ate the lunch the Kerstetters had packed them at a roadside picnic table in the park. There were tufted eared grey squirrels in the trees above them. One threw or dropped, there was a question of intent, little pieces of pine cone on them, and chattered angrily as he, or she, did so. Their lunch box contained tuna salad sandwiches, on whole wheat bread, with lettuce and tomato (Mrs. K was a dream) of course, and fresh fruit. The tuna fish sandwiches made Elaine flash back to the picnics of her youth. Before the invention of blue ice, her mother would pack tuna fish sandwiches in baggies and place them in coolers filled with ice cubes. By the time they ate lunch many hours later the baggies would be floating in ice water and the sandwiches had usually been baptized a bit. This was all kinds of gross as she thought about it now, but at the time they loved it. Those were the days before wet wipes and hand sanitizers, when people either didn't believe in germs or fear them as much.

When they got back to the B&B it was after dark. The Kerstetters were reading in the living room. They talked for a while about all the animals they had seen. That is, Elaine, talked about the animals. Paul talked about taking pictures of the ground squirrels. Then the four sat in the dining room drinking glasses of warm spiced milk. After this snack, they all went to bed.

That night Elaine had another dream about sex, but this time she remembered it.

***

Elaine regarded herself in the great mirror behind the bar. At first, she did not recognize herself. For one thing she was very young, for another thing she was Chinese. As she concentrated on her surroundings and her image she became aware of who she was. "My name is Dai-yu," she said aloud, as if to convince herself. "I'm 20 years old. I'm in Colorado, in Silver Spring, at the Silver Spring Saloon. It's a brothel. I'm a prostitute. And I have a lover. His name is Estefan. He's handsome, charming, and he has a wife, but it doesn't matter. Because he loves me, and I love him."

Suddenly, as often happens in dreams, the scene changed, and she was upstairs in her room. And Estefan was there with her. They were kissing. He was chewing her lips as if they were edible. He was nibbling at her breasts. Biting them. Kissing her neck. Biting it. She felt his mouth warm and wet, his breath hot and smoky like a mythological dragon's. He was incinerating her, turning her body into ash.

And she wanted him to, to destroy her, to reinvent her, to reconstitute her into whatever kind of being he chose.

His tongue touched the flesh of her neck, burning it, searing it; his saliva was the glowing white hot metal in a crucible. Then he was scorching her with his fingers. Fingers of flame. They were hot and burning, blazing a way down from the mountains that were her breasts to the valley that was her belly. Flickering orange and red embers ignited the expanses of flesh bordering the path, torching the stand of light brown trees guarding her secret hiding place. As if doused in kerosene, the trees burst into flame. The hilltop was laid bare, defenseless.

The fire continued to burn out of control, all the way to the mother lode. His fingers penetrated slowly, melting a new portal into her body. Drilling open a shaft, mining for gold. As he teased the door wider, she squirmed with pleasure.

She felt an orgasm coming on and she tried to stave it off, tried to keep from losing control, tried to keep from erupting in release. But it was no use. When she came, she squeaked like a mouse, and she and Estefan both burst into laughter. Somehow, even though the exclamation had surprised both of them, it seemed appropriate, and he smiled broadly.

Then she started to cry. Estefan was alarmed.

"What's wrong?" he said quietly, trying to not to make it worse.

She couldn't say anything.

"What's wrong?" he asked again. He started to panic. Everything had seemed so perfect, wonderful, exciting, and new. Almost too perfect, as if preordained, as if the goddess of Love had finally acquiesced to smile upon him. He had finally found *it*, *it* being that elusive ideal. *It* being the love written of in literature; the love of

Shakespeare's Romeo and Juliet. *It* being a woman that he was in love with who loved him back. Not a woman he married for a horse and a couple of silver pieces. Love for someone he could cherish, celebrate, and worship.

A woman no longer possessing earthly defects. She had been soiled and yet, she was reborn, with his protection, and his love.

"I do not want to feel this way," she cried. "I do not want to love you."

There it was; she had used the "forbidden" word. The word he was so afraid to say out loud. The word that doomed lovers throughout time to live only in the pages of literature, as slaves fulfilling the needs of others, slaves eager to abandon their selves.

"I love you, too, Dai-yu," he said, and the words were out of his mouth before he could stop himself from saying them.

And he smiled because he knew that when he said them to this wonderful China Doll, they were true.

***

When Elaine awoke, she was happy. Then she grew sad when she realized it was only the girl in the dream who was happy. She got out of bed, and padded barefoot downstairs to the kitchen. To her surprise and relief, she wasn't alone. Mrs. K was there waiting with a pot of coffee brewing on the stove. It smelled delicious.

"Good morning, my Dear," she greeted her.

"What time is it?" Elaine asked, although she was wearing her own watch.

"Why, it's just after midnight, the witching hour."

"You don't really believe all that superstitious nonsense, do you?" asked Elaine.

Mrs. K chuckled. "No, of course not," she added. But her eyes twinkled.

"Well, I didn't use to," Elaine stammered.

"So, what are you doing up at this hour?" asked Mrs. K.

"I couldn't sleep; I had a dream."

"Ah, just as I suspected," Mrs. K said quietly. "They usually come to us, but ah, well…"

Elaine looked puzzled, so Mrs. K went on. "I'm not trying to frighten you, and I guess that's always a possibility, but, you see…" and she used the same tone of voice she would have used if she were informing Elaine that the lawn needed mowing, "The Silver Spring is haunted."

Elaine wanted to laugh at first. She scowled instead. She wanted to react angrily, but she couldn't. She knew, no matter how much her logical brain rebelled, that this insane fragment of information was exactly what she wanted to hear. It would mean, no matter how ridiculous it seemed, that she was not crazy. Even though she had often feared that she would be a first-class passenger on the crazy train one day, this possibility meant that today wasn't that day. This single, albeit crazy answer, explained everything. The weird otherworldly dreams, the mysterious peaches, and the sexual interlude she and Paul had had in their sleep. And even though she suspected she ought to be terrified, or at least alarmed, at this very moment, instead she felt light and free.

She wasn't going nuts! Instead, she was merely a part of some macabre reenactment of Rosemary's Baby and she was Mia Farrow and Paul had been possessed by the devil!

As Mrs. K got up to fetch them both cups of coffee, the reality of the situation set in. Then she reacted. First she shuddered; then she started feeling as if she might be having an anxiety attack. Her throat started to tighten and she felt something in her chest; it was her heart, beating a little too loudly. Then there was nothing. She was numb. Calm.

She tried to take her cues from the older lady, who was humming absentmindedly to herself as she headed to the refrigerator and pantry to retrieve cream and sugar for their coffee.

Elaine tried to activate her logical left brain begging it to come up with another reasonable explanation. It was silent.

Then her right brain popped in and advised her, *Just go with it!*

Her left brain added, *Ask her to prove it.*

Just go with it?? Prove it!? Elaine fired back. *Are you both nuts!?* There was a lot of hollering going on inside her head.

The racket caused by both sides of her brain trying desperately to assist her conscious self, was halted as a third voice cut in.

"Please, Dear, drink some of this. You'll feel better." It was Mrs. K's voice, the voice of reality.

To Elaine's chagrin, the coffee had only been imagined. That was excessively strange, for she had even smelled coffee brewing. Now it was tea. Or had the caffeine bearing beans been transformed in the same way the apples had morphed into peaches? She wasn't eliminating any possibilities at this point. But she agreed, as her left brain reminded her, that was just silly. She had read one too many Harry Potter books and seen one too many episodes of Bewitched when she was a girl. All she knew for sure was that Mrs. K believed the bed and breakfast to be haunted.

And wouldn't that explain everything? she pointed out to herself. After all nothing really bad had happened to them, at least not to their bodies.

She took the tea that Mrs. K. offered and finally opted to take the advice of her overly imaginative right brain. *Right is right, right?* she reminded herself. She repeated this truism with conviction as if to convince herself it was so.

"So, what do you mean haunted?" she asked Mrs. K. She caught herself wondering why this conversation seemed to be stretching into infinity. Had it only been a couple of minutes since the older woman's odd pronouncement? Maybe time itself was warped in this space, in this house, in this part of the universe.

Mrs. K said, "Well, it is a longish story, so we'll need sustenance." And she disappeared back into the kitchen to retrieve a couple of pieces of the peach pies they had baked. Had it only been two days ago or had it been two years?

It was all because of that stupid dream. The dream. Time had temporarily been altered. She had been living the life of a person that had lived and died many years ago. She had experienced another person's reality, seen life through another person's eyes, felt the feelings of another living being. It was disorienting.

How long had they been at the B&B? In Colorado? On vacation? What day was this? Again her right brain broke in and this time it was firm, *Just go with it...*

Shut up and listen! added her right brain with authority.

"Whipped cream?" That was Mrs. K's voice coming from the kitchen and cutting through her mental fog.

"Is it fresh or is it canned?"

"Canned."

"Then, no thank you." She didn't know why she had even asked. At home she didn't use whipped cream in any form.

She was ready to hear the ghost tale, and yet, she too was dragging out its beginning. Maybe she wanted to try one last time to dig her heels into the reality she had started with. Maybe she wasn't ready to hear that everything she had believed up until this time, every certainty she had known about life, the universe, and everything was WRONG! Or, if not entirely wrong, at least very much different than what she had previously believed.

She didn't really want to know the truth, but like a cat that sticks its paw into a flame anyway because it has to know what fire feels like, she had to listen.

"So, tell me the story," said Elaine.

"Do you want the long version or the short version?" Mrs. K laughed.

Was this all some sort of twisted joke? thought Elaine. "Just give me the whole thing!" she said aloud. Elaine was exasperated. She was beginning to suspect she might go into hysterics at any moment.

"Drink your tea, Dear. Have a bite of pie." Mrs. K suggested. "I was only teasing you, Dear; there is no short version. I'm just trying to lighten the mood. After all, I and the Mr. have been living with this reality for longer than you have been alive. It isn't often I get to tell the story, because most people don't stay long enough to hear it."

"What do you mean?" asked Elaine.

"Well, most people don't stay here long enough for the ghosts to get to know them. And if they don't know you, they won't really ever like you, and if they don't like you, they try very hard to make you leave. That's what happens to most of our guests. They stay for a night or two, then they leave and they never come back. For some reason," she continued, "And I think this means you and Paul are very special, the ghosts liked you right away."

"Liked us!?" Elaine gasped.

"Well, 'like' is a weak word in your case." Mrs. K went on. "They 'adore' the two of you."

"Adore!?" This was just getter stranger and stranger, and being "adored" seemed even worse than being "liked" by spirits. "They adore us?" she repeated.

"Yes, they've taken quite a shine to you both. Why do you think they've been making you dream all those dreams? Why, you are the only other couple they have even tolerated in this house for more than two days since, it must have been 1898, yes, I remember it was right before the big storm hit Galveston."

Elaine began subtracting numbers in her head but she was terrible at doing so. She tried rounding off the numbers. She rounded 1898 to 1900 and 2012 to 2010, and she got…2010 minus 1900. That couldn't be right. That meant the K's were more than 110 years old!

Her mouth dropped open. Mrs. K smiled as she saw this tidbit of data register itself in the banks of Elaine's short term memory.

"That means…" she began.

"Yes," confirmed Mrs. K, "I'm a little bit older than I look." And she laughed.

"But how?" cried Elaine.

"Magic, sorcery, the unexplainable; I have no word for it. I just know that it has everything to do with our ghosts. They have been coming to us, in our dreams, for years. And we never seem to get any older. Remember the good old days everyone is always going on and on about? Well, Mr. K and I remember those good old days." She finished with, "We've been living in this house for over 100 years. Before that we were just regular people like you and Paul, and we aged just like you do. Once upon a time, we came here on vacation when we were about the same age as you and Paul, but we never left."

"So you want to know about the ghosts? Well, there are only two of them. Living in this house, that is. There's a third ghost, the ghost of Estrellita, but she doesn't show up often. Oh, and I almost forgot, there's the ghost of poor Margarita, but she lives elsewhere. And nowhere. You see, she was a suicide, and her body is buried at a crossroads, beneath the spot where Highway 1 and Cemetery Road intersect."

"Buried!?" said Elaine. "Under the pavement!?"

"Yes, my Dear. You see in the good old days that I was alluding to, things weren't so good if one suffered from depression or any other mental illness. If someone committed suicide it was not permitted for him or her to be buried in sacred ground. The body of a suicide would be buried under a crossroads. That way its soul could not find its way back to the place it lived or to the people it once loved. They buried poor Margarita under the dirt street, and since that time the road has been paved over with asphalt."

"So when did she die? And when did the others die?" Elaine asked.

"Well I think they all died around the same time. In the 1890's. Or thereabouts. I'm not sure of the years, and the ghosts haven't told me, so I guess they don't know. Or maybe they don't recall. It's hard to say with ghosts. I guess they don't remember, because you know they must have known at the time."

This was too much for Elaine. Absent-minded ghosts. Suicides. Dream invasions.

Mrs. K laughed. "Silly ghosts, but you know they aren't very much interested in dates. All these ghosts think about is sex."

"What!?" exclaimed Elaine.

"Yes," Mrs. K laughed again. "We have a couple of horny, sex-starved ghosts living, or should I say, not living, under our roof. And you might be asking yourself, so why do they stay here? Well, they have to; they died here, and this is where their energy is trapped. Or to be more truthful, this is where they were murdered!"

"Murdered!?" Elaine spit out the word.

"Yes, they were both killed by our poor lost ghost. You see, I told you it was a long, drawn out tale. But it was a love story too, and everyone likes a good love story, don't they?"

"I guess," agreed Elaine.

"So, anyway, this is how it all began. Our beautiful B&B used to be a well-known and very popular brothel called the Silver Spring Saloon, quite probably named after the town itself."

"Silver Spring used to be a bustling mining town. They didn't find gold at first, and they had a few false alarms because someone salted a mine near Mt. Pisgah with gold, but in the 1890's someone hit a mother lode. Overnight, there were 55,000 people living in the area surrounding the towns of Silver Spring, Cripple Creek and Victor. Most of the miners lived in tents, and those few who struck it rich built massive Victorian homes in the town proper. Homes just like this one. People came from all over the country and the world to try to find gold here. The men were lonely; many left their wives and families behind, intending to send for them once they had enough money. But the vast majority of them were young single men with nothing but fancies of fortune in their heads."

She continued, "They came here to the Silver Spring to find companionship, to drink, to dance, to see a show, to gamble and have fun. Once upon a time, a bordello, or whorehouse as they are so indelicately dubbed, was more than just a place to buy sex. There was a stage, and world class entertainment. There was drinking, and gambling to be sure. But a brothel was, above all else, a place to gather, to be among friends, to have a good time, and if need be, a place to find solace in the arms of a woman."

"This is how our two resident ghosts came to know one another. Estefan was a wealthy landowner, and a rich mine owner by the time he met his beloved, Dai-yu. She was one of the sporting girls, which is what they used to call women of the night."

"Isn't that a lovely name, Dai-yu? It means blue-black jade in Chinese. And Estefan and Dai-yu fell in love. It wouldn't have been a tale at all if it hadn't ended badly. Poor Margarita was Estefan's wife, and one night she followed him to the Silver Spring and went up to the room where Estefan was making love to his beautiful Chinese princess and shot them both dead while they were still in the act."

"Then the poor distraught Margarita hung herself. "Alas," sighed Mrs. K., and Elaine could tell Mrs. K very much sympathized with the betrayed woman. She said, "Margarita must have truly loved her husband to have killed him just so another woman could not have him."

Mrs. K ended the story. "And that is why their ghosts are still so, for lack of a better word, randy. You see, they were brand new lovers. They had just fallen in love, and as it is so often in real life, they hadn't had a chance to get tired of or disillusioned with one another. So now, they are forever stuck in that time, the time of lovers falling in love, the time of giddy unexpected demonstrations of devotion, flowers left anonymously on porch steps and ballads sung beneath balconies. It's the time that spawns bad poetry, but heartfelt sentiment. It's the time when every moment is as charged as the first one when lovers glimpse one another from across a room. And it's the time when every kiss is just as powerful and knee-weakening as the first.

Like Romeo and Juliet, Estefan and Dai-yu spend the hours of darkness together praying for the nightingales to sing and the sun to refuse to rise.

"How romantic, but so sad!" said Elaine. She tried to remember the first time she saw Paul. And she did vaguely. Suddenly she recalled what it felt like to be so in love with him that seeing him dancing with another woman made her heart ache. With a jolt, she felt that feeling again; it was remarkable, so powerful and so strong. She actually felt the pain that accompanied that moment.

"So that's why I'm having these dreams about sex?" she asked.

"Yes, I'm sorry about that, but I can't do anything to stop it. These ghosts have minds, or should I say ectoplasms, of their own." She smiled at her own lame jest. "Most of the time, they just use me and the Mr. to fulfill their sexual needs. But as I said before, and I would be flattered if I were you, they have obviously taken quite a liking to the two of you."

Elaine didn't know what to think now. "So what do we do about it?" she begged the other woman.

"Do about it?" Mrs. K seemed genuinely confused.

"Well, I wanted to resurrect my non-existent love life, but this is ridiculous!" Elaine exclaimed.

"Is it?" smiled the older woman.

***

While Elaine and Mrs. K talked, Paul was dreaming. He dreamt that he was Estefan the man who had been murdered in the Silver Spring. He dreamt that he and Dai-yu were making love.

When Paul awoke he was smiling. It was good to be rich and popular and desirable. Then he remembered he wasn't really any of those things. It was all a fantasy and he wasn't in fact the charming character in the dream. He was just a regular guy, working hard to make a living, and married to a woman who was not interested in him. Not interested in his stories. Someone who didn't think he was funny.

Paul was alone. He reached over to the place where Elaine had been sleeping and felt the sheet. It was still warm. That meant she had only just left. He lay there and wondered for a few minutes if he should get up and go after her. Then he remembered a snippet of the dream he had just departed and decided against it. So vivid was the sexual energy of the dream, that he was seduced into remaining beneath the covers. He closed his eyes and willed himself to return to Silver Spring.

***

He was Estefan and he found himself downstairs in the game room where the piano player was pounding out a lively tune. One of the girls was singing along with the music. She was a little off key but what she lacked in tonal expertise she made up for in enthusiasm. Dai-yu was standing and staring into the mirror behind the bar when he walked up behind her. He looked at their reflections, at her small form and his larger one towering over it. He closed his eyes, gently stroked her hair, and inhaled her perfume.

In a flash, all the other patrons had disappeared. The music had stopped. His breath on the back of Dai-yu's slender neck was all that remained. He carefully pulled back the strands of long black hair that covered her ear and whispered, "I need you. You are so beautiful," and as he did so the hairs on the back of her neck stopped waving at random and came to attention.

"Come with me," he said as he took her hand and led her into a room with a roaring fireplace. He knelt down before the fire and bade her to kneel down with him. Then he kissed her, on the mouth, on the neck, between her breasts. His breath was hot, sticky. Then he realized it was she that was hot and sticky. As his hand slid down between her legs it came away wet and he brought it to his nose and sniffed. As he did that, he changed into a wolf. The light in his eyes glowed. His pupils grew; they became huge and predatory, but she was not afraid of him. She was ready for him to take her, to conquer her. To become a beast herself.

The scene changed once more, and he and Dai-yu were alone in her tiny room above the dance floor. He was no longer a wolf. He was a man again. And she was a woman again. But now that she had discovered that pleasure was associated with sex she was determined to take over and lead the dance.

She slid the head of his cock into her mouth. As she did this she sucked it as if it were a mother's teat, first gently, then harder, then gently again, but always she maintained a constant insistent pressure. She sucked him until beads of his fluid began to ooze onto her tongue.

But instead of allowing him to release himself, she stopped. He groaned almost as if he were in pain. But she maintained control of the situation, and bade him to sit up with his back against the headboard of the bed. Then she faced him, and straddled him, and the single effort he made to enter her succeeded with ease. Slowly she began to ride him up and down, moving side to side as she squeezed and teased only the tip of his cock with her vaginal muscles. She continued to move slowly up and down, but never let him penetrate her entirely. It occurred to him that maybe he was too big to fit inside her all the way. Maybe he was hurting her.

But suddenly she dispelled that fear. She surprised and delighted him when at long last he discovered what she had been up to. All at once she plunged her body downward until his entire manhood was enveloped, buried deep inside her. At that moment, there was nothing else of consequence in the universe. The entire cosmos shrunk as if by magic in that single instant into a space only large enough to encompass his self within the garden of the China Doll and the physical sensations that resulted from that union. Everything around them, the sheets, the bed, the room, the brothel, the town of Silver Spring, the state of Colorado, the United States, the world, the sun, the stars, the galaxies, and every other thing that made up the universe, disappeared. Everything else ceased to exist.

He came with an orgasm unlike any that he had ever experienced before. Or lived through. His whole body shuddered. Convulsed. Shook the bed, shook her. Again and again he convulsed. Then he fainted, for lack of a better word, for that is what happened. He fainted because his body could take no more. No more pleasure, or pain, or sensation of any kind.

***

Paul slept the rest of the night without waking. When he woke up it was already light out. He felt more relaxed than he had in years. Happy. Warm. And safe.

***

Meanwhile, Mrs. K went back to bed, but Elaine couldn't sleep. She spent the rest of the night downstairs in the living room doing crossword puzzles, and playing solitaire. Every so often she would get up and check the time on the clock in the hallway. It was a lovely antique grandfather's clock that was probably hundreds of years old. It might have originated in Germany or Switzerland; she had no good idea about things like that, but it was apparent that the wood had been carved by hand. Now she wondered, in light of the new knowledge she possessed about the Kerstetters' longevity, whether they had brought it with them from wherever they came from by covered wagon. No, probably not. She was still confused about how old they were. If they had lived in this house for a more than a hundred years, and if they had been in their fifties when they got here, that meant they were born in the 1850's or 1860's and had lived through the Civil War, the California gold rush, the Victorian era, the gay 90's, and World War I.

No, they had probably not arrived by covered wagon. But not by automobile either. So they must have brought the clock in some sort of horse-drawn conveyance. Other questions filled her head. Where did they come from? Why had they chosen to stay here? Had they known about the ghosts at the time? Did they stay because of the ghosts? It was perplexing. She hated mysteries. A mystery was just one more thing that she couldn't control. One more item that needed to be added to the list of things she had to fret over.

She hoped things wouldn't seem so difficult once it was morning. Things almost always seemed worse at night...in the dark. She listened to the steady ticking of the old clock. If she timed her breathing just right, matched it to the rhythmic sounds emanating from the wood, she found her body, despite an imagination that was actively running off its leash, relaxing. Becoming calm.

Day Five

The first light of morning brought the sound of birds singing into the old house. The call of mourning doves alternated with the animated chirps of purple finches, mountain bluebirds, chickadees and other small songbirds. Elaine couldn't identify which birds were which because she had forgotten to bring a pair of binoculars and her eyes had never been that good. From a distance they were all "LBJ's, or "Little Brown Jobs," as she had once heard a Brit call them. Worse than that, she had never learned to separate one bird song from another. She only recognized the sound of doves. All the little peeps, cheeps, and chirrups of sparrows and warblers pretty much sounded the same to her. When it came to her feathered friends, Elaine was definitely a visual person.

As she looked out into the yard she was delighted to see a nuthatch zigzagging its way down the trunk of a pine tree that lived behind the B&B. She reminded herself to ask Mrs. K if she had a pair of binoculars she could borrow. The morning clouds were rapidly morphing form purple and pink to white, and the pale background of sky was turning a robin's egg blue. It promised to be another dry cloudless day in the Rockies.

Elaine walked down to the carousel. In the early morning light, it was eerily calm. She checked out the animals. They seemed altogether a little too sinister as they watched her with their shiny painted wood eyes. Most of them were smiling at her, with many teeth showing and she highly suspected their motives. What had they to smile about? They had no life, no soul; they couldn't eat, or sleep or play. They would never love or be loved, and then it dawned on her why no one else felt sorry for her. She was fortunate beyond measure, for she had creature comforts in abundance, and she had her health, at least in its physical manifestation. And someone loved her, even if it was *only* Paul.

As she sat and studied the animals, it seemed that the carousel was a huge noisy, multi-colored metaphor for her life. Things went round and round, but they always ended up in the same place. Even though these spinning animals seemed to be moving quickly, in reality they weren't moving at all. Just like her. Instead of moving forward, nothing had changed. She noodled at her art, wrote poetry only intended for herself, started novels she never finished, took photographs she never hung on the wall, and attended a writer's club but didn't show her work to anyone, because she didn't dare subject her scribbling to the scrutiny of her fellow writers. She even took watercolor classes at the local community college, but she didn't have the nerve to enter her finished paintings into art exhibitions. Every time she displayed a piece of artwork she was devastated by any criticism, no matter how small or constructive it might be.

It seemed her life itself had stopped moving forward. Nothing she did had any real consequence. Nothing she did made a difference to the world. And having had no children, she didn't feel she had any real connection to the future. She lived her life for no one in particular. In other words, she lived her life entirely for herself.

It was a selfish existence, one strangely similar to the one she had lived in her 20's. That is where the metaphor of the carousel became almost too blatant to contemplate. Yes, it seemed life was a cycle of life and death, death and rebirth, a recycling of energy from one generation to the next, but what about her life? What about her energy? Where would it end up?

She sat on one of the benches that surrounded the carousel. After a while she went over to the ticket booth where there was a plaque that told a little bit about the origins of the merry-go-round. She was ashamed of her own sloth when she learned that one man had worked for 26 years to produce the colorful collection of animals before her. This was a man with a purpose, with a goal, with a vision. This was a man who had left a legacy, a mark on the world. Was it something that had changed the world? Who could say? Did he die and leave the world a better place? In the great scheme of things, would his existence prove to be more important than hers?

As she recalled the joyful faces of children and adults as they enjoyed the ride, she had to admit it certainly seemed that his contribution to the universe had been a positive one.

She wished she could get on the carousel and ride. But, like all the spinning rides at the carnival or amusement park, the merry-go-round only made her dizzy and sick to the stomach. In fact, if she even tried to watch the animals as they whirled past her eyes, she got queasy.

It all made sense if she extended the metaphor of her life to its logical conclusion. Of course, going round and round should make her sick. Going in a straight line, therefore, should be the goal. Progressing, moving forward in life, and avoiding the same mistakes, should be the antidote to the stagnation that she equated with her white-bread unimaginative existence.

Why couldn't she just enjoy the moment? Why couldn't she watch the laughing children and share in their joy? Why wasn't she a part of the shared reality of parents and grandparents and children and grandchildren? Why did the cries of "Look over here!" and the accompanying frenetic clicks of camera and smartphone shutters annoy her as these "amateur" photographers captured blurry image after blurry image?

Why did she find herself standing outside watching like an observer from another universe? Why didn't she enjoy these simple human interactions like everyone else? Instead she hated these happy people. She envied them their simplistic, unexamined existences, for they were happy purely to be, purely to carry out their biological imperatives of eating and reproducing.

What a cynical wretch I've become, she muttered to herself. *I have become the epitome of self-loathing*, she added melodramatically. It was hard to garner pity when she was so abrasive. *I need to stay at home when I'm in one of these moods and not inflict myself on others*, she concluded.

With that last gloomy thought, Elaine left the building that housed the carousel and walked back to the B&B. When she entered the house, she found Mrs. K busily preparing breakfast. As soon as she smelled the bacon, fried eggs, and coffee brewing, she felt better. It smelled like home…and love.

As they munched on toast, bacon and eggs, Elaine asked Mrs. K about the B&B.

"How did you ever wind up here and how did a brothel change into a hotel?" she wondered.

"Oh that," said Mrs. K, "that was a labor of love."
She continued, "After the gold rush ended and most of the
miners departed, the town of Silver Spring experienced its
own economic downturn. Almost everyone left, and the
Silver Spring had to close its doors. The entire town of
Silver Spring turned into a ghost town. It wasn't until the
1970's that someone got the idea to market the neighboring
town of Cripple Creek as a "ghost town." As a ghost town,
it became a bit of a tourist destination. Silver Spring
decided to do the same thing, promoting itself as a ghost
town.

"Armando and I came on a whim to see the
"ghosts." We spent one night in Cripple Creek and decided
to stay in Colorado forever. That was in 1950. We looked
all over Cripple Creek and Silver Spring and stumbled
upon this old brothel. It was in considerable disrepair. But
we fell in love with its Victorian charm. So we bought the
building and restored it. In the 1990's we decided to turn it
into a bed and breakfast. I loved to cook and entertain
people, and Armando loved to carve ducks. It was the
perfect combination," she laughed.

"Anyway, the remodeling took a great deal of
planning and many man-hours. When the Silver Spring was
a whore-house, there were six bedrooms upstairs, four
smaller ones and two larger ones. The small bedrooms
couldn't really accommodate much furniture aside from the
bed and a free-standing wardrobe. These rooms were
ultimately converted into four equally sized bedrooms that
could comfortably accommodate queen- or king-sized beds,
furniture, and closets."

"Even more importantly, restrooms had to be added
to all the upstairs suites. This meant tearing down interior
non-load bearing walls, constructing new walls, adding
closets, and installing plumbing in all the new bathrooms.

The original Silver Spring had a single small communal restroom upstairs for the use of all the patrons. Most of the patrons still relied on chamber pots. Not only that, but the entire house had to be wired for electricity because in the old days they used oil lamps for lighting."

"The downstairs was also drastically reconstructed. The gambling room was expanded and converted into a large kitchen, dining room, separate restrooms for ladies and gents, and a living room where Mr. K now houses his substantial wooden duck collection." And she laughed again.

"It must have taken you forever to do all this work," said Paul.

"You have no idea," added Mrs. K. and she winked.

***

After breakfast, Elaine excused herself and went upstairs to take a nap. She couldn't stay awake any longer.

And she dreamed.

***

Elaine woke. She felt good. She realized she might have been touching herself. She smiled a little self-consciously before she realized she was all alone.

Then she got dressed, looked at herself in the mirror and smiled deviously as she briefly recalled the highlights of the dream she had just left. Then she got dressed, smiled at herself, told herself she still had it, and went downstairs.

***

There was a good deal of daylight left so Paul suggested they take a drive up Pikes Peak. As Paul drove, Elaine read from the guidebook. According to the section on Pikes Peak, the mountain was named after the army officer, Zebulon Pike, Jr., sent by the United States government to explore the southern part of the Louisiana Purchase. From 1806-1807, Pike led the Pike Expedition from St. Louis Missouri, into Nebraska, and across the great plains to Colorado where they first sighted the distant "Grand Peak" (which later came to be known as Pike's Peak). In November of 1806 they attempted to scale the great peak in knee-deep snow. They hadn't eaten in two days, but they made it as far as Mt. Rosa (with an elevation of 11,499 feet) or Mount Miller, a peak 15 or 16 miles from the summit of Grand Peak. Even though Pike and his men never made it to the top of Pike's Peak, the mountain described in his travel journal was later given his name.

The expedition continued on to track the headwaters of the Red River, but they got lost. While they wandered about they stumbled upon the Rio Grande and mistook it for the Red. In northern New Mexico, they were captured by the Spanish authorities who governed that state. From there they were taken down to Chihuahua, Mexico, and held for questioning. No harm done, they were released, and Pike's book describing the new territory became a bestseller.

"Well that was a good story, said Paul.

"Yes, agreed Elaine." They were all good stories. That's why she liked history so.

From Silver Spring Paul and Elaine drove north on County Road 61 until it ran into Highway 67. They stayed on 67 until it came to Highway 24. This is where they came to a sign that read PIKES PEAK HIGHWAY. There they joined a long line of cars whose license plates revealed the identities of the various sightseers in them. Some were native Coloradans, or sneaky aliens driving rental cars, but the vast majority appeared to be foreigners from other states waiting for the people in the cars ahead of them to finish their monetary transactions with the woman manning the toll booth. Meanwhile an old dude with a palm full of tens, twenties and singles came up to their car to ask if they wanted to pay with cash or credit card. When they said credit, he directed them to the person in the toll booth.

There they paid the somewhat steep fee, $12 per person, to drive up to the top of the mountain, and Elaine was again reminded of why her family had never taken this expedition when she was a child growing up in Golden, Colorado. It was the same reason she and her siblings had never learned to ski. It was just too expensive. The same reason they had never visited any of Colorado's many renowned tourist traps, like Seven Falls, or Cave of the Winds, or taken the famous train ride across the Royal Gorge on the narrow gauge railway that ran from Durango to Silverton.

Pike's Peak Highway took them 19 miles to the pinnacle of the 14-footer as the locals called all peaks in Colorado with an elevation exceeding 14,000 feet. Pikes Peak was [and still is] visible for 90 miles, from all parts of Colorado Springs and the areas surrounding the rapidly growing metropolis. The road wound itself back and forth in a series of switchbacks that brought them slowly up the northern slope of the mountain. The speed limit varied from 20 to 25 mph and a bevy of warning signs reminded drivers to keep their automobiles in low or first gear.

There were places where recent fires had decimated the spruce armies and laid bare the mountainside. They passed cars laden with bicycles, and clusters of bikers riding down from the top of the mountain. There were drop-offs that took one's breath away or would have if Elaine hadn't grown up in this state and taken so many trips just like this one. And she smiled as she recalled how as a child in the back seat of their station wagon she would lean the other way, away from the drop-off, as if her paltry weight might cause the Oldsmobile to fall off the road if it were not balanced just so.

At Mile Marker three they passed a sign that said BIG FOOT X-ING which had a silhouette of a Big Foot-like creature on it. Underneath this sign was another sign with an official looking message that warned people that a being resembling the abominable snowman had been sighted in the immediate area and visitors should exercise caution.

"Hilarious!" laughed Elaine; and they stopped to take the mandatory "grab" shot.

After the Big Foot sign, they passed a series of mile markers with different animals native to Colorado on them. They passed the Crystal Creek reservoir, the first of three bodies of water that graced the journey. The view of the scenery below was intermittently obscured by a sprinkling of somewhat sickly looking pine trees that bordered the road on either side. After the pine trees dwindled away, the views below were mostly blocked by clouds.

At Mile Marker 14 the terrain changed. They were now above tree line, and had entered an ecosystem of tundra, which meant, if she remembered her biology lessons, the only plants that could survive at this altitude were scrawny lichens. Elaine couldn't help but notice there were other small flowering plants up here even past the tree line.

Even though one was supposed to be able to see all the way to the state of Kansas from this elevation, they could not see much of anything below because dramatic storm clouds were starting to come in as if they were anxious to dump cold raindrops on the clumps of motorists trekking up to the top of the mountain.

At the very top of Pike's Peak, Elaine and Paul got out of their cars, like all the other tourists busily plugging quarters into the telescopes strategically aimed at the city of Colorado Springs and the Garden of the Gods. The first thing Elaine did was visit the potty. Paul was ordered to come with her because there were a lot of tourists and she was afraid they would get separated and not find one another again. Even though Paul pointed out, quite logically, that they could always meet up again at the Summit House if all else failed, he went with her.

As Elaine circled the summit taking pictures of the clouds below she couldn't help but wonder what the first people up here had seen after they finished their grueling trip by horseback or in wagons. It must have been truly spectacular with no clouds and no cities below, just miles and miles of unbroken wilderness.

How disappointing it must have been for poor Zebulon Pike who never stood in the place Elaine and Paul were standing. He never beheld the sights they were seeing. And even if he had been standing here, it would have been the middle of winter, and the mountains would have been covered in snow. He and his men would have been freezing to death and in no mood for sightseeing. On the other hand, Elaine reasoned, people still climbed Mt. Everest and other tall peaks; even numb and freezing cold they still managed to take pictures and celebrate their accomplishments. They still managed to stand on the "roof the world," reveling in the wonder of it all.

Here at the top it was cold. The temperature was supposed to be 35 degrees. Luckily Elaine and Paul both had warm woolen coats and ski hats on. Most of the year the summit was covered with snow; but today was an exception. It did start to sleet briefly as the rain couldn't decide what it wanted to do. As it started to rain, they dashed into the Summit House along with dozens of other tourists. To kill time they browsed around and Elaine bought a souvenir to take with them; it was a stuffed marmot.

As the rain ended, and the sun came out again, sort of, they fulfilled their other tourist obligation and posed to have their picture taken by strangers as they draped their arms around one another and stood in front of the sign that proclaimed Pikes Peak, Elevation 14,110 feet. As they stood there another couple walked up and asked them to take their picture with their camera. More people came up and Elaine offered to take pictures of them. Suddenly there was a line of people in little family groups all wanting their pictures taken with their own cameras. Elaine gladly obliged, and she got to sample a variety of different cameras; this is when she discovered there were still digital cameras with viewfinders available that made it easy to see what one was taking as one snapped away.

The trip down was better, even though it rained most of the way. They did manage to see a marmot, perched high upon a rock almost as if he were a sentinel. He was in silhouette, just like the yeti on the sign. This is what Elaine had been waiting for. This was what she kept her eyes peeled for as they drove past the vast fields of red colored boulders.

It was a little bit of a letdown to see only the one; she remembered a trip twenty years earlier before the highway was paved. On that trip the marmots were thick as fleas. Perhaps it was a function of the weather. Perhaps marmots don't like to get wet.

On the way down, they stopped to take some pictures of the winding snaking road below. The red rock formations brilliantly contrasted with the dark blues of the sky and the bright whites of the clouds as the sun made another cameo appearance. Elaine once again was struck by how difficult shooting with a digital camera often was, especially when it was bright out. In fact, even with the rain, the clouds reflected so much light it was still too bright to clearly see her camera's sensor. So Elaine resigned herself to shooting blind, as she liked to call it, because she really couldn't see what the camera was seeing. Despite her visual limitations and the limitations of her camera, Elaine did manage to get some really good landscapes starring the clouds and menacing skies, juxtaposed against the dramatic drop-offs, vast valleys, and moonlike rock screes. Paul of course, captured his usual award winning vistas.

By the time they drove all the way back to the B&B Elaine was exhausted. She fell into bed and fell asleep immediately. Paul stayed up reading.

***

In the middle of the night Elaine found herself wide awake. She lay in bed for 20 minutes before she decided it was hopeless. So she went downstairs to the kitchen. And there was Mrs. K. with a glass of warm milk. It was almost as if she had been expected.

"Here Dear, try this," said Mrs. K. She handed Elaine a glass of frothy white liquid. The milk tasted a little of cinnamon, and she sipped it slowly and let it warm her from the inside out.

Elaine wanted to know more about the ghosts, about the lovers, about the murders, but she had this weird feeling she wasn't in control of when or how she received this information. She suspected, however, that the ghosts would tell her everything eventually. In fact, she believed, they were anxious to tell her their stories. She was the one who was running from the truth. She wondered if she should say something to Paul. Then she wondered if he too were having the same dreams. Was Estefan coming to Paul as he slept? That would explain a lot.

She asked Mrs. K., "Do you think Paul knows about the ghosts?"

"Oh, he's met them. I'm just not sure he's ready to accept them."

"You mean?"

"Oh, yes, he's having dreams about Estefan."

"How do you know?" asked Elaine.

"Because Estefan told the Mr. and the Mr. told me," smiled Mrs K.

"Oy!" exclaimed Elaine. "It's a regular ghostvine around here!"

***

After that revelation Elaine bid Mrs. K good night and climbed back up the stairs with determination. She would go to sleep. She was on vacation, each moment mattered.

She practiced deep relaxation until her breathing was slow and regular. Four counts in, hold for four, four counts out. She kept track of each completed cycle on her fingers. Then she lengthened her breath even more, eight counts in, hold for eight, then eight counts out. By the time she had used up all eight fingers and both of her thumbs she found herself dreaming of Dai-yu. And as she dreamed of Dai-yu, so did Paul.

***

Estefan was making much progress with the China doll. Once so unschooled in matters of romance she was a quick study. Estefan's goal was to teach her how to enjoy physical pleasure, how to make love, not how to serve someone else's needs. He already had a woman for that, his wife, Margarita. And he already had a woman who pretended she liked sex and did whatever he wanted in order to receive gifts. She was an excellent actress, his little Estrellita.

Estefan wanted a woman who enjoyed sex, and had it because she liked it, not because he gave her money or presents. He wanted a woman who knew what she wanted and was not afraid to ask for it or take it.

So the lessons continued. First he touched Dai-yu with his fingers until she gasped with pleasure. He was amazed to see that she could have one orgasm after another in his way.

Then he decided it was time to graduate his student to the next level. As she lay on her back and looked towards the ceiling, he knelt down between her legs and moved them apart slightly.

"Do you trust me?" he asked.

"Yes," she said.

And she did. Then he brought his face close to the small patch of fur there. He inhaled her perfume. His lips touched her gently and the wiry hairs of his mustache mingled with the fuzz at the place where her two legs came together to unite. He kissed at her until she began to writhe with discomfort.

***

Paul jerked awake. He was smiling. He was in love with a girl. And she laughed when he laughed and she glowed when he glimpsed her tiny catlike teeth. And she was in love with him. She was so close, just within his reach. And all he had left to do was slide over and kiss her, and she would yield beneath him…

Then he was aware it had all been a dream; he was just Paul again. There was no suave Estefan, no mysterious Oriental maiden, no China Doll anymore, no kiss, nothing. The room was dark.

He glanced over at Elaine; she appeared to be smiling but she was sound asleep. He didn't dare wake her. Even though she was just an arm's length away, he felt very alone. He willed himself to return to the dream he was just dreaming… Foggily he tried to recall the details, but they were evaporating quickly. In a twinkle they were gone altogether; bread crumbs beneath a flock of hungry crows. He couldn't help but notice he had a raging hard-on.

***

Elaine dreamt too. Of a snake.

Her consciousness intruded into the dream and instead of watching Dai-yu and Estefan make love, she turned into one of the main characters. She was Elaine but

Estefan was still Estefan. *Why not?* she thought. *It's my damn dream!*

As she transformed into a participant, Estefan's face, mouth and tongue changed into a serpent, and slowly it slid, wet and alive, closer and closer towards her tiny hole. She stared down at her belly, at a snake as it undulated back and forth, winding and unwinding its coils across her skin. It was fascinating, not frightening, even though it seemed the snake was huge and she could clearly make out every detail of its scales and gleaming green-yellow eyes.

The serpent's body oscillated once more from side to side like a rope as it ended its oblique approach. Then it headed straight for the goal. As it reached the edge of her precipice it began its attack, gnawing at her like a coral snake, and her tiny hole grew until it was a great crevasse. For some reason, she could not feel its teeth. Then the snake dropped inside her as if it had been pulled.

This doesn't make sense, Elaine's subconscious spoke up then. But her conscious kicked in and decided she didn't have to be a film critic for once. She groaned with pleasure. For some reason Elaine woke then, and she realized she was touching herself. *Whatever works*, she thought.

She glanced over towards Paul to see what he was doing. He was sound asleep. *Rats*, she thought. *Oh well, maybe later*. She willed herself to return to Estefan's world.

The snake was back and it was still hungry. It continued to feed, taking the petals of her flower into its mouth and sucking each one suggestively and carefully, as if the pink and delicate shutters, as translucent as a mouse's ear, were made of the same material from which butterfly wings are crafted. As if too much handling might tear them apart. The snake sucked and sucked until she was helplessly lost, at the mercy of Estefan, and she reached a powerful orgasm.

This time the shuddering was a lot more enthusiastic. This time she made quite a bit of noise. Estefan laughed out loud when he heard her. With a jolt of disappointment, Elaine found that she was no longer Elaine eavesdropping into the lives of two lovers. She was definitely Dai-yu again.

Dai-yu blushed with embarrassment as Estefan gushed with pleasure.

"No, it's great! It's wonderful! You are incredibly erotic!" he assured her.

"Erotic?" she asked. "What is this?"

He tried to explain, "Erotic, it's like a feeling. It's a feeling where you make me feel powerful and strong. You make me feel like I can do anything."

Now, it was Dai-yu's turn to laugh.

"You are funny man. You are already powerful, and strong. How do I make you feel that way?" It was clear she was interpreting his words in their most literal sense.

"It's a strange concept isn't it?" he said. "But letting me make you feel good makes me feel…and he could not find the right word. You make me feel…(and he settled on a word) *important,*" he finished.

"That is funny," she said, "You are important. You are most important man in Silver Spring."

They kissed again…

***

Elaine woke up and she was smiling. *Now that was great dream* she thought. She was anxious to dream some more so she went back to sleep. But this time she had a nightmare.

***

When she woke up the second time, Elaine had the feeling that something was really wrong. The feeling was in her stomach. She turned to Paul and woke him up.

"I had the worst dream, she whined.

"What happened?

"I dreamt I owned the most spectacular necklace. It was so cool. And I've never seen anything like it in real life.

"What did it look like? asked Paul.

"Well, it had small pear-shaped rubies set in sterling silver. They were about five mm long.

"Are you sure it was sterling? Was it stamped?"

"Oh Paul, don't be silly. It was in the old days, they didn't stamp silver."

"Oh yeah, you're right," said Paul. So tell me about this necklace."

"Well, it had five pear-shaped rubies on either side and one huge pear-shaped ruby at the bottom. There were five round bead-set diamonds, about two points each, on either side of the big stone. The cool thing was all the stones were oriented so they looked like teardrops."

"So why was that a bad dream?" asked Paul.

"Because I lost the necklace. One minute I was wearing it, then I took it off, then we had sex," she smiled slyly, "Then it was gone. "

"So was the sex good?"

"Oh Paul, quit; you are such a dork! I want some sympathy here!"

"Okay, I'm sorry you lost your necklace. Do you think you could draw it for me? Maybe we can make one like that for you.

"Oh Paul, you romantic thing you."

Day Six

At breakfast the next day, Elaine told Mrs. K the dream about the lost necklace. The only thing Mrs. K said was, "I remember that necklace…"

***

After breakfast came the inevitable suggestion Elaine had been dreading. Elaine knew it was only a matter of time before Paul brought up the subject of…casinos!

Unfortunately, the closest casino was only six miles away.

Yes, there were casinos up the road in Cripple Creek. Elaine had been there before, when she was very young, back in the 1970's. In those days Cripple Creek had been a ghost town. There was virtually nothing to see along the main street, just boarded up houses, and buildings that looked as if they had collapsed in on themselves. Many old abandoned shaft houses dotted the hills surrounding the town nestled peacefully in the bowl of a valley between mountains. The old mines reminded visitors of Cripple Creek's event filled past.

Elaine wasn't sure if gambling was legal statewide, countywide, or just city by city. She suspected it was the latter since Silver Spring seemed to be free of them.

Apparently gambling had injected life back into Cripple Creek.

After a couple of minutes of debate, and a quick read through the guide book, Paul went on the offensive; he reminded Elaine of the abundance of cheap food on the all-you-can-eat buffets, the cold boiled shrimp and cocktail sauce, the juicy slices of rare prime rib. And he refreshed her memory with respect to the endless array of desserts, cherry covered cheesecake, chocolate layer cakes, cookies, bread puddings and brandy sauce. Whatever she was fond of was sure to be there in abundance. Elaine licked her lips and relented.

It was decided they needed to visit the old mining town. Elaine even agreed half-heartedly to squander a few dollars on the slot machines, in the spirit of conciliation of course, not because she enjoyed it.

She didn't even like slot machines. There were no longer handles to pull and that was part of the thrill. These days one sat down on a stool and turned into a Skinner rat compulsively pushing on a button. Where was the excitement in that? At least when one pulled a lever one got a bit of exercise for the biceps and triceps. Granted it was not a measurable amount, but Elaine told herself repeating any motion enough times would eventually give one's right arm a workout, assuming one was right-handed.

That wasn't really the problem with slot machines. She always felt manipulated, like a subject in an experiment, when she pulled a lever and was rewarded intermittently by a coin or two. She knew perfectly well some scientist had spent a lifetime figuring out just how much reward, she, the subject, needed in order to compel her to continue pushing the button until all of her money was gone. She knew it was a science. And she hated the fact that she was just irresponsible enough for them to get away with it.

She didn't remember a lot from college but the concept of operant conditioning had managed to imprint itself permanently into her gray matter.

**

The first thing they did when they got to Cripple Creek was to hit the Heritage Center. Even though the front of the building was clad in fake man-made rocks and might be called tacky, it was well worth the visit. It was like a combination museum/visitors center, and had many informative and interactive displays on every aspect of Cripple Creek's history. There was even a replica of a stegosaurus because one was found in the area.

The history thoroughly covered the gold rush days. As Paul and Elaine pored over the text to the displays, and watched the short historical films, they learned that once gold was discovered in Cripple Creek, many out of work silver miners from other regions in Colorado flocked to the district. The mining process was difficult and dangerous. Men had to go down into the mine shafts and cut out chunks of ore that was then brought to the surface in buckets. The ore was sent elsewhere to be assayed, then it was processed or milled in order to relieve it of its valuable gold. Oftentimes miners, or the foremen themselves, would smuggle out a little bit of gold ore for themselves. They might hide the gold in their lunchboxes or in their clothing. This practice, called "high grading," was a costly problem for the mine owners, as it deprived them of up to 10% of their profits. To counteract high grading, miners were searched as they exited the mines.

"Come check this out," Paul called to Elaine and they read the section on high-grading together.

"A miner who fell down in the mines had to be helped to his feet, because, just like a medieval knight in armor, his clothes were so laden down with ore that he couldn't get up by himself. Even the mine owners themselves might be in cahoots with the thieves stealing gold. An entire industry was set up to assay and buy this stolen ore. The problem was rampant because high grading wasn't even technically considered illegal because 'ore' was considered 'real estate' and therefore one could not steal it. A person caught taking high-grade could not even be prosecuted for larceny, only for trespassing."[5]

"Wow!" said Paul, "No wonder they called it the Wild Wild West."

The weirdest thing Paul discovered in the Heritage Center was a copy of a Castle Rock newspaper from the day.

"Come check this out," he said as he called Elaine over. The paper was dated 1907. An odd headline read, "Boys Wreck a Train for Fun."

It was not strange that hoodlums would do such a thing; it was strange because the two boys were so young, only nine years old. Not only did they derail a train, and get

_____
[5] Sprague, p. 205

away with it, they had a four-year old accomplice who helped them put rocks on the track. They only got caught because they became so bold they tried to do it again. Apparently, juvenile delinquency was not a new thing.

Before they left the Heritage Center Elaine and Paul sat down in the small theatre to screen several short movies about Cripple Creek history that cycled continuously on a loop. There they learned that even though mining was a difficult occupation there were so many miners needing work that the mine owners didn't have to pay them very much. In 1894, the miners in the Cripple Creek district only earned $3.00 a day to work an eight-hour shift.

By 1893 the first miner's union had formed in Montana. It wasn't long before John Calderwood, union organizer, reached Colorado. Calderwood organized eight hundred miners into the Western Federation of Miners (W.F.M.).

In February 1894, after the mine owners attempted to institute a nine-hour work day 500 miners in the Bull Hill area went on strike and shut down several of the most important mines, including Winfield Scott Stratton's Independence. In the beginning, Stratton, Colorado's first millionaire, and Jimmie Burns, the owner of the Portland mine, defended the cause of the miners. They made sure the miners were fed. The strike started out well, the miners were civil, well behaved, and well organized. Funds were carefully raised to feed the out-of-work miners.

The mine owners tried to send in scabs to keep working the mines. The scabs were beat up. The sheriff sent six deputies up to the mines to put an end to that. The deputies were captured but released unharmed.

King Calderwood and the strikers had effectively captured Bull Hill, two miles due east of Cripple Creek, and established their own little kingdom there. All went well until Calderwood left to go spread the cause of the unions elsewhere. While he was gone, rival gangs took over the kingdom. Gangs of thugs began wrecking the town of Altman. This time the local sheriff raised an army of 125 ex-policemen and firemen from Denver and went to confront the miners.

The miners decided to try and scare them off and they did by blowing up the shaft house of the Strong Mine. In addition, they sent a flatcar filled with dynamite to stop the advancing police force. When the flatcar derailed and blew up, the casualties included an unlucky cow and three innocent goats who found themselves in the wrong place at the wrong time.

This is when things began to get out of hand. The strikers, drunk with power, took over the Independence mine. That was it for Stratton and other mine owners. Stratton turned on the miners and public sentiment for them disappeared. The good people of Colorado Springs were led to believe that the miners were coming for them next so a force of 1200 vigilante deputies was organized to protect the fair inhabitants of that city. The force was supposed to be led by Sheriff Frank Bower but he lost control of it to a self-proclaimed rabble rouser, County Commissioner Winfield Scott Boynton.

The populist governor of Colorado, Davis H. Waite, and King Calderwood tried to reestablish order but it was no use. So finally, Sheriff Bower was forced to ask the governor to send in the militia. The militia headed for Bull Hill to head off the deputies. When the militia reached the miner's kingdom, the miners peacefully laid down their weapons and the strike organizers were arrested. There was no battle, but there was a great parade in Colorado Springs celebrating the end of the strife. The strike had lasted 130 days, and cost $3 million, most due to lost production. The militia went home, the mine owners backed down; the eight-hour work day was put back into effect, and the miners celebrated.

However, the miners' victory was short-lived. In 1903, the W.F.M., under the leadership of William Haywood, organized another strike. This time the newly elected Republican governor and the newly formed Mine Owners Association were loaded for bear. The mine owners resorted to terrorist tactics. They rigged a track so a train carrying scabs would derail, they tampered with a hoist so a cage full of miners (15 in all) fell to their death, and they set off explosives in a mine and killed two people. Another bomb on a platform killed 13 scabs and wounded another six. These acts were blamed on the union so public sentiment for the unions would disappear. It worked.

Mob rule took over, the union headquarters were trashed, and the union newspaper was shut down. Another five people were killed during an anti-union protest. Finally, the management-friendly governor called in the militia; the violence only ended when union men were rounded up by the hundreds. More than 200 were herded onto trains and stranded out in the prairie near the Kansas/Colorado border.

After this colorful chapter in Colorado's history, gold continued to be mined in Cripple Creek and the surrounding towns. But miners were forced to work for whatever wages and working conditions mine owners offered them. Once the price of gold was fixed, it wasn't profitable to keep working the old shaft mines. Cripple Creek and the surrounding towns became ghost towns as the miners moved away.

The history of Cripple Creek became a little anticlimactic at that point. In the 1970's tourism was revived as Cripple Creek got national attention as a ghost town. In 1991 gambling casinos were legalized in the town.

This is where the movies ended.

Elaine and Paul wandered out into the light.

"Unbelievable," was all Elaine could say. "I feel like we've just traveled back in time 100 years."

"Make that 120 years," said Paul.

***

The second thing they did when they got to Cripple Creek was to hit the Mt. Pisgah cemetery. Paul stayed in the car as Elaine wandered along a highway that led into a past filled with other people's lives and dreams.

It was a huge cemetery, not at all what Elaine had expected. More than 1500 people had been interred on the hillside which had been allowed to virtually return to its natural state. A grove of aspen trees hovered over the dead. A mule deer sprouting fuzzy new antlers rested among them. Although Elaine was surprised to see him, he didn't seem surprised or alarmed at all by her appearance; apparently this was an oft frequented place.

She did see two cars full of visitors driving slowly past the plots as if they were looking for certain ones. There was even a photographer with a very long lens and an oddly dressed female companion hanging around certain graves and taking pictures.

The oldest stones that were clearly marked were from 1901 or later. There were many small wooden placards sticking up everywhere among the marble stones, but they were mostly located in the center of the cemetery. Elaine imagined these marked the graves of people who had died before the turn of the century.

Elaine looked for patterns. There were a bunch of people who had died around 1907 and another bunch that died around 1918. Influenza outbreak? The Spanish flu? An epidemic? World War I? What had happened to them? Most sadly, there were many graves of children, often surrounded by their own little metal fences. Some of these monuments were only two or three feet long and looked like casket lids sticking up out of the ground. These stones were cut from marble and the age of each child was precisely spelled out in years, months, and days.

It must have been hard to survive as a child in those harsh times, each day was a milestone.

The separate family plots were surrounded mostly by chain link fences which had been added in recent times. There were large areas set aside for groups like the Masons and the Elks. The elk plot featured a life-size statue of an elk in it. And though Elaine was sure the local elks were very proud of this attempt to appear *cultured*, it was, in Elaine's opinion, a crude bit of artwork. From what she could tell, the noble black beast had been cast from bronze. On closer inspection a bit of its nobility trickled away as Elaine beheld globs of yellowing glue indicating that at some point in the poor synthetic cervid's life, he had suffered a great trauma; the doctors had only semi-successfully glued its antlers back on. Why they had fallen off in the first place was anyone's guess.

Several other large monuments drew Elaine's attention. There were tree trunks made of concrete or marble that appeared to be chopped off at the top, perhaps to signify that death was a "chopping off" from life. Or perhaps to signify another bit of aesthetic disability. Either way, Elaine found them ugly, visually displeasing and somewhat disturbing, though she wasn't sure why.

One gravesite couldn't help but draw attention to its self. Like a tombstone she had once seen in the Terlingua cemetery near Big Bend National Park, which had been strewn with empty beer bottles, dead cigars, and bottle caps, or the tomb of "The King" in Graceland, with its motley collection of ugly Elvis memorabilia, the concrete slab in Mt. Pisgah cemetery was almost completely covered up with modern day *crap*, for that was the only way to describe the random arrangement of items which must have had some significance for those who left them there. Perhaps, like Elvis' many fans, they wished to pay homage to the dearly departed. On further inspection one could see a heart-shaped marble headstone with the name Pearl de Vere on it. That name rang a bell in Elaine's brain, but for a moment she wasn't sure why.

Pearl's collection included colorful bras and thongs, dildos, vibrators, tubes of K-Y jelly for HIM and for HER, a copy of the lover's manual, *The Joy of Sex*, and other sexually oriented objects. Elaine wasn't sure if the people who left the items were complimenting Pearl or making fun of her. For now she remembered who Pearl was; she had been one of the madams of the finest brothel in Cripple Creek. Elaine couldn't help but ask herself, would Pearl have been offended or flattered by these gifts? Did she have a sense of humor? Only the dead could answer a question like that.

Elaine snapped a few photos, said a few silent prayers and returned to the car.

***

After the cemetery, Elaine and Paul decided to tour Pearl's historic brothel. Actually Elaine decided. She loved the idea of it: the romance, the intrigue, the scandal. Paul was curious but he tried not to act like it.

The brothel, known as the Old Homestead, was located on Bennett Avenue, the main street of Cripple Creek one block from Myers Avenue and ran parallel to it. The brothel itself had closed down in 1917, then it became a boarding house until 1957, and finally it was turned into a museum.

For five dollars each Paul and Elaine and a couple of other tourists took turns peeking into the rooms to see the various items on display. The photographer from the cemetery and his girlfriend were just leaving as they got there. The shutterbug proudly informed them that he was a ghost chaser and had experienced an otherworldly encounter while in the cemetery. He had seen "orbs." Elaine and Paul raised their eyebrows and smiled at one another surreptitiously behind his back.

As they peered inside the different rooms of the house, two little old ladies regaled the group of tourists with well-practiced and often delivered monologues detailing the rooms and the objects within them.

As they learned from one lady, the Old Homestead had catered to the richest men in the Cripple Creek district and only the most beautiful girls worked there. In order to even become a patron, a man's financial resources had to be verified ahead of time. Most of the girls worked only by reservation. More than three hundred other prostitutes supplied the needs of the other men in the district, that is, the thousands of miners working in the gold fields. As the houses got further up the hill and farther away from town, the prices for a girl's services went down accordingly; those on Myers Avenue charged the most.

The tour began downstairs with three rooms: a parlor, a room with a bar in it, and a game room. In the parlor there were couches, a little table with a kewpie doll cigarette dispenser on it, and two mannequins dressed in period attire. According to the tour guide the "sporting girls" had to dress in yellow whenever they walked the streets of the town so everyone would know what they were. Prostitution was "technically" illegal so every month each girl had to pay a fine of 6 dollars to the city and each madam had to pay a fine of 16 dollars. In addition to paying fines, the girls had to have monthly medical exams.

In the bar, there was a piano for musical entertainment. At the back of the house was the game room, and it contained a card table and chairs, and a fireplace, as well as a "fainting couch," where women sometimes needed to recline, because their corsets were too tight. There was also a "corset horse" in the hallway and the tour guide gleefully described how a woman would sit astride this contraption and hold on while a servant would pull the corset strings until they had achieved the mutual goal of a 16" waist, the fashion at the time. Elaine pictured the scene from Gone with the Wind. In the corner was a small table which contained a petticoat mirror located beneath it. This mirror was about 2 feet wide and 1 ½ feet high, and was used by women to check the condition of their floor-length skirts.

The tour group headed upstairs to the bedrooms where four girls and the Madam lived. The madam was a working madam which meant she also serviced clients. One of the four-poster full-sized bed frames was made of brass. The other four bedframes were made of wood and had ornately carved headboards. Each bed had ropes which crisscrossed one another, and were tied to pegs attached to the bed frames. Each network of crisscrossed ropes supported a mattress filled with feathers. Over time the ropes would sag and, as a result, so would the mattresses. According to the docent, people then had to get up in the nighttime and tighten the ropes, and this was the origin of the expression "Sleep tight."

The tour guide continued with this interesting piece of trivia, "The Old Homestead was run by a young woman named Pearl de Vere, who was listed as the 'proprietor' on a roster of employees working at the brothel. This list included the names of cooks, and housekeepers, and other workers. If an employee was not white, besides his/her name there was a citation that read, 'Colored.'"

"Wow, things sure have changed," someone said. There was a murmur of agreement and a lot of head nodding as this truth sunk in.

Besides the beds the rooms were furnished with dressers, and porcelain wash basins and bedpans. Not only that there were white porcelain "pigs" in each room. According to the docent, these would be filled with hot water and placed under the covers to warm up the sheets in cold weather. The madam's room had a folded screen, decorated with Japanese art, in it; perhaps she had changed her clothes behind it. The guide didn't elaborate. There was also shaving equipment in some of the rooms, including long menacing razors, available for the use of patrons who spent the night. The guide explained women didn't shave their legs or underarms at the time; it was only men who shaved their faces.

There were two other rooms upstairs: a closet, and a "previewing" room. A woman would go into the previewing room and take off all her clothes. Then the client would look at her through a piece of sheet glass and decide if he wanted to sleep with her. *What a way to make a living*, mused Elaine sadly.

As the tour wrapped up, the old lady told the story of Pearl's tragic end. "One night Pearl de Vere threw a grand party. She wore a very fancy green chiffon dress with seed pearls on it. The dress cost $800. Then Pearl went upstairs to rest where she took some morphine to help her sleep. Later that night, one of the girls went up to check on her and found her breathing heavily. The doctor was called but Pearl never woke up."

"It was soon found out that even though Pearl had run the most expensive brothel in Cripple Creek, charging her clients 50 to 250 dollars a night, she was broke. Pearl's only sister came from out East to claim the body, but was shocked to find out that Pearl was not a seamstress at all, as she had been told, but had been running a house of ill-repute. When the sister discovered the truth, she left and refused to take Pearl with her. So all the local working girls in the town got together to try to raise enough money for a proper burial. Luckily an anonymous letter arrived in the mail from Denver. It was from one of Pearl's rich patrons and included a thousand dollars in it. He insisted Pearl be buried in the lovely chiffon gown. Pearl had a grand funeral and everyone in town showed up, some out of respect, others just to gawk. She was only 36 years old when she died," she finished.

"What a tragic story," said Elaine. The other woman in the group sadly nodded her head in agreement.

Even though questions did not seem to be encouraged, Elaine just had to ask. "What about the grave in the cemetery? It's all covered with junk," she continued. "Who puts all that stuff there?"

"We don't know," said the old lady. "But they clean it off from time to time." She went on, "The stone that is there now was put there in the 1930's because the original wooden cross eroded away."

Lost, but not completely forgotten, thought Elaine.

***

As they returned from the old brothel-turned-museum and were driving around the town Elaine spotted a herd of donkeys. The donkeys were crossing the street as if they didn't have any place to be and weren't in a hurry to get there.

"Stop the car!" screamed Elaine, as if it were a real emergency.

Paul obliged as quickly as he could and Elaine jumped out of the vehicle and started clicking away with her point-and-shoot. Paul joined her and they took pictures of one another standing with the donkeys. The burros were all different colors; one was black and white, and the rest were mostly brown and white.

Later that night they asked one of the locals about the donkeys. They were told that the donkeys were *not* descendants of the original donkeys brought in by the prospectors. *Whatever,* thought Elaine.

***

Since the day was spent doing things Elaine wanted to do, that night they had to do what Paul wanted to do. Paul wanted to go to the casino. There were several casinos in town so they had several to choose from. Elaine wanted to go to the new fancy casino, and of course, Paul wanted to go to the older ones, so in the interests of prolonging the peace, they had to do both.

As they approached the newest casino the doors opened automatically. Elaine was again reminded of the thing that bothered her most about gambling and casinos. It was the tension created by a combination of bright colors and loud noises, in the form of flashing lights and ringing bells. The degree of tension was always the same.

Whether it was good tension or bad tension didn't matter to Elaine. She reacted badly to tension in any form. Desperately she endeavored to reduce the effects of the tension on her nervous system.

The first thing she did was dig into an outer pocket of her purse to retrieve a napkin or Kleenex tissue. Then she tore off small pieces, going with the grain of the paper, to get straight edges as best she could. Then she wadded up the pieces, and stuffed them into her ears. Thus she mitigated the problem of excessive noise.

The second thing she did was head for a quiet place to regroup. That was most often the closest restroom. She notified Paul, "I'll be right back," and went inside to check her face, comb her hair, and decompress for a few minutes.

The light inside the restroom in places like this was always deliberately, she had to conclude, exceptional, and she always looked good in these mirrors, which were usually surrounded by a marquee of Hollywood style lights. Strategic use of incandescent light bulbs flattered each woman who sought salvation at the shrine known simply as the "Ladies Room." The casino operators were well aware of one truth: the last thing any woman wants, especially one who has just spent the night gambling, drinking, and smoking, is to see her complexion honestly, with each line, wrinkle and blemish revealed. And the great sin of green-blue florescent lighting is that it makes even the tannest of complexions appear pasty and pale. So the lights in the Ladies Room had a soft red glow akin to candlelight, and the ladies who visited it were happy to behold warm healthy reflections. Happy women keep on gambling.

The restroom was also an oasis of good smells, a medley of unidentifiable flowers and ocean air. She didn't know how they did it; she just wished she could take some of it home to her place in Texas.

After Elaine checked her face one last time, she applied a fresh coat of lip gloss with the consistency of Vaseline, followed by a light coat of lipstick, in that order. She preferred to do it that way, backwards, according to the gurus of beauty. Elaine didn't care; she was now ready to make her entrance into the chaos of the casino itself. Paul was still waiting obediently outside the restroom door.

The new casino was called the Wildwood and it was like the ones in Vegas, in that there were rows and rows of slot machines, awaiting unwary gamblers. On the other hand, it was not like the casinos in Vegas because there were only a handful of blackjack tables, one roulette table and a single craps table. The dealers were not young and handsome either. Neither were the waitresses.

The casinos in Cripple Creek were a lot smaller than those in Vegas. This was supposedly because of the way they were taxed which was by the number of machines; so each large casino was divided up into several smaller ones.

The Wildwood did have the all-you-can-eat buffet but the smaller casinos that lined Bennett Avenue had small cafes inside the casinos themselves. These cafes were nice and quiet. Instead of all-you-can-eat, they had "dirt cheap," especially at breakfast time. One casino featured a 49 cent breakfast; another had a choice of breakfasts with great food for a dollar ninety-five.

Like in Vegas, all the casinos offered free drinks. These were brought to you by young scantily clad waitresses. These girls fetched beer or hot chocolate, if one preferred, but only if one remained stationary for any period of time. Paul ordered a beer from the first wench who happened by; Elaine was moving too quickly, so she had to fend for herself. Luckily she homed in on the freshly popped popcorn in the self-service machines. The kernels of corn were slathered liberally in hydrogenated coconut oil and the secret ingredient known as Flavocol. Elaine filled a couple of bags with popcorn and headed back to find Paul. He was camped out at the craps table, watching. She watched for a while too, munching small handfuls of popcorn. Then she bummed a twenty-dollar bill off of Paul and headed for the penny and nickel slots. They agreed to meet back at the restaurant to partake of the dinner buffet at a quarter to six.

The sound of slot machines still managed to assault Elaine's well-defended eardrums. After a couple of minutes of listening to the distinctive clicking, clacking, and clinking song she was helplessly singing along with the refrain, imitating the sound of coins dropping as each machine, in its turn, hit the jackpot. It was a symphony; nearby machines played the melodies and distant machines harmonized with them. But instead of creating pleasant music, all the machine noises merged into one discordant avant garde mess. Dink Dink Dink...Dink Dink De Dink Dink she sang along. The constant repetition was not nearly as difficult to endure once she internalized it in her head.

Paul, on the other hand, seemed to thrive on the noise. To Elaine this was all part of the *Bennie and the Jets*, *Crimson and Clover*, and Burger King *Have it your way* jingle conspiracy of earworms designed to drive people like herself crazy. People like Paul seemed to love repetitive songs with repetitive refrains. She vaguely remembered reading something about a study where they determined men liked repetitive songs while women didn't. Or maybe, like all the rest of the mental flotsam and jetsam filling her head, she made up that bit of information.

Craps was the only game Paul played. It took a minimal investment and if one were lucky, one could play along for hours. And one thing about Paul, Elaine could not deny, was that he was lucky. Absurdly so. What did they say? God takes care of gamblers and fools? Perhaps Paul was a little of both.

Elaine chose the penny slots because she hoped this would make her cash last longer. She had no expectation other than that of donating all of her money, that is, Paul's money, to the cause of the casino and she was not disappointed. Elaine could not figure out how the slot machines worked, so she selected the option "One Line, One Push" for a while until she was down five dollars. As she stared at the magical symbols without comprehension, she felt herself being drawn into the hypnotic state that was induced by the rhythmic ping-ping-pinging of the machines, and the flashing lights that were all around her, sucking her in, interfering with her thought process. Bell, bar, double bar, triple bar, cherry, wild card. The symbols flashed faster and faster. She deliberately changed her pushing speed to try to make it last longer. That didn't help. She was losing, one penny at a time.

She knew she was powerless, defenseless against the will of the machine. Those who designed these machines were experts at influencing human behavior. They had spent considerable time and money to learn exactly how to make someone like Elaine do exactly what they wanted her to do, to wit, deliver her money into their machines. She was down to her last 10 dollars.

It was no good, so she changed her strategy. She upped each bet to 20 lines, but stayed with one push at a time. That meant instead of going down one penny at a time, her fortune was now decreasing at the rate of 20 cents. Each time she selected 20 cents, 20 lines would appear across the screen connecting the symbols in weird configurations. This meant a lot more opportunities to win, and she started winning, however, she was still losing faster than she was winning. One push, 20 cents. Win 5 cents. Net loss, 15 cents.

Eventually she was down to 80 cents, then 60 cents, 40 cents, 20 cents. She could no longer make 20 cent bets. She tried the 15 line, and made a 15 cent bet. She tried the 10 line, and made a 10 cent bet. She could see the end coming. But still she hung on, penny by penny, push by push. At last she had exactly one penny left. She cashed out, and kept the one cent voucher as a memento.

***

After the money was gone, Elaine wandered around the casino again. She passed a gift shop selling sequin-spangled clothing, spandex tights, huge tacky pieces of costume jewelry, and knick-knacks with the word "Colorado" on them, that were, for the most part, manufactured in China and other foreign nations. It was easy to tell the casino was firmly committed to keep all the money that passed through its doors.

She browsed through the T-shirts and blouses, checking price tags. Whenever she found something particularly attractive, something she would even venture to say she loved, it was much too expensive. In contrast, everything on the clearance racks and tables reeked of cheap tawdriness. She knew that assessment was all in her mind. She suspected that if the shop keeper were to blindfold her and switch all the tags from the expensive items to the cheap items, she would most likely be swooning over the ones that presently found themselves relegated to the bargain table.

This had something to do with another issue brought up by her therapist, that is, that she didn't feel "worthy." According to her therapist, this is why she had trouble spending money on herself. Even here in this casino on vacation she felt guilty spending money gambling, because it seemed like she was wasting it. She couldn't eat the fruits of gambling. She couldn't wear the fruits of gambling. Gambling was the fruit of gambling. Supposedly, there was pleasure in trying to win, as well as in the actual winning. Gambling was an entity known as "entertainment" and entertainment, also known as fun, was something Elaine had trouble rationalizing. She didn't enjoy having fun. When she tried to explain this problem to other people, they just looked at her like she was nuts. And maybe she was.

So like all the rest of her crazy thoughts, she kept the fear of fun to herself.

She was a little disappointed to find that casinos in Colorado were pretty much no nonsense affairs. There were no rooms for performers to perform, and there didn't seem to be any pinball arcades for the kids. Maybe it was illegal to have children in casinos in Colorado. She certainly hadn't seen any, as she thought it over.

***

When they arrived at the buffet, there was a long line. As a rule, Elaine never stood in lines, but it was a new day, and she just decided to go with it. The line moved as quickly as it could, considering the large lumbering people ahead of them appeared to be selecting food in slow motion, using the tongs and ladles to transfer food to plate as if they were Neanderthals learning to master the use of tools.

As soon as they reached the seafood section of the buffet, Paul began his assault on the bumpy bright salmon-colored king crab legs. He piled his plate high with the spindly spiky appendages, and filled a little bowl with drawn butter sauce, as Elaine filled her plate with cold boiled shrimp, a luxury she didn't "deserve" at home.

Their plates filled to overflowing, Elaine searched around for the right table. Elaine always picked the table. It really mattered to her where they sat. Not so much for Paul.

Once they were situated at the correct table, Paul's attack on the crab continued as he cracked open each leg to extract the tender white meat hiding within. As Elaine watched what always seemed akin to a religious ritual to her, Paul speared each morsel securely with a fork before dipping it in the butter sauce. Then he allowed the excess butter to drip off; lastly, he levitated each portion to his waiting mouth. As if by magic, none of the oily sauce landed on the front of his shirt; it always managed to land elsewhere. To Elaine, this seemed a miracle, because when eating anything at home, small pieces of solid or liquid matter always landed on his shirt front. Elaine often imagined a bib there to protect the front of his shirt.

After two or three helpings of crab legs, Paul went back to the buffet to finish the battle. He gorged himself on fresh fruit, especially the locally grown Rocky Ford cantaloupe, strawberries and other berries. Paul, who rarely ate a meal without occupying himself otherwise, either by watching television or reading a book, truly seemed to be enjoying the moment.

As Paul savored the crab, Elaine packed in the cold boiled shrimp, liberally dunking each white pink bottom feeder in red cocktail sauce. It was a real treat since they hardly ever sprung for such a delicacy at home. She had to admit, even if one were not rich, it was hard not to feel rich, at a casino feeding trough. Elaine finished her meal by returning to the buffet tables covered with desserts. There she mangled a few pies, cakes, and bread puddings by cutting off little slices of several different kinds just so she could sample more of them.

After each bite, Paul picked up a napkin, and dabbed at his lips and mustache. One good thing about Paul was he did have manners when dining in public.

Elaine flashed back to one of their very first dates. As the sun went down over Galveston Bay and they sat in the shadow of the Kemah/Seabrook Bridge, she watched Paul eat blue crabs at a local seafood dive. The place no longer existed and had probably been torn down long ago. It had been aptly named the Crab Shack, because that's what they specialized in. The picnic tables were outdoors and the waitresses dropped the crabs in metal buckets on the tables along with little mallet hammers to crack open the crab shells. They also delivered red plastic mesh baskets filled with cold boiled potatoes and chunks of corn on the cob, and glasses of the overly sweet iced tea served everywhere on the Texas Gulf Coast.

There she sat in the warm glow of summer and watched Paul hammer each blue crab body and claw open so he could pick out the tiny pieces of whitish meat. He hammered like a little elf making toys for Santa. Tap, tap, tapping for hours it seemed. At the time she didn't really know him very well, but everything about him in those days had seemed cute and charming.

After they got married all those charming things, like the way he chewed ice, or potato chips, or raw carrots, had become annoying. Now she realized they were never annoying, in and of themselves; it was only her perception that had changed.

Suddenly Elaine felt something weird in her heart. It was the realization that she was still in love with this man. Despite all his quirks, despite all his oddities, despite his cheapness, despite his ability to go without seeing people for days at a time, despite all her fantasies of killing him, despite everything. She loved his pickiness and his mustache that twitched up and down like a rabbit's whiskers as he chewed and the way it turned up on one side when he smiled. His mustache reminded her of that old grey cat they used to have. She could still see Paul and Dusty rough-housing and playing swat paws as if Dusty were a dog. She smiled at Paul, and finally he stopped chewing, looked up, and noticed she was watching him.

"What's wrong?" he asked.

"Nothing," Elaine said, "Everything is great, as a matter of fact," and she used Paul's own favorite expression. "Everything is great," she repeated. And for once it was.

***

After they ate dinner, they headed back to Bennett Street to check out the older smaller casinos there. It was getting dark outside, so Elaine wandered down the street taking night pictures of the brilliant neon lights that screamed "EXCITEMENT," while Paul chose a casino and went inside to play. Elaine shot for an hour or so; then she decided to find Paul to see if he was ready to go back to the B&B.

She found him, of course, at a craps table. Paul always decided ahead of time how much he was willing to lose. Today it was 40 dollars.

The minimum bet was $2. Paul was playing now. He liked to play PASS/NO PASS, which meant, as nearly as Elaine had it figured out, this was the "safest," translation *conservative*, bet one could make. In other words, one could "count" on winning about 50% of the time. Actually, one could not ever "count" on winning, but as far as casino games go, the odds were as "good as they got" for the player playing that way. The return on the bet was low, but like a mutual fund or a savings account, one usually still got paid something. By playing PASS/NO PASS the odds of winning were a little lower than 50%, because the house always wins, or at least, the house always has to have the advantage. Otherwise, gambling couldn't work and casinos, dog tracks and other gambling establishments couldn't stay in business.

PASS or NO PASS essentially meant one was betting either on or against the person throwing the dice. Elaine didn't remember which was which. All she knew was that if you wanted the person to win, you wanted him to make his "point." Otherwise, you wanted him to throw a seven, which was known as "crapping out." Making a point meant that the person with the dice had to throw the same thing he threw the first time he tossed the dice. The number of the first throw was called the "point." If he threw an 8 on his first toss, then the point was 8, and he kept on throwing until he threw another 8, which meant he made the point, or he threw a 7, which meant he "crapped out." As soon as he threw a 7, his turn ended and the dice went to the next player. In between throws, players made various bets, which got pretty complicated. The throws got complicated too. If you threw things like snake eyes (two ones) or boxcars (two sixes), on the first toss, those were winning and losing throws too. She wasn't really sure about all the rules in craps; all she was sure about was Paul's winning strategy. He always bet against the person with the dice, because his engineering brain knew that the 7 was more likely to show up before the point did. It was a good strategy and Paul was lucky, especially with money.

When she got to the table, Paul had $100 and was up $60. He kept $40 out and stuck the rest in his wallet so he would still come out ahead. He used the $40 to continue placing his PASS/NO PASS bets. As Elaine watched, a couple of other players tossed the dice two or three times each and crapped out. Then the dice were passed to Paul. He threw a 9. Then he threw again. It was a 3. He threw again. It was a 5. Again he threw. It was a 6. Paul threw again and again. No 9's or 7's. He threw everything but 9's or 7's. People started betting with him as he kept rolling. He kept betting against himself. People stopped leaving the table. They stayed to watch. People at other tables started drifting over to see what was going on. Excitement began to build. People were chanting under their breath, "No Sevens, No Nines." Paul kept rolling. His $40 was gone, so other people started covering his bets for him. And still Paul rolled and other people kept winning off his tosses. Forty-five minutes went by. The people were standing three thick at the table.

"Come on, Paul let's go!" whined Elaine. "I'm hungry. Let's go eat!"

"I can't leave right now," said Paul.

"Okay!" she said in a huff, "I'll be at the cafe."

Elaine left. She sat at an empty table and waited.

When she finally saw Paul, he was grinning broadly.

"What happened?" asked Elaine.

"I crapped out!" He was still smiling as he said this.

"I thought that meant you lost?" she said.

"It does, but check this out!" He had three blue, green, and red striped chips in his hand.

"What are those?" asked Elaine

"Hundred dollar chips!" Paul laughed. "Let's go cash out!"

"Where did you get those?" Elaine was confused.

"Remember all those guys who were winning when I was throwing? These are the tips they gave me!"

"Wow!" was all Elaine could say.

He really is lucky! she added to herself.

***

That night, Elaine dreamt once more.

She felt him long before she saw him. He was staring at her from the far side of the room, staring at her with lifeless eyes. They sparkled to be sure, in the same way a diamond sparkles. They were shiny, but they were inanimate. The huge black pupils seemed to displace the irises. His eyes gleamed with animal energy, but they were dead, just the same. Behind the spark was no thinking being, no humanity, nothing at all. Yes, as she tried to describe it, all she could think of were mindless, predatory shark eyes.

Her eyes met his eyes once and instinctively, she lowered hers. But she had to look again. He was still staring at her intently. She could feel his gaze, his glare, burning into her skin, into her brain, calling her, trying to contact the part of her that was pure reptilian, pure instinct.

She tried to ignore the call, but it was too strong. She met his eyes again. She averted her eyes quickly. But again, something made her look. He was still staring at her. His eyes never left her.

And then it was too late. He had somehow crossed the room, in an instant, had plunked down a pair of silver dollars, and had taken hold of her upper arm, in a grip that was firm and unyielding. She tried to pull away, to say, "I'm sorry, I'm already taken," or "No, thank you." But it was no use. Turning down a customer was not an option in a place like this. In alarm, she realized this place was not the Silver Spring. She could not recall the name of the place. She could not even recall her own name.

She tried one last time. Her eyes searched wildly for those of the madam. Their eyes met briefly; she beseeched the older woman silently, frantically, but the madam only shook her head, slowly, from side to side twice, and she realized there was nothing she could do and there was no one there to save her. A chain of unstoppable circumstances had been set into motion.

She led the way upstairs to her chamber. He
followed without making a sound, without saying a word,
without touching her. He never said anything. He just
pushed the door open as soon as she had unlocked it and
pushed her forward into the room.

She had been warned this might happen. She had
known all along this might happen. And yet, she had kept
that knowledge well guarded in the fortress-like bastille of
the deepest recesses of her brain. She had known this
would invariably happen if she kept on doing what she had
been doing. But nothing, no warnings, no tales of horror,
nothing could have prepared her for the actual event.

Unlike the first time she had had sex which had
been enormously exaggerated and had woefully under-
fulfilled her expectations, this experience grossly
overshadowed her expectations. Not that she had had
expectations, good or bad, but she *had* idly thought about
the thing.

She had even fantasized about rape before, when
masturbating, sometimes even when engaged in the sexual
act, with some John who was particularly boring. She had
even used rape fantasies to arouse herself when she wasn't
aroused, but the reality of rape was like so many other
things. Something best left forever to the realm of fantasy.
It was not exciting; it was not erotic; it was scary. It was
akin to falling off a cliff, and looking forward to eventual
death, just so the falling would stop.

She shut her mind off. She watched him hit her
face, punch her in the stomach, grab at her breasts roughly,
force his rigid member into her tightly closed opening, and
make little slices into her soft flesh with a knife. She
watched everything from above. She didn't feel a thing.
Each time he stopped fucking her, her mind returned to its

body, and she prayed silently, *Please let him be finished. Please let him go away. Please don't let him kill me. Please let it be morning.*

Each time in despair she'd realize he was only resting, waiting for the devil to commandeer his body, waiting for the devil to resume the onslaught on her innocence. For this could not be a man attacking her; it had to be a demon. It had to be pure evil.

He'd stop for a few minutes or an hour. Time lost all meaning. Then he'd awaken and begin biting her or groping her, or squeezing her neck until she blacked out. He'd have an orgasm; then he'd fall asleep on top of her so she couldn't escape. Then he'd wake up, and begin another destructive foray into her tender young flesh, and her mind would quickly retreat into the air above the bed, where it watched in silent disbelief.

At long last the night was mostly over, and he was finished. He dressed in silence. Yes, she noted with detachment, he had gotten completely undressed. She watched him put his clothes on, and as he did so, she studied his wiry body. She didn't dare meet his eyes again but with clinical curiosity she examined his tanned flesh. There was a long scar crossing his upper right leg and another scar in the middle of his chest that resembled a wound from a bullet. And she prayed one final prayer, *Why, God, why didn't you let that bullet kill him?* But she already knew the answer.

God didn't care about her. God didn't care about whores. God didn't care if people like her lived or died.

He grabbed the rest of his clothes and headed out the door. He never said a word to her and he didn't leave a tip.

***

Elaine woke with a start. She couldn't breathe. She was crying silently. She had had the most horrible dream. Or was it a dream? It seemed a little too real. She jumped out of bed and went to look at herself in the mirror in the bathroom. She examined every inch of her face and her body. She looked for bruises on her neck and face and breasts. She looked for the gashes left by a vicious knife blade. There was nothing.

Thank God it was just a dream. But why did she feel sticky down there? She reached her hand down and touched her pubic hairs. They were wet with something thick and gooey. She sniffed at her fingers in disbelief. Yes, it was cum. She stared with horror at her husband still asleep on the bed. The covers were all pushed back and the sheets were rumpled and twisted in a knot. What had happened just now?

And was that a smile crossing his lips?

***

She went back to bed but she couldn't relax. There was a tightness in her chest. She struggled to breathe. It felt as if her airway had decided to go on strike. She realized she was having an anxiety attack. She wanted to say something but the words wouldn't come out.

She flashed back to her first genuine panic attack. She was back in junior high. It was the first day of the semester, and she was starting at a new school. That morning she and her brother walked to the bus stop and got on the right bus. She went to school, and the day itself was uneventful. The only thing she remembered about that day was what happened after the classes ended.

As she exited the building she saw at least 20 buses lined up in front of the school, all identical, except for the little number on the dashboard so the children could identify them. As she walked along the long line of buses, she realized she didn't know which one was hers. All the bus drivers looked unfamiliar. She started to feel frightened. She went up to one of the buses and tried to ask the bus driver where the bus was going.

She opened her mouth to speak but she couldn't talk. Her words were frozen in her upper chest. Her heart was beating frantically. She was unable to move. The bus driver just stared at her, not doing a thing to help. She didn't get up off the seat and come outside to ask Elaine what she needed. She didn't say those four little words, "Can I help you?" The bus driver just didn't care.

Elaine felt abandoned and all alone. All the other kids knew where they were going. They moved with purpose. She looked around for the face of a student she recognized. Finally she spotted one that looked familiar so she got onto the same bus as he did. It was the wrong bus! As she watched with growing alarm, the bus took her farther and farther from her home.

The bus drove the children all over town, and all the children got off, one by one, until she was the only one left on the bus. She was so scared that she crouched down in the space in front of her seat to hide from the ever present eyes of the bus driver in the large rear view mirror.

After what seemed like many hours, the bus stopped at the high school to pick up the high school kids. One of the big kids spotted her hiding there and pointed her out to the other children. Some of them laughed. She was embarrassed. By some miracle one of the older kids was the babysitter that used to lived next door at their old house.

Her ex-babysitter gave Elaine's new address to the bus driver.

The driver drove her right up to her house and dropped her off across the street. It was the worst day of her young life. She was very late, but instead of being relieved to see her, her parents screamed at her, chewing her out for not knowing which bus to get on, and for not speaking up once she realized she was on the wrong bus. Now as an adult, she could look back at this incident and see it from her parents' points of view. Maybe her parents were just as scared as she was. Maybe that's why they were so angry; their fear had turned into anger.

Elaine stopped thinking about her lost 12-year old self, and returned to the present. The anxiety attack had passed. She came to the full awareness that it had all been a dream. But she also decided it was time to do something, anything, about it.

She woke Paul, even though it was still the middle of the night.

"Did you have a strange dream?" she demanded.

"I don't remember my dreams," he began. Then he vividly recalled a snippet of the dream about the Grand Salon. "Now that you mention it, I do remember a recent dream," he added.

"Was it a sex dream?" she asked bluntly.

"How did you know?" he asked.

"Because I had the same dream," Elaine finished.

"Are you sure?" he asked. This information was a little too off-the-wall for his engineer's brain to accept. It started to jump the steel tracks.

"Did you have a dream about, and she hesitated before she said the word...*rape*?"

He stared at her. He was wide awake now. "What? How did you know?" he started. He seemed uncomfortable.

Now came the difficult part, getting his logical, scientific, skeptical brain to accept a concept that was completely foreign to it. Paul didn't like to watch shows about ghosts, or reincarnation, or ESP, or UFO's or God, for that matter. It was all superstitious hogwash to him. Elaine was asking him to suspend belief in his perfectly ordered universe and to take a ride on a zip-line straight into the improbable.

She didn't expect him to believe without reservation but he surprised her when he said, "Thank God, and I'm not conceding there is one, but for a time there I thought I might be losing my sanity! The dreams I've been having were so real, I was beginning to have trouble distinguishing my dream persona from my real one."

"Me too!" exclaimed Elaine. "So, she asked, have you met Margarita?"

"My wife?" he added. "Yes, I have," and he blushed. "She loves me, you know."

"I know," laughed Elaine. "And no, I'm not jealous."

"I wasn't saying you were," said Paul.

They both laughed at the absurd notion of being jealous of a dream.

For the first time in 10 years, Elaine knew she was in love with Paul again. They had shared something, were still sharing something; they had a secret, and as crazy as it sounded, this secret was bringing them back together.

In the darkness, Elaine decided to be brave.

"Can I ask you a question?" she said. Her voice was almost a whisper. She had agonized about bringing it up, but she just had to know. She was scared of what Paul might say and what she might hear.

"Of course," said Paul.

"So, who's *Islandgirl*?" she asked. She knew that it was a bad idea to let Paul know that she had snooped into his personal life. But she didn't know what else to do. She needed to know the truth.

"Oh that," and then he added, "Wait, how did you know about that?"

"You left your smartphone open. It was an accident. I never meant to spy on you." She tried to appeal to the mercy of the court, a court of one, aka, Paul, the wronged husband.

"Oh Elaine, I'm so sorry!" Paul went on the defensive. But he continued, "There is no Islandgirl. Not like you think. She's just a friend, someone whose husband doesn't listen to her anymore. Someone who needs someone to confide in and that someone is me, because I'm the only person at work who will listen to her.

"You mean?"

"Yes," said Paul. "It's my boss' secretary."

"You mean, Maryann?" Elaine laughed with relief. *Maryann was no threat* she reassured herself. Paul said it again, "I love Maryann, like a friend," he added quickly, "but Maryann is a lush."

"I see," said Elaine. And she accentuated the words as if to seem jealous. Then she went further, "Do I have *anything* to worry about?" She wanted Paul to know she was concerned.

"No, Elaine. You are the only girl for me. I love you. You are the only woman I *ever* married, the only woman I ever *thought* about marrying, and the only woman I ever *will* marry."

"Even after I die?" Elaine asked.

"Yes, even after you die."

They both laughed.

"Oh Paul. Thank you for saying that. I know I haven't been the most caring or demonstrative wife in a very long time. But that is going to change right now." And with that declaration, she leaned over to kiss him at the same time he leaned over to kiss her. Morning, or midnight breath be damned, their lips met in the middle.

Day Seven

At breakfast, instead of digging into the delicious smelling bacon and eggs on the table, Elaine started right away asking the Kerstetters more questions about the ghosts. She needed to know about the bad dream.

"So tell us about the murders," begged Elaine.

Mrs. K was happy to oblige.

"After Estefan dumped Estrellita he began coming to the Silver Spring almost every night to see Dai-yu. His wife, Margarita began to worry. Estefan had had many women before but none of them were a threat. Now she sensed something was very wrong."

"How do you know all this?" asked Elaine.

Mrs. K went on...

"You see Dai-yu came to me in my sleep, so everything she knew I knew."

You mean?

"Yes," said Mrs. K, "I dream about the ghosts too."

She went on with the story. "After the murder, there was a minor uproar. There was an official inquiry and the murder was ruled unsolved. No one, but Estrellita, had seen anything. Nobody was arrested. The next day Estrellita disappeared. It was rumored that she had killed the two lovers; then she had killed herself in sorrow or in guilt. But her body was never found. Then six months later Margarita was found dead. It was obvious Margarita killed herself, and as was the custom of the day, the townspeople buried her body at the crossroads."

"Business at the Silver Spring went back to normal. Everyone said it was a shame about poor Estefan. Everyone said it was a shame about poor Margarita. Some said the China doll got what she deserved. Everyone said Estrellita should be burning in hell."

"Estefan's estate went to his oldest son, Estefan, Jr. who was not a cowboy or a ranch hand. He was a spoiled son of a wealthy man who had worked hard all his life. Unlike his father, Estefan, Jr. was "unmotivated" when it came to manual labor. He was a scholar; he liked to read books. So he left Colorado and went to study at a college out East. The other two sons took over Estefan's affairs."

"Unfortunately, Estefan's great monetary wealth was missing; it was rumored Estefan had hidden his gold somewhere on the vast property. The sons still had part ownership of a mine, the land itself, and Estefan's prized horses. However, the estate was soon embroiled in legal matters as people popped up out of nowhere to lay claims to Estefan's fortune."

"It took years to settle the lawsuits. Meanwhile the two sons sold the horses in order to raise money to pay the lawyers. Eventually they had to sell the estate, and Estefan's original four homesteads were platted into the township of Stephenville."

"But there is no Stephenville anymore," pointed out Paul.

"Yep, that's what happens sometimes," said Mr. K sadly. "A town is born and a town dies."

"So what's left of Estefan's great hacienda?" asked Elaine.

"Not a lot," said Mrs. K, "Like many wooden structures around here, the mansion house burned down after the turn of the century."

"Until that time, Estefan's two youngest sons and their families lived there. But once the house burned, they didn't really have the wherewithal to rebuild. By that time they were living modest and rather obscure lives. However, they are buried out there in the cemetery with their father. And that's another story."

"But I didn't finish telling you about the murder," Mrs. K returned to the earlier topic.

"After Estefan and Dai-yu were killed, the townsfolk held a huge funeral for Estefan. Everyone who was anyone showed up to pay their respects and to say the obligatory nice things about the deceased. Estefan's sons sold a couple of horses to pay for a grand marble headstone, the tallest one in the cemetery. Estefan's name was carved into the hard stone of the obelisk. Beneath his name, etched into the white expanse, were his vital statistics: Born 1850. Died 1895. And beneath Estefan's name was the name Margarita."

"Poor Estefan was only 45 years old when he left this world, but, I must point out, she added, "That was a ripe old age for those days."

Mrs. K went on, "Estefan's sons purchased plots for the rest of the family. The one immediately adjacent to Estefan was reserved for Margarita. The others were saved for the three brothers."

"Lastly, you might very well wonder, what became of the poor Chinese working girl from San Francisco? She had no relatives nearby to claim her body and nobody bothered to look for any so she was buried in the town cemetery without a proper funeral. The undertaker planted a plain wooden cross at the head of her grave. Her name and the date of the year she died were crudely scratched into the cheap wood."

"That is such a sad story," said Elaine, "Does it have a happy ending?"

"We'll see", said Mrs. Kerstetter and she smiled slyly.

"I wonder what she means by that," thought Elaine.

***

Elaine looked longingly at the uneaten food sitting on her plate and poked at it with a fork. She tried to drink the coffee in her cup, but she was having difficulty. Her appetite was on strike.

"One more question," said Elaine. She began, "Last night I dreamt," and she hesitated, partially out of embarrassment, partially out of fear.

"Yes?" said Mrs. K.

"I dreamt I was raped," said Elaine.

"Oh that," said Mrs. K and she frowned. "I'm afraid that's a chapter from poor Estrellita's life. She had a very bad time before she came to the Silver Spring and she wants everyone to know about it."

"But I dreamt about it too," said Paul, and he couldn't even say the word. Elaine's fears were confirmed.

"I know," said Mr. K, "I've had that dream, too."

"But what does it mean?" asked Paul. "Does it mean I'm evil? That I want to do these things in real life?"

That's a relief, thought Elaine. *At least he's worried about it.*

"No, don't worry about it," said Mr. K. "It's just the ghosts. They dream what they need to dream, and we have to dream it with them.

Mr. K continued, "Dreaming the same dream is just another weird thing about this place that we can't explain.

Call it synchronicity. Call it whatever you like. Sometimes at night the Missus and I share dreams; sometimes we dream alone."

Paul and Elaine were left to wonder if they would ever figure out the rules of the ghosts.

***

After breakfast, Paul and Elaine decided to do a little sightseeing to clear their heads.

"Let's go on a drive today," suggested Paul

"Where to?" asked Elaine.

"Does it matter?" Paul returned.

It was decided it didn't matter. They stopped at the first gas station they came to. There they bought day snacks: cookies, potato chips (for Paul), juice, bottled water, and a map of Colorado.

Paul didn't seem to have any particular destination in mind. He never did on these "side trips" or "adventures," as he liked to call them. Elaine still called them "ordeals," like the time he locked their keys in the car at the top of the Continental Divide in Rocky Mountain National Park in the middle of winter, and they had to bum a ride off of two complete strangers, she might add, down to the ranger's station. What if the two strangers had been ax-murderers instead of nature-loving tree-huggers? They hadn't been psychopathic killers, but that was beside the point. Instead, they turned out to be very nice tourists like themselves and they soon dropped them off at the ranger station, and a very nice and handsome young ranger, proficient at the use of a Slim Jim, opened the car door, and they were on their way again.

Or the time they got lost in Mexico while on an "adventure" with a rented Volkswagen beetle and had to spend the night at a place that had no hot water, and she had to take an "ice cold" shower with soap that wouldn't lather and wouldn't wash off. Her heart felt as if it might stop. Then they tried to make love on the deserted beach and after getting bit by sand fleas, two passersby walked up on them while they were both stark naked, which definitely ruined the mood!

On the other hand, without Paul and his "adventures," she wouldn't have nearly enough material to write the novel she was going to write one day.

Each adventure was an unforgettable memory as she relived it later on. Perhaps she should thank him after all.

They started up the main street of Silver Spring, which was not surprisingly named Highway 1. Perhaps, as they discovered on their long ago honeymoon to the Virgin Islands, there was only one highway on the entire island, and even though this same highway changed direction many times, it was still always referred to as Highway 1. It would have been completely impossible to navigate on the island if one had to rely only on the numbered road signs. Luckily, there were other signs that read, quite unimaginatively, but succinctly, TO TOWN and AWAY FROM TOWN.

Otherwise, people on the island navigated by using natural landmarks, such as very large trees. It made sense and served the purposes of the island dwellers, even though that "sophisticated" system would never work in a bigger city.

So, likewise, here in Silver Spring, where there was not a lot of pavement and no reason to have a lot of signage, it also seemed fitting to call the only sizable chunk of pavement in the place, Highway 1.

They headed west into the hills surrounding the town. They soon came to the road that led to the cemetery, which, in most small towns in Texas, was usually named Cemetery Road. Here it was called Highway 1A. Go figure, thought Elaine. Elaine requested, or more correctly commanded, Paul to stop the rental car. She got out, camera in hand, to take pictures of her favorite subject, dead people, that is, the places where dead people were laid to rest.

They had a well-practiced routine at such times. Paul too, was a photographer, so when he needed to stop and take pictures of something, Elaine would whip out the binoculars and study the local birds. Paul, in turn, would sit in the car, and read whatever book he was currently absorbing with his boundless curiosity, as she snapped the shutter. She smiled to see he had one of the duck carving books with him.

She loved old cemeteries, and new ones for that matter. What she liked about the old ones were the weathered wooden crosses, whose names had long ago been eradicated. She would wander among the marble and granite headstones and other monuments. She would read each inscription, examine and analyze the data before her. Each name and set of dates represented a unique story from the past, a living breathing individual, a life that was no longer. She fantasized about each person buried beneath the soil, using the clues carved in stone to fuel her imagination.

Here was a carved headstone with a girl's name. The birth year and the death year were identical. A girl baby was buried here. How had she died? Had her parents been heart-broken or relieved that her suffering had ended? Were they buried here beside her? She took comfort as she saw that, indeed, the parents of that small child were close at hand. That discovery made everything all right in Elaine's rigidly ordered universe. In Elaine's world, people who loved one another should spend eternity sleeping next to one another. That was how it should be and it distressed Elaine when she found that not to be the case.

To this end, she also searched each cemetery to find those people who were buried without their loved ones. She said a little prayer for these abandoned individuals. It didn't make any difference why they wound up alone; maybe they were so unpleasant their relatives wanted nothing to do with them. Maybe they were crazy. No matter, she still felt badly for them.

Then she captured images of her favorite home-grown shrines. Some of them had little benches of marble or some other hard substance. The newer ones were fashioned of cement or concrete. It made her feel good to know there were newer ones. That meant someone still came out here to visit the people who had passed. Someone still made sure they were not forgotten.

Almost all the shrines were bedecked with cheap plastic flowers. Most appeared to be much older than they were, because the harsh Colorado sun quickly robbed them of their vibrant reds, blues, and yellows. The faded flowers huddled like tiny soldiers at the tombs of unknown soldiers, braving all the extremes of weather: snow, rain, wind and sun.

The last things she captured with her Nikon Coolpix were the monuments embellished with angels. She loved these flying creatures. She especially liked the angels with wings outstretched as if readying for takeoff. These resembled Greek or Roman statues, and she imagined the creators in their workshops doing their best to encapsulate the essence of real life peasants as they chiseled away at the rock. She fully realized these cemetery statues were probably mass produced copies, but she still appreciated them because they were so detailed; individual feathers stood out from one another and the seraphim wore soft serene expressions on their faces. These winged beauties went into Elaine's collection of cemetery shots along with the homemade shrines. They symbolized the happiest of endings for Elaine.

Like Paul, she didn't very much believe in any specific God, but she did believe there was an order to the universe. She strongly believed in karma and that good things came to those who did good while bad things happened to those who did wrong...eventually. All things in the universe balanced themselves out. There was evil in the world, it was true, but every evil thing that happened, in Elaine's opinion, ultimately happened for a good reason.

At least it had been so in her own life, so this is what she chose to believe.

Elaine continued to cling to this simplistic, even childish, view of the world. It was the only thing that helped when she heard the news of some crazy person going into a movie theatre and shooting 70 people. It had happened right here in this state, so full of beauty, just weeks ago. She told herself he must have had a good reason, or perhaps one of the people he killed was supposed to die. Perhaps the gunman was in so much pain himself that he couldn't see any other way out.

Why hadn't he shot himself after he killed so many other people; why had he let himself be apprehended? Those were the real mysteries to Elaine.

Perhaps there was something much greater at work. Perhaps the universe had a plan for that particularly heinous event. Maybe it would be the impetus for new gun laws to be passed. Who could say? Certainly not Elaine.

All she knew was no one else would understand the sympathy she felt for the lone gunman. She didn't feel as badly for the victims. She knew there were millions of people feeling sorry for the victims so it would be her job to feel pity and shame for the man, more closely resembling a boy, who would do such a thing. Elaine felt very sorry for him, and she didn't care if she was the only person in the civilized world to take on this responsibility. Someone had to do it. So it might as well be she. She kept these feelings and thoughts to herself.

Suddenly Elaine froze. There before her was the grave of Estefan. *The* Estefan! A tall white marble obelisk marked the place where he was buried beneath the hard red ground. As she made to take a picture, she was overcome with the strangest feeling. It was a mixture of arousal and deep sadness. It was as if she was feeling Dai-yu's excitement and sorrow. She had to sit down but there was no bench so she sat down heavily on the ground. She crossed her legs Indian style. Then she felt even weaker, and drowsy, as if she had been drinking. She lay down on her side in a fetal position. It was then that Paul looked up from his book and saw her lying there. He dropped his book and ran to her. As a rule, Paul didn't run.

As he reached her, he cried out, "What's going on!? What's wrong!?" Paul was really alarmed which made Elaine smile in a drunken sort of way. She had never seen such emotion from Paul before. As she lay there, feeling disconnected from the real world, she smiled. At least Paul would miss her if she was gone.

Paul sat down beside her and stroked her shoulder and arm. "Are you okay?" he asked her again and again.

"I'm fine," said Elaine and she kept smiling. Finally Paul looked up and noticed the stone that was before them.

Paul too was overcome with emotions. He flashed back to the dreams, and he saw through Estefan's eyes. He felt weak. Lifeless. All the energy left his body and he found himself lying next to Elaine in the scrubby grass that filled the cemetery. Then he put his arm around Elaine and hugged her with his whole body, and she snuggled into his embrace. They lay there side by side for a long time.

At last, the feeling of sorrow began to pass from Elaine's heart. She got up first, and reached down to help him up.

"Are you okay?" Paul asked her again.

"I am," she replied, "What about you?"

"I'm fine too," said Paul. "That was weird," he added.

"Understatement of the year," she said.

They both smiled.

The mysterious ocean of sorrow had retreated as quickly as it had arrived.

It was as if nothing had happened, but Paul didn't dare leave her side. As Elaine reached for her camera and began clicking away again, he followed her. Elaine noticed then that the monument to Estefan was surrounded by the graves of more of Estefan's clan. Here were two graves but they were not marked. Here lay Estefan, Jr., Gilberto, and Oscar. Where were their wives and children?

Then Elaine remembered something else; before the strange emotional tidal wave washed over them, she had seen some wooden crosses in the midst of the other stones and monuments. There was no longer any writing on them. Could one of these crosses mark Dai-yu's grave? There was no way to be sure. She returned to take a closer look at the crosses. All the writing and numerals had long ago been scratched away by the wind. As her eyes touched one particular cross, she felt a sharp stab in the center of her chest. With certainty, she knew she was standing before Dai-yu's resting place.

"Look Paul," she said, "Dai-yu's grave." Paul's face grew sad and Elaine knew that he felt Estefan's sorrow.

Elaine and Paul returned to the car. "Are you sure you're okay," he said one last time.

"I'm fine," she said. "Let's keep going. But let's not tell anybody about this."

"Agreed," said Paul.

***

They continued west along Highway 1 until they got to Saddle Mountain Road. Then they veered to the left. *That was strange*, thought Elaine. From that road, they turned left again onto Spring Ranch Canyon Road. All bets, it appeared, were off on this particular vacation, for Paul invariably turned to the right. In the many years they had been traveling together as husband and wife, this was the first time he had not taken the road to the right!

As a strategy it seemed to work for Paul. In this way, he made sure he didn't miss anything. They would drive along a main road, then take a right turn, then follow each right turn until they found something to see, or found there was nothing to be seen. Then they'd return the way they'd come, taking every right turn in its turn.

In fact, going to the right was how Paul shopped. He walked into a store, turned to the right and went up and down every aisle, looking at things, even if he didn't need anything in that particular aisle. Paul was a creature of habit, as she herself was becoming.

She started to question this odd behavior, but decided to stick to the mantra that had served her well so far on this trip, *Just go with it*. So she said nothing. It was indeed peculiar behavior. They drove until the road came to an end in the middle of what seemed like nowhere.

Paul hauled out his camera and tripod and made as if to take a picture. Then he said, "I'll be right back," left the camera standing where it was atop the tripod, and took off walking on foot. He headed up into the trees on the hill.

This is strange, she thought again, *even for Paul. Maybe he needs to use the facilities and doesn't want anyone to see him.* She waited until he was almost out of sight before she got out of the car and started after him. He kept on walking with a purpose, with a definite goal in mind. He wound in and around trees and she lost sight of him every so often, so she hurried to keep up with him.

They walked for at least an hour and a half, maybe longer, she couldn't tell and she didn't have a watch on. She was thirsty and of course, she hadn't brought any of the water that was in the car. Abruptly Paul came to a halt before what appeared to be an old mine. The shaft was sealed with old timbers, rocks and dirt. Paul sat down, checked the GPS on his smartphone and pulled out the little notebook he used to write messages to himself. He scribbled something quickly in the notebook. She assumed he was recording the coordinates of this spot. She had seen him do this multiple times before, when they were geocaching[6].

Now that beat all!

"What are you doing?" she demanded finally. There was irritation in her voice, despite her new mantra.

Paul turned to look at her, and she didn't recognize that look in his eyes. It was as if he were in a trance. He blinked a few times, looked about him; then asked, "Where are we?" Elaine became frightened when she realized they were miles from nowhere. How on earth would they find their way back to the car?

---

[6] Geocaching is a hobby where individuals, known as geocachers, look for prizes, or tokens, concealed inside little metal canisters. Geocachers all over the world hide these canisters for one another to find. Then they write puzzles to help other geocachers find the hidden canisters. They post the puzzles on geocaching sites on the Internet. Once a geocacher solves a puzzle, he, or she, is rewarded with the GPS coordinates that instruct him, or her, where to find a hidden cache. The two main goals of geocaching are to try to collect as many prizes as possible from as many places as possible and to try to get to be the first geocacher to get to a cache before anyone else finds it. All one needs for geocaching is a computer, a GPS, a puzzle-solving mind, and a means of transportation to get from one cache to another.

It was with a huge sigh of relief that she looked back the way they had come and spotted two tiny figures off in the distance, far below, approaching them.

"Thank god!" she exclaimed, as the figures got close enough for her to make out the old but spry forms of Mr. and Mrs. Kerstetter.

**

The Kerstetters easily managed to lead them back to the place the automobiles were parked. It was almost as if they had been there before. This was a little odd, Elaine noted, but compared to everything else they had seen and heard on this vacation, this little bit of weirdness barely registered on the Scale of Strange. As strange went, this was merely something to ask Paul about later on when they were alone again.

The Kerstetters got in their car. Paul stowed his camera equipment; the tripod was still standing forlornly next to their vehicle, as if watching for stray bighorn sheep. Elaine and Paul got in their car and followed the old couple's car back to the B&B. So much for "adventure," thought Elaine as they drove; that little sojourn had almost turned into another "ordeal." The odd thing, now that she thought about it some more, was that the K's had found them there in the first place. Had they been followed?

Of course, they had been followed! How else could the K's have known where they were? This entire ordeal was beginning to change from puzzling to alarming. Why would the K's be following them in the first place?

She very much wanted to ask Paul what he thought about the whole matter, but she knew what he would say. He would say she should be glad that they had shown up when they did.

Instead, as they drove, the awkward silence was broken by Paul's voice. He said, "What just happened?"

"You're not going to believe it, but you and I were out there in the hills," and she pointed back the way they had just come, "And you found an old sealed-up mine shaft."

"What!?" was all Paul could say.

"Yes, you found a mine. You got out of the car and just started walking. Then we walked and walked and you knew exactly where it was."

"That can't be," said Paul, the engineer, "I've never been here before."

"I know that!" exclaimed Elaine. "But maybe Estefan has."

"That's right," said Paul, "I've dreamt something about a mine. Or mines. And something about gold. But I can't remember what it was."

When they got back to the B&B it was late afternoon. Elaine just couldn't let it go. She liked the K's, was even starting to love them a little, and she hated secrets, especially when the secrets kept something from her.

She decided to take the direct approach. She asked Mrs. K if they had followed them up to the hills surrounding Silver Spring.

Instead of denying it, Mrs. K smiled. Happily she admitted it. "Yes, dear, you see, the ghosts, well they are mischievous. This is just the kind of trick Estefan might pull. We were worried about you. Estefan has been behaving strangely of late and we didn't want the two of you to come to any harm." *In other words*, thought Elaine, *the K's are not going to let us out of their sights.*

"What do you mean?" said Elaine.

"Estefan's hiding something from us and he always has been. But you know what I think? I think he told Paul what it is."

"That's crazy!" said Paul. "I don't know any secrets of Estefan's."

"Oh, on the contrary, my Dear, you know everything Estefan knows."

"Well, I sure would be curious to find out what Estefan is trying to tell me," said Paul. That had to be the scientific curiosity in Paul's engineering brain weighing in.

"Well, why don't we try an experiment?" suggested Mrs. K. "Why don't we hold a séance and ask Estefan ourselves?"

"A séance!?" That was too much for Paul's logical skeptical brain.

"Call it hypnosis instead," said Mr. K. "I used to be pretty good at this," he added.

"I don't know..." said Paul.

"I promise it won't hurt," said Mr. K.

"I think it would be an adventure," chimed in Elaine. "C'mon, Paul, don't be a chicken!" and she knew with those words, Paul would succumb. Once upon a time, someone must have called him chicken one time too many, for now it was the only surefire way Elaine knew to get him to try something. Especially something that was blatantly silly, purely for fun, and with no ostensible purpose.

"Okay," agreed Paul, but he was visually not happy about it.

***

As they convened in the living room, Elaine asked, "Don't we need to light a candle?"

"No, that's just for the movies. It isn't necessary," said Mr. K. "All we really need is a quiet place so Paul can relax." With that announcement, Mrs. K drew the blinds and turned off the overhead lights.

"Just relax and close your eyes," said Mr. K, in a gentle soothing voice. He kept his words slow and evenly spaced apart. He lowered his speaking voice, rendering it full and pleasantly resonant.

He began, "Imagine a staircase. You are at the top of the stairs and you are going to descend the steps, one by one. And as you go down, imagine you see the number '100' in your mind's eye. And as you imagine the number '100,' picture it clearly, and as you picture it, imagine the number '100' slowly fading away until it is gone altogether. And as you step down onto the next stair, imagine the number '99,' and picture it clearly in your mind. Then picture the number '99' slowly fading away until it's gone…"

He continued in this way, repeating the numbers in decreasing order until Paul's breathing became slow, deep and regular; then he said, "Paul, when I clap my hands, you will awaken. You will feel very relaxed. You will not remember this conversation. All you will remember is that you feel refreshed, content and rested."

Now, it was time to talk to the ghost. He said, "Estefan, are you here?"

"Estoy aqui," said Paul/Estefan.

"En ingles," commanded Mr. K.

"Yes, I am here," said Paul/Estefan.

Elaine did not recognize Paul's voice anymore. He had a Spanish accent and his voice was higher; apparently, Estefan was a tenor, while Paul was definitely a baritone. *This is wild!* thought Elaine.

Mr. K continued to talk to Paul/Estefan. They spoke as if they were very close friends, but the tone of the conversation was serious. "Where have you been, Estefan? I've been worried about you," said Mr. K.

"I've been around," said Paul/Estefan cagily.

"I've missed our time together," said Mr. K.

"I am sorry, but I have had many important matters to attend to." Paul/Estefan was deliberately avoiding this line of questioning.

"I see," said Mr. K. "When do you think we might be able to discuss our business together?"

"I'm not sure there is anything left to discuss," said Paul/Estefan.

"I see," said Mr. K. He was visibly angry.

Elaine kept waiting for Mr. K to ask Paul/Estefan why he was out at the abandoned mine and what he had been doing there. But he never asked him, so Elaine began to suspect Mr. K already knew what Estefan was doing there, and he and Mrs. K were up to something.

"You know you have something we want and we have something you want and the sooner you tell us what we want to know, the sooner you'll get the thing you want."

"I can't do that at the present moment," answered Paul/Estefan.

"I see," said Mr. K, you know you are running out of time. I suggest you sleep on it, and we can talk about it tomorrow night."

"We will see," was all Paul/Estefan said.

"Impatiently," Mr. K clapped his hands and Paul awoke. Paul stared around himself, and said, "Okay, I'm ready to start then."

"It's already over!" exclaimed Elaine.

"You're kidding!?" said Paul. "Well, that wasn't bad at all. I feel great. I wouldn't mind doing that again. You should try it Elaine!"

Now Elaine was even more confused. She didn't have any idea what Mr. K and Paul/Estefan were discussing but it certainly sounded important.

***

That night Elaine turned to Paul and said, I think it's time we got out of here."

"Why?" said Paul, "Things are just getting interesting. It's an adventure!" he finished.

"Whatever you say," Elaine groaned. She was not at all certain that she was even speaking to her husband anymore. Maybe she was actually having a conversation with that scoundrel, Estefan.

Then she began worrying again over the mystery she had unwittingly become a part of. Questions flooded her head. What were Estefan and Mr. K arguing about? What did the K's have that Estefan needed? What did Estefan have that the K's wanted? What were the details of this bargain they were trying to hammer out?

***

Soon after Paul and Elaine fell asleep, a ghost came to Paul. The ghost urged Paul to wake up, get dressed and put on hiking boots. The ghost instructed Paul to find a shovel, a pickaxe, and a flashlight. Then the ghost instructed Paul to drive back to the mine in the hills. Paul got out of bed and searched for the requisite tools. As he was clunking around and knocking things together noisily in the toolshed behind the B&B, the sounds awakened Mr. and Mrs. K. They got out of bed quickly and dressed.

Elaine just kept on sleeping. She dreamt.

Instead of waking Paul, the K's watched him; then they followed him. Paul loaded the metal, wood and plastic implements into the trunk of the car, got in, started the engine, backed the car out into the street, and headed off down Highway 1. The Kerstetters got in their own car, and went after him. They followed from a safe distance and kept their headlights off so he would not notice them in his rear view mirror. There was a full moon so the landmarks that dotted the foreign landscape were lit almost as brightly as during the day. There were no other cars out in the middle of the night. Or in the daytime, for that matter; Silver Spring was known as a ghost town for good reason.

The K's also knew exactly where Paul was going. He turned onto Saddle Mountain Road and again onto Spring Ranch Canyon Road. He continued all the way to the end of the road. There he parked the car, retrieved the shovel, pickaxe, and flashlight from the trunk of the car, hoisted the tools onto one shoulder, attached the flashlight to his belt, and headed off up the hillside towards the abandoned mine. Again, the Kerstetters followed at a safe distance so he would not see them.

Paul reached the mine and dropped the tools on the ground; then he unhooked the flashlight and dropped it at his feet. He rested for a few minutes. Then he picked up the pickaxe and started prying away at the logjam of rotten timbers that clogged the opening to the mine. He pried away log after log until they lay splintered in a large pile by the entrance. Then he put down the pickaxe, picked up the shovel, and began digging. The fill dirt went back several feet. The mine had been sealed with intent, not necessarily to keep someone out for all time, but definitely to keep some casual passersby from entering, although the chance of a passersby wandering through this remote area was astronomically miniscule. Paul was not aware of anything but his digging. He dug mechanically, mindlessly, automatically, and tirelessly. For hours he dug until the pile of dirt removed from the mine shaft towered over the pile of broken up timber next to it.

Still Paul kept on digging. He was now so far deep into the shaft that the Kerstetters could not see him until he emerged with another seemingly endless shovelful of dirt and rubble.

Finally Paul rested. He came out of the dark mine shaft, and picked up the flashlight he had left lying on the ground.

Then he entered the portal of the newly opened mine. The Kerstetters got up then and scrambled over bramble and boulder to reach the place where Paul had disappeared.

"Let's go after him," said Mrs. K.

"After you," said Mr. K.

They entered the mine to search for Paul. They walked about 100 yards when they came to a fork in the path. They shined their flashlight beam towards the thin layer of soil that covered the floor of the mine. There they could see Paul's tracks heading along the corridor to the right. They turned right and went after him. They followed the drift until they came to a stope, a large open room. They listened. They could hear the sound of someone speaking in a low voice.

"I'm sorry, Estrellita, I'm sorry about everything. Where are you, pobrécita?"

Then they heard the sound of digging. They heard metal scraping against rock. They heard a shovel crunching deep into dry dusty earth. Again and again. It was getting very stuffy in the mine and still the digging sounds went on and on.

"Let's go back and get some fresh air," hissed Mrs. K.

"I'm with you," whispered Mr. K in return.

The K's returned the way they had come and waited by the mine entrance.

After a while, they heard Paul coming towards them. When he saw them standing there, he froze. He made to go back into the mine but Mrs. K ordered him to stop. "How do you intend to make me, old woman?" Paul laughed. It was obvious they were now speaking to a ghost who laughed heartily as if it had just delivered the punch-line to a joke.

"This is how," said Mrs. K and she leveled an old pistol directly at him. It appeared to be a very old revolver. It had a long black-grey barrel and a shiny wooden grip. Six 44-caliber bullets were snuggly fitted into the chambers of the cylinder. It might have been so old that it no longer worked. Paul wasn't interested in testing that theory. Mrs. K gestured with the gun towards the entrance.

Paul played stupid, "You want me to go back in there?"

"Yes," ordered Mrs. K. "Now, make it snappy!" She waved the gun at him.

He turned and headed into the mine. The K's were right behind him, practically treading on his heels.

"Where are we going?" Paul asked.

"I think you already know" said Mrs. K.

***

Meanwhile, Elaine dreamt.

"Wake up! Hurry!!" The ghost inside her head was pleading.

Elaine got out of bed. Her eyes were bleary and she was dog tired. She felt as if her body were not her own, but she couldn't stop it from moving. She went down into the kitchen and opened an old porcelain cookie jar. Inside it was a set of car keys. Out behind the B&B, in the garage, she found an old slightly rusted beater from the 50's. It was a '57 Ford Thunderbird with tiny affected aerodynamic wings. Its original color might have been cherry red. The paint was missing in many spots, the upholstery needed to be repaired, and the tires were low. It looked as if it hadn't been driven in years.

Elaine plugged the keys into the ignition and tried to start the engine. The engine didn't turn over. Elaine tried again. There was a clicking sound as if the battery was dead. Then a strange otherworldly thing happened. Elaine put both hands on the steering wheel and channeled all her psychic energy into one command.

"Start!"

As if the car had ears and a brain, and the willingness to obey, the engine roared into life. Elaine slowly backed the long vehicle out into the driveway and onto the street. Then she drove towards the hills.

***

Paul and the Kerstetters were now deep inside the mine.

"So," began Mrs. K, "Where did you hide the gold?"

"What gold?" said Paul.

"The gold you've been stealing from everyone ever since you got to Silver Spring." She waved the gun at him.

"I don't know what you are talking about," Paul said coyly.

"We know you took it and we know who helped you do it. And we know you died before you could get it out of here. Now where is it?"

She flourished the gun menacingly at Paul's head, right at the spot between his wide-open eyes. "If you kill me," Paul started, "You'll never find the gold. I never told anyone about it. No one knows where it is but me."

"I see," said Mrs. K. "Well, obviously you could care less if we kill Paul here. So who do you care about? Let's see…"

They had been walking for several minutes. It was hard to believe they knew where they were going, until they came to another large underground chamber. The beams of the flashlights zig-zagged erratically along the walls and the ceiling of the stope, then came to rest on the floor. There on the ground was a heap of earth. Next to it was a recently excavated hole. A shallow grave? And once Mrs. K leveled the flashlight at the pile of dirt on the ground, they could see what appeared to be a mummified human. The face was so distorted it was hard to tell if the person had once been male or female. Further inspection of the shreds of fabric clinging vainly to the shriveled body told the rest of the story.

The wearer had once been a lady. And then something else caught the light from the flashlight. Something shiny. It was a necklace studded with silver and green stones.

One more thing grabbed everyone's immediate attention. Coins. Gold coins. They were scattered around the heart of the dead woman. Mr. K reached down and picked up one of the coins. It wasn't particularly shiny anymore because it was covered with dirt and oxidation. But, nonetheless, he could tell it was gold.

Paul cried out then. "Oh, Estrellita! Estrellita, I'm so sorry! I never meant to harm you!" He knelt in the dirt and cried. Paul felt tears running down his cheeks even though he had never met Estrellita. He felt pain in his own heart.

"Now, do you want to leave her here for another hundred years? Or do you want to bury her in the cemetery for what is left of eternity?" asked Mrs. K.

"Oh Estrellita," Paul continued to weep softly. He reached down and gently picked up the necklace that once encircled the neck of the dead girl. He held it to his breast as he cried. Finally, he blurted out, "Yes, yes, I want to take her out of here!" The gold is here!" And he started to lead them down one of the other mine shafts. They followed him closely again, almost stepping on his heels, for the beams of the flashlights barely illuminated the way.

Mrs. K never stopped pointing the weapon dangerously at the middle of Paul's back. Finally, Paul stopped. There was an oddly shaped indentation in the wall where someone had left an identification mark. Paul reached into a natural grotto in the wall and pulled out...nothing. There was nothing there. Then the flashlights illuminated something white on the floor by the wall. It was a piece of paper. Paul reached down to pick it up. He stared at the paper in confusion. He showed it to the Kerstetters. On it were scrawled the words, "Better luck next time."

There was silence.

"Noooooo!" Paul screeched. His voice was high and shrill, almost as if it belonged to a woman. Paul continued screaming the same words over and over again.

"He screwed us! He screwed us! He screwed us both!" It sounded as if Paul was having a temper tantrum!

As Mr. and Mrs. K stared at him in shock, Paul lunged at Mrs. K and easily snatched the pistol away from her. Then he pointed it directly at her heart.

"This is your fault!" he screamed at her. "You stupid bitch!"

Paul cocked the trigger and made ready to fire...

***

Suddenly, there was a loud clicking noise behind them.

"Drop it, Puta!!"came Elaine's voice. But it was not her voice. She was speaking a mixture of Spanish and English, and she had a thick accent. Her voice was firm and no nonsense.

All eyes turned to the form of Elaine standing there with a shotgun in both hands. The clicking was the sound of Elaine pulling the hammer back. She had both barrels pointed squarely at Paul. But instead of dropping the pistol, he squeezed the trigger. There was a clicking noise, but no explosion of gunpowder. He squeezed the trigger two more times. But the gun would not fire. He dropped it to the floor, but instead of surrendering and admitting defeat, Paul did something crazy.

He charged directly at Elaine. He grabbed the shotgun with both hands and the two of them struggled. Elaine's fingers squeezed the trigger. The gun exploded with a deafening roar as the weapon discharged into the hard ceiling. Pepples, dirt, and small rocks dislodged by the buckshot rained down on them. Everyone was stunned by the loud noise and temporarily blinded because the flash was so bright. The air quickly filled with a cloud of dust.

The noise was enough to wake the dead, or the ghostly possessed. Paul and Elaine woke up.

Paul dropped immediately to the ground – exhausted. Elaine was still holding onto the weapon. Then Mr. and Mrs. K reacted. Almost at the same time, Mr. and Mrs. K grabbed onto the shotgun.

Elaine, who was no longer possessed, let go and surrendered peacefully. Mrs. K let go too. Mr. K was left holding the gun.

Then, like a puppet pulled by invisible strings, Paul rose up again behind them.

He heard Estrellita's panicky voice inside his head.

"They will kill you and leave you here with me forever! Do something!!!" With that message burning into his brain, Paul grabbed Mr. K from behind and tried to wrestle the shotgun away from him.

Mr. K dropped the gun as he tried to get Paul off of him. As Paul and Mr. K struggled, Mrs. K resorted to guerilla tactics. She came up behind them and knocked Paul on the head with a rock. He staggered, let go, and dropped once more to the ground. First his head dropped to his chest; then he passed out.

***

Everything stopped then. Each of the four found themselves alone with their thoughts. Elaine was filled with terror, *What if Paul dies? What will happen then?* She realized, more than life itself, she didn't want him to die!

She loved him. As she knelt beside him, she held onto his hand and starting begging.

"Paul! Paul! Come back. Come back to me. I love you!"

Tears crept down her face; she didn't even realize she was weeping. As the clock ticked away Elaine hovered over Paul, Mrs. K hovered over Elaine, and Mr. K hovered over Mrs. K who apologized over and over again.

"I'm sorry Elaine," she was weeping as she spoke the words. "I didn't know what else to do. I'm so sorry."

Elaine couldn't say anything. She was silent as the time slowed down, and the minutes seemed to drag on, turning into hours.

The darkness was stifling, and frightening. A lone flashlight on the ground barely illuminated the inert forms of Paul and the others.

Suddenly, as if in a dream, Paul sat up. He had a strange look in his eyes. He smiled cunningly. Like a person on speed, his eyes were wild, like those of an animal.

They realized it wasn't Paul in charge. It had to be…Estefan.

"Venga con migo! Come with me," he bid the others.

Mr. K helped Mrs. K to his feet. Paul was off in a hurry. Elaine and the Kerstetters could hardly keep up with him as he almost sprinted from the mine, to the cars, and back to the cemetery in Silver Spring.

When they reached the top of the hill where the cemetery kept watch over the town of Silver Spring, Paul hopped out of the car and headed directly for Estefan's family plot. In the moonlight, within the little square of territory set off by a chain-link fence, they could just make out a pair of unmarked graves to one side of Estefan's ghostly white monument. Paul pulled out a pocketknife, stabbed it into the hard ground atop one of the unmarked graves, and started to dig with the blade.

"Aqui. Aqui," he said.

After a moment, Mr. K ran back to the car and retrieved a shovel and a tire iron from the trunk of his car. He started to dig too. Elaine and Mrs. K stood, arms around one another's waists, and watched with growing concern. The men were down about three feet when they hit something. It was either wood or metal, it didn't sound like rock. Mrs. K and Elaine came over to the grave to look then.

Not the coffin, surely, thought Elaine. *That would be too much.* But no, it was not the coffin, it was a wooden box and it was heavy. That was obvious as Paul and Mr. K together tried to lift it, but could not. So Paul pried the lid off with the tire iron.

Inside were coins, gold coins. Hundreds of gold coins!

Now that the price of gold had reached $1,600 an ounce, everyone realized there was a substantial fortune in gold in that little chest. It was then that Mrs. K realized this was not her gold at all. There was far too much of it. Her gold must have been the gold they found in the mine along with the body of the poor dead Estrellita.

Suddenly, Paul's knees seemed to give out and he sat down on the dirt next to the grave. As if he was just awakening from a deep sleep, he asked, "What happened?"

Mr. K exclaimed, "We found it! We found Estefan's gold!"

***

"Let's get the heck out of here!" said Elaine loudly. What if the local police happen to drive up and spot us desecrating a grave?"

"That would not be a good thing," agreed Mrs. K, "but," she added, "They hardly ever come out here. But you are right, let's get out of here!"

It was almost sunrise, so they decided to fill the hole back up and come back to get the rest of the gold out later. But first they stuffed as much as they could carry into their pockets and made a couple of trips back to the car. Like starving children stumbling onto a sack of Halloween candy, they all went a little nuts.

They practically ran back to their cars, buoyed by the thought of the gold in their possession.

***

When they reached the cars, Mr. K turned to Elaine and said, "How on earth did you get the old T-bird out here? That thing hasn't been driven in years. I didn't even think the battery worked anymore."

"That is a mystery," said Elaine. She didn't really remember how Estrellita got the car started. She remembered the drive out as if it were a dream sequence in a movie.

Mr. K got in the Thunderbird and turned the key. The engine started easily.

"Well, I'll be darned!" he exclaimed. "Elaine, you must have the magic touch."

"I think it might have been a bit of *ghost* magic," Elaine giggled uneasily.

***

When they got back to the B&B they were in no mood to sleep. It was just after dawn but they were all wide awake. They piled their bonanza onto the coffee table in the living room and stared at the gold coins for a while. Finally, Mrs. K got up and headed for the kitchen. Elaine followed her. They snagged four slices of pie and four cups of hot coffee and the four of them stayed up talking, or debriefing, until well into the morning hours. They discussed the events of the evening, and the secrets guarded by the ghosts who had haunted Silver Spring for more than a century.

"So let me get this straight," Paul said. "Someone stole gold from you? So that means YOU were the Madam of the Silver Spring? You were the woman who ran the brothel? I can't believe it! You seem so nice! You seem so *young*!" Paul feigned surprise.

"I am nice," said Mrs. K and she sparkled as she said it. "You have to be nice to run a whorehouse. You have to be nice to your customers, and more importantly, you have to be nice to your girls. As for young..." and she laughed loudly.

"But how did you keep people from finding out?" Elaine asked.

"Finding out what?" Mrs. K sounded puzzled.

"Finding out *you* were the Madam of a whorehouse that must have closed its doors years ago?" said Elaine.

"Well, you know, Elaine, being a Madam of a brothel wasn't the same thing as it is today. It's not like being a pimp. A brothel was 'almost' a respectable establishment in days gone by. Sometimes it's difficult not to apply our puritanical 21st century mores to the cultures of the past. It's hard not to pass judgment on people who do things differently than we do. Let me just say, I was proud of being a Madam. I was proud of the Silver Spring. And I was proud of my girls, most of them anyway."

"I thought you told us you came to the Silver Spring when you were in your fifties," recalled Elaine.

"Oh that, that was a just a little white lie. I didn't think the truth would be something you needed to know at that point in our relationship. The truth is I came to Silver Spring when I was in my 20's. That must have been"…and she tried to do the math. Then it became apparent that a date just popped into her head…. "1862…that was the year they passed the Homestead Act. We came a few years after that. Probably around 1870, after the United States government had removed the one obstacle to the settlers, that is, the Native Americans that were already calling the Colorado territory their homes."

Paul began doing the math. "That means you were 20 years old in 1870; so you have to be…162 years old!! What!! That can't be right!" he exclaimed in disbelief.

"Well, I've heard that numbers don't lie," replied Mrs. K simply. "And I don't look a day over 100," she joked.

"But how? How is that possible? How is it you haven't aged?" asked Elaine.

"That," she said, is a very good question, and I have no good explanation. Suffice it to say, I believe it is the ghosts who are responsible. Maybe once the ghosts get hold of you, you stop aging. I don't know, but that's what has happened. I know it's not scientific and I'm sure no one would believe me if I told them that is how it is, but, that *is* how it is," she finished.

"All I know for sure is that I was a young bride when my husband and I came West like many others to take advantage of a once-in-a-lifetime opportunity; the United States government was practically giving land away to people willing to come out here and settle it. We all had one thing in common; we wanted a piece of the American Dream, to become landowners."

"We were given a plot of land, 160 acres, on which to build a house. We both worked hard to make the soil suitable for farming. It was very rocky and dry. We moved hundreds of rocks, dug a well, and planted a few seeds. We were so excited, enthusiastic, and idealistic. Unfortunately, my young husband died soon after we came here. I was left a young widow with no one to take care of me. I couldn't care for our homestead all by myself and it was much too dangerous for any woman to live alone on the plains or anywhere else in the Colorado territory. So I came to town to live."

"The Madam of this very brothel gave me a job working in the kitchen. I became a scullery maid. I refused to become one of the saloon girls. When the Madam found out I was good with numbers and mathematics, she let me take care of her bookkeeping chores. Eventually, she came to trust me completely with all her finances. I took over most of the business transactions that kept the Silver Spring going day to day. After many years, the Madam got sick with consumption. I was the closest thing she had to a relative, or daughter, so she trained me to take over the operation of the Silver Spring. When she died, after many months of suffering, I was at her side, holding her hand. I still miss her. She was a good woman, and always did right by her girls. That's what I learned from her. Do right by people and they will do right by you. So I always did right by my girls."

"But how did you explain to people the fact that you never got any older?" Elaine continued with her questions.

"Oh *that*..." Mrs. K sniggered as she emphasized the word *that*. "No one ever seemed to care about *that*. Or make note of it. From my experience, no one cares about things like age after a woman reaches a certain point in her life. You know what I mean." She winked at Elaine. "Once a woman gets past 50, it's almost as if she becomes invisible." Elaine and Mrs. K both nodded at this private shared truth.

"On the positive side, it makes things incredibly simple," said Mrs. K. "A woman our age can do whatever she wants. She can act like a small child if she feels like it, or make a complete fool of herself in public, and everyone just smiles and forgives her actions, no matter how inappropriate. She can wear a mini-skirt or a red hat, die her hair purple or green, drape herself in gypsy scarves, or ride the carousel, and everyone just goes with it. It's very freeing."

"You're right," said Elaine. "I guess there are advantages to being this age."

***

"So, said Mr. K, "Who killed Estefan and Dai-yu?"

"I think I can tell you that," offered Elaine.

"You remember Estefan's regular 'girl Friday'? The one called Estrellita? She was the girl he kept before the China doll's arrival. After Estrellita had to give up her room to Dai-yu she was furious with the Madam even though it was really all Estefan's doing. She decided to punish the Madam by getting into the till and stealing her gold."

"I knew it," said Mrs. K, "I knew she was the one who robbed me but I never could prove it. Like I told you before, everyone knew Estrellita was a thief, and a sloppy one at that. But when it mattered, like when she took my gold, I guess she was a little more careful."

"Anyway," continued Elaine, when Estrellita was Estefan's girl, he told her where he hid his gold. At least that is what Estrellita believed. That's one of the reasons why Estrellita wanted me to go to the mine. To find Estefan's gold. The other reason of course, was to find her body."

Elaine went on, "After he dumped her so abruptly, Estrellita was furious with Estefan. She felt betrayed, and her heart was broken, so she wanted to punish her three-timing boyfriend. As I'm sure we can all agree Estefan was a bit of a sociopath. He didn't really care about any of his girlfriends or lovers, but he talked a good game so they were often taken in by him and convinced of his sincerity. The truth was Estrellita knew that taking valuables from Estefan was the only way she could truly punish him."

"Somewhere along the line, Estefan told Estrellita he had hidden his gold in that old mine. He even told her that no one, not even Margarita, his own beloved wife, knew where he kept his fortune. Estefan even gave Estrellita instructions so she could find the money if anything ever happened to him. Even though she knew Estefan was a liar and a cheat, Estrellita convinced herself that Estefan trusted her and loved her enough to give her his money. Of course, she was only fooling herself."

"Anyway, Estrellita was happy to keep Estefan's hiding place a secret as long as she was Estefan's woman. And all would have been peachy keen if Estefan could have kept it in his pants. But he had a wandering eye…and a wandering you-know-what. Unfortunately, a wandering eye has been the downfall of many a man with a huge ego. And Estefan did have a huge one."

"A huge what?" Mrs. K couldn't help herself.

"Ego…girl, where is your mind?" They all laughed.

Elaine went on. "If Estefan hadn't been so delusional about his own invulnerability he would not have been murdered, in my opinion. After Estefan dumped Estrellita, I believe she went a little mad. Not only was she insanely jealous of Dai-yu, but she now hated Estefan as much as she once loved him. And that was a lot."

"So Estrellita shot Estefan and Dai-yu?" asked Mr. K.

"Not exactly"…said Elaine.

"I don't understand," said Mr. K. "Who killed Estrellita? And how did she get in the mine?"

"I can answer that," said Paul. "The reason Margarita took me out to that old mine, was that she was still trying to locate Estefan's gold. And she wanted everyone to know what happened to Estrellita. She felt guilty. I think she got stuck in that time with those two goals foremost in her mind."

Paul went on, "That's the other twist to this sad tale. Apparently after Margarita found out about the necklace that Estefan had given Dai-yu, she too went a little insane."

"What necklace?" asked Mr. K.

"Estefan bought a necklace for his wife and another exactly like it for Dai-yu," Paul added.

"Oh, that's asking for big trouble!" Mr. K groaned. "But how did Margarita find out about the second necklace?"

Paul went on, "Margarita followed Estefan to the Silver Spring and saw it with her own eyes!"

"Oh that couldn't have been a good thing!" said Mr. K.

"No kidding," said Paul.

"Then what happened?" prompted Mr. K.

"Then Estefan experienced the wrath of Margarita. But we're getting a little ahead of ourselves..."

It was then that Elaine chimed in to add, "After Estefan dumped Estrellita, Estrellita went to visit Margarita. She rode a horse out to Estefan's estate, knocked on the door, and confronted the wife of her long-time lover. Margarita was shocked to see her. They stood and stared at one another like a couple of female cats locked together in a room. There was a little hissing at first but no nails. Finally, Margarita asked Estrellita in. Estrellita at once broke into tears and Margarita found herself consoling the other woman despite the fact that they were in essence competing for the love of the same man."

"And once Estrellita told Margarita about the China Doll, Estefan's latest behaviors, and the goings on at the Silver Spring, the two betrayed women found themselves commiserating. They even cried a bit in solidarity. They lamented, *Estefan was such a bastard*. You know what they say? The enemy of my enemy is my friend. Sometimes enemies become strange bedfellows."

"Estefan was in big trouble from that moment forward. It was only a matter of time. For there's only one thing worse than having a woman scorned coming after you; that's having two of them. And so it was with Estrellita and Margarita. They were eager to get even with Estefan. Estrellita told Margarita everything she knew…about the gold, about the mine, about the China Doll. And then they planned a perfect murder. Estrellita knew which room was her old room, so she gave Margarita that information. Estrellita 'borrowed' the Remington revolver the Madam kept downstairs behind the bar and gave it to Margarita to use."

Mrs. K lovingly picked up the pistol. "This is the very gun they used. And, no, it doesn't work anymore, but the ghost of Margarita didn't know that.'"

Elaine continued to unravel the story of the murder. "Estrellita kept a lookout in the hallway outside Dai-yu's room and then signaled the 'all clear' to Margarita who was waiting on the back stairs at the end of the hall. Margarita slipped into the room where the two lay sleeping and closed the door behind her. As I recall," and Elaine winked at Mrs. K then, "You told me that they were having sex when they were killed," pointed out Elaine.

"Oh that," said Mrs. K, "That is what we call 'poetic license.' Makes for a better story though, doesn't it?"

"Anyway," Elaine continued, "After Margarita sneaked into the room where the two lay *sleeping*," and she emphasized the word, "in one another's arms, she fired two gunshots."

"This is the part that I remember," and Mrs. K jumped in. "Once the shots were fired, there was pandemonium at the Silver Spring. A few of our overnight 'guests' came running out into the hall brandishing loaded weapons. I was asleep in my room, but the sound of gunfire woke me up. I ran out into the hallway, like everyone else, to see what was going on. As soon as the shots rang out, Estrellita, who was still standing out in the hallway, started screaming and pointing. She insisted she had seen a man carrying a pistol, running down the hall and down the back stairs where he made his escape."

"No one was certain where the shots had come from. All the doors to the rooms stood wide open but one; that was Dai-yu's room. Finally someone opened that door and there they were. It was a bloody mess. Some of the girls screamed. But everyone still took a peek. When Estrellita saw the bodies she started crying and screaming hysterically."

"The only lead we had was Estrellita's. Some of the men ran out into the alley and the main street to search for the mysterious man with the smoking gun. But of course, they didn't find anyone."

This is where Paul broke in again and picked up the thread of the story. "After she shot them, Margarita hid under the bed in the room where the dead lovers lay. She waited until the hall was empty and Estrellita came back to give her the 'all clear' once again. Then she slipped down the back stairs and got on her horse and rode away. She was dressed in men's clothes so no one would notice her, and she escaped when all the other men took off."

Then Mrs. K added, "That night, after the men gave up searching for the mysterious gunman, the sheriff came back to the Silver Spring, and started interviewing eyewitnesses. Of course, no one saw anything, no one but Estrellita. He took her statement, did a cursory examination of the crime scene, and went home and went back to bed. The next day the undertaker came by to claim the bodies. The Silver Spring was closed for a week. Black curtains were hung out front to signify mourning."

"Then what happened?" prompted Mr. K.

Paul picked up from there, "That very night, Margarita and Estrellita rendezvoused on the outskirts of town and rode out to the mine together, where Estrellita promised to show Margarita where Estefan had secreted his gold. The plan was for the two of them was to retrieve the gold that Estefan had hidden and to leave town and start all over again. The gold was supposed to be in the grotto where they found the note."

"When they reached the grotto, there was no gold. No silver. Nothing. Just a piece of paper with a snide note on it. First they stared at one another in disbelief. Then Estrellita burst out laughing, because it was just like Estefan to pull a stunt like that."

"It was all too much for Margarita. When she saw the note written by Estefan, Margarita just went crazy, she was so angry. First her husband had fallen in love with another woman; then there was the ultimate insult: he had screwed her out of her rightful inheritance! There wasn't any money!"

"The beautiful spoiled Margarita, the recipient of one final insult from the vainglorious Estefan, grabbed a shovel and smashed Estrellita on the head with it."

"Then she sat down and cried. When the tears finally stopped, she looked down to see what she had done, and was filled with remorse. Quickly, she buried Estrellita's body, not that anyone would ever find it, because Estefan was the only other person who knew where the gold was supposed to be hidden. And Estefan was dead."

Paul finished the long convoluted tale, "Margarita never found Estefan's gold. The gold we discovered with Estrellita's remains must have been the gold Estrellita swiped from the Silver Spring."

"So Margarita never intended to kill Estrellita? They actually intended to split the gold?" asked Mr. K.

"That's what she told me, said Paul. Then he continued, "After she killed Estrellita, Margarita finally realized she had lost everything. She no longer had Estefan, who loved her in his own selfish way. She no longer had her place in society. The murder was a disgrace. She no longer had Estefan's fortune because it had evaporated into the atmosphere like so much water vapor. She couldn't eat, she lost weight, she couldn't think about anything but dying. She wasted away. After six months she couldn't take it anymore..."

Mrs. K added, "Poor Margarita, and believe it or not I feel sorry for her, no longer had any reason to live so she hung herself. The worst part was, Margarita's family wouldn't take her body because suicide was a venal sin back then. Instead, the poor girl was buried at the crossroads, so her soul could not find its way back to town, which was a superstition people had at the time. Now her lonely soul haunts the hills, the buildings, and the people around Silver Spring. Sometimes she comes to me in dreams."

She added, "It was also a shame about poor Estrellita. Her life was over, even before Margarita killed her. I knew she was the one who robbed me. I couldn't prove it, but I knew it. All she had was the handful of gold she stole from me."

"At first, everyone blamed Estrellita for killing Estefan and Dai-yu, and then when she disappeared, everyone assumed she had escaped and gotten away with it."

"After Margarita killed herself, people started thinking maybe she was the one who killed the lovers. Public sentiment fluctuated over the years. Now, of course, more than a hundred years later, no one even cares. But," and Mrs. K winked at Elaine, "it would make a good ghost story."

"One last question," asked Mr. K, "how did Estrellita wind up wearing Dai-yu's necklace? That *was* Dai-yu's necklace, wasn't it?

"I can tell you that," said Paul, "Margarita took it off the nightstand after she shot her. She gave it to Estrellita when they reached the mine. Twins in deed and in heart they were wearing the matching necklaces when they reached the place where they were supposed to find their fortune."

"So I guess that only leaves us one question. What do we do with Estefan's gold?" asked Mr. K.

That is a very good question, thought Elaine and Paul.

***

That afternoon Elaine and Paul walked back down to the carousel. They held hands as they strolled.

"Let's ride it," said Elaine.

"You're kidding, aren't you? Don't you always get sick on the spinning rides?" asked Paul with concern.

"I do, but let's try it anyway. It will be an adventure!" she declared.

They bought five tickets, because that was the minimum purchase. Each ticket said, "Welcome to the Carousel of Fun." Elaine waited nervously until the carousel operator, who looked a lot like a homeless person, opened the gate and let the people in. Luckily she didn't have to wait long. Then she climbed up on top of the rabbit. There were rungs that led up to its shiny painted black saddle. The rabbit looked as if it were flying, front and rear legs extended as far apart as they could go. Paul chose to ride his favorite, the swan. There was no ladder on the swan, just a little seat.

The operator walked around and buckled in all the children and Elaine, who was fumbling with the seat belt. She was excited and eager to ride. The musical calliope began to play. It played an old song, something from the turn of the century, the one that separated the Victorian Age from the Industrial Age. Then it played another old song. Elaine sang along, even though she didn't really know the words. "In the good old summertime" and "Wait til the sun shines Nellie…"

She caught herself laughing, despite herself, as the rabbit went up and down. She kept her eyes on the large hoofs of the zebra immediately in front of her fleet steed. All the animals went up and down and round and round. She watched the zebra until she was dizzy and starting to feel sick. Then she looked out the windows and waved at the little kids who were watching. Most of them waved back timidly with their free hands, the ones that weren't clutching their parents' or grandparents' hands. They all seemed to be wearing the same expression, a mixture of fear and confusion.

Elaine laughed some more. When the ride was almost over, and the animals slowly came to a stop, Elaine started to untie the seat belt so she could climb down the ladder. The operator yelled at her to wait until they were completely at a standstill. It was just like being a kid again. She smiled guiltily. Paul asked her if she wanted to ride one more time.

"No, once is enough. I just wanted to see if I still got sick."

"And did you?" asked Paul

"You better believe it!" said Elaine, but she smiled weakly anyway.

Elaine took the extra tickets and put them in her purse as another reminder of this wonderful and unforgettable week.

***

That night Paul dreamt of Estefan and Elaine dreamt of Margarita. Apparently, the two ghosts were eager to talk with one another. Estefan was penitent. Margarita was still furious. Estefan went on the offensive.

Estefan began, "You shot me!?"

"Yes, but you deserved it!" said Margarita.

"I deserved to be murdered!?" he said self-righteously.

"Yes, you shouldn't have given a necklace to another woman!" To Margarita, it seemed, it was all about the jewels.

Estefan tried to explain. "It wasn't given with the same intent."

"What do you mean?" Margarita was at a loss.

"I gave the necklace to Dai-yu so she would not be so sad. I gave you the necklace because I love you." He continued, "I love you. You are the only woman I ever loved. Te quiero, mija. And I miss you."

"You have a rotten way of showing it," said Margarita.

"But I do," he assured her.

"Love is not taking other lovers," she reminded.

"Ah, but they meant nothing to me," he tried to cover.

"So you say." She was still hurt and angry.

"I love you, I miss you, I want us to be the way we used to be," Estefan implored.

"We will see, said Margarita.

Estefan sensed a weakening in Margarita's resolve so he jumped once more to the offensive. "Tell me you did not miss me!" Estefan demanded.

"I did not miss you," Margarita lied.

He knew she was not telling the truth. "You did not miss me?" he pressed her.

She relented. "Yes, I missed you. Every moment of every night," said Margarita.

"You didn't act that way," said Estefan.

"You wouldn't let me be enough for you," she said.

"But you were enough. You were the woman I loved most of all."

"Most of all!?" Margarita was angry; then she became thoughtful. "I'm not sure that's enough," she said. She sounded sad and disappointed.

"But it is. I do love you. Sometimes you wouldn't let me be with you. I had to be with someone."

Margarita was silent.

"Will you ever forgive me?" Estefan asked pitifully.

"We will see." Margarita was wavering.

"I love you, you know? I will always love you. I'm sorry for what I did. I'm truly sorry for the pain I caused you," he groveled.

"So you say..." Margarita seemed uncertain.

"I do, you know."

"I know, but…"

As Paul reached over to kiss Elaine, it was Estefan kissing Margarita.

***

That night Elaine and Paul made love. First they made love as Estefan and Margarita, two old lovers whose bodies were familiar and comfortable with one another. Then they made love as Estefan and Dai-yu, two new lovers, still learning the nuances of one another's bodies, two people still very much in lust. Then they made love as Paul and Elaine in charge of their own bodies, their own minds, and their own hearts. Slowly and gently they made love, not sex. It was wonderful, tender, and caring.

They kissed like they had never kissed one another before. It felt brand new. And maybe, thanks to the ghosts, it was. Elaine felt loved. And so did Paul.

Perhaps it is true what they say, love never truly dies.

Aftermath

It took some doing but eventually the bones of Estrellita were recovered from the mine and buried in the cemetery of Silver Spring.

It took even more doing, and a heap of ghostly intervention, to right another wrong. An earthquake cracked open a chunk of concrete right at the intersection of Cemetery Road and Highway 1. When the road crew showed up to make repairs, they were shocked to find a skeleton. They had discovered what was left of poor Margarita. After some DNA testing it was determined that the small white bones belonged to Estefan's suicidal spouse. She was dug up and moved to the place next to Estefan's.

Then came the hardest part, that is, what to do about Estefan's gold. For all Paul, Elaine, and the Kerstetters knew, the gold belonged to the state of Colorado.

A little research revealed the gold actually belonged to the "residents," for lack of a better word, of the plots in the cemetery.

But how were they to find Estefan's living relatives? No one had visited the family plot in years. But Paul, Elaine and the Kerstetters knew Estefan had to have living relatives somewhere.

They decided to make the discovery public and called the local media outlets. Once the gold in the cemetery made international news, and it quickly did, Estefan's relatives came out of nowhere and everywhere. All were eager to prove that they were related to the "Man under the Millions" as he was dubbed by the press. Estefan had distant relatives in places like Mexico and others in Texas. A little too readily they gave permission to the authorities to dig up Estefan's grave.

The body of Estefan was disinterred and DNA tests were performed on it.

As it turned out only one person could directly trace his lineage back to Estefan…Estefan's only living son, known to everyone as…Armando.

More DNA tests were in order. Armando was tested and it was found, to the amazement of all, that Armando was indeed related to Estefan. Then the whole supernatural and ghostly truth came out.

Armando wasn't just any cattle drover. And he was more than a hundred years old.

Mrs. K, formerly the madam of the Silver Spring, knew there was something special about her husband. He bore a striking physical resemblance to the man who caused all the grief and suffering that took place at the Silver Spring, that rascal Estefan.

For years, Mrs. K had kept her suspicions to herself. But now it became necessary to uncover the truth.

After the DNA tests were completed, all doubts were laid to rest, along with poor Estefan's bones. Armando was indeed the heir to the fortune buried in Estefan's family plot. In fact, his mother had been one of Margarita's many handmaidens. One of the reasons Margarita was so mean to this woman was that she knew Estefan had an illegitimate son with the woman.

***

The Kerstetters offered to split their good fortune with Paul and Elaine. At first, Elaine and Paul said no, but then they realized *that that was just crazy.*

The necklace they found around Estrellita's neck was worth a small fortune. The emeralds alone were appraised at more than $30,000. They unanimously decided to donate the necklace to a museum as a historical artifact.

It also turned out there were quite a few silver coins in the bags along with the gold coins. Some of them were worth quite a bit to collectors. They decided to sell them off a few at a time to numismatists, in order not to flood the market.

It was difficult to estimate, but, considering the current price of gold and the value of the silver coins, Estefan's fortune was worth a little more than half a million dollars. The press was off a bit, but it made better headlines.

***

Then the K's made Paul and Elaine another offer they couldn't refuse. Elaine and Paul moved lock, stock, and barrel to Colorado and went into partnership with the K's on the B&B. With the new found fortune of Estefan, the four didn't need to make any real money with this business venture, at least not for a few years. They could concentrate on more important matters.

Elaine decided to write a book about her dreams of ghosts in Silver Spring and it became a bestseller. They decided to make a movie from the screenplay. Benecio del Toro was approached to play the role of Estefan, Dennis Quaid and Andie McDowell would star as Paul and Elaine, and Eva Longoria would be the beautiful spoiled Margarita. Ming Na was suggested for the part of Dai-yu and America Ferrera would play the mad Estrellita. Julianne Moore would portray Mrs. K and the role of Mr. K, or Armando, at the time of this writing, was still up for grabs.

Paul took up duck carving.

The ghosts continued to visit Paul and Elaine, as well as the Kerstetters, in the wee hours of the night.

Paul and Elaine's sex life improved dramatically.

The End

About the Author

Ivy Kaminsky was born in Denver, Colorado, in a year to remain unspecified. She attended high school in Golden, Colorado and graduated with a plan to study engineering. After flunking a few science classes at Rice University in Houston, Texas she decided to become a Liberal Arts Major. She has a degree from Rice in Psychology and works as a Writing Tutor at the University of Houston Clear Lake and Houston Community College.

She has had several careers, including secretary, computer technician, and freelance writer and photographer for the Houston Chronicle. She also has edited newsletters for clubs and books for friends. Her articles and photographs have appeared in the Houston Chronicle and High Technology Careers magazine. She has published three books of original poetry, and edited textbooks, photography books, an anthology, and a biography for friends and acquaintances. This is her first novel.

She resides in Clear Lake, just southeast of Houston, Texas.